Merit Niemeitz was born in
culture and media studies, sh
but found she preferred imme
She loves autumn days, flea ma

Caroline Waight is an award-winning literary translator
working from Danish, German and Norwegian. Her translations
include books by Laura Vogt, Ingvild Rishøi, Maren Uthaug,
Caroline Albertine Minor, Asta Olivia Nordenhof and Dorthe
Nors. She was a finalist for the 2023 PEN Translation Award and
received a special commendation at the 2023 Warwick Prize for
Women in Translation.

Berlin in 1995. Whilst studying
started working in publishing
herself in her own stories,
books and writing.

STARLING NIGHTS

MERIT NIEMEITZ

TRANSLATED BY
CAROLINE WAIGHT

One More Chapter
a division of HarperCollins*Publishers* Ltd
1 London Bridge Street
London SE1 9GF
www.harpercollins.co.uk
HarperCollins*Publishers*
Macken House, 39/40 Mayor Street Upper,
Dublin 1, D01 C9W8, Ireland

This paperback edition 2026
1
First published in Great Britain in ebook format
by HarperCollins*Publishers* 2026

Copyright © Merit Niemeitz 2026
English translation copyright © Caroline Waight 2026
Merit Niemeitz asserts the moral right to be identified
as the author of this work

A catalogue record of this book is available from the British Library

ISBN: 978-0-00-874147-1

This novel is entirely a work of fiction. The names, characters and incidents
portrayed in it are the work of the author's imagination. Any resemblance to
actual persons, living or dead, events or localities is entirely coincidental.

Printed and bound in the UK using 100% Renewable Electricity
by CPI Group (UK) Ltd

All rights reserved. No part of this publication may be reproduced, stored in a
retrieval system, or transmitted, in any form or by any means, electronic,
mechanical, photocopying, recording or otherwise, without the prior
permission of the publishers.

Without limiting the exclusive rights of any author, contributor or the publisher
of this publication, any unauthorised use of this publication to train generative
artificial intelligence (AI) technologies is expressly prohibited. HarperCollins
also exercise their rights under Article 4(3) of the Digital Single Market Directive
2019/790 and expressly reserve this publication from the text and data mining
exception.

For my family.

For the books, the travelling, the worlds.

Dear Readers,

This book contains potentially triggering content, including depictions or references to physical, psychological or sexualised violence; death/loss; murder; suicide; depression; rape.

Also note that some elements of Cambridge University's college geography and protocol have been changed for dramatic purposes.

We wish you the best possible reading experience.
Yours, Merit

PROLOGUE

Then

There were many myths told about Cambridge. Stories woven from rumour and skewed half-truths, the thin fabric passed from hand to hand in the shadows. Students whispered them along the queues in the throne-room-like dining halls, lecturers recited them to the rows of awed and faintly anxious faces seated before them, anecdotes embroidered for each new class.

Most of these stories skimmed barely a hair's breadth across the surface of the truth. The true secret-keeper was Cambridge itself. The city and its winding lanes, and above all, the university. The buildings that gleamed gold, the lawns braided through the stone fabric of the colleges, the smooth-flowing Cam.

The lifeless heart of the city was the most vital part of it, because for centuries it had outlasted generation after generation of students. It had watched as countless, different yet similar faces passed it by, while its own face altered little. No wrinkles, only a weary blink of the eyes as the years went by and wafer-thin layers of its façade were worn away.

The university kept the true, unfiltered secrets of this place. Only a select few were capable of understanding what it had to tell. People like us. We understood, because we were part of it. Because we were the biggest secret of all.

~

'Are you hiding from us?'

I held back a sigh. It had only been a matter of time before one of them found me here. We knew each other too well: our minds were maps we had studied closely over the years, and by now none of us needed signposts to know what the other person was thinking or feeling. Or where they were.

I turned to face the young woman striding purposefully towards me down the aisle. 'Like that's even possible. Sometimes I just need a break. Crazy, huh?'

She stopped in front of me, grinning broadly. The light falling through the stained-glass window cast blue shadows on her symmetrical face, the gap between her teeth a dark chink in a row of luminous white. 'You can take a break when you're dead.'

I rolled my eyes. 'Considering what you guys have planned, that's sounding less far-fetched by the minute, don't you think?'

'Well, now you're just being insulting.' She gave me a teasing look, her fingers toying with the thin chain around her neck. The plain ring that hung from it glinted every time the vivid moonlight struck the gold. She must be thinking of the person who wore an exact duplicate of it. 'And don't be a wet blanket, okay? Not today.'

'What's so special about today?' Our days were beads on a never-ending necklace. All of them were beautiful, precious, unique, yet at the same time somehow ... alike. Sometimes I wondered to myself if one could tire of beauty. Or of happiness. It wasn't always at the foreground of my mind, more an underlying anxiety. A muted fear of the future, which I was always quick to fill up with as much of the now as possible.

'Nothing. I just want ... I need this. All of you.' Coming closer, she put her hands to the collar of my shirt and smoothed the fabric. An oddly tender smile played across her lips. 'My best friends,' she whispered, the pads of her fingers brushing over the scar on my temple. 'The four-headed love of my life.'

I took her hand, which was burning hot, and squeezed it gently. 'Your life isn't over yet. Maybe you'll find something better than us.'

'No, never.' Her smile widened, but something behind her eyes clouded over. If I hadn't known her better, I'd have mistaken it for sadness.

I frowned. 'Is everything okay?'

She was silent for a moment, then pulled away from me and took a step back. Red light instead of blue, an exaggeratedly cheerful grin instead of genuine happiness. 'Sure. Always. I just want to make this a night to remember – if that's all right with you?'

I was briefly tempted to ask more questions, but I knew her as well as she knew me. 'Of course,' I said, with a glance at my watch. 'Let's—' I broke off, realising that the hands weren't moving. I tapped the golden dial, but nothing happened. 'My watch has stopped.'

She took a deep breath. 'Holy shit.'

I looked up, narrowing my eyes. 'Don't.'

'I can't help it, that's so obviously a sign.' She tapped the glass with a fingertip, clutching her other hand theatrically to her chest. '*Ex hoc momento pendet aeternitas.*'

My mouth twitched at the corners: the meaning of that phrase was always on the tip of my tongue, nuzzling itself up against my lips in the same pleasingly warm way. It was just an empty phrase, an old Latin platitude – but to us, it was also a promise.

Eternity is poised upon this moment.

Nobody loved or lived those words quite like the woman in front of me. She spoke them often, mostly when they were demonstrably untrue. On nights like this, when we were planning to break God knows how many rules, climbing onto the roof of the university's tallest building to see the meteor shower, it would have been more accurate to say: *our lives are poised upon this moment*. Still, I never contradicted her. None of us did. And sometimes, in the very best moments, it felt like the same thing anyway.

This time I simply shook my head and followed her out of the chapel. The evening outside smelt of rhododendrons, of the water in the Cam and the aromas wafting from the open windows of the student housing: incense sticks, paper and ink, washing powder and perfume. Fragments of innumerable lives, all of them throwing into greater relief how exceptional ours were.

I tilted back my head until my face was bathed in pure moonlight. And I smiled and breathed and *lived*, realising yet again: eternity might not depend upon this moment, but our whole lives did.

Later, much later, I came to wish I'd realised something else: if our whole lives rested on a moment, then a moment could bring them crashing down as well.

CHAPTER 1
MABEL

'W ait for me!'
I wrapped my coat around me more tightly as I trotted to keep up with Zoe. Her blonde hair fluttered in her wake, bouncing in time with the glittering silver tulle of her dress. The tip of my nose was stinging in the icy evening air by the time I caught up with my best friend and fell into step with her. 'This is a really bad fucking idea.'

Zoe sighed and hooked her arm through mine. Her coat was expensive, cut in some velvety fabric, and significantly warmer than mine. My own hole-ridden black jacket was really only meant for spring and autumn, so in winter I combined it with thick woolly jumpers, my sole protection against the cold. It was still only October, but the crisp autumn air was doing a pretty good job of creeping through the material and bringing the gooseflesh out on my skin.

'All the best stories start with bad ideas.'

Grinning broadly, Zoe handed me the half-empty bottle of wine, and hesitantly I took it. I'd had no time to cook between getting back from the library and when Zoe came striding into the kitchen, reminding me that I'd promised in a moment of weakness to come with her tonight. I'd had nothing but half a bar of chocolate since breakfast, so I knew the wine would go straight to my head. Then again, I'd never get through tonight if I was sober.

Making up my mind, I took a long gulp. 'Name one,' I choked, stifling a cough.

Zoe began to chew on her full bottom lip, steering me around a corner. 'When I was fifteen years old, I had this idea to throw a party at my neighbours' house while they were on holiday. That night was the first time I kissed the hottest guy in the whole school.'

'Didn't that story end with you falling off the balcony, breaking your leg and getting grounded for three months?'

I smiled faintly, my eyes fixed on our shadows darting across the walls next to us. We had reached Trinity College, younger but much bigger than Trinity Hall, where Zoe and I lived and studied. I felt a lot more at home there: the buildings were more compact, the courts ringed by pale stone, and dotted in summer with rose bushes left to run wild. The river Cam flowed just outside the windows of our rooms, and in the evenings, we watched the sun sink slowly into the water. I loved it for its cosiness, the way it had immediately felt like home. Trinity College, only a few minutes away on foot, was larger, more imposing, wealthier. *Less charming*, I had thought on my first visit to the University of Cambridge. Although it did have a better library.

The Wren Library was closing, the last handful of people leaving the building and scurrying away down the colonnade. In the lamplight they looked like ants, scattering across the college grounds and back to their rooms. Most days, I was one of them. One of the students, startled from their work by the gong, hastily packing up. Slinging book-crammed satchels over stooped shoulders, the bags so heavy it felt at any moment like you might collapse onto the paving. Hair stuffed under the collar of your coat, because you'd forgotten in the morning sun that you might need a scarf once you'd left the library. Just then, I wished I was one of them, instead of hurrying next to Zoe.

'I was just a kid back then. We're adults now.' She clacked her fingernails against the bottle, imperious.

I reluctantly obeyed and took another sip. The wine was too sugary, but that was how Zoe liked it. *Semi-sweet*. A word that happened to suit Zoe herself. With those big cornflower-blue eyes, long lashes and pale blonde hair, she was femininity incarnate. All her outlines were softly drawn, as if seen through a filter. Her movements were lithe, her laugh never too boisterous, her clothes beautifully fitted and flowing. She was always wearing something with a sparkle. Today it was the oversized hoop earrings, which had snagged several times while she was getting dressed.

'We're twenty, Zoe. And last week I saw you trying to melt butter in the microwave with the wrapper still on,' I reminded her, passing back the bottle.

She rolled her eyes. 'And did anything bad happen?'

I snorted. 'No, because *I* unplugged it in time.'

'There, you see.' She gave me a wink. 'And that's exactly why I asked you to come with me tonight. So, you can pull the plug, if it comes to that. But only if it does – and not before anything's actually happened.'

She gazed up at me, an eloquent look. Her gold-painted eyelids shimmered as we passed beneath one of the rust-eaten lamps. She had offered to put some on me as well, but I'd declined. The only make-up I owned or ever used was my collection of lipsticks. Whenever I wanted to reward myself, I went to the department store in the town centre and treated myself to one of their overly expensive products. I knew it was unwise to spend so much money on something I could have bought for less, something I barely used day-to-day. Yet I loved everything about them: the innumerable shades, the frivolous

7

names, the extravagantly designed packaging. Most of all, I loved the way it felt to go through the world with their borrowed flush on my lips. I felt beautiful. Beautiful, sensual and strong. Lipsticks were the only luxury I allowed myself. Today I was wearing *Mona Lisa Smile*, a dark matte red that reminded me of the brick buildings in my hometown. A colour for trips to the museum, autumnal walks in the woods, or cosy nights in with a film. Not particularly suitable for an exclusive and highly illicit party in a university building.

I was pretty sure the college administration knew nothing about it. The rules didn't leave much room for interpretation when it came to what was – and was not – permitted on college grounds. Unlike Zoe, I had read every last paragraph of them, and I'd tried to point out to her that our plan was in direct violation of at least a dozen regulations. Not that it had any effect, of course.

It was less than a week since Zoe had come bursting into my room while I was getting ready for bed. Her hair was tousled, her eyes glassy with alcohol and anticipation. *It's like super secret and exclusive*, she had said. She'd seemed nervous, her voice even higher than usual, but this was less about the party and more about the person who'd invited us.

I cleared my throat. 'Wait, remind me again where you met this guy?' I was trying to hide it from Zoe, but somehow all my misgivings ended up spilling over into that one teeny little word: guy.

She heard it, of course. And suddenly she sounded annoyed. 'At that party the other day, the one you wouldn't come to. And for the last time: Ashton is not a dangerous psychopath!'

I grabbed the bottle and took a swig, trying to wash down all the strings of letters I didn't want to come blurting out. Zoe wasn't the most pleasant person to argue with. Even when she didn't have a leg to stand on, she always managed to get the last word. And usually it was one that bothered me for days. 'I never said that.'

'But you were thinking it.'

I rolled my eyes but said nothing. As far as I was concerned, all the guys we met at student parties were potential psychopaths. Or arrogant, self-absorbed arseholes, at the very least.

Our outlines, drained of colour, were reflected in the tall windows as we left the library behind us and turned towards Great Court. The rest of the way we were silent. When Zoe was upset it was best to leave her alone. She wasn't one to bear a grudge, and I knew she was too excited about the evening ahead to stay angry for very long that I didn't feel the same way. We'd only been friends for a year, but since we were both studying English, we knew each other pretty well.

The building we arrived at after a few minutes' walk was not one I knew. Most of the university's architecture looked more or less the same: Gothic structures that loomed like castles into the sky. Long, stone passages that cast back your footsteps in a never-ending echo. Spiral staircases that coiled vertiginously upwards and twisting corridors that made you feel like you might at any moment stumble onto something hidden.

The ivy-clad façade ahead of us looked like any other in Cambridge, except that a few windows were lit, even though the college had long since gone to sleep. Before we reached the wooden door, Zoe turned to me. She looked me sternly up and down, fiddling with my dark hair and picking some lint off my coat. I was well aware that her fingers were always itching to dress me up in her own clothes when we went out. Not because she was ashamed of me, but because she thought I was ashamed of myself. Except I wasn't. I made no secret of the fact that I didn't have much money. Zoe's parents were rich, mine were dead. That's just the way it was.

'Look, try and make an effort, okay?' she said, putting the empty bottle behind a pillar. 'Just keep an open mind, don't start judging them straight off the bat. They're nice people. Really.'

I didn't trust my voice, so I went with a dutiful nod. Zoe had only known this guy a couple of weeks, and frankly, there were a lot of people she considered 'nice' who I'd have preferred to give a wide berth. Zoe approached everybody with an open mind, unbiased. She could find the good in anyone within minutes. I, on the other hand, had a knack for nosing out the bad. Not that I was especially proud of that. I'd have preferred to be more like my best friend, although at the same time I sometimes wished she was more like me. Then we wouldn't disagree so much on how to spend our Friday nights.

Zoe shook out her hair and undid the top button of her coat before she straightened her shoulders, strode determinedly up to the door and knocked. A few seconds later, it swung half-open. The dull thud of music flowed out of the gap, in which a broad-shouldered boy leant against the frame, his hood pulled up. His eyes wandered down our bodies. When he reached the run in my tights, he frowned. 'Password?'

I bit my lower lip to hold back a snort.

Zoe jabbed a warning elbow into my ribs and beamed at him. '*Sturnus vulgaris*,' she said, voice lowered.

He nodded slowly and opened the door wider. 'In you come. Down the corridor, turn right. Just follow the music.'

Before I could think better of it, Zoe grabbed my arm and yanked me inside. '*Stu* ... what?' I asked under my breath.

'*Sturnus vulgaris*.' She was dragging me impatiently down a long corridor. The floor was patterned like a chess board, the walls hung with gold-framed portraits in oil. Whatever kind of building this was, it certainly lived up to the college's traditionalist reputation. 'It's the scientific name for the common starling. You know, like the bird.'

This time, I didn't bother holding back the snort. 'Seriously?'

Zoe threw me an exasperated look. 'Mabel, you promised!'

'Fine, fine.' I was undoing my coat as we turned the corner. 'At least we didn't need to bring birdseed to get in, I guess.'

'Starlings are a lot more impressive than you think,' said a deep voice ahead of us.

Zoe and I both stopped short, staring at the young man leaning against a plinth a few yards in front of us, his head level with the bust on top of it. Both had wavy hair and a faint smile on their symmetrical faces. His eyes swept over Zoe before he turned his attention to me. While her face broke into a radiant smile, I felt the skin pucker on my arms. This must be Ashton.

'Oh, yeah? How's that, then?' I asked.

With a languid movement he stepped away from the plinth and walked towards us. 'They're incredibly intelligent and very observant. They also have the best-trained syrinx of any songbird, which means they can mimic almost anything.'

'They usually move in flocks, don't they?' With an effort I dredged up the only piece of information I had about the species. 'I think I read that in many places they're considered vermin, so people take measures to keep the population down.'

'People often tend to destroy things they feel threatened by. In this case it seems like a rather vain effort. There are still starlings everywhere.' He smirked, then his eyes were scrutinising Zoe again. Reaching out, he brushed a stray lock of flaxen hair from her face with the tips of his fingers. 'If you ask me, they're the true kings of the sky.' Gently, he kissed her on the cheek. 'Hello, Anima.'

I didn't even bother to ask if that was a term of endearment or if he'd simply forgotten her name. Probably it was just another one of those *sturnus* type things.

Zoe blushed, murmuring a soft 'hi' and smiling rapturously. She seemed to have forgotten I was there.

Ashton had not. He turned, looking at me with interest. 'So. You must be the fabled friend. Zoe's told me a lot about you. Says you're the cleverest person she's ever met.'

I couldn't quite tell if that was a trace of mockery I caught in his voice. Everything about him was so perfect, so glossy, in a way that felt unreal. It was like I was staring at a façade, and there was no telling what – or *who* – was concealed behind it. Erring on the side of caution, I made no attempt to return his smile. 'If I was, I wouldn't be here. I'm not keen on being kicked out of uni because I got caught at an illicit party.'

Zoe stared at me, aghast, but Ashton laughed, the sound flowing warm and golden through the dim passageway. 'Oh, don't worry about that. We never get caught.' He winked before turning around and beckoning us to follow.

We made towards a room at the end of the corridor, the music drifting from underneath plain double doors. Ashton waited until we came to a halt right behind him before pushing them open.

If Zoe hadn't dragged me over the threshold, I probably would have stayed there, rooted to the spot, overwhelmed by all the sensory input. It was just so ... unexpected. I didn't go to a lot of student parties, but I knew they weren't generally like *this*.

A large room, almost a hall. Music, slow, not much bass, and not so loud that snatches of conversation couldn't filter through. Dim pools of light around candles placed on wooden tables. Velvet sofas and dark carpets. Oil portraits on the walls, the faces scowling down at us disapprovingly. Muted tones, both the furnishings and the clothes of the guests. Swaying dresses, blouses with ornate stand-up collars, skirts tight at the waist. Plain rollneck jumpers, here and there a jacket tossed over the back of a chair. Straight-cut trousers, leather shoes, socks with embroidered hems.

In seconds I had spotted the odd ones out. Roughly a dozen

of them, actually: people who did not fit in. Shirts too pleated, dresses too colourful. Zoe was one of them, because her dress gleamed silver. So was I, because ... well, everything.

I curled my fingers into the stretched-out hem of my grey wool jumper, ill at ease. The safety pin I'd used to fasten my skirt poked uncomfortably into my waist as I followed Zoe.

I couldn't get a sense of how many people were there. Some were lounging on soft furniture, others reclining against the pale grey walls. Two young men played chess at a table at the back of the room, while on the opposite side a couple kissed by the slightly open window. In the middle of the room, two women were playing a piano, the lid of which was cluttered with glasses and candles.

Well, this is weird, I thought, as Zoe whispered to me, her eyes huge, 'Isn't it the coolest thing you've ever seen?'

I was about to answer when I saw I'd already lost her attention. Ashton had taken her hand and was drawing her towards an old drinks trolley at the other end of the room.

As I lost sight of her tulle dress among the mass of shadowy figures, I had a bad feeling. Zoe had met her fair share of oddballs, sure, but this one seemed to be in a class of his own.

For a minute or two I just stood there, worrying at the fabric of my jacket, which was draped over my arm. The more I looked, the more I began to feel like this wasn't a party at all. More of a cult meeting. What I really wanted was to fish out my mirror compact and take a look at myself – that was the only thing that even remotely helped when I felt this isolated and out of place.

I jumped as someone appeared in front of me. A boy with shoulder-length black hair and a sly face. Or maybe it was just his smirk, which deepened as he scrutinised me more closely. 'Hello, Anna Karenina. You look lost.'

'Yeah, well I've got no interest in being found.' I took a step back. 'And I always choose war over peace.'

I heard a whistle, and moments later a second boy was standing in front of me. His reddish hair was shorter, but his grin was just as wide as his eyes slid from me to his friend. 'Books *and* bite. The perfect combination. Your contribution, Victor?'

Contribution? I was too perplexed to think of a retort. The other boy shook his head regretfully. 'Sadly not. Jack?' He tapped the guy standing behind him on the shoulder, and he turned around. 'She one of yours?'

It just kept getting better. My mouth opened, but yet again I was too slow. Jack took two steps towards me, his eyes sweeping over my face. 'I'm afraid not,' he said with a shrug. 'But if no one's called dibs, I will.' Lifting his hand, he ran a lock of my hair through his fingers.

Right. Enough was enough. I slapped his hand away, stepping back. 'This might be difficult for you to get through your head, but not everything in this world belongs to you, all right? The next person who lays a finger on me gets smacked upside the head with one of these fancy candlesticks.'

They didn't seem very impressed, their collective grin only growing more challenging. Victor sighed theatrically and rested a hand on his friend's shoulders. 'Damn, we'll have to find out who she belongs to. I'll give my latest winnings at poker for a share.'

My cheeks flushed with heat. I had only two options. Either I really did grab the nearest blunt object, or I got the hell out of here. At least temporarily. My eyes darted towards Zoe. She was with Ashton, leaning against a wall, laughing at something he was saying. She didn't look like someone who wanted to be rescued. And she probably wouldn't be too thrilled about me starting a fight within five minutes flat.

I turned on my heel without a word and barged my way through the crowd. Music and voices drifted in my wake until the door fell shut behind me.

The more distance I put between myself and the strange party, the more my pulse began to quieten, and after a couple of minutes I was calm enough to examine my surroundings. If I ignored the reason I was here, maybe I could get something positive out of the whole fiasco after all. It wasn't every day I got to spend time alone in a building like this. There was a loftiness to the halls of Cambridge even during the day, and by night they were more enchanting still.

I went up a spiral staircase and began to wander down the corridors, past dark walls and copper-coloured light fittings. There were doors left and right, all of them unlocked, opening onto studies and empty teaching rooms furnished with nothing but chairs. When I reached the end of the corridor, I paused.

The last door was the only one that was locked. Gingerly I turned the handle, but nothing happened. Biting my lip, I glanced back over my shoulder. Apart from the distant music, all seemed quiet. Vacant. I should have gone back to find Zoe, but something stopped me. It wasn't just the prospect of another pointless conversation – I was itching to know what was behind that door. Curiosity had always been my fatal flaw.

Muffling a sigh, I gave in and removed the hairpin that held my overlong fringe in place. I was breaking the rules just by being here, so I thought I might as well go all in. And anyway, there are certain skills that benefit from practice.

After my mum died, I moved in with my aunt and her son. They lived in a small town not far from Brighton, where there wasn't a whole lot for teenagers to do. Which is probably why, before he'd even left school, my cousin had amassed a substantial criminal record. I was fifteen when he taught me how to open a lock with a piece of wire. Or a hairpin.

It took me thirty seconds to pick the lock, which opened with a click. Smiling triumphantly, I slipped inside. Slowly, my eyes adjusted to the dim light from the corridor.

It wasn't a large room. The only items of furniture were a

heavy oak desk and matching chair, placed in the middle of the room, and a velvet wingback with a side table by the window. The night outside was barely visible through the ivy growing over the pane.

The room was full of books, the air thick with the scent of old paper and printing ink. My pulse slowed and my shoulders dropped as I took a few deep breaths. The bindings were muted, mostly grey or black. A few had gold numbers on the spine, elaborate initials or words in Latin or Ancient Greek. This was no ordinary college library. The books exuded a certain nobility: each one seemed exquisite and important. Even this pocket library was elite.

I set the pin down on the desk before wandering closer to the floor-to-ceiling shelves. I ran the tips of my fingers cautiously over the spines, hesitating for a long time before I ventured to pull out a book. It felt like removing an organ from a body. These volumes formed a work of art; one I desperately wanted to understand. Carefully, I stroked the anthracite-grey binding. The gold lettering embossed on the cover gave shape to words my schoolgirl Latin wasn't good enough to read. I smoothed one damaged corner consolingly.

Before I could open the book, I heard a cough behind me. I whipped around, startled, the book clamped protectively against my chest.

He was standing in the open doorway, his face in shadow. I looked him hastily up and down, taking in his build, his tall, lean body, his crossed arms, his faintly tousled hair. When he took a step towards me, I saw his face. A decidedly attractive face, with a defined jaw and a pair of expressive dark eyes. They narrowed slightly as they surveyed me.

His voice, however, was calm. 'Strictly speaking, this area is off-limits to guests.' He stepped unhurriedly into the room, the door falling shut behind him with a creak.

'And you're not a guest?' I replied with equal composure, although my heart was pounding. Whoever he was, he didn't seem overly intent on chucking me out. Which could be either good or bad. Good, if he simply wasn't interested in me. Bad, if he had something else in mind.

'Not as much as you are.' I felt his eyes on me, although his features had sunk back into darkness. By now he was almost at the window, leaving my escape route well and truly clear.

My muscles relaxed. 'I didn't mean any harm. I just got lost,' I said, giving what I hoped was an embarrassed smile.

'Lost?' He sat down in the reading chair. The green velvet matched the olive shade of his pullover. 'Usually that door's kept locked.'

'Then I guess someone must have forgotten.' I was slowly stroking the tattered corner of the book, trying to avoid his searching gaze.

'You're not a very good liar.'

I thought perhaps I heard the trace of a smile in his voice. Annoyingly, I knew he was right. I'd never had an issue telling the truth. The opposite, actually, although it would have done wonders for my social life if lying came more naturally. 'I don't get much practice, I suppose.'

He leant forward, resting his forearms on his knees. 'I see. An honest burglar. Were you planning to steal anything?'

I shook my head. 'I was just curious.'

He frowned, a deep crease appearing between his brows. They were dark, like his hair and eyes, which were framed with thick lashes. There was a quiet, classical quality to his face. It reminded me of the silhouettes illustrated in old novels. 'Curious about what?'

'About what someone who has everything is most eager to protect.' I nodded towards the bookshelves. Their energy was pressing up against my spine, pushing me to stand taller, and my eyes wandered over them with unaccountable pride. 'I'm pleasantly surprised. Protecting books, that's ... sweet.'

He laughed – a harsh, throaty sound. 'I don't want to disappoint you, but I don't think it's to do with their intangible value. These are all first editions. The one you're currently holding is on its own worth more than any painting in the front hall.'

I jumped, staring at the book I'd been fidgeting with for the last five minutes. Hurriedly I turned and slid it back into place before it could crumble to dust in my hands. 'Dammit.' I wiped my fingers on my jumper, as if to remove any lingering evidence of my potential guilt. 'They should put up a warning.'

'I think the locked door is supposed to clue you in,' he answered sardonically.

I sighed and pulled out the desk chair to sit down. Perhaps it would have been wiser to go back, but for some strange reason I enjoyed his company more than the others'.

'So,' I began, after I'd got comfortable. 'What brings you up here?'

'Peace and quiet. And whisky.' He reached over to the side table and picked up the half-full crystal decanter, raising it enquiringly in my direction. I shook my head and watched as he poured two fingers of the golden fluid into a bulbous glass. 'Which college are you at?' he asked, settling back into the chair.

'Trinity Hall. And you?'

He gestured at the room. 'Trinity College. Which makes us neighbours. Although, I don't think I've seen you around.'

I laughed. There were nearly 25,000 students at the university. I spent most of my time outside of classes studying, so except for the people on my staircase, the only students I really knew were the ones I kept bumping into at the library. 'Probably best to forget you did. I'm pretty much just a parasite at a fancy party like this, anyway.'

'I'm sure my friends would be impressed by your choice of words.'

The corners of my mouth drooped. *Friends*. Of course. Not sure what I'd secretly been hoping. That he was a cleaner's son who'd snuck in unnoticed? I should have known; he wasn't the odd one out here, he fit in perfectly. His presence here meant he belonged. Another explanation for why we'd never met. Even if I got out more, I'd never have crossed paths with someone like him. Some things just aren't meant to go together.

'Got it. You're one of them.'

He raised his eyebrows, leaning towards me so that the light fell across his face. There was a faint scar across his right temple. A silvery thread on his otherwise perfect skin. 'When you say it like that it sounds like a crime.'

'No.' I gave a half-hearted smile. 'At least, not one I can blame you for. We don't choose the world we're born into.'

'And what world were you born into?'

'Not one you'd like to get better acquainted with.' My fingertips were groping along the run in my tights, which ended in a blob of nail polish above my knee. Seeing the quizzical look in his eyes, I sighed. 'Fine. Just look at me.' I stood up and moved past the desk, stopping a few steps away from him. 'Look at my clothes. Worn tread on my shoes, dull patent leather. A hole in my tights, and I'll still be wearing them until the day they fall apart. Vintage skirt – not because I shop at hip second-hand shops, but because it belonged to my nan.' I lifted the black fabric, which I'd hemmed myself. Then I gestured to my tattered fringe. 'See how uneven that is? Looks suspiciously like kitchen scissors, doesn't it? Dark circles under my eyes, ink stains on my fingers.' I gave him a nod that was both invitation and challenge. 'What does all that tell you, then?'

He didn't hesitate. 'That you got here on some sort of scholarship?'

I bowed with a smile and leant back against the desk. 'Total cliché, isn't it?'

'We're all clichés in one way or another. Everything about us is inherently repetitive, no matter how special and unique we'd like to be. We're only ever a copy of someone else.' For a moment the expression on his face was so forlorn that it disconcerted me. I swallowed, hard. Before I could answer, he shook his head gently. 'But at least you're a cliché to be proud of.' And that was all. No jeering, no arrogance, no mock-approval. His reaction astonished me. And I liked it. More than I wanted to let on.

I tilted my head, contemplating him again. Everything about him was clean and neat. His clothes weren't flashy, but although I could see no obvious branding, they were clearly expensive. His skin looked healthy, flawless, even – except for the delicate scar. His hair was glossy, and I knew that if I looked at his hands, they'd be soft and well-manicured. Every aspect of him was somehow like a painting. A perfect snapshot of a human being. Yet I couldn't help thinking that the most perfect-seeming images were usually the ones with the most chaos underneath the surface. And I'd have bet money there was chaos under his. I could see it in his eyes, in the subtle, pensive air he'd emanated ever since he set foot in the room. Everything about him saddened and fascinated me all at once. I'd never met anyone like him before. Someone who felt so present, even as a part of him was clearly elsewhere.

'Mind if I take a stab at your cliché?' I didn't know why I was asking. I only knew that I wanted urgently to find out if what I saw in him was the truth.

He sipped his drink, caught a little off-guard. 'You're welcome to try.'

I twisted a lock of hair, grasping for the right words. 'You're the son of wealthy parents. The kind who had your whole life planned out before you were even born. You've always done your best to live up to their expectations, but you've never had the chance to figure out what you really want. You don't know who you want to be, and it's eating you up inside. You're studying...' I paused, examining him closely: the impassive face, the slightly tense shoulders, the glass gripped tightly, the melancholy cast to his features. 'Philosophy. You're hoping it will guide you to the right questions, but the more you learn, the fewer answers you find. You're afraid of wasting your life, but it's even more difficult to admit that you don't actually know what you want to use it for.' I stopped and gave him a quizzical look. 'Am I on the right track?'

He said nothing, but gradually his shoulders relaxed as he held my gaze. I even thought perhaps I saw the trace of an appreciative smile at the corners of his mouth.

'So, what brought you here, then, if you think so little of our world?' he asked at last, dodging the question. Maybe I should take it as a sign of how close I'd got – very.

'The same thing that always makes people put someone else's needs first.' I lowered my voice to the dramatic tenor of a horror movie. 'Love.'

'Your boyfriend?'

'Oh no, I'm talking about a much deeper connection than that.' My smile felt more genuine when I thought of Zoe. Hotheaded, impulsive, heart-on-her-sleeve Zoe – although we often disagreed, she was the closest confidante I'd ever had. 'My best friend asked me to come.'

'Ah, I see,' he responded softly, running his little finger along the rim of the glass. 'And where is she now?'

Good question. Glancing at my watch, I realised it had been more than an hour since I'd left the party.

'With the reason she wanted to come in the first place, I suppose.' Ashton's name was on the tip of my tongue, but I swallowed it. There were a lot of people downstairs, but I couldn't be sure the two of them weren't friends. 'The guy who looks like a Michelangelo statue come to life,' I said instead, deliberately vague.

He frowned, as if something I'd said had surprised him. Or displeased him. 'So you were invited.'

'How else do you think we got past the guy at the door? Convoluted scientific names for animals aren't part of my standard vocabulary.'

'I thought you had a knack for getting into places that are technically off-limits to you, Pica.' Despite the restlessness in the shallows of his eyes, this time I was sure I saw a smile on his elegantly curving lips.

'Pica?' I replied, baffled.

He didn't respond, merely sipped his whisky and eyed me thoughtfully.

Reluctantly, I went on. 'I mean ... yeah, I am. But this isn't an event I'd attend by choice. I didn't last two minutes down there.'

The smile was wiped abruptly from his lips. 'What happened?'

'Your *friends*.' I shrugged casually, although the memory brought back a surge of fury. 'It's the principle, you know? I don't like being referred to as a "contribution", or treated like something you'd win at poker.' It was meant to sound sarcastic, but I could feel my bottom lip quiver.

We were silent. My anger pulsed between us – I could see the waves of it lapping against his face. His expression twisted into a faint grimace, as though the emotion had crawled beneath the skin. 'I'm really sorry about that. I'd like to tell you they didn't mean it that way, but—'

'But you're not a good liar either?'

'I'm an excellent liar. I just prefer not to,' he corrected me flatly. It didn't seem like he was proud of it – more like it was a fact he simply couldn't deny. Something about it made me smile.

I looked again at my watch. It was time to go. Partly because I didn't want to leave Zoe alone any longer, but also because I didn't like how comfortable I was getting. This conversation was going to be a one-time thing, and the more intense it got, the longer it would take to put it behind me. I didn't have time for distractions – I needed to focus every glimmer of attention on my studies.

'I should go.' I snatched my hairpin off the desk with a determined gesture and turned towards the door, but something stopped me in my tracks, and I looked back at him again. 'What's your name, by the way?'

'Cliff.' The word was barely out of his mouth before he clamped his mouth so tightly shut that I saw the muscles in his jaw go rigid. He wouldn't meet my eye, frowning as though annoyed.

I gave a terse nod and strode over to the door, although everything about the room was tempting me to stay. It was absurd, but leaving it knowing I'd never see it again, felt deeply, painfully wrong. It was like I'd forgotten something. Something my mind didn't remember but my emotions did. It was almost literally blocking my path, and I had to force myself to keep moving. 'Well, I hope you have a lovely evening, Cliff.'

'Wait.' His voice held me back. When I turned again he was standing beside the armchair, his hands buried in his pockets, his enigmatic gaze fixed on me. 'You didn't tell me your name.'

I tucked the slightly bent pin back into my hair. 'What's the point? You're better off forgetting all about this conversation, anyway. A name without a face means nothing, right?'

He shook his head earnestly, taking a step towards me. 'I don't see it that way at all.' The glow from the corridor fell in a slender oblong across his face, illuminating the deep brown of his eyes.

For one long moment I stared at him, felt myself committing him to memory. A snapshot of a snapshot of a human being, someone I knew I would remember much longer than I cared to admit. Then I turned and opened the door wide. 'Don't forget to lock up when you leave. You never know what kind of riffraff might be prowling the halls.'

As I walked off down the passageway, I thought I heard him laughing softly.

CHAPTER 2
MABEL

The rain turned the colleges to silver, studding the paving stones with little puddles that cast back the midday sun. Tiny flecks of light on dark stone, the glitter of them dazzling.

It had rained solidly throughout the last seminar, but as soon as we left the building, it stopped. A few last drops trickled down onto our heads as Zoe and I set off towards Trinity College. I did my best to avoid the puddles, whereas Zoe tramped straight through them. Her suede boots were already soaking wet, but she didn't seem to notice. For the last hour or two she'd barely said a word, gazing out through the window of the teaching room, the rain mirrored in her glassy eyes.

Although I sometimes found it hard to listen to her constant chatter, I missed it now. A silent Zoe was unsettling. 'Everything all right?' I asked her for the umpteenth time – the last being a good ten minutes ago, as we were queuing up at Nero's to buy lunch for ourselves and Davie. I'd had to repeat myself more than once to get an answer. Now, when she didn't react, I poked her in the ribs.

She jumped and gazed at me, startled. 'What?'

I stared at her with concern. Her eyes seemed duller than usual – the blue washed out – and not even the concealer she applied each morning could hide the exhausted coffee-coloured rings beneath them. 'Everything all right?' I asked again.

Zoe rolled her eyes and returned her attention to the path ahead – only to go splashing straight through the next puddle. Grimy water was seeping up the hem of her trousers.

'I'd be better if you weren't asking me that every other minute,' she replied crossly.

'You nearly fell asleep in that seminar, Zoe.'

She groaned and threw her hands in the air. 'Right, yeah, how crazy. Shakespeare's sonnets don't exactly send me into ecstasies.' She kicked a stone sulkily across the path and it skittered onto the lawn. In summertime, students would lay out their jackets and sit on the grass between lectures, turning their library-wan faces towards the sun. Now, it, too, was dotted with puddles.

'Why don't we ever analyse anything contemporary? There's good poetry being written today, you know. Like, we could talk about Rupi Kaur, for example. She talks in plain language about stuff that actually speaks to me. I'm so sick of listening to the same old crap spewed by dead white men.'

'Shakespeare is one of the most important dramatists in the history of world literature.' I eyed her sceptically. Zoe loved Shakespeare, I knew she did. In the single year we'd been friends, she'd talked me into going to see three separate productions of *Romeo and Juliet*.

But, judging by the look on her face, she had forgotten all of that. 'Rupi Kaur is a modern-day internet icon,' she added stubbornly.

I shook my head. 'You shouldn't be studying English if you wanted to read stuff from this century. Anyway, not all poems are sonnets and—'

'Stop it.' Zoe interrupted, taking the cup out of my hand. 'I love you, but if I don't get another dose of caffeine I won't be able to handle another minute of you being a smart alec.'

I watched her down my coffee – her third of the day – with a furrowed brow. 'Are you sure you're okay? You've been knackered all week. Since Friday night, to be exact.'

Frankly, 'knackered' was a euphemistic term for Zoe's state of mind since the strange party. After leaving the book-lined room and going back downstairs, I'd eventually found her and Ashton on a velvet sofa in the corner. For a moment I thought they were kissing, but when I looked again I saw that Zoe wasn't really with it anymore. She was slumped against his shoulder, eyes closed, her face peaceful and relaxed. It took a few minutes to get her upright and on her feet. I declined Ashton's offer to walk us home. Zoe had been so out of it the whole way back to college that I started running through worst-case scenarios in my head – what had she taken? But the next morning, she said she hadn't even had that much to drink, and wasn't sure why she was so tired. All weekend long, she had headaches and nausea, spending most of it in her room. Still, she did say she'd had a 'great night'. I found her optimism uncanny.

Now she shrugged, yanking at the belt of her coat. 'I just had a late night, that's all.' Her voice grew softer, less defensive. A sign that she was ready to talk about it.

'Did you go out again?'

'No.' She paused, chewing her lip. 'Ashton said maybe we could do something. But then he didn't get back to me.'

Bitterness welled up into my mouth, furring my tongue. 'So. You stayed up half the night waiting for him to call.'

I tried not to make it sound like an accusation, but immediately Zoe tensed up again. 'Yeah, and? I'm twenty years old, Mabel. Not all of us want to tuck up in bed with a good book every night, put the lights out promptly at ten and spend the whole night dreaming about *even more books*.'

My cheeks flushed, my heart on fire. I gripped the leather strap of my bag more tightly and focused on the paving stones ahead. Zoe got like this sometimes: when she fought, she hit below the belt. She had a sixth sense for her opponent's weak spots, and when in an impulsive mood, she used it.

She knew how important this degree was to me. I loved to learn, and I was certainly learning a lot – but I didn't do it just because I wanted to, I did it because I had to. My bursary depended on me doing well, and my future depended on my bursary. I knew I should be grateful simply for the opportunity, but I couldn't help but feel the pressure. Every time I got the sniffles and couldn't study properly for a day or two, I panicked. Basically, she was right: I couldn't afford to lose out on sleep, unless I was pulling an all-nighter at the library.

For a few minutes we were silent. The blue-bellied clouds parted slowly to reveal the sky, bathing the buildings around us in sunlight and streaking the brown stone with threads of gold. Gold and silver. On days like these, I couldn't imagine a more beautiful place than our university.

After a while, Zoe let out a huge sigh. 'God, that was so mean. I'm acting like a diva from one of those American high-school movies. I'm sorry.' She linked her arm through mine and blinked up at me contritely. 'That was the exhaustion talking. And the coffee. And the psychological wounds inflicted by Professor Walton's heinously boring lecture. Do you forgive me?'

I rolled my eyes, but couldn't repress a tiny smile. 'It's fine.'

Usually I found it more difficult to be forgiving. But with Zoe I could never stay angry for long. As my mum used to say, *'To truly love means to forgive'*. Since meeting Zoe, I'd come to realise what she meant.

Before I could say anything else, I heard a long, drawn-out

whistle coming from somewhere near by. Zoe gave a snort of annoyance and wheeled around, obviously gearing up for a tirade. But then, abruptly, she stopped.

Confused, I did the same, following her gaze. Only six feet away from us, sitting on the steps of the iconic fountain in the middle of Great Court, was a group of people. My eyes were drawn automatically to the young man on the bottom step. The hem of his coat grazed the stone and his shoes were sodden with rain, but he still managed to exude a particular grace. His hair gleamed in the light. A bit like the buildings, but more golden.

Ashton smiled languidly up at Zoe, although his eyes were watchful. 'Anima, how nice.'

It was all he needed to say, and in an instant, the exhaustion was banished from Zoe's face. She blushed prettily. 'Hi,' she answered in a dreamy tone. Evidently she'd forgotten all about being stood up.

I cleared my throat, and Zoe jumped. Ignoring my meaningful scowl, she shot me a look of aimiable severity. 'Well, well, well, what a coincidence! Mabel, these are the lovely people you would have met at the party if you hadn't gone AWOL for hours on end.'

Suppressing an eye-roll, I surveyed the rest of the group. Sitting on the step behind Ashton was a girl who seemed vaguely familiar. Maybe we'd met on Friday, or maybe I'd just seen her around town somewhere. She had one of those instantly recognisable faces – no matter how briefly you'd noticed her, you could still pick her out of a crowd. Delicate features, high cheekbones. Large, pale blue eyes. An elven face in shades of pastel. Her fox-red hair, playing across her face in the breeze, struck a vivid and contrasting note that made her all the more attractive. She paid me the briefest flicker of attention before returning to her phone.

My eyes drifted to the young man next to her, and before I'd even registered what I was seeing, my heart began to thud. I stared for three or four seconds before it really sank in what I was looking at. *Who* I was looking at. Cliff.

Black rollneck, plaid coat, a tattered book in his lap and an uneasy twist to his mouth. He wasn't looking at me, but I could tell from the crease between his brows that he'd noticed me. Noticed me and recognised me. Not that he wanted anyone else to know, that much was obvious. The way he was ignoring me, he didn't exactly seem pleased to see me again. I shouldn't have cared, but I felt my stomach knot unpleasantly, and I hurried to look away.

When I saw the guy sitting next to Ashton, my lips narrowed. His shoulder-length hair was pulled back into a topknot, but I recognised him at once.

He recognised me, too – and unlike Cliff, he didn't seem to mind showing it. A sly grin crept across his lips as he regarded me closely. 'My, my. Anna Karenina.'

About ten different retorts shot through my head, but they'd have pissed off Zoe as well. Thankfully, Ashton beat me to the punch. He tutted and shot his friend a look of reproach. 'Don't be rude, Vic. Her name is Mabel.' With a blithe smile, he turned to me. 'It means "lovable", doesn't it? Pretty name.'

'I'm not the one who chose it,' I replied matter-of-factly. A nudge from Zoe made me add, 'But on behalf of my parents, thank you very much.' Possibly I wasn't hiding my cynicism as well as I thought, because Zoe's fingers dug deeper into my side. My coat gave me a bit of cushioning, but I bit my lip to hold back any further remarks.

Ashton was still smiling. 'So, lovable Mabel. In case you missed the introductions last week: this is Victor, Norah and'—he turned and jerked his head at Cliff, who was still staring fixedly at the book, as though the letters might jump out and rescue him—'Blake.'

For a few dogged seconds, my brain wouldn't budge.

Sometimes, when you hear something totally unexpected, your mind acts momentarily like it didn't even notice. I only realised I'd been holding my breath once the five bogus letters had sunk to the bottom of my sea of thoughts. I exhaled a bit too loudly.

'Blake.' The name skidded off my tongue, floundering. Half a question, audibly bewildered, and instantly I wished I could take it back.

Slowly he raised his head to look at me. He made no response, but his eyes told me more than I wanted to know. In them I saw pure indifference: only the taut muscles in his jaw betrayed the tension he was feeling. He looked angry. Angry because I was forcing him to join the conversation, because I had made it obvious – if only to him – that we'd already met. Or perhaps he was simply angry with himself for allowing it. He probably regretted not immediately throwing me out on my arse. Thank God he hadn't been reckless enough to tell me his real name. Where would the elites of this world be if they showed the slightest spark of interest or decency towards people like me? And why was I even surprised? He did tell me he was an excellent liar.

I felt the back of my neck grow hot, a single-minded spreading warmth. It dug the burning tips of its fingers into my cheeks, warped the corners of my mouth and etched itself into my vocal cords. 'Another pretty name. It means "honest", doesn't it?' I said, keeping my tone friendly.

He arched his eyebrows, but otherwise his expression did not change. '"Dark", actually.'

The sound of his voice made me flinch a little. It was deep, a little rough, and – worst of all – familiar. Maybe part of me had been hoping he had a surly twin brother.

'Ah,' I said, drawing out the syllable. 'My mistake.' The smile I'd plastered on my face was becoming increasingly painful, as was the piercing gaze he had fixed on me. A mute, *stay quiet*.

I had more to say but choked it back. It was true: it *was* my mistake. My mistake to think even for a split second that someone I met at a party like that could be anything but a lying bastard.

Ashton had been following our exchange closely, and now he tilted his head. 'Would you like to join us?'

Zoe's mouth flipped into a sickle moon, lighting up her whole face. Apparently, she hadn't noticed that his friends seemed less enthusiastic about the prospect of spending their free time with us.

I wished I still had a coffee to throw at them, wipe the looks of resentment and irritation off their smug faces. Instead, I laid my hand protectively on Zoe's arm. 'We've got plans.'

Zoe sighed. 'Come on, you know I don't really need to be there. Anyway, I'm sure Davie would love to have you all to himself for half an hour.'

My cheeks grew hot. 'He's your friend too, Zoe.'

She shook off my hand, glaring at me stubbornly. 'Yep, so say hi for me. I'll see you later, Mabel.'

I hadn't even opened my mouth to reply before she was walking away from me. Ashton shifted readily aside to make room for her on the step. Suddenly I felt an urge to reach out and stop her. A hint of foreboding, the tip of an unfathomable fear darting through my mind. I did nothing. Just gripped the strap of my bag until I felt the leather flex.

As she sat down I turned to go, and for a moment my eye caught Cliff's. No, *Blake's*. The colour of his irises seemed even blacker than before, although it was much brighter out here than in the little library.

At that moment, I was struck by the thought that certain things seem darker in the light of day than they do by night. And that I still very much wanted to throw coffee in their faces. Especially his.

I turned on my heel without a word and left. Zoe's laughter was ringing in my ears, quickening my steps until the sound was lost amid the hubbub of the other students. The university fanned out before me, but the further I walked, the more I had the creeping feeling that I was leaving its centre behind.

~

The editorial office of the *Blue News* was tucked away in a corner at the far end of Trinity College, nearly a ten-minute walk from the main entrance. Davie's usual joke, whenever he was grumbling about another rejected grant application, was that the location of the office was a metaphor for how little the university appreciated its student newspaper.

Still, when the door swung open to my knock, I remembered immediately how much I liked the room's seclusion. It was roughly twenty square metres in size, with four work stations crammed between filing cabinets, archive racks and trolleys stacked with long-overdue library books.

In summer, the windows were thick with wisteria, but by now its tendrils had lost their blossoms, and the noonday light fell serenely across the carpet. Specks of dust danced in the narrow bands of sunshine, which seemed to be everywhere. Davie was by the open window, standing in a patch of light. Eyes closed, head back. The breeze had brought out the gooseflesh on his bare arms. The old radio on his desk was playing, tinnily blaring a song by The Smiths.

'You know you can air out the room every once in a while, even when you *don't* have visitors, right?' I shut the door behind me with a teasing grin and walked towards him.

Davie turned. The sun shimmered on his brown skin and the depths of his dark eyes. 'I just spend my whole life trying to make you feel special, Mabel.'

'Right back at you. Hence the fancy sandwiches from Nero's.'

I set down the paper bags on Davie's desk. Positioned

directly in front of the draughty window, it was the reason for his semi-constant cold. Unlike everybody else on the editorial staff, Davie spent the most time in this room. He was the only one with a key to the building and a permanent desk, the one who spent hours cooking up ideas for new articles and proofreading the layout of the upcoming edition for the twentieth time. Davie insisted there was no editor-in-chief at the *Blue News*: they aimed to be a democratic, everybody's equal type of publication. But ever since I'd heard the others calling him 'Commander', I hadn't given that much credence.

'My hero.' Davie shut the window and collapsed into his chair.

I sat down on a chair on the other side of the desk. He always put the chairs out when we were meeting for lunch. Over the past few months, it had become one of my favourite rituals.

We had met at the Cambridge v. Oxford Boat Race. One of the biggest events of the year, it took its celebration of the long-standing rivalry between the two elite universities to the point of absurdity. I hadn't been able to muster up much enthusiasm at the idea of travelling all the way into London for it, but Zoe declared that you couldn't call yourself a proper Cambridge student until you'd experienced it for yourself.

After two hours spent shivering on the freezing cold banks of the Thames, waiting for the boats to pass by, I still didn't get it.

'Does it make me a bad person if I want one of them to fall in?' someone next to me asked as the long rowing boats finally shot past, to an eruption of cheers and whoops around us.

'Depends,' I said, with a glance at the camera he was pointing towards the water. 'Is that for personal or professional reasons?'

He sighed deeply. 'Sadly, I don't think the answer will make me any more endearing.'

He was wrong about that.

'Where's Zoe?' asked Davie now, unwrapping his avocado sandwich from its greaseproof paper.

Immediately my smile faltered. My eyes flitted to the bag containing Zoe's veggie wrap, which I had reflexively placed in front of the chair next to me. 'She got held up,' I said, doing my best to sound guileless. 'She told me to say hi.'

Feigning guilelessness never worked on Davie. Journalistic instinct, he called it. I called it being an exhaustingly good judge of character. He arched his eyebrows, lowering the sandwich. 'Did you two fall out?'

I picked some watercress out of my sandwich. 'No. She just got waylaid by one of those arrogant pricks from Trinity College.'

Davie cradled his chin in his hand, his interest piqued. The sandwich evidently forgotten. Typical Davie: no matter how hungry he was, when he was on the trail of a good story, everything else went by the wayside. 'And you don't think much of him?'

'Dunno really. I haven't spoken to him much.' Anything else would be a lie. I couldn't say what kind of person Ashton was. Lurking underneath that marble façade might be a kind-hearted man of unexpected depth. I wanted to believe that, for Zoe's sake. But the truth was, I could sense something wasn't right about him. He put me on edge.

'Then why are you concerned?' Davie asked.

I sighed, glancing briefly up at the ceiling. 'It's Zoe. She's so sweet and ... good. And that just doesn't mix well with a hot, self-absorbed guy who thinks the whole world revolves around him.' I hesitated, picking out more watercress to avoid meeting Davie's sharp scrutiny. 'Plus, you know when you just see someone and immediately know they're bad news?'

'Sure.' Davie nodded earnestly. 'I think they call that being prejudiced.'

I rolled my eyes in mock you-got-me-there exasperation and threw my napkin at him. Davie caught it and tucked it into his shirt pocket before he gave me an encouraging smile.

'Look, don't worry about Zoe. Only the other day I saw her tearing a strip off some kid who tried to jump the queue at the coffee cart. That guy will never be the same again, trust me. That woman can take care of herself.'

'You're telling me.' Zoe didn't need protecting. If she felt like she was being treated unfairly, she was more than capable of standing up for herself. If anybody else had done what Ashton did yesterday, Zoe would already have kicked him to the kerb, but she obviously found something about him so alluring that she couldn't stay away.

I wrestled my face into a smile. 'Sorry, I didn't mean to rant at you.'

Davie waved it off. 'That's what friends are for.' Reaching a hand into his bag, he put a small box on the desk in front of me. 'And for this, of course.'

I caught a whiff of the sugary smell before I'd even opened the cardboard flaps. Chocolate cake from Bridget's, the outrageously expensive bakery near St John's College. The cake for which I'd gladly go hungry for two days, and which I couldn't really afford. One miniscule slice cost my weekly coffee budget at the dining hall.

'God, you really are perfect, Davie Waverly!' I reached for the fork in the box. One bite and my mood lifted, my smile became more genuine. As a general rule I didn't like gifts that I couldn't afford myself, but for this I made an exception. The taste was worth swallowing my pride.

Davie watched with satisfaction as I divided the cake into tiny pieces in reverent silence, allowing each bite to slowly dissolve on my tongue.

'Anyway, let's talk about something more pleasant. What's

new in the world of Cambridge?' I put the fork down, leaving half the slice for later.

Davie folded his arms behind his head. 'Are you sitting down?' he began in a low, dramatic voice. 'Because the law-school café is switching to a different catering company.'

I clutched at my heart. 'Say it ain't so.'

'Yep. Apparently some faulty refrigerators resulted in a teensy tiny outbreak of salmonella.'

'Well, it's a good thing we eat lunch on this hallowed ground instead of stooping to the level of the café.' I made a sweeping gesture that encompassed the hodgepodge of papers littering Davie's desk.

He raised his hands defensively. 'Hey: one word from you and I'll bust out the tealights, give you a full-on candlelit dinner.'

I laughed and batted the idea away. 'Thanks, but I'm just fine. Besides, I think it might be a fire hazard, what with this giant mountain of paper.' Curious, I leant forward to read the label of the topmost file. It was so thick that the clip had popped open. 'What is all this, anyway?'

Davie casually slid another folder on top, covering the label. 'Research.'

I tried to catch his eye. Suddenly his face was wary. 'That's a lot of research for an article about the law-school café.'

'I'm a conscientious journalist.' Davie scrunched up the paper bag and tossed it at the bin next to the desk, missing narrowly. He didn't go and pick it up. Part of me was sure he didn't want to leave me alone with the files.

Which only made me more curious. Davie wasn't usually secretive about his articles. In fact, he normally liked to talk about them at length, giving me several rough drafts to read. This was weird. And I'd always been a sucker for weird.

'And a terrible liar. What is it really?'

He said nothing. Outside, the clouds had drawn in again, casting a dove-grey light through the window and dropping a soft filter between us. The heap of paper had taken on a bluish glow, and something in Davie's eyes flashed silver. I knew that look: an ominous mixture of anticipation, nerves and emotional strain.

'What are you up to, Davie?'

He sighed, then leant in closer and lowered his voice. 'Okay, fine. I'm working on a new story. Something really big.'

'Sounds intriguing.' My heart began to thud, and I shifted to the edge of my seat. The excitement in Davie's voice was contagious.

He nodded, leaning back again. 'It is.'

'Now you're really making me curious.' I tried again to reach for the file, but Davie was too quick. He grabbed my hand and squeezed it, smiling at me apologetically. 'Leave it. It's all pretty vague, and ... that's all I can say about it at the moment.'

'Even to me?'

His smile softened, and he stroked the back of my hand with his thumb. '*Especially* to you.'

As I gazed down at our fingers, I felt a slight flush of self-consciousness. Davie and I were friends, so inevitably we ended up touching sometimes – no big deal – but in moments like this, I understood what Zoe meant when she raised her eyebrows suggestively after seeing me with Davie and whispered, 'Uh-oh.' I didn't know exactly what this thing was between us, but I knew I didn't want to find out. Davie was the best male friend I'd ever had, and I wasn't going to let anything change that. Not that I had the time for a relationship anyway.

Pretending to pout, I drew back my hand and reached for my bag. 'Fine. Whatever you say. Guess I'll leave you to work in peace, then.'

'As soon as it's ready to print, you'll be the first to read it,' he promised, with an anxious grin.

I tried to shake it off, and opened my mouth to reply when my phone buzzed. Skimming the message, I groaned.

'What is it?' asked Davie with concern.

'Zoe.' I dropped the phone into my coat pocket. 'Ashton's invited her to some sort of thing with his friends again. She wants me to come too.'

'Was it really that bad last time?'

I hesitated. Until about an hour ago I would have said the evening was mixed but not exactly *bad*. Despite the circumstances, the moment I'd shared in that strange room with that strange man had been somehow beautiful. Special. Memorable. But now that I knew 'Cliff' had been a mirage, I was even more impatient to put it all behind me. 'It was just kind of weird. Those people are ... I'm not sure what the word is. Elitist? Snooty? Like something out of a horror movie?'

'Again, all I'm hearing are your preconceptions,' said Davie. And in some ways he was right, of course.

I poked my tongue out at him anyway and flounced over to the door. 'You'd get it if you'd been there too. They made you give a password to get in, Davie. And it wasn't like 'apple punch' or some other corny bullshit, it was *Sturnus vulgaris*.'

I heard Davie exhale sharply. When I turned around, he was on his feet. 'As in ... starlings?'

I raised my eyebrows, impressed. If even Davie – who knew absolutely nothing about nature or animals – had heard the name before, then I must have a gap in my knowledge. 'Did you switch to natural sciences or something?' I asked, amused.

He didn't return my smile. 'Zoe's boyfriend. What's his full name?'

I frowned, trying to recall. 'Ashton Griffin, I think. But why–' I broke off when my phone buzzed again. This time it was my alarm, reminding me that the next seminar was about to start. I'd have to get a move on. Quickly I switched it off and shot Davie an apologetic smile. He was still staring at me blankly.

'Guess I'd better run. Thanks for the cake and the conversation. Text you later, yeah?'

It wasn't until I'd left the building that I realised I'd left the half-eaten cake behind. And that Davie never said goodbye.

CHAPTER 3
MABEL

Zoe was sitting on a kitchen chair, hunched over the table. Her chin resting in her hands, she stared at me wide-eyed. Even with the lingering drowsiness and in the neon glare of the ceiling lamps, her gaze was intense and piercing.

I could never hold out very long when she looked at me like that. I turned swiftly away, stirring the pot of spaghetti with a fork.

We'd bumped into each other thirty minutes ago, in the shared kitchen. It was after nine, and at this time of night we usually had the space all to ourselves. On Fridays, the others generally headed into the town centre, to spend the evening at one of Cambridge's countless pubs. Usually, Zoe was one of them, but today she had other plans. For twenty minutes now she'd been talking about the 'event' that Ashton had invited her to. Or rather, us, if I was going to believe her.

'Zoe, honestly,' I began, when I could no longer ignore her eyes boring into the back of my neck, 'don't you think you'd have more fun without me?'

She snorted. 'Without my best friend? No, I don't think so.'

I resisted the urge to point out that, last time, we'd spent all of five minutes together before I'd ducked out and she'd swanned off with Ashton. I didn't really like the idea of telling her where I'd been. And with whom. So far, I'd been evasive, explaining that I'd gone for a nose around the building, but I was afraid that running into not-Cliff again might lead me to reveal more.

Zoe would probably say the poor guy had a self-esteem problem, and that's why he gave me a fake name. That I should give him a chance to explain himself. But I didn't need any explanations from him. The way he'd reacted to me earlier told me everything I needed to know. He was simply a liar who thought he was better than me. And I didn't want to talk or think about somebody like that. Let alone spend another evening in his company.

I put the colander in the sink. 'Right. And what kind of event is this, exactly?'

'Don't say it like that,' Zoe replied, sounding disgruntled.

'Like what?'

'You know, like'—she drew air quotes—'*event*.'

I chewed my lip, avoiding her eye. Hurriedly I drained the pasta, grateful for the cloud of steam that rose up and veiled the look on my face. How were you even supposed to say that word without the air quotes? And wasn't it kind of snobby to refer to a Friday night hang with friends as an 'event'?

'So, what happens at these … get-togethers?' Admittedly, the euphemism still sounded suspiciously air-quotey.

'No idea.' Zoe shrugged. 'Something amazing that we absolutely cannot miss out on?'

'He didn't tell you what they're planning?' I eyed the look of childish euphoria on her face with concern. I didn't know anybody with as little innate mistrust as Zoe.

'I didn't ask.' She shook her head. 'Why do you always have to know everything? Just take things as they come.'

Right, sure. Because I had such a great experience last time. Silently I put the pasta into two bowls and added a tablespoon of walnut pesto to each. Zoe smiled gratefully as I sat down and slid her a portion across the table.

'Why are you so keen to go, anyway? It was only yesterday he stood you up,' I said carefully, after she'd taken the first mouthful.

'Ash didn't do anything wrong, not when you really think about it. I mean, he didn't say he was *definitely* going to call. A maybe isn't a commitment.'

It took a lot of effort not to contradict her. I knew it was what she needed to believe if she wanted to like Ashton, but I still thought she was wrong. A maybe can mean lots of things, but usually it's a way of giving someone false hope. Especially if what you really mean is never. It was inconsiderate and selfish. Definitely not what I wanted for my best friend.

Zoe sighed. 'Okay, don't give me that look, like I'm some pathetic woman letting herself get taken advantage of. Ashton isn't a bad person, Mabel. In fact, he's been a total gentleman. We haven't even slept together yet. He hasn't even tried it on. I think he genuinely likes me, you know?'

'All right, then why aren't you spending time alone, just the two of you? Don't you think it's weird he's always dragging you along to see his friends, like he's bringing them a present, like you're his little "contribution" to the fun?'

The word was out of my mouth before I could think twice. I could have bitten off my tongue. Zoe had seemed so unlike herself after the party that I never told her about my lovely little chat with Ashton's friends. Before I had time to explain or backpedal, she raised a hand and glared at me, her eyes flashing fury.

'Okay. You know what? I'm going to go out tonight and do whatever the hell I want. And I'd really like you to come with me. Because I love you, and because I think it would do you good to switch off for a bit. But if you don't want to, that's absolutely fine.' She stood up so abruptly that the wooden chair rasped unpleasantly over the linoleum. 'But stop making me feel guilty about it. I don't have to justify why I'm doing stuff that makes me feel good, Mabel. Not even to you.'

I opened my mouth, but she was already storming out of the kitchen. Slumping back into my chair in resignation, I stared at her empty seat. Guilt throbbed dully somewhere behind my ribcage, mingling with a vague anxiety that refused to dissipate.

I was prodding morosely at the tepid pasta when I heard a sudden knock behind me, making me jump.

The best thing about our kitchen was the patio. In summertime we often used to eat outside, sitting at the picnic table in the shade of the pink magnolia trees. In autumn and winter, however, we usually kept the sliding doors closed. You could use that door to reach the college, but we tended to prefer the main entrance.

I was surprised to see the outline of a figure through the glass. I stood up uncertainly and walked over to the door. It had begun to rain again a few hours earlier, blurring the night outside into a near-impenetrable veil of blue and grey. It took me a second or two to realise who was there.

I hurried to slide the door open, letting in a rush of chilly air, and clutched my wool jacket more tightly to my chest. 'Davie, what are you doing here?' I shook my head, staring. He was soaked to the skin. 'You're wet through. Come in.'

Davie shook his head. The greenish kitchen light cast dark shadows across his features, and I couldn't read his expression. 'I just have to—Okay, listen.' His voice sounded rough, and halting. Oddly unfamiliar. Leaning in, he fixed me with an urgent look. I could make out the expression on his face now: concentration, and a deep undercurrent of anxiety. 'I just wanted to quickly tell you something.' He took an audible breath. 'I think you were right. Ashton isn't a good guy. And nor are the people he hangs out with. That ... that group is bad news, Mabel. Really bad. The kind of people you want to give a seriously wide berth.'

I stared at him, perplexed, trying to make sense of his words. 'What do you mean?' I took a step towards him. Water was soaking into my socks, but I barely noticed. All of a sudden, I was cold, and not just because of the rain: I was shivering more inside than out.

Davie ran a hand over his cropped black hair. 'I can't tell you any more right now. Just trust me, okay? Stay away from them. And whatever you do, don't go to any more of their parties.'

I couldn't quite decide whether to be amused or disconcerted. The result was a crooked grin. 'Wait, so you're telling me the guy Zoe's hanging out with tonight is – what? A threat? And you expect me to let her go alone?'

He shook his head vehemently. 'Tell Zoe she can't go either.'

My pulse began to race, although I still wasn't sure what Davie was really telling me. Part of me didn't doubt him, because he was putting into words exactly what I'd felt all week. The feeling I couldn't explain to Zoe because I didn't understand it myself. 'It's *Zoe*. You know what she's like, Davie. In what parallel universe would she listen to me? Especially if I don't even give her a reason?'

I took a deep breath. This whole thing was silly. Sure, Ashton probably wasn't the decent, kind-hearted person Zoe wanted him to be, but that didn't mean he was *dangerous*. We were talking about a bunch of spoilt, cliquey undergrads here, not the mafia. Besides, I knew how Davie could get sometimes. When he was working on a story, he had a tendency to get carried away, so whatever he thought he knew about Ashton, it might turn out to be nothing.

I forced my lips into a placid smile, perhaps as much to reassure myself as him. 'Come on, Davie. What's really going on here?'

His brow creased deeply, the muscles tense in his jaw. I could almost hear the cogs whirring. Then he shook his head jerkily and focused on me. 'I'll explain everything, just give me some time, okay? I want to be completely sure.'

'God, you sound like we're the main characters in some cheap horror flick. You know, low on budget, high on gore. That kind.'

I crossed my arms, trying not to shiver. I wasn't sure if it was the cold rain against my skin, or Davie's warning. As much as I tried to think rationally, to explain away what he was telling me, the look on his face made me uneasy. I felt like I was under threat from something I couldn't see. Like I could be attacked at any moment, and there was no way to tell what it was or where it might come from.

Davie gave a hoarse laugh. 'Jesus. You don't have a fucking clue, Mabel.'

I frowned, confused, but he was already backing away. The grey rain obscured his shape, and I caught only a hazy glimpse of his eyes, still fixed on me intently. 'Keep away from those people. Please. Promise me.'

There were several retorts and questions on the tip of my tongue, but something made me bite them back. Even in the bluish dusk, I could see his pupils were clouded with worry. So instead, I gave a weak smile. 'Sure. Fine.'

He nodded, relieved, and turned to go. 'I'll text you tomorrow. Look after yourself.'

'You, too,' I replied, but he was already leaving, passing through the arbour on the other side of the patio and vanishing into the night.

Just as I slid the door shut, heart pounding, Zoe walked into the kitchen. Without so much as a glance in my direction, she dumped her bowl in the sink and opened the fridge to take out a bottle of wine.

I girded my loins. 'Zoe.'

She turned to me, the gleam of irritation in her eyes as striking as the shimmer on her lids. 'For the hundredth time: I'm going, Mabel. I respect that you don't want to come with me, but you also need to respect the fact that I'm not staying here, okay? You can't—'

'Fine,' I interrupted, giving up. There was no point trying – it was impossible to persuade Zoe not to go. Besides, how could I explain something I didn't even understand myself?

Listen, Davie was just here, and he said your new boyfriend is a really bad guy. He wouldn't give me any details, but would you mind breaking off all contact with him anyway, pretty please?

Even I wouldn't buy that. There was nothing I could say to stop her. And nothing, after what I'd heard from Davie, that could stop me going with her.

Sorry, Davie, I thought, then I cleared my throat and put on a conciliatory smile. 'I actually just wanted to ask if I can come with you after all.'

CHAPTER 4
CLIFF

The white moon was suspended in the sky beyond the large east window. Its light broke through the stained glass, casting a mosaic on the floor of the chapel. I examined my pallid fingers in their borrowed finery. Blue and red and yellow and green. Strange how colourful one can appear when inside everything is grey.

To me, King's College Chapel was the most beautiful place in the whole university. You could see the work that had gone into the building over the hundred years it took to finish it. During our first week at Cambridge, I'd spent a lot of time here. At night, when tourists and believers alike had vanished, I stayed on alone, devoting hours to my study of the Gothic chapel. The fan vault, the altarpiece, the windows, the organ – every detail told its own story.

Everywhere I went, I began by seeking out a church. I'd always liked them. Not because they made me feel closer to any higher power, but because I felt closer to myself. In those vast halls, surrounded by columns, cool stone and vivid glass, the world receded. There were no distractions, no sea of smells or sounds or other stimuli. The world was loud, but churches were places of silence. It felt as though the universe had pressed pause as soon as I stepped through their wide-flung doors.

Churches soothed me, but I had never really understood what they did for people of faith, what it was that kept drawing them back. Sometimes I wished I could feel it, too. To know what it was like not to be alone. To believe that everything happened for a reason. That all sins could be forgiven. But I felt nothing. I didn't believe in God. I didn't believe in anything anymore.

When I heard footsteps and cheery whistling behind me, I shut my eyes. I didn't need to turn around to know who it was. I only knew one person who could walk through a chapel so heedlessly, without a care in the world. There was nothing Ashton held sacred. Well, almost nothing.

'Why do I always find you in such depressing places?' He stopped short beside me, throwing a swift glance at the window before moving to stand directly in front of me so that I couldn't ignore him. Even in the shadow of night, I could make out his features clearly. That subtle radiance in his eyes, which told me what he'd just been doing. 'We can start. It's done. The porter is taking a well-earned nap.' Pale clouds of breath danced between us, his much more visible than mine.

'Did you have to?' I backed away until I felt the pew behind me. Ashton was often hard work, but I found it especially difficult to be around him in the immediate aftermath. My stomach clenched, and the place just below my heart began to pulse unpleasantly. I put my hand there and pressed, trying to contain the feeling.

'No,' Ashton replied mockingly. 'I could have invited him to join our little celebration. But I prefer the company of our other guests.'

'Who are you bringing this time?' I didn't really want to know. It didn't matter anyway. All the names and faces blended in my mind into a river of inconsequential details. They came and went. We stayed.

'Zoe.' The smile that appeared at the corners of his mouth seemed almost genuine. He was good at dissimulating, whether about what he felt or what he was. Once, I'd envied him. Now, I could sense that a part of me despised him for it.

'Again? Aren't you over her yet?' I tried to remember how many times he'd mentioned her. As far as I knew, he'd been seeing her for a couple of weeks – much longer than normal, and it was starting to verge on the problematic.

'Why? She's sweet. Quite exceptionally exquisite, actually. I can't get enough of her.' He gave me a suggestive wink.

'Ash, please.' I looked away, irritated, and rubbed my forehead with the heel of my hand. The throbbing in my chest had eased, but the one behind my temples had worsened. The fickle weather made my head ache. A predisposition to migraines – one of the body's more taxing habits.

'What? You asked.' Ashton grinned and jabbed me in the ribs. 'You can even have a go yourself, if you like. I don't mind sharing. Since it's you.'

'Ashton.' The word was little more than a breathless growl. At that moment I would have gladly taken a migraine if it let me get away from him.

'All right, all right, calm down. We don't have to.' He paused theatrically, then cocked his head to one side. 'She's bringing her friend, too.'

My heart skipped two beats. When it picked up again, the throbbing was more intense. Painful. I hesitated. Three, maybe four seconds, but even as they passed, I knew they were disastrous. Ashton would register the least hint of inner struggle. He knew me too well.

'Who?' I asked, still hoping to sound like I didn't care.

A knowing smile played across Ashton's lips. Arms folded, he leant against the wooden pew beside him. 'Don't bother.

You know *who*. I saw the way she stared at you. You know her.'

Reflexively, I balled my fists, but relaxed them instantly when I noticed his eyes drifting in that direction. 'I can't be held responsible for people staring at me. It's not like I chose my face,' I snapped.

I'd been afraid he'd picked up on the moment of tension between Mabel and me by the fountain. I'd made every effort not to look at her. But I'd wanted to.

I'd wanted to see if her dark hair was still lightly tousled, if her cheeks were flushed with that same delicate veil of pink, if her bare lashes were still as thick and wild. I'd wanted to see if I'd imagined the trail of beauty spots on her left temple, or the smattering of freckles across the narrow bridge of her nose, strangely out of keeping with her February face. I'd wanted to see if her eyes still held such depths in daylight, and if I would glimpse again that rare curiosity in the way she looked at people. At *me*.

What she'd seen in me that night, what she'd said about me, had come dangerously close to the truth. Dangerously, but also refreshingly. It was a long time since I'd felt like I didn't have to pretend. The way she stared at me earlier was different. Startled, bewildered, angry, challenging. And ultimately disappointed. I couldn't blame her for it, and I shouldn't let it bother me, but somehow the idea was intolerable.

Ashton studied me intently before at last he nodded. 'Whatever you say. I thought I was doing you a favour. It's been a while since you got *close* to anybody.' He clicked his tongue meaningfully. The sound echoed through the chapel, making the hairs on my arms stand on end under my jumper.

'That's not your problem.'

'Isn't it?' Ashton gave a grim smile. 'I'm the one who has to spend my free time with you, don't I, my little ray of sunshine?'

'Nobody's forcing you to,' I said tonelessly, although that

wasn't true. I would have given anything to be alone. Far away from Ashton, far away from all of it. But they would never permit it, we both knew that. There were some things you couldn't escape. One of them was yourself.

Ashton groaned noisily. With a fluid movement he pushed off from the pew, grabbed me by the shoulders and gazed urgently into my eyes. The light was a wash of colour across our faces: Ashton's cheeks shimmered red, his hair blue, but his eyes were dark and searching.

For a few long seconds we held each other's gaze, then he shook me gently. 'You're my best friend,' he said, unexpectedly serious. 'We are your family. I only want the best for you, okay?' He waited until I nodded weakly, then laughed. 'Good. So. Maybe you could forget for just one night that you're the world's wettest blanket and have a bit of fun?'

Without waiting for an answer, he turned on his heel and strode off down the aisle towards the exit. He didn't need to make sure I was following. We both knew that sooner or later, I would.

'If you don't want Mabel, do you mind if I offer her to Victor?' he called out, already so far away that his voice distorted as it echoed through the nave. Yet I caught the gist of his words, and the pulse in my temples throbbed harder. Strangely, so did my heart. 'Evidently, he's taken a shine to her – what was his poetic turn of phrase? – to her "appealing bitchiness".'

'Ashton,' I repeated simply, although something in me had flinched. I hadn't failed to notice the way Victor reacted to Mabel earlier. Putting two and two together, I realised he must have been one of the people she was talking about in the small library.

'I don't like being referred to as a "contribution", or treated like something you'd win at poker', she had said. I could still see the look on her face. The mute defiance, the steely self-assurance – this wasn't someone who let other people define her, that much was unmistakeable. She had impressed me straight off the bat. Maybe it was why I'd forgotten, for a fleeting moment, who I was. Who I was supposed to be.

Ashton laughed. The sound mingled with the echo of his footfall and trickled hollowly to where I stood. 'Since when did you start using my name as an insult?'

Since you started acting this way, I thought, but said nothing out loud. I knew it wasn't true. He hadn't changed, at least not much. The problem wasn't what he did but what I *didn't* do.

I had forgotten how to fit in. With my family, my world, my ... life. And I had no one but myself to blame. A part of me had slipped through my fingers. The shard that had bound me in some fundamental way to Ashton and the others.

I knew he felt it, too. It was why he kept insisting all the more resolutely that we stick together, planning one evening after another. 'Give it time', he'd said the other day, patting my shoulder reassuringly. '*Tempus curat omnia.*' As I turned to go, his words came back to me. *Tempus curat omnia*. Time heals all.

Wherever that lost part of me had gone, I wasn't going to find it here. And although I didn't dare say so in front of Ashton, I doubted time would make much difference.

CHAPTER 5
MABEL

The Cam was criss-crossed by bridges, and in summer there was an endless stream of punts passing underneath. Zoe had talked me into doing a tour with her during freshers' week, even though I wasn't particularly keen on water. In the end, though, I had to admit it was worth it. Being carried past the colleges, seeing all the students sitting on the banks, letting my fingertips graze the slate-blue water and the low-hanging bellies of the bridges – it lent the university an even greater magic.

At night, however, I found it hard to see anything more than a chilling warning in the black river. Perhaps, in part, it was the people. It wasn't just their presence there. In summertime, the meadows around the Cam were crowded well into the evening. But in autumn, most of the students retreated to the pubs in town. It was also the *manner* of their presence. Most of the bridges were on college grounds, and students weren't usually allowed to gather there after dark. Parties would be rudely broken up by the porters.

Just like the week before, however, these students didn't seem to care. There were fewer than last time, about fifteen or so, but they made no effort to be quiet. Or inconspicuous. A speaker was playing somewhere, Edith Piaf's voice drifting out across the water.

As Zoe and I stepped onto Clare Bridge, my eyes were drawn to the riverbank below. A group of students were sitting on the grass, which must surely still be damp with rain. Four of them were distinctly underdressed. While I was shivering in my layers – shirt, sweater dress and coat – they weren't even wearing jackets. Only two of them had pulled the sleeves of their coats down over their hands, their rapt faces turning from one host to another.

I grimaced. I knew that look. It was the same one that appeared on Zoe's face as soon as we laid eyes on Ashton, standing halfway across the bridge. We were late, because Zoe had kept changing her outfit. I had simply reapplied my lipstick: a deep, gleaming red called 'Deep Wish' – ironic, because my only wish was to get through the evening in one piece. Davie's words kept playing in my head, overlaying the scene with a dismal grey pall. I had no idea what he'd meant when he said these people were 'bad news', but I was feeling in pretty bad shape myself by the time we reached them.

'There you are.' Ashton drew Zoe into a half-hug, planting a kiss on her cheek.

Even in the dark I could see her blushing. I was only half-listening as she explained why we were late, my eyes sweeping across the people gathered on the bridge. A couple of them I thought I vaguely recognised, although I couldn't put names to the faces. Well, only two. I felt a tiny stab of disappointment, and despised myself for it. I folded my arms and took a step closer to the balustrade. On the bank below, a few party-goers were dangling their feet in the water – just watching them made my own toes feel like ice.

The girl next to Ashton was pouring herself a glass of wine. 'Every time I come here I feel like the whole thing is about to collapse beneath our feet. I mean, when was this even built? Like in the 1800s?'

'1638,' I corrected her automatically. 'Clare Bridge is the oldest surviving bridge in Cambridge.'

Zoe smiled at me in a way that made me feel embarrassed. 'Told you she was smart.'

The girl twisted a finger in her black bob, murmering something that sounded a lot like 'smart-arse, you mean', but it barely registered. I'd been called a lot of names in my life, and 'smart-arse' or 'know-it-all' were among the more polite ones.

Zoe's eyes narrowed, but I broke in before she could say anything. 'So ... your event'—I cleared my throat to get rid of the gooseflesh—'it's taking place on a bridge, is it?'

The girl surveyed the run in my tights, then the fraying hem of my coat. 'Would you feel more comfortable *under* the bridge?'

I almost let out a groan. Not because she'd hit a nerve – 'poor' was also one of the more pleasant words I'd been called over the course of my life – but because I knew not everybody present would take it lying down. As if on cue, a jolt ran through Zoe's body, and she took a step forward. 'Excuse me?'

I reached for her hand, trying to defuse the situation. 'It's fine, leave it.'

'No.' She tore her hand away, still bearing down on the girl. I didn't know anybody else for whom loyalty was so closely intertwined with impulsivity. 'If she's got a problem with you then she's got a problem with me.'

'Hey, relax. I don't have a problem with your friend.' The girl shot me a look that added: *She's not worth the effort.*

Zoe planted a hand on her hip. 'Oh, really? Because I could have sworn that being around someone three times cleverer than you are was making you feel threatened.'

Now it was the girl's turn to take a step forward. 'Are you calling me stupid? That's a bold thing for a naïve kid like you to say, *moth.*'

Soft creases furrowed Zoe's brow. 'What's that supposed to mean?'

'Enough, Clementine.' Ashton gave her a warning look. 'Behave yourself.'

'You forget – you're not in a position to order everybody else around,' she replied dryly. Her eyes darted from Zoe's face to mine, before she turned away and stalked off.

Ashton ran a hand over Zoe's tense shoulders, bringing it to rest on the back of her neck. I thought of predators grabbing their prey by the scruff, and suddenly I felt queasy again. 'Sorry about that,' he said, once Clementine was out of earshot. 'My friends can be a bit weird about meeting new people. They don't mean any harm.'

I felt like retorting that a lack of calculation or intent didn't make it any less harmful, just more pointless. 'No big deal,' I said instead. Not to make Ashton happy, just to step Zoe down from DEFCON 1.

Judging by the look in her eyes, she was still toying with the idea of going after Clementine. Zoe never shied away from confrontation when defending her values and opinions, even at the risk of her own safety. I loved that about her, but often it worried me as well.

Ashton seemed to notice it too. His hand shifted to her throat, and he stroked his thumb across her skin. Within seconds Zoe's gaze had softened, and the noise she made was suspiciously like a sigh. He responded with a satisfied smirk. 'What do you reckon, Anima – come for a swim with me?'

I was about to laugh, but Zoe's arrow-swift, 'Sure' held me back. I stared in bewilderment from her to Ashton, who was already unbuttoning his shirt. 'In the Cam? It's the end of October, the water's way too cold for that.'

He grinned. As he undid the last button, my eyes went automatically to his collarbone, where my attention was caught by the mole immediately below it. It was oddly angular, and much darker than the ones a little further to the right. It looked almost like ... a tiny puzzle piece.

'I'll make sure she doesn't feel the cold, I promise,' he said. Zoe's face reddened again, but I felt myself turn pale. 'You're welcome to join us,' he added. 'A couple of my friends down there would love to see you again.' Something about the way he said it made me involuntarily draw my coat more tightly around me.

'Mabel's scared of water, especially in the dark,' Zoe said before I could reply. 'When she was a child she got pulled downriver in a rowing boat and they didn't find her until the middle of the night.'

I threw her a warning look, but she missed it: too busy staring at Ashton's hand in hers. Raptly, as if it didn't even occur to her she was merrily spilling all my secrets.

Ashton regarded me with interest. 'Sounds like quite a story.'

'Just your standard-issue childhood trauma,' I said dryly, although the mere memory of the day sent a chill down my spine. 'But no, thanks, I'll pass.'

Ashton shrugged. 'Up to you.'

As he made to lead Zoe away, she pulled back from him and came to stand in front of me. 'Are you going to be all right by yourself?'

The fact that she still had the wherewithal to ask dispelled the last of my exasperation, leaving only concern in its place. I glanced at Ashton, waiting a few feet away. He was still smiling, but with a strange impatience that made me uneasy. 'Zoe,' I began uncertainly, not knowing how to stop her. I could see in her eyes how unreservedly she trusted Ashton to keep her safe.

'You have my permission to give Tangerine or whatever her name is a smack in the mouth if she starts acting like a bitch again.' She prodded me in the ribs and smiled, so radiantly that the corner of my mouth twitched in return.

'Look after yourself, okay?'

'Always do. And have fun, yeah? I'll be back soon.' She gave me a hug and let Ashton lead her away.

I stayed by the balustrade, watching them go. Ashton's shirt dissolved into the night before they'd even left the bridge, but I could see the pale glow of Zoe's beige skirt until she shimmied out of it on the bank. I watched, unsettled, as Ashton jumped into the water and threw his arms wide to catch her. No sooner were they in the river than the others started stripping down to their underwear too – evidently this was a team effort to catch a cold.

My eyes wandered to Clementine at the other end of the bridge. She was standing in the light of a lamppost, talking to a girl who looked distinctly nervous. Ashton's friend placed her hand on the other girl's throat and began to stroke. The longer she let her hand linger, the more I saw the apprehension in the girl's eyes fade. But not only that. Everything else faded a little, too: the colour in her cheeks, the smile at the corners of her mouth, the tension in her posture.

I frowned and took a step towards them. 'So wary?' a voice whispered into my ear.

Whirling around, I bumped straight into someone's chest. A wide, bare chest, because the person was wearing only boxer shorts. I lifted my gaze to his face, which was very close to mine. Victor placed his hands either side of me on the balustrade, smiling down at me. It took every ounce of willpower not to ram my knee directly between his legs.

'Something tells me you lot don't really care what happens to your guests.'

He laughed, his breath hot on my face. It smelt like peppermint toothpaste, but somehow I got the feeling he was drunk. 'That's where you're wrong. We're meticulous when it comes to our "guests".'

I hesitated. Victor definitely seemed like he was on

59

something, if not drunk then high. Enough, perhaps, that he'd accidentally let something slip. 'And who are "you", anyway? Clearly not your average group of friends.'

Victor blinked, but his face betrayed no emotion. If I caught a glimpse of anything, it was a flicker of curiosity. 'Oh, yeah? And what makes you say that?'

'Well, for one thing, you walk around the college grounds like you own the place. Where are the porters when you do stuff like this?' Victor tilted his head to one side, but said nothing. I decided to take a shot in the dark. 'As far as I'm aware, you're all studying at different colleges, but you act like you've been inseparable for years. Then there are the tattoos.'

'Tattoos?' I didn't fail to notice the attention creeping into his eyes. His pupils seemed to contract, as if his mind were clearing.

The thought had just popped into my head, but now it was solidifying into certainty. I gestured to the mark just below his collar bone. 'Ashton's got the same one. Something tells me you all do. They look like they belong together.'

Victor grinned broadly, although it didn't reach his eyes. 'You're very observant, Anna Karenina.'

I stared at him, exasperated. 'Stop calling me that.'

'Would you rather I used Mabel Emilee Golding?' He rolled every single syllable around in his mouth, leaning in. Instinctively I shrank back, but the balustrade pressed mercilessly into the small of my back. 'Daughter of Rowan Golding and Simon Lore, both deceased. Born in Bath but resident of Hamsey since the age of fifteen, in the care of her guardian, Clara Golding. Second-year English undergrad on a full bursary at Trinity Hall, currently living in West Court, J2.'

Suddenly my heart was pounding against my ribs, thudding harder every time he recited a fact he couldn't possibly know. Wasn't *allowed* to know. My mouth went dry – I swallowed. 'How—'

'Like I said,' he interrupted with a sneer. 'We're meticulous when it comes to our guests. Especially when we've taken a liking to their company.'

'I haven't given you any reason to like me. I hope.'

'I'm afraid you have. You're so gloriously closed-off. It has a certain charm.' He lifted his hand and coiled a lock of my hair around his fingers. His nail polish gleamed blue as I felt a surge of red-hot panic. He lowered his thumb towards my carotid artery. He didn't touch me, but his nearness felt almost tangible. Despite the cold night, his skin radiated a strange heat. Almost like he had a fever. Victor tutted. 'Unfortunately, you've been declared off-limits. Such a shame.' Suddenly he glanced to one side, then promptly drew back. With an exaggerated gesture, he put his hand to his temple as if in salute.

Confused, I followed his gaze towards the person standing at the end of the bridge, nearer the main college buildings. Hands in his coat pockets, his face a mask of greyish night and flickering lamplight.

Blake was so obviously staring at us that my body tensed. Before I could decide whether to wave provocatively, he had already turned away.

'Doesn't matter. My June girl is waiting for me,' Victor murmured beside me, and a moment later I felt a breath of wind. When I looked up, I realised he was climbing onto the balustrade. 'Are you completely fucking plastered?' I blurted. 'The water's not that deep, if you're unlucky you could break your—'

'People like us don't have bad luck,' he broke in, grinning.

Panic began to stream into my muscles, and I reached out instinctively to grab him, but he'd already spread out his arms, let out a yell and … jumped. I gasped and grabbed the balustrade, leaning over it. As my gaze fell on the water's surface, it was already parting again. Amid a swirl of waves and black, Victor's head emerged.

Somebody called to him from the bank, and others laughed as he swam towards the middle of the river, up to one of the women who a short while ago had been among the few people thickly swaddled on the bank. Now she was treading water in vividly white underwear, laughing as Victor drew her closer to him. She threw her arms around his neck as he buried his face in hers. My artery thrummed at the memory of him almost touching me just minutes earlier.

I looked towards the bank, where Zoe was now sitting nestled into Ashton's chest, wrapped in a blanket. He hadn't buttoned his shirt back up yet, but he was rubbing her shoulders as if to keep her warm. *That's nice*, I tried to think, but what I felt was: *That's dangerous*.

Probably what Victor had said was true. People like them didn't have bad luck. But at that moment I realised what Davie had meant: people like them *brought* bad luck.

If I wanted to make Zoe realise it too, I'd have to understand it better myself. I'd spent pretty much my whole life learning new things, so if anybody was going to find out more about this group of friends, it was me. It was just a matter of identifying the right source material. As if of their own accord, my eyes drifted to the far end of the bridge. It was worth a try.

I knew where I'd find him even before I'd set foot on college grounds. Cambridge at night was a densely woven darkness, shot through with darts of light from lanterns and illuminated windows. Now and then you heard the voices of returning pub-goers or bursts of laughter from student rooms, but otherwise the colleges at night were mostly one thing: silent. You heard no music there. Especially no organ music.

I wasn't completely sure until I was standing just outside King's College Chapel. By now the low notes reverberating through the imposing walls weren't just audible but tangible, and the ground shook beneath my feet as I approached the main entrance. I knew it would be wiser to stay away from the chapel. It was only a matter of time before somebody noticed me poking around where I wasn't supposed to be, and I didn't want to be accused of trespassing, disturbing the peace or possibly blasphemy. Still, I didn't hesitate to turn the handle. Like I said: curiosity has always been one of my most helpful yet problematic qualities.

I'd only been to the chapel a few times before, mostly to hear the choir. There was something magical about it: the way the fan vault filled with voices as the sun falling through the stained-glass windows cast a motley carpet of light across the floor, or when the interior was lit with scores of candles. This time I was met with darkness. When I first arrived at Cambridge, I'd gone on a guided tour of every college, including King's. As part of the tour they had taken us to see the organ, so it didn't take me long to find the stairs that led up to the organ loft.

The higher I climbed, the louder the music became, until eventually I felt like I was standing in the very mouth of the instrument. I recognised him immediately. The dark hair curling at the nape of his neck, the way he carried himself, at once graceful and tense. Blake and I had only met twice, but somehow I could sense I'd know him anywhere.

It was fascinating to watch him. His fingers danced over the keys with astonishing fluidity, his shoulders moving as though swimming in the sound, his feet operating the pedals with such practised skill that I wondered how often he played. From the first moment I saw him, I knew there was something strange about him, but I'd never have guessed he used his spare time to break into one of Cambridge's most famous landmarks to play the organ.

When I took a step forward, he stopped abruptly. The last

note resonated powerfully between us, but I could still hear myself swallow loudly.

Blake was still for five seconds, then he took a deep breath. 'You really have a knack for showing up where you're not wanted.'

So. Now I knew where we were going to pick up. It took an effort of will not to respond in kind. If I wanted to get anything out of him, I'd have to tread carefully for a while. I walked up to him. 'Aren't you worried about getting caught?'

He stared obstinately straight ahead of him, not giving me so much as a glance. 'We never get caught.'

I stopped beside him and crossed my arms. 'Oh, yeah? How come? Do you bribe the porters? Or do you donate so much money to the university that they let you do whatever the hell you want?' I paused, but Blake didn't react. 'Where do you know the others from? You're not doing the same course, are you?' As far as I knew, Ashton was studying economics. Not necessarily a subject where you were likely to cross paths with a philosophy student. Although I couldn't be sure if that's what 'Blake' actually was.

'You ask a lot of questions.' Although he wasn't looking at me, I thought I saw a flicker of something at the corner of his mouth.

'Yeah, well I've got more where that came from.' I observed him closely. His cheeks were pale in the wan light, almost bluish, and the scar on his temple shimmered silver. The jumper he was wearing was dark and hid his collarbone. I got the impulse to yank it down. 'For example ... do you have one too?'

'One what?'

'A tattoo.'

He closed his eyes and let out a deep sigh, evidently reluctant to answer. So I persisted. 'What's the point of these parties you throw? Why can't you just get hammered down the pub like normal students?'

My last word was drowned out by a low bass note, as Blake depressed a key. I jumped and tried my question again, but he just kept playing. Pretty much exactly where he'd broken off.

I rolled my eyes, but couldn't hold back a deep surge of awe. It wasn't just the acoustic in the chapel – it was his face. It was the look he wore of utter devotion. It was ... beautiful. *He* was beautiful. The minute the thought crossed my mind, I wanted to run. Instead, I arranged my face into an expression of indifference and waited for him to lift his hands from the keys. 'That's not half as impressive as you think.'

This time the grin was unmistakeable. 'Oh no?'

'No.' I hesitated, then sat down on the edge of the bench and turned to look directly at him. I saw the way his body tensed, but I had no intention of pulling back. A negative reaction to me was still a reaction. 'I mean, an organ is basically just a giant piano. Even if it does have the biggest range of any instrument.'

He shifted along the bench until he was at the other end. 'So you're an expert on organs too, are you?'

'I told you – I read a lot. And don't forget: unlike you, *Blake*, I'm not a good liar.' The name came out of my mouth so acerbically that I wasn't surprised to see him frown. He turned away, his face mirrored in the gleaming pipes of the organ: pale skin, dark eyes, the expression in them darker still. I kept talking, unable to stop myself. 'Will you at least answer me one question? Why didn't you just tell me your real name?' My voice didn't sound as combative as it was supposed to. Even I had to admit what I was really feeling – what I'd been reluctant to acknowledge ever since I saw Blake and his friends that afternoon in Great Court: I was hurt.

The muscles worked in his jaw, then he shrugged. 'If I remember correctly, you didn't give me any name at all. So you've got no reason to be upset. You really shouldn't let me get under your skin like that. Either way, I'll forget you after tonight as quickly as I did the last time. Neither your name nor your face mean anything – you said so yourself, didn't you?'

'I ... you're not under my skin,' I stammered, taken aback, while my face – my meaningless face – began to redden.

'No? Then why are you always trailing around after me?'

'I'm not...' Furious, I clenched my fists. 'Is that what you think? That I'm desperate for your company because of a ten-minute conversation and one moment of breathtaking rudeness?'

'I have no idea what you're desperate for. All I can tell you is that you're looking in the wrong place. I'm not interested.' He paused and turned to face me. My heart leapt as his eyes locked with mine. His mouth opened, but as I watched, he paused. For two or three long seconds I gazed at his lips, which were quivering almost imperceptibly. Then he cleared his throat. 'At all,' he added hoarsely.

His words were at odds with the way he was looking at me. Too alert, too intent, too ... *interested*. No matter what Blake claimed, at that moment I knew he wasn't quite as good a liar as he thought. 'Don't bother.'

He blinked. 'What?'

'You don't need to try and chase me off. I'm only here because Zoe is. And because I don't want to leave her alone with'—*a group of potentially dangerous people*—'you lot. So if you want to get rid of me, make it so she doesn't have a reason to stay.'

Blake was staring into space again. 'I don't need to do anything. It'll wear off all by itself. Ashton tends to lose interest in his "girlfriends" pretty quickly.'

'Let's hope so,' I muttered, rubbing my arms to ward off a sudden chill. 'What about you? This is the second evening I've spent with your friends, and yet again you've ditched them.'

'I could say the same to you. If you're here to look after your friend, then why are you with me and not with her?'

Point to Blake. My cheeks grew hot again, and I hated myself for it. *Because I want answers*, a part of me thought. *But you've stopped asking questions*, another part of me shot back with a sneer. 'I prefer nocturnal churchgoing to a swimming lesson that's practically guaranteed to give you pneumonia,' I replied hesitantly, tucking my fingers under my thighs. As I did so my hand brushed his, and I felt a tingle race up my arm. I saw the hairs rise on his skin as well.

Instantly, he jerked away and got to his feet. 'Pneumonia would be the least of your problems.'

'Wait, what—' I began, but he was already gone. Without stopping to think, I stood up and followed.

I caught up with him as he reached the middle of the nave, between the rows of pews in the broken moonlight. 'You can't just drop a hint like that then cut and run!'

He sighed but didn't stop. 'I was hoping it might make *you* cut and run.'

In two strides I was level with him, eyes glinting. 'I'm not afraid of you.' It was strange how true that was, even though Davie's words were still echoing at the back of my mind. Ashton gave me a bad feeling, but with Blake what I felt was more like restlessness. At its core, it wasn't fear. It was more like ... curiosity. Maybe he was right: he had got under my skin. His behaviour was so odd that I was determined to know what was behind it. Why was it so contradictory? Why the brooding stare, the melancholy expression, the general air of gloom?

Blake's mouth twisted. 'You're exhausting, you know that?'

'If I'm getting on your nerves, why don't you leave?'

'I'm trying.'

I planted myself in front of him. 'No you're not. You can leave the chapel at any time. And you were drawing a lot of attention to yourself for somebody who wants to fly under the radar.'

He looked at me, visibly grudging. His lashes cast shadows

on his skin. His eyes seemed brighter than usual in the blue light of the window, the scar on his temple somehow darker. 'What are you implying?'

'Victor said he's been told to stay away from me. Who told him that?'

My heart was thudding so hard I was afraid he could hear it. For a few long seconds we were silent, staring hard into each other's eyes – before Blake lowered his gaze. I felt it on my freckles, although in the dark they must have been less obvious than usual. 'It wasn't me.'

At his words I felt a dull pang of disappointment in my chest. 'No?'

'No.' He hesitated and took half a step towards me, dropping his voice. It grew softer, more fragile, almost – like he was conceding something, lowering the mask he'd been clutching so fiercely, just a fraction. 'But that doesn't mean I wouldn't advise you to keep your distance from him.'

'Why?'

Blake's body radiated a palpable warmth, but as he stepped in, I felt a chill. 'We're not good people, Mabel. I thought that would be obvious. Or have you forgotten how they treated you at the party?'

I barely registered his last words. My attention had snagged on a different one. One that – for the first time that night – brought a genuine smile to my lips. 'Don't tell me you remember my meaningless little name.'

It was a gentle jab, and it coaxed Blake's mask even lower. Just enough to reveal a faint but very genuine grin underneath. 'Hmm. And I was perfectly content to call you Pica.'

He put his head to one side, as if expecting me to pounce on the clue. But I had no intention of it: I liked puzzles, and I especially liked solving them without help.

Biting my lip, I swept past him. 'You fit right in here. From a distance, the chapel looks almost perfect. But when you look more closely, you find all these tiny flaws. Shoddy workmanship and carvings, bits of the foundation missing.'

'Then let this be a reminder that you should never judge a book by its cover.'

'What do you mean?' I turned back to face him.

Arms behind his back, he trod slowly towards me. His manner was still tense, but he no longer seemed as dismissive as he had in the organ loft. 'You thought you saw me in that library, didn't you? I mean really saw me. But that's not possible. We only ever see what we're allowed to see. That's the thing – do you understand? We can choose how others see us. Everything we reveal about ourselves, in the end it's no different from these windows.' He jerked his chin towards the colourful stained glass above our heads. 'Every phrase, every glance, it's like a tiny window into our inner selves. But it's up to you which curtain you draw back when you're around other people. If you draw one back.'

Evidently he wasn't lying about being a philosophy student. I frowned, trying to follow his logic. 'Are all the glimpses through those windows real? Or are they deceiving, too?'

He traced the scar on his temple with his fingertips. 'Most of them are deceiving. Who'd willingly reveal their true self when there are so many opportunities to be someone better?

'So you're deliberately fooling people?'

'We all do it. To other people and ourselves. You wouldn't be here otherwise. You wouldn't be trying so hard to see something in me that isn't there.'

Perhaps some part of what he said was true. Perhaps I'd come not merely seeking answers about his friends but to also answer some questions of my own, questions that had been nagging at me ever since the night we met.

I had been looking for something I thought I'd glimpsed in him. What he was trying to show me now was unequivocal: *You were mistaken.* And yet, doubt lingered in my mind, a trace of *Maybe not completely, maybe not about everything.*

'I think you're forgetting one salient point,' I said, padding closer to the vast sheet of windows.

For a moment there was silence, then I heard him follow. 'Which is?'

Coming to a halt at the end of the row of pews, I couldn't help but smile. I lifted my chin so that the moonlight cast its splintered colours across my face. 'When we show people what we want them to see, we can't help revealing something of ourselves as well. Even if it's only for a moment. For a fraction of an evening.' I narrowed my eyes in the warm golden light. 'Surrounded by old books, in the company of a stranger you think you'll never see again.'

For a few seconds more we held each other's gaze. Even in the mottled light it felt a little too intense. Again, it was Blake who broke it. This time, by looking up.

'Which one is your favourite?' I asked, following his gaze.

'The Last Judgement.'

'You believe in that stuff? That when we die we'll have to answer for our sins?'

'No.' All at once he seemed exhausted. 'Comforting as the thought would be.'

I stared incredulously at his profile. 'You find it comforting, do you, the thought of being judged? You must be pretty confident you're a good person.'

'You need to learn how to hear the things you don't want to hear. I already told you – I'm not a good person.'

Before I could reply, there was a clatter behind us. I jumped before I even heard the voice, so bright and powerful that it drowned out even the footsteps. 'Typical.' I hadn't even turned around before the face of a red-headed elf popped into my head. 'When I'm looking for Ashton, I head to the bar. When I'm looking for you, I head to the nearest empty church.'

Blake stiffened and flinched away from me. 'Norah,' he began, but she cut him off.

'You've got to help me. Victor's overdoing it again. If we don't stop him we'll have a—' She broke off the moment she caught sight of me. 'Oh.' Within seconds, her delicate features had transformed. Cool indifference, mild condescension. She knitted her eyebrows, glancing irritably at Blake. 'I didn't know you were—'

'No,' he interrupted tersely, moving towards her and putting himself between us. 'She's nobody.'

He was right: I really should learn to listen. Right now he was making it pretty fucking easy for me. He couldn't really have made it any more obvious how he saw me. The way all these people saw me: as somebody beneath them.

Summoning what was left of my dignity, I held my chin high and strode past Blake and his friend. 'Right. Well, *nobody* is leaving. Have a great night.'

As I stepped out into the chilly October air, I felt my mind clear. Suddenly I didn't know why I'd let myself get so carried away, why I was wasting my time on Blake at all. He clearly had no intention of giving me any relevant information about his friends, and that was all I wanted from him. All I was supposed to want. *Allowed* to want. If I took that away, then it was true what he'd just said: I was nobody to him and he was nobody to me.

It was time to focus on what really mattered. First: take care of Zoe. Second: find out what Davie knew. Third: eliminate any last lingering part of me that wanted to see Blake as anything but what he really was: an arrogant bastard.

CHAPTER 6
MABEL

I often thought of Cambridge as a bit like a secret compartment, with a false bottom. There were places so heaving with tourists that you could barely put one foot in front of the other – and there were others so carefully concealed that few people ever laid eyes on them. Places you discovered by chance and were wary of sharing with others, knowing that the magic that clung to them would be further worn away with each inquisitive stare. Sometimes, I imagined that the city, like the university, had evolved these secluded nooks and crannies all by itself: small fortresses steeped in history, where silence and reclusion defended the last vestiges of atmosphere from the flash of tourists' cameras and students' Instagram profiles.

My favourite of these secret places was tucked away in the Wren Library. At the end of a corridor between two bookstacks was an unassuming wooden door with a sign that read *No Access*. For the most part it was kept locked, but this morning when I tried the handle it turned easily. I knew immediately that Davie must be inside. It was the same place he always went to ground when he needed peace and quiet, either because he was deep in the weeds of research and didn't want to be interrupted or because he was in the mood to hide. Even, lately, from me. Or so it seemed.

Cautiously I opened the door a crack, until it caught on the latch. I took a biro out of my pocket, slid it through and lifted the small metal hook until it sprang out of the eye. With a last look over my shoulder, I pushed the door wide and stepped through.

I refastened the hook and climbed a set of stairs. The higher I climbed, the more the smell of old paper was overlaid by Davie's distinctive cologne and the aroma of his favourite eucalyptus sweets. Upstairs, I glanced into the narrow room with the bay window, the walls of which were lined with books. They were all very old, and the library staff had stashed them away up here to minimise how often they were handled. If you wanted to look at them you had to fill out an application form, which happened so rarely that nobody ever really came up here.

Nobody except for Davie, who had stumbled across the books – and thus the room – while researching an article. Afterwards he'd brought all his charm to bear on the librarian, who agreed to let him keep a key. He told me the story the second time we met, swearing me to secrecy. After my first visit, I understood why. In here, the clamour of the university seemed so far away, although you only had to lean out of the window to be reminded that you were in the heart of Trinity College.

The light that streamed through the casement window fell directly across the wooden table in the middle of the room, where Davie sat on one of two chairs, leafing through a stack of papers.

I cleared my throat and stepped into the room. 'Davie Waverly, you're hiding from me.'

He jumped, startled, and looked up at me. A look of surprise flitted across his face, soon turning to resignation with a trace of guilt. 'That's not true.'

I walked over and put my bag down beside the table. 'You've

been ignoring my calls. And this morning you were out of your room by seven, even though I know that on the weekends you don't get up before eight.'

He shrugged, but I saw the way his eyes darted to the heap of papers. 'I'm busy.'

I sat down on the chair opposite. 'Yeah, I know. You're supposed to be explaining what the hell happened yesterday when you came barging into my kitchen. You promised.'

Davie rubbed his face with the back of his hand. The circles under his eyes seemed especially dark today, yet his expression was oddly harried. I had a suspicion he hadn't slept at all since last night's visit. 'I thought you might give me a bit more time.'

'You thought wrong.' I opened my bag to take out my notebook. 'But I didn't come empty-handed. I'll give you my information in exchange for yours.'

In a flash he seemed considerably more alert. 'Did you talk to Zoe?' He tried to reach for my notebook, but I clamped it to the table with both hands.

'Not exactly. But I did a bit of fieldwork of my own.' I forced my mouth into a guileless smile, knowing he wouldn't be happy to hear what I was about to say – frankly, I wasn't too thrilled about the memory of it myself. 'I went to a little get-together with Ashton and his friends last night.'

In an instant, the last traces of drowsiness were wiped from his face. 'What? You promised me you'd stay away from those guys! How long did that last? Five minutes?'

'Look, I'm sorry, okay? But I had no choice. Zoe wouldn't let me talk her out of it. What did you expect me to do, let her go in there alone? Anyway, nothing bad happened. Apart from a UTI, maybe.'

'Not yet.'

'What does that mean? Davie, you really need to explain to me why you're so worried about this.'

We stared each other down. The daylight pouring into the

room was keen and wintry-silver, sharpening the edges of Davie's face. He narrowed his lips. As he put his arms around the stack of papers in front of him, I saw the corner of a file peeking out from underneath. Two, three seconds, then it dawned on me: that was the file I'd seen in his office yesterday.

Suddenly the pieces were coming together. Davie, who was working on a new story – *something really big*. Davie, who stared at me in horror when I mentioned Ashton's name. Davie, who had made me promise to stay away from them – because they were *seriously bad news*. I'd imagined those two things were separate, but now I realised: it was all connected.

'Your research,' I said bluntly. 'It's about Ashton and his friends, isn't it?'

Davie hesitated, but he didn't deny it. Instead he eyed me dubiously, almost unhappily. 'If I tell you about this,' he began at last, in a low voice, 'you have to keep it between us. Promise?'

'In case you haven't noticed, my social circle isn't exactly huge. Who am I even going to tell?'

'Zoe,' replied Davie soberly. 'You'll want to tell Zoe.'

'If it's about the people she's been hanging out with, then surely she should know, shouldn't she?'

'She should, but she can't.' He leant across the table and took my hand, which had been moving instinctively towards the file. His grasp was tighter than yesterday, but this time I could sense no hidden layers of meaning. 'You know how fond I am of Zoe, but ... she's impulsive, she wears her heart on her sleeve. If she really likes this guy, she'll definitely say something to him.'

'Something about what, Davie?' I repeated tensely. I couldn't promise to keep something secret if I didn't even know what it was.

I saw the tussle going on behind his eyes, until at last he let go of my hand and slid the topmost pile of documents aside to reveal the file. 'A couple of weeks ago I took over one of

Cassidy's articles,' he began, flipping back the ragged, light blue cover. 'She was getting too busy with her dissertation and wanted to take a step back from the newspaper. I offered to edit her article and polish it up for publication.'

'Which is Davie for rewriting it, I suppose?'

He grinned wryly. 'You could say that. It was about the tradition of student clubs at Cambridge. Cass had made an intriguing start, but her research was superficial and – without wanting to be mean – sloppy. I'll never understand why some people think the ability to use Google qualifies you to be a journalist...'

'Davie,' I interrupted firmly.

He sighed. 'Right. Well, anyway, I got stuck back into the research. I started poking around, digging up dirt about the big, established secret societies, I'm sure you know the ones: the Apostles, the Ferrets, the Pitt Club and so on. I read through old reports, pored over articles, scanned through any records I could find in the university archives. A lot of it was old news. These societies often tend to go a bit overboard – they make newbies jump through all sorts of hoops, take part in embarrassing rituals, you know the drill. But ... I stumbled across a few things that piqued my curiosity. And as you know, I do tend to get a bit obsessed with stuff like that.'

'You don't say.' I suppressed a grin, although I could feel my whole body tensing eagerly as he spoke.

'So I did a bit more research. I went to the National Archives in London and nosed around in some of their really old files.' Wetting his bottom lip with the tip of his tongue, he leant in over the table again and lowered his voice. 'For some time now, there have been rumours circulating of a secret society that seems to have been connected to Cambridge for over a century.'

I frowned, confused. 'Okay, but you just said it yourself: there are tons of clubs like that at Cambridge.' Not that I'd ever met anybody in one, but all of us were aware of their existence.

For many students, joining one of these exclusive societies was a lifelong dream. Induction into their inner circles, it was rumoured, practically guaranteed a broad network of alumni who could be called upon to help members after graduation. Personally, I knew from the very beginning that I didn't want to get mixed up in an organisation like that. Those groups were all about money and power, and although they were relatively small spotlights, they still drew clear distinctions between light and shadow. It was all about positioning, and I was painfully aware that people like me would never be allowed into the light. Close as I might stand, I was always in darkness.

Davie nodded. 'Yeah, but this one ... isn't affiliated to the university. It sounds more like it's popped up at various universities across the country, sort of in cycles. It started more than a century ago, when the same inscription began appearing on memorials, the same motif on clothes worn by students at various institutions, the same name cropping up in connection with alumni. They call themselves the League of Starlings.' He arched his eyebrows, obviously waiting for the penny to drop.

It did. Very slowly, reluctantly, because it was all so absurd. 'Starlings as in ... *Sturnus vulgaris*?'

Davie leant back with a nod, folding his arms.

I could tell he was serious, but I couldn't bring myself to feel the same. The mere memory of the password prompted a smirk I fought to suppress. 'Isn't this all a bit silly?' I asked slowly. 'If you were trying to set up a big-shot secret society, wouldn't you choose an animal that's a bit more impressive? The League of Lions, or something?'

Davie's mouth didn't even twitch. 'This isn't a joke, Mabel. And what they call themselves is irrelevant. It's what they *do*.'

'Which is?' I asked sceptically. Frankly, I wasn't sure I could respect any secret society that deliberately compared its members to a bunch of harmless birds.

'If you believe the rumours, they've got quite a rap sheet.

Theft, vandalism, plus various other crimes that were never officially solved, even when it sounds like there was clear evidence. It's like they can do whatever they want, simply because they're in the wealthiest two per cent.'

'Okay ... and what does all that have to do with us?'

A draught came rattling through the window. 'I think they're back,' said Davie, his voice so guttural that for a moment I couldn't tell why I was shivering.

I fought to keep the feeling at bay, refusing to let myself be intimidated by that sort of cheap scare. Real things had happened in my life: dark, tragic, sad things. I wasn't going to let myself be cowed by some silly urban legend.

'The starlings have flown in, you mean?' I asked, keeping my face deadpan.

Davie's eyes darkened. 'Mabel.'

I forced a grin. 'Fine. What makes you so sure?'

'I was at the pub the other day. Overdid it a bit, to be honest – I was pretty drunk at one point. I went outside to find a quiet corner, thought I might have to ... well, you know...' He gestured. 'Anyway, there were these two lads chatting. One of them, a blond guy, sprayed something on the wall.' Davie flipped through the file and slid a photograph towards me. The lamplight had painted the bricks yellow, making the dark lines even more apparent. I was no biologist, but even I recognised what it was: a bird with a leafy twig in its beak.

'Okay ... and you think this is evidence that the two lads belong to some ancient organisation? All because they graffitied a bird onto the wall? Probably just reliving the glory days of their Art A-level.'

Davie reached again into the file and took out a sheaf of photographs. Some were blurry, others sharp, but all were unmistakeable: each was of the same motif. The same bird in the same pose with the same twig in its beak. My smile grew leaden at the corners of my mouth, dragging them downwards.

'When you trace the group, this image keeps cropping up.' Davie tapped one of the photos, which depicted the bird on a door – unless I was very much mistaken, it was the door of a church.

A face appeared in my head, but I pushed it resolutely aside. I didn't want to to think it. I didn't want to understand it. Any of it. 'What makes you think Ashton's one of them?'

Davie smiled grimly. 'Because I've done my research. As soon as they went back into the pub, I followed them. Watched to see where they hung up their jackets, and found an ID in one of them. Ashton Griffin. That's the name of Zoe's friend, isn't it? Besides, you said it yourself: the whole group is weirdly secretive and elitist. It all fits, don't you think?'

I wanted to say no, but all I could manage was a weak nod. My head was swimming, my thoughts lagging behind the truth I'd just been told. *Ridiculous*, said a voice inside me. But I couldn't muster so much as a chuckle to myself, because my insides felt stiff with cold.

Davie took a deep breath. It seemed as though telling the story had lifted a weight off his shoulders. 'Okay, now your turn. What's your read on them? Apart from the fact that you think they're arrogant twats who act like something out of a horror movie.'

I hesitated, fiddling with the ribbon page-marker in my notebook. It was hard to put my thoughts about Ashton and his crew into words. Especially because it wasn't Ashton who first sprang to mind. It was Blake. And because my conflicting feelings about him confused me more than I wanted to admit. Davie's theory sounded absurd, yet at the same time it was almost eerily logical. I had sensed right from the start that there was something off about them. Was it so far-fetched to imagine that they belonged to a special club? And if I let myself think along those lines, what was the next rational step? *'We're not good people'*, Blake had said yesterday. Was that code for: *We're in an exclusive secret society whose members thinks they're superior to everybody else and flout social conventions at will, regardless of how much havoc they wreak?*

'It's complicated,' I began slowly. 'They're strange, but they're not doing anything I can put my finger on. It's like they're communicating in a secret language merely by virtue of existing. Even when they're not looking at me, I feel like I'm being made fun of.'

'But they haven't ... got too close to you?'

I had to smile. 'I can look after myself just as well as Zoe can. Anyway, I don't think I'm their type. Poverty isn't something they find attractive.'

I'm not interested. There it was again, that soft voice in my head, where it absolutely did not belong. I screwed up my eyes until it dissolved away, and flipped my notebook shut. The corners of the paper were ragged, some pages wrinkled with damp. I'd jotted down most of my thoughts by the Cam last night, keeping an eye on Zoe. After my frustrating conversation with Blake, I'd gone back to the bridge and spent the next hour trying to eavesdrop as inconspicuously as possible. Until Zoe returned to me, hair dripping riverwater and eyes drowsy, asleep on her feet. Ashton had offered yet again to walk us home, and yet again I declined, wondering as we left what it was about his company that made Zoe so tired, her mind so clouded. This time, I'd seen for myself that she had nothing but a few glasses of wine all night. It must be Ashton himself who had such a powerful sedative effect. I supposed in a way it was nice that he had such a calming influence on her – but still, I found it odd. I found the whole thing odd. I had *so* many questions. But Davie's theory, as improbable as it first seemed, might actually offer some answers.

'Okay, let's say you're right, and Ashton really is a member of this secret club. What's your plan? Where does your research take you next?'

He let out another short laugh – gentler this time. 'We're talking about a society that has remained a mystery for more than a century. There are no official records, no lists of members, no verified photographs, or really any proof of its existence beyond hearsay and rumour. To this day, nobody knows how the League decides when to move on to a different university, how it selects its members, how it's financed, what its traditions are. They're ghosts, Mabel. Ghosts who have been haunting England for donkey's years but somehow have never been caught. If I'm right, and they're currently here in Cambridge, then you tell me: am I going to stop now?' His voice was rougher with each word, his fingers drumming agitatedly on the edge of the table. I knew what that meant: although Davie was genuinely worried about the group, it only made him more eager to keep digging. And as strange as it seemed, I understood him.

'Great, in that case I have something for you,' I said, unfolding a sheet of paper. 'A list of names I've collected so far. I'm missing a lot of last names, but maybe we can figure those out. I've noted down as much information as I could. Subjects, colleges, appearance...' When Davie reached out to take the piece of paper, I yanked it back. 'Hang on. First you have to promise me something. I want us to work this case together.'

'This case?' He laughed. 'Mabel, I'm the editor of a student newspaper, not a CIA agent.'

I leant back, unimpressed. 'All the more reason why you could do with some help.'

We stared at each other. *Different shades of brown, same kind of stubborn*, Zoe liked to say when Davie and I were arguing. Finally, Davie rubbed his forehead with the back of his hand. It was flecked with ink, leaving tiny smears. 'Nope, no dice. If I'm right and they're somehow dangerous, there's no way I'm dragging you into all this.'

'I'm already neck-deep in it, Davie.' After last night, I was more aware of that than ever. 'Zoe is my best friend. As long as she's hanging out with these ... people, so am I. And I know Zoe well enough to be pretty sure that this'—I tapped the folder—'won't keep her away from them. I'll need to get more conclusive proof. With or without your help.'

He regarded me unhappily, and I lifted my chin. I wasn't about to cave now. For one thing, it was true – I knew Zoe wouldn't let a few half-baked rumours keep her away from Ashton. For another, frankly, I was curious. If Davie was right, then I had to find out more. I *wanted* to find out more.

After a while, Davie let out an exasperated sigh. 'You're so fucking stubborn, Golding.'

I permitted myself a tiny, triumphant grin. 'Then spare us both the effort and back down, Waverly. You know you need me. It's public knowledge that you work for the newspaper. If you start trying to infiltrate a group that's managed to keep itself a secret since forever, they're not exactly going to welcome you with open arms. You need someone low-profile. And that someone just so happens to be sitting right in front of you. Let me be your informant.'

He gritted his teeth, but I could tell he'd been thinking the same thing. I didn't doubt that he'd prefer to keep me out of harm's way, but we both knew that his journalistic instincts would always win out over concerns for his – or anybody else's – safety.

'Fine,' he replied at long last. 'You can help, but only under certain conditions. One: no going rogue. Everything you do, you discuss it with me first, okay?' He waited for my hesitant nod before carrying on. 'Two: no unnecessary risks. That means no obvious prying, no snooping, no getting creative with hairpins.'

I pulled a face, amused. 'Hairpins?'

'I was there the other day when you forgot your key and didn't want to wait for Zoe, remember?'

I bit my lip. 'Sure. Anything else?'

'If things get too dicey or we stumble across something really bad, we pull back. No hesitation, no argument. Promise?'

'Promise.' The word fell too glibly from my lips. I wasn't a good liar, but although I wanted to mean it, I couldn't in all sincerity make that promise. Ever since that first night with Ashton and his friends, part of me had known I was on the threshold of something. Something so murky and opaque that I couldn't tell where the next step would lead.

It wasn't that I felt no fear. But the dull sense of panic that had been coursing through me ever since that first night was nothing compared to how I felt when I imagined leaving Zoe alone with those people. She was the most vibrant person I knew. And she was worth venturing into that darkness for, even if I still couldn't make out what lay in its shadows.

I could tell from Davie's face that he'd heard the lie in my voice. 'Try and keep this promise better than the last one, okay?'

I hope I can, I thought, as I slid the list towards him with a faint smile. 'Let's get started.'

～

I raised my hand with a frown and knocked for a third time on Zoe's door. When I'd got home earlier – around nine – I texted her about returning a book she'd borrowed from me. Just an excuse to check in on her, really. Then I made myself a coffee and changed into more comfortable clothes, but by the time I was finished Zoe still hadn't answered. The walls were pretty thin, so I could hear her music. Cigarettes After Sex, her favourite band.

Zoe almost never bothered knocking, so I felt only a slight twinge of guilt as I turned the handle. The ceiling lamp was off, but the fairy lights over Zoe's bed bathed the room in a warm yellow glow. Drops of rain were spattered across the half-open window next to her desk, which, like always, was a mess. The candles on her bedside table guttered in the autumn wind, and I shivered. 'Can I—' I stopped abruptly when my eyes fell on the bed.

Zoe was lying fully clothed on her lavender duvet, eyes closed, her arm wrapped around the person next to her. For a few seconds I stared at her fingers, which were twisted, claw-like, into the collar of his white shirt, until at last I tore my gaze upward.

Ashton was smiling at me. 'Good evening, Mabel.'

'Sorry, I ... just wanted to grab a book for my Shakespeare essay. I didn't realise...' Again, I looked at Zoe, who still did not react, although I could hear her breathing. 'Is she asleep?'

'Mmm.' Ashton ran the pads of his fingers along the sliver of shoulder revealed by her rumpled sweater. For a brief second, it occurred to me that Zoe's choice of music might have clued me in on what they'd been doing, but Ashton was also fully dressed. 'She was pretty tired, so I told her to have a rest.'

'She gets tired a lot when she's around you. Something for you to consider, perhaps.'

It was just so ... odd. Zoe got so animated whenever Ashton's name came up that I was surprised she was willing to miss a single second of the time they spent together. Besides, this was Zoe – she was almost never tired. She was one of those people who started the day in unbearably high spirits and kept them at an eleven until late into the night. Or she used to be, anyway, before she started hanging out with Ashton's clique.

He smirked. 'You can't stand me, can you?'

I had to give him credit: at least he was direct. 'I don't know you well enough to answer that.'

Gently, Ashton lifted Zoe's head so that he could sit up. As he did so, his shirt slipped, baring more skin. From what I could see, his body was as eerily flawless as his face. He felt so ... unreal. *Wrong*, I corrected myself inwardly, *he feels wrong*.

'And yet you've come out with us twice now. Didn't you have fun yesterday?'

I felt like snorting, but if I wanted to find out more about them, I probably shouldn't let him know I thought they were nuts.

'Sure,' I said matter-of-factly, taking a few steps further into the room. 'I did. Your friends are ... interesting.'

His smile broadened as he toyed lazily with Zoe's hair. 'A couple of them would say the same of you, were you aware of that?'

Again, a familiar face crossed my mind. I hated myself for it. After last night, it was painfully obvious that Blake wasn't interested in me. *She's nobody*. His words had dug a pit in my chest, and no matter how hard I tried to fill it with dislike, what remained was a dull wound that ached when I prodded it. With an effort, I suppressed a frown. 'How do you mean?'

'There's something about you. You seem ... older than you are. As if your personality were mature beyond others of your age.'

This time I couldn't resist the snort. 'Others of my age? If I recall correctly, you're only twenty-two.'

'She's told you about me?' Ashton looked down at Zoe, who nuzzled closer to him at that moment. Part of me wanted to shake her awake, wipe the complacent smile off her face. Even in her sleep, it was obvious how much she adored him.

'We tell each other who we're seeing. We look out for each other.'

He bit his lower lip. 'That's good. But I wish you'd accept that you don't have to worry about me. Come on, ask me something.'

In a flash, hundreds of questions were racing through my head. But I remembered what Davie and I had just agreed. If I pushed too hard now, I risked making myself unwelcome in their group. So I pointed at Zoe and asked, 'What's going on between you two?'

'I like being near her.'

'Why?'

He raised his eyebrows. 'Do I really need to explain to you what's so attractive about your best friend?'

'No.' I knew the effect Zoe had on people. Especially men. But the way Ashton looked at Zoe was different. Less admiring, more ... greedy. Which made no sense, given that according to Zoe, he had never tried it on. She'd mentioned them kissing once or twice, but in a way that was so innocent I couldn't quite square it with his expression. 'But you do have to explain why I'm not buying it,' I added.

Ashton laughed softly. 'Maybe because you have trust issues.' He lifted Zoe's head again, settled it carefully on the pillow, and shifted to the bottom of the mattress. I tensed as he came closer to me. 'My turn now. Answer me one question, will you?'

I took a nonchalant step backwards and promptly felt the edge of the desk pressing into my bare legs. 'Go for it,' I replied, in as cool a voice as I could muster.

Ashton was still a foot or two away from me, his eyes fixed on mine, insistently, unpleasantly intense. As if trying to read the answer before I'd even heard the question. And perhaps he could, because I knew immediately what he wanted to know before he'd even opened his mouth. 'Where did you first meet Blake?'

My cheeks flushed with heat, eating through my skin and directly into my tongue. The next word was trembling. 'Who?'

Ashton chuckled again, although the laugh did not reach his eyes. 'Funny. He reacted the same way when I asked him about your little run-in at the fountain. However you met, it must have been fascinating, or you wouldn't be acting this strangely.'

I exhaled with relief. He seemed to know nothing about our

other encounter. Or all the questions I had asked. 'Or maybe we genuinely don't know each other.'

'Hmm. Unfortunately, he's my best friend. He can't lie to me. And *you*'—he leant in—'don't take this personally, but I'm afraid you can't lie at all.'

I lifted my chin. 'Right, well, don't take this personally, but I'd like you to go now. I'm not leaving you alone with Zoe while she's asleep.'

Ashton grinned, and suddenly he was looming over me. I flinched, but instead of touching me he reached past me to the desk. Shakespeare's face on the cover of the book, Ashton's very close to mine as he held up the paperback. '*Hell is empty and all the devils are here.*' He smelt of Zoe's scented candles, Zoe's washing powder, Zoe's perfume. Not of himself at all. 'That's my favourite quotation. Do you know it?'

I swallowed and reached for the book. 'Yes.'

One corner of Ashton's mouth curled, and he drew back. 'Goodnight, Mabel. I'm sure we'll be seeing each other soon.'

I couldn't stammer out a reply before he left the room. All I could think was: *You can count on it.*

CHAPTER 7
CLIFF

I examined the goosebumps on the ribbon of skin visible underneath my jacket sleeve. There was a time when I couldn't remember what it felt like to be cold, but over the last few months, I had forgotten what it felt like not to be.

I quelled the shiver that was building up in my muscles. It was nearly ten p.m., and Trinity Hall lay deserted around me. The red-brick building towering before me in the night-blue sky was garlanded with magnolia, the leaves gradually turning brown. Lights were on in many of the student rooms, while others were already dark. A fine, evening mist hung above the lawn where I stood.

My attention kept being drawn to the second floor, to a window where the curtains were drawn. The light within shone through the pale grey fabric, and I glimpsed a silhouette that moved occasionally across the room. I hated myself for every second I stared up at it. I hated myself for holding my breath the minute I saw her. I hated myself for my racing heart when I forced myself to look away.

What am I doing here? I'd been asking myself that question ever since I'd left my flat an hour earlier. Unlike Ashton and most of our friends, I'd deliberately chosen not to live on college grounds. It was one thing to sit through a few hours of lectures but quite another to feel like my every move was being watched. Not just by the students, but also – and lately, especially – by Ashton. To the extent that I could, or was allowed to, I avoided him. So it made even less sense that I'd called him several times tonight and got through to his voicemail every single time. Or that I'd left the flat as soon as I realised what that meant.

So: why did I do it?

Once again, my eyes went to the second floor. She was sitting down again, presumably at a desk. I could see her outline through the curtains, just on the other side of the window: back stooped, hand reaching forward every now and then, the blue light of a laptop mingled with the gold of the reading lamp.

I knew it was her room. Victor had given me her room number after Norah and I took him back to his staircase last night.

Why so rough? he'd asked me as I shoved him unceremoniously through the doorway. His pupils had been large as pennies, his body much too hot. *I was a good boy. She's all yours.*

I'd said nothing. For one thing, Norah was standing right behind me, and for another, Victor wasn't in any fit state to listen. Norah was right: he'd overdone it. *Again.*

The mere memory of the flicker pulsing off him made my chest tingle unpleasantly. I pressed my hand to my sternum and focused again on the window where she was sitting. Although I couldn't see her clearly, I recognised her. It was mad, but I'd had the same thought yesterday when I heard her footsteps in the chapel. I'd known her instinctively just by her tread. There was no wariness to her movements, no uncertainty or fear. None in her voice or expression. Only that mute defiance and apparently indestructible resolve.

I wanted to believe it hadn't impressed me. I wanted to

believe this wasn't about her. That I hadn't walked for half an hour on her account, without even knowing why I was coming here. That I hadn't fled the bridge last night on her account. That I hadn't gone into the chapel and sat down at the organ on her account – knowing she could find me if she chose. That I hadn't simultaneously feared and hoped she would.

Part of me insisted it was fine. I knew what would have happened if she'd stayed with the others, and I didn't like it. Compassion wasn't a sign of weakness. Another part of me, however, knew it was more than that. I hadn't just wanted her to stay away from the others: I'd wanted her to come to me.

I despised myself for thinking it – I felt ashamed, disgusted with myself. Hurriedly I shifted my focus to something more bearable: seeing her wasn't an option, so I had to make sure it never happened again. And since she'd told me yesterday that she lived on the same staircase as her best friend, that meant I had to talk to Ashton.

Just as I was about to try his number again, a door opened. Ashton's hair gleamed in the lamplight. His coat was under his arm, his shirt half unbuttoned. He took two steps down the gravel path and paused, tilted back his head and exhaled – a sigh so long and deep that it shrouded his face in a cloud of breath. Even from this distance, I thought I could feel the heat pouring off him.

Even if I hadn't already known who lived here, I'd have guessed by now who he'd been to see. His whole aura was different. Brighter, more intense. Ashton was right: there was something exceptional about Zoe.

Again, I pressed my fingers hard against my chest, then I pulled myself together and strode up to him.

Ashton was just lighting a cigarette when he saw me. Surprised, he raised his eyebrows and let the hand holding the lighter drop. 'What are you doing here? You barely leave the house these days unless I force you to.'

'I need to talk to you. And somehow I had a good idea of where to find you.' I nodded at the building behind him, but forbade myself a glance at the second floor.

Ashton sighed and clicked the lighter. As he took a drag, the cigarette glowed. Exhaling smoke, he grinned lopsidedly. 'You got me. What now?'

I crossed my arms and tried to subdue my shivering. Being this close to Ashton made me even more aware of how cold I was. 'It's too much, Ashton. You just saw her last night.'

He waved a hand dismissively and began to walk away. 'I don't need you to tell me the rules. I'm not interested in them.'

'But you're interested in *her*?' I persisted, sceptical. What I'd told Mabel yesterday was true: Ashton usually discarded his girls more quickly than I could learn their names. Not that I made much effort. We couldn't let them mean anything to us.

Don't tell me you remember my meaningless little name? Mabel's sneering voice popped into my head. I tried to shake it loose.

Ashton flicked the cigarette onto the lawn and stubbed it out carelessly with the toe of his shoe. There was a path a few feet away from us, but he meant what he'd said: he didn't care about the rules. I'd never questioned it before, because for a long time it had worked to my advantage too. 'Don't be silly,' he said scathingly. 'You know it's not about that.'

Of course I knew. It was never about them and always about us. 'Then find somebody else. Otherwise it's too big a risk.' I tried to sound casual, but I could feel my heart begin to pound. Thankfully, Ashton was still too wrapped up in himself to notice.

He lit another cigarette and took a drag so deep it made him cough. 'There is no risk,' he croaked. 'I'm very fucking good at what I do. Do you know why? Because I've had a lot of practice. Because I'm living my life. *Our* life. And I'm not going to take orders from you just because you've decided to play dead.'

I heard the warning in his voice, and felt myself wanting to back down. I knew Ashton far too well to delude myself that I could make him do anything he didn't want to do. He loved me, yes, but he loved himself more. He would never deny himself anything for someone else's sake. The only reason he ever considered deferring to other people's demands was when it suited his purposes. Or ... if it helped keep him out of trouble.

'What about Henry – would you take orders from him?'

Almost before the words were out of my mouth, I knew it was a mistake. For a few seconds there was silence, then Ashton's hand shot out and stopped me in my tracks. His breath was warm and smelt of smoke, his skin of scented candles, women's perfume, a distinctive floral fragrance that did not belong to him. I breathed through my mouth and tried to hold his gaze.

'Are you fucking serious?' he growled, his voice soft and menacing, and he jabbed me in the chest so hard I took a half-step back. 'You're threatening me? After everything I've done for you? When I've had your back for *months*? You wouldn't even be here if I wasn't lying for you, covering your arse every fucking day! They'd have locked you up ages ago if they knew you wanted to leave!'

Even in the dark I saw the the blaze of fury in his eyes. And as much as I hated to admit it, he was right. I had Ashton to thank for every step I took by myself, every breath of fresh air, every decision I was able to take, which he usually didn't like but tolerated.

'Look, I'm sorry, okay,' I said, with a glance at the vein pulsing in his neck. 'I'm just worried.'

Ashton snorted, but he already seemed less hostile. He tapped the ash off his cigarette onto the grass before he walked on. 'About who? Zoe?' The jeering note in his voice was unmistakeable. Ashton had long since ceased to feel compassion. On good days I despised him for it – on bad ones, I envied him.

'About us,' I replied, because it was the only thing he cared about. 'We can't afford a scandal.'

'Relax. I know what I'm doing. And Zoe is so naïve it's pathetic. She's totally harmless. I've got it under control. Besides, I've got other things to worry about.'

'Like what?' I frowned as we passed under an archway, reentering the grounds of our own college.

'Like your little friend.' He threw me an amused sidelong look, and inside I froze. 'You know, the girl you keep saying you don't know. She's annoyingly suspicious, and I'm afraid we won't get rid of her so easily. Could be trouble.'

'All the more reason to steer clear of Zoe,' I advised him dryly, although my mind was whirling. I didn't know if Mabel had spent any more time with Ashton and the others last night. After our conversation in the chapel I'd gone to Clare College with Norah to stop Victor doing something stupid – he was heading up to the room of the girl he'd invited that night – and when I went back to find the others, Zoe and Mabel had already left. Whatever had happened between him and Mabel, it was wrinkling Ashton's forehead. *Irritation lines*, Norah called them. *Worry lines* wasn't quite right: Ashton didn't worry because he knew there was no problem we couldn't solve.

'Oh, I don't think so,' he said casually, turning a corner. In the distance, the building where he was living this year – when he wasn't crashing on my sofa unannounced – loomed into view. The spare key to my flat had been his sole demand in exchange for not telling Henry I was living alone.

'We're good at getting rid of nuisances, aren't we? You haven't changed your mind, have you? I could tell Victor he has free rein.'

I paused, staring at him, aghast. 'You are joking? Only yesterday he came within seconds of a serious fuck-up.'

Ashton sighed and shrugged on his coat, although he still radiated a palpable heat. 'He's a bit too keen at the moment, sure. But he's interested in her. And frankly? If something goes awry, it would be one less problem on my plate. Anyway, why are you getting so worked up if you don't want her yourself?' There was a flash of suspicion in his voice.

I wasn't sure if Norah had told him about our meeting in the chapel, but for whatever reason, Ashton seemed convinced that something was going on between me and Mabel. He couldn't know what – I didn't even understand it myself. But the mere fact that he suspected something was enough to make me uneasy.

My eyes darted, my heart thudding. I knew I should just shake my head and let it be. Ashton was unwittingly offering me a solution to my problem. If Victor took care of Mabel, then I wouldn't have to worry about her for much longer. For any reason. It was the best option, the simplest, the most logical. Yet I couldn't bring myself to take it. Something held me back.

I didn't know what it was, but something about Mabel stirred an emotion in me that I hadn't felt in a very long time. It didn't matter so much which emotion – any emotion at all was the surprising thing. One so strong it could not be ignored. I'd sensed it from the moment we first met, and this something made it impossible for me to simply stand and watch as what always happened, happened.

'I'll do it.' Not until I'd heard the words did I realise I was saying them.

Ashton's brows knitted. 'What?'

I forced myself to remain impassive, although my heart was pounding in my throat. 'I'll take her.'

'Just like that? Why?'

I shrugged. 'Like I said, we can't afford a scandal. And I don't fancy a surprise visit from Henry any more than you do.

Anyway, as you remarked yourself only yesterday, it's been a while.'

Tentatively I raised my hand and grasped Ashton's wrist. I was so cold he winced. Frowning, he looked at the hairs risen on my skin, then at my shoulders, which began to shiver violently as soon as I stopped trying to control it. 'See?' I asked, my voice rasping. 'I ... can't deny it would be good for me.'

Ashton nodded slowly as I unwrapped my fingers and took a step back. There was a trace of concern in his eyes, but most of all he looked suspicious. 'You know I can tell when you're lying to me.'

'I don't intend to. You were right, she ... I do like her. If she's a problem, and clearly I've got a problem of my own, then maybe we can kill two birds with one stone. Right?' I didn't even have to try to make the words sound sincere, because apart from the first bit, they were true. Unpleasantly so. If it wasn't for the fact that everything inside me bridled at the thought of using her.

Ashton regarded me for a long time before sighing. 'Fine by me. But do it properly. The bitch is getting on my nerves.'

'No problem,' I said tonelessly, watching him disappear into his staircase.

Do it properly. The words were still racing through my head long after I'd left the deserted college grounds and been swallowed up by the bronze streets and Saturday-night clamour of the town centre.

Do it properly. Do it properly. Do it properly.

As if any of us knew anymore what that even meant.

CHAPTER 8
MABEL

The midday sun fell through the three arched windows, casting soft dappled light onto my notepad. One half of the bird was bathed in white, the other dipped in shimmering lead pencil. I'd been pressing down so hard that the paper was beginning to ripple. No surprise that my hand had drawn the image of its own accord: I'd stared at it so much over the past few days that its contours felt burnt into my retinas.

Normally I tried to stay focused in class, but during this supervision I allowed my mind to wander for a few seconds, if only because I knew that each doodle and every glance out of the window would throw off the person talking. And it did. Matthew had just finished speaking, and now I felt his eyes burning into me. I had to hold back a smile.

The room was lined with books, and contained an oak desk and two velvet armchairs placed across from each other.

Professor Ruiz leant against his desk, eyeing me over the top of his glasses. 'Miss Golding? Perhaps you'd like to respond?'

'Sure.' I concentrated on Matthew, who was sitting opposite me, wearing a plaid shirt. He had one leg crossed over the other, but behind the studiedly casual pose I could see he was readying himself for my response. His expression, as usual, was poised somewhere between boredom, haughtiness and tension.

Matthew and I had ended up in supervisions together – classes where we discussed the course content in small groups – last year, too. Neither of us was happy about it, because we'd realised after the very first session that we definitely did not like each other. I sensed this was why Professor Ruiz had paired us up again: he believed it encouraged deeper discussion if you hated the idea of yielding even an inch of ground to your opponent. And I really did. If I hadn't already disliked Matthew, any lingering impulse to be polite had evaporated the first time he referred to me as *Cinderella*.

Eventually I shook my head. 'Sorry, but I'm not sure where to begin. It feels like we're talking at cross purposes.'

Matthew knitted his blond eyebrows. 'What do you mean?'

'Your argument misses the whole point. You obviously haven't understood the real crux of the theory.'

He uncrossed his legs with a jerk and planted both hands on his knees. 'I understood it perfectly. Maybe you're just not capable of following my train of thought.'

I shrugged, smiling. 'Yeah, maybe. Why don't you try summarising your argument in two sentences? Slowly and clearly, so I can understand it, too.'

Matthew was silent. With every second that passed, his face turned a deeper shade of red, until he leant abruptly forward, fingers clenching around his knees. Something in his eyes told me he wished they were around my throat. 'You stupid, arrogant—'

'Mr Bassett,' Professor Ruiz broke in sharply, fist slamming down onto the desk. 'If you please.'

Matthew leant back in his chair, exhaling. 'Sorry,' he muttered grudgingly.

'No problem.' I smiled as good-naturedly as I could, knowing it would rile him up even more.

'Good.' With a glance at his watch, Ruiz got to his feet. 'Our time is up. Mr Bassett, I'd like you to prepare an essay for next week that persuades us all you have indeed understood the point. Good work, Miss Golding.'

Matthew was practically skewering me with his glare as I stuffed my things into my bag and slipped into my coat. I eased the collar of my blue floral-patterned top out from underneath the saggy jumper I was wearing over it. Zoe had given it to me. Judging by how new the fabric felt, she'd barely worn it. I knew Zoe sometimes gave things to me that she pretended she simply didn't want anymore. But ever since I'd found a tag on a pullover she'd supposedly not worn in years, she at least went to the effort of putting new clothes on a couple of times before she offered them to me. It did make me a bit uncomfortable, but given that several items in my wardrobe were now more moth-hole than fabric, I forced myself to see it as a grey area, dignity-wise. Especially because I knew Zoe didn't think of it as patronising or superior. *It's really not a big deal*, she had said last spring, when I angrily dumped the pullover onto her bed. *I help you with stuff like this, and you help me when I'm stuck on an essay or whatever. That's what friendship is, Mabel. We support each other in whatever way we can.* I didn't have enough experience of friendship to know if she was right, but I was pretty sure that as friends went, Zoe was rare. And precious.

I ran the tips of my fingers over the bird drawing at the corner of my notepad before I shoved it deeper into the bag and left the room. Ruiz's office was in Trinity College, which didn't give me much time to get back to my own college in time for the next supervision.

I was plaiting my hair into a hurried braid as I speedwalked down the corridor. Just as I reached the stairs, I felt someone tread on my heel from behind, so suddenly and so hard that my foot got stuck and I pitched forwards. By sheer good luck, I managed to grab onto the banister and catch myself before I fell down the steps. Heart hammering, I stared into the void on the other side of the railing, then at the floorboards beside me. My toes had slipped out of my shoe and I'd dropped my bag, spilling half its contents noisily down the stairs.

Before I realised what had happened, Matthew was standing next to me, pressing my shoe into my hand. I grasped it reflexively, flinching as he leant towards me. 'Careful, Cinderella. If you lose this you won't be able to afford a new one.'

My heart was racing so quickly that I couldn't think clearly, let alone come up with a half-decent retort. A moment later, Matthew was barging past me, but not without kicking one of my folders even further down the stairs. I waited until he was out of sight then slipped my foot back into my patent leather shoe and knelt down to gather up my things. Two girls deep in conversation gave me a wide berth, and someone else tutted irritably as they stepped over my belongings. I clamped my lips shut, trying not to say anything.

I swept a few elderberry sweets and several hairpins haphazardly into a pile and scooped them into my bag. My brain knew that Matthew was an idiot, but somehow my body still reacted with surprise that he would show it so obviously. I was used to distainful scowls and even insults from him, but this was new.

My fingers shook and I dropped a pen that rolled down the stairs. It only got two steps down before it was stopped by a shoe. Dark leather, gleaming buckle, the dusty hem of a pair of trousers.

'Thanks,' I said, then froze as I looked up.

Blake glanced briefly down at me, then crouched to pick up

the pen. Instead of straightening back up, he stayed at my eye level, and set it in front of me before reaching for the folder next to him. 'I saw what happened. Charming lad.' He tucked a few loose sheets back in and held the folder out to me.

I took it with a snort, which I regretted the moment I heard the lingering tremor – in my movements as well as my voice. 'If you enjoyed that you should see our supervisions.'

He frowned. 'Does he always treat you like that?'

'More or less.' I got to my feet, slid the folder into my bag and took a deep breath. Only then did it hit me what was happening. This wasn't just anybody: this was Blake. Blake Ames, if Davie's research was to be believed. The person who had made it excruciatingly plain to me four days ago that he wasn't interested in exchanging so much as a word with me, let alone being seen with me. And yet. Not only had he been the only one to help me – he'd showed no signs of leaving.

Part of me didn't like that he'd seen what happened. I hated looking weak. Especially in front of somebody who already thought I was needy and pathetic. Another part of me knew there was an upside. It couldn't hurt to speak to Blake if I wanted to find out more about him and his friends. And as long as he felt sorry for me, he wouldn't take me seriously enough to be wary of spilling secrets.

'You should report him,' he said as we walked downstairs side by side.

I rolled my eyes. If I told Zoe about it she'd be filling in a misconduct form before I'd even finished the story. Davie, on the other hand, would probably tell me to talk to my college tutor and keep my distance from Matthew for the time being. I had no intention of doing either. All I wanted was to keep my head down, get through the next few years and come out on the other side with the best possible degree. I had neither the time nor the energy for someone like Matthew. And I wasn't going to dim my own light so that he could feel better about himself. 'The university doesn't care about a little bit of rivalry. Anyway, it doesn't matter. He's just threatened: I work harder, I get better marks, I beat him every time we have a debate. If he needs to act like a neanderthal every now and then to make up for it, fine by me.' I shoved the double doors open and turned to let Blake through.

He paused in the doorway and scowled at me, exasperated.

'What?' I asked.

He blinked, then walked past me. 'Nothing, just ... you really don't care what other people think, do you?'

I shrugged. I wanted to answer with a firm, *No, I don't*, but I knew better than that. When it came to the people who mattered, I did care what they thought of me. Which might be one reason why I'd given up on friendships for a while. Loving someone makes you dependent on their opinion. If you don't let anybody get close to you, you'll never be rejected, never be made to feel like you're not enough, or too much, or too wrong. Plus, when they die, it won't nearly destroy you.

My aunt had dragged me to see a therapist after my mum died, but I didn't need her to figure out why I made no effort to put down roots in my new home. I was sick of loving people and then losing them. It didn't have to be a heart attack or a car accident – there were plenty of ways for someone to disappear from your life.

So no, I wasn't oblivious to what other people thought of me. I was just selective about whose opinions I valued. And Matthew's opinions definitely didn't make the cut.

I squinted up at Blake. The sun was behind him, and his hair gleamed. Raven-black. Or rather ... starling-black. 'Like my mother used to say, *If people are badmouthing you, it says nothing about you but a lot about them.*'

'Sounds like she's a smart lady.'

'She was,' I corrected him automatically. Blake's brow furrowed, and I sighed. 'She's dead. So's my dad. I never actually met him – he had a heart attack before I was born. Bursary kid *and* an orphan. Extra cliché, isn't it?'

I sped up a little, not wanting to see the expression I always got in response to those words. Pity, awkwardness. Clumsily stammered condolences.

To my surprise, that wasn't Blake's reaction at all. 'I see,' was all he said, catching up to walk by my side. The cobbled paths were dotted with puddles again today. A few feet away, the fountain shimmered in the noonday sun breaking through the clouds.

'No, *I'm so sorry*?' I studied his expression, and read neither pity nor unease. Only thoughtfulness.

He'd tucked his hands into his coat pockets, but his jumper revealed a glimpse of collarbone. I tried to see if I could spot a black dot, but as he turned to me the fabric covered his skin. 'I can tell you from experience that sorry doesn't help.'

'Dead parents?'

'Something like that.'

I waited, but when he showed no sign of elaborating I sighed. 'You're really doing your best to give the serial-killer vibe, aren't you?'

'Mmm.' The corners of his mouth twitched, but I noticed that his eyes were grave. And that his attention wasn't on me but on the group seated on the fountain steps. I didn't have to look to know who they were. There was something revealing about people who considered themselves the cream of the university crop always choosing to hang out at one of its most famous landmarks.

Irritated, I stopped and waited until Blake had turned to face me. 'Okay, level with me. What do you want?'

He tilted his head slightly. I wasn't sure if I saw a trace of amusement in his expression. 'Who says I want something? These are college grounds. My college, actually.'

'In case nobody's told you this yet: it doesn't belong to you. Or to your friends over there, watching us from barely twenty feet away.'

Blake stiffened, although I was sure he'd seen them, too. He was probably going to meet them right now. The last couple of times he'd done everything he could to avoid being seen with me – why was he so keen to take a walk with me now?

It made no sense that Blake was talking to me. And while I was happy he was letting his guard down, I wasn't going to blindly take the bait. I had no interest in being made a fool of twice in one day. 'So: what do you want from me?'

For a moment he shut his eyes, then he took a step towards me – so suddenly that I jumped. Without a word, he raised a hand to my hair. His fingertips brushed my neck before he pulled back, turning a leaf between his fingers.

I was too perplexed to react. Perplexed and ... overwhelmed. I was very aware that his friends were watching us, but most of all I was aware of his touch. I'd thought *I* was cold, but although his coat was significantly thicker than mine, his skin felt almost icy. I tried to tell myself that was the only reason for the goosebumps under my jumper, and not the strange, unexpected heat that surged through my body.

'There's only one thing I want from you,' he said tonelessly, examining the red leaf in his hand. 'But I'm afraid you won't oblige.'

'I assume it involves us never seeing each other again. In which case, Ashton's the one you should be telling – it's him who keeps inviting Zoe.' I stepped aside to let a group of girls pass. One of them was staring at Blake with such obvious interest that it almost made me uncomfortable. He, however, didn't seem to notice: he was studying his hand as it balled into a fist around the leaf. There was a crunch. I hesitated briefly, then braced myself. 'What does he want from her? Zoe says they're not sleeping together, but then I don't get why he wants her around all the time.'

Blake's expression relaxed into amusement. 'You can't think of any reason to hang out apart from sex?'

I couldn't stop the heat rising into my cheeks. 'You know what I mean.'

His lips curled slightly. 'Do I?'

Two simple words, and I felt like he'd switched into a different language. One I hadn't thought he spoke. Caught off-guard, for a moment I didn't understand – or maybe it was because I was so out of practice myself. 'Are you flirting with me, Blake Ames?'

There was a quiver in my voice – and, strangely, in my heart as well. The way his gaze ... wandered. From my eyes to my mouth, to the sweep of hair that fell across my face. To my mouth. Secret Whisper, a brown-hued matte red. The name of the shade kept repeating in my head as Blake looked at me. The whisper running through my mind was so enigmatic that I couldn't quite make sense of it. I only knew one thing: the thought behind it was new and intense and ... dangerous. And alluring. A little too alluring.

Before I could examine it more closely, Blake shook his head. 'No. I'm not.'

Good, I thought, but my chest tightened. I crossed my arms and waited for the tightness to fade. Then I took a deep breath. Whatever that was, there were more important things to think about: 'So ... what would I need to do to make Ashton ... lose interest in Zoe?'

'Is that what you want? She likes him, doesn't she?'

'Better a broken heart than a broken neck. You said it yourself. She's not safe with you lot. And I'm not going to lose her. Not Zoe, too.' The last words were out before I could stop them.

I could feel Blake's gaze scratching at my forehead, but I didn't dare look up. What I'd just said was the varnish on a deep, underlying truth I'd been trying to hide for years – even from myself. I wasn't ready to reveal any more of it just yet. Or any more of me.

'Just wait it out,' Blake said. 'Emotions are fickle, Ashton's more than anybody's. Give it a couple of weeks and he'll have forgotten her name.'

I brushed my misgivings aside and plastered on a grin. 'You've got a thing about names, haven't you?'

'There's nothing more important than a name.'

Suddenly, I remembered what we'd been talking about that night in the little library.

A name without a face means nothing, right?

I don't see it that way at all.

'What makes you say that?'

'I mean ... people do research into how bodies function. How blood, hormones and cell types interact, which muscles are where, how particular organs develop. But there's something the models can't capture: a person's psyche, their ... soul. We'll never be able to understand it fully because each one is made up of different things. Inborn characteristics, personal experience, the hopes, fears and dreams we're taught by society or develop for ourselves. Researchers have always underestimated the power of the human soul. It is the core of everything that makes us ... who we are.' His voice trailed off, his gaze becoming unfocused. For a few seconds, the sadness was back in his eyes, much deeper than I'd seen before in anyone my age.

I realised that what he'd just said struck to the heart of his grief, although I still didn't fully understand it. Even in his most apparently honest moments, Blake confused me. It was exhausting and frustrating and, unfortunately, intriguing.

'So you think of names like labels for souls, or something?'

He blinked. 'Maybe. Probably sounds a bit silly.'

'No, actually it sounds astonishingly wise.'

Blake laughed. A short, warm, very frank laugh that I liked a little too much. 'You've certainly got a knack for backhanded compliments.'

I couldn't help but grin. 'Okay, you got me, I'm not good at being nice. Just be happy you're not trying to flirt with me.'

He laughed again, husky and a little ... desperate, somehow. 'You're the one who should be happy about that.'

'You've certainly got a knack for piquing my curiosity with all those creepy lines,' I said, wondering what was wrong with me. It didn't repel me – in fact, I felt more words rising unbidden to the tip of my tongue. Words that sounded less provocative and more halting than I wanted them to. 'So ... would you mind if we saw each other again soon?'

Abruptly the smile on his mouth faded. Slowly he opened his hand and let the scarlet shreds of leaf drop. *Blood rain*, I thought, shuddering. 'Would it stop you if I said yes?'

The trace of a pang burned in my chest at his words. And I despised myself for it. Like I said: I didn't care what other people thought, as long as I didn't care about them. So obviously it didn't matter to me if this dipshit didn't want me around. *He* didn't matter to me – but the pain in my chest told me something I didn't want to acknowledge: I did care. It was ridiculous. I didn't even know him, and I wasn't going to let myself get all upset just because he didn't like me. I certainly couldn't let it stop me from doing what needed to be done.

'Nope. And now I've got to go.' I skipped over a puddle next to us to get past him. Part of me wanted to take the long way round, avoid Blake's friends, but I steeled myself. *No cowering, no hiding – not from anybody*.

I'd taken barely two steps when Blake's voice held me back. 'That guy from the supervision. What's his name?'

Confused, I turned to face him. His hand was clenched into a fist. The one he'd used to crush the leaf. The one he'd used to touch me. It was so stupid: a trivial, two-second memory and my heart was pounding so hard I couldn't think straight. 'Matthew Bassett. Why?'

Blake merely shrugged before he turned and walked away without another word. A dark fleck on the autumn-vivid courtyard, slowly receding. Away from his friends. Away from me.

CHAPTER 9
MABEL

The wind whipped against the draughty windows.

Tugging the neck of my woolly jumper up over my chin, I looked outside. The college grounds were dark and serene beyond the glass, as if the image were cast in lead. The last drops of ebbing rain beaded the vaulting windows, and a current of November air swept unchecked through the corridors – one of the reasons why this library was usually half empty, and why I loved it so much.

It was past eight o'clock in the evening, and apart from a few weary faces occasionally scurrying by in search of a book, most students had already gone home. I didn't know how long I'd been sitting there, but my stomach felt hollow and there was a sharp, stabbing pain between the vertebrae in my neck. I dug two fingers into the place where it hurt and circled my shoulders before returning to the open book.

I'd come to the library straight after the last seminar to work on an essay. My laptop had gone to sleep ages ago, but every now and then the ancient fan would spring to life, as if trying to tell me with an exasperated groan where my priorities should lie. Unfortunately, my brain refused to agree. Whenever I tried to concentrate on work, my mind began to wander. The deeper I burrowed into Davie's research, the more I understood why he was so nervous.

There were plenty of clues pointing to the existence of the League of Starlings, but no proof. Rumours of parties in lecture halls and on faculty roofs, of statues looted from college grounds, professors' offices ransacked and porters rescued from storage rooms the morning after, stripped of their uniforms and their memory. Tales passed along the grapevine, stories that under normal circumstances I'd have dismissed as legend for lack of hard evidence. But then again: there was the symbol. Photos of the bird scrawled on the doors of student flats and faculties, on toilet walls and monuments to great philosophers. Moreover, the League of Starlings was mentioned in several university newspapers in the same breath as other societies and clubs, although never in detail.

The universities where rumours of the name cropped up were scattered across England: Oxford, Kent, London and Cambridge. Over and over, Cambridge. The closer I got to the present day, the more sporadic the references became. Almost as if the club – if it had ever existed – had dissolved. Or ... as if its members had grown more cautious over time.

I was leafing pensively through the University of Cambridge yearbook from 1982 when my phone lit up. Davie.

DAVIE

Hungry? I have half a tray of chips left over from dinner, and I could throw in a slice of apple pie to make the schlep across town worth your while.

I smiled as I cast my eye over the message. Mostly he only sent me texts like that towards the end of the month, when he knew my funds were running low.

MABEL

Tempting, but I've still got stuff to do here.

DAVIE

I don't think you're understanding me. They're curly fries.

I bit my bottom lip to keep from laughing, which I knew would irritate the student at the other end of the table.

MABEL

Seriously I can't. I've got to finish this essay.

I felt a stab of conscience as I flipped my phone screen-down and hunched over the book. Partly because my laptop had just started humming again and partly because I was deliberately lying to Davie.

He knew I wanted to help him with his research, but I'd downplayed the extent to which this research had mushroomed over the last few days. Either I was trying to find out more about the people in Ashton's circle whose names I'd learnt, or I was digging into the sinister society, hoping that the two strands would eventually intertwine.

So far, there was no sign of that happening, except for Davie's experience outside a pub. We'd gone back a couple of days ago, but the bricks had long since been scrubbed of graffiti. It could all be a coincidence. Ashton could have seen the bird symbol somewhere, like we had, and sprayed it on the wall just on a whim. He and his friends might be a common-or-garden bunch of spoilt, new-money brats who simply happened to use the name of a species of bird as a password to get into their parties. We might be wrong. And yet: we didn't think so.

The low-hanging lamps illuminating the desks at the back of the library blazed up for a moment, casting a dappled peach light across the paper in front of me. I glanced up at the old-fashioned fittings as I continued to leaf through the book, and very nearly turned the page without noticing it. At the last moment I stopped, and went a page back. The section was about a Trinity College anniversary, and it included photographs from the celebrations.

It took me a moment to realise which one had caught my eye. It was at the very bottom, spread across half the page: five people against a brick wall, all looking directly into the lens. The photograph was in black and white, but I was certain they were all wearing black. *Starling-black*, I thought, and in the next breath I remembered Blake's hair. Narrowing my eyes, I examined them more closely. Three men, two women, all in their early twenties, and at first glance not only strikingly attractive but also so obviously self-assured that they could only have led lives of privilege.

They looked no different from the students I crossed paths with every day, yet there was one detail that stopped me in my tracks. One of the women was wearing a brooch at the neckline of her dress. A brooch in the shape of a bird holding a twig in its beak.

Heat rose to my cheeks and blurred my vision. I blinked it away, then bent hastily over the book to read the caption.

The new generation of the Cambridge elite. From left to right: Quentin Middleton, Ellen Lucille Meester, Cedric Landon Wells, Arthur O'Brien, Amelia Victoria Wallingford.

I had to reread the last name several times before I realised why it sounded so familiar. Once it clicked, I reached for the stack of books in front of me and found the one I'd just been looking through. It took me a minute to find the page again. Next to an article about the most scenic views in Cambridge were several photographs. One of them was of a bench next to the Cam. I'd dwelt on the picture earlier because I always paused to look at benches – at least, I did if they had a commemorative plaque. My mother always used to stop and read the inscriptions. Sometimes there were just names, sometimes dates or quotations. *Funny, isn't it? When somebody dies, people often don't know what to do with their love*, she'd told me once.

Is that sad or beautiful? I'd asked.

That, my darling, she had answered, linking her arm through mine, *is life's most fundamental question.*

Barely two months later, her old Volvo had been T-boned by a Porsche. Since then, I too had been at a loss, not knowing what to do with my love. If I had the money I'd have put up a dozen benches in her memory, but as it was, I just stopped for a moment at the ones I found, and read my mother's name in each inscription.

I'd done the same with this one earlier, but the actual name on the plaque had stuck in my head.

In memory of Amelia Victoria Heaven Wallingford
ex hoc momento pendet aeternitas

I picked up my phone, opened the translator app and typed in the Latin phrase.

Eternity is poised upon this moment.

Frowning, I entered the woman's name into the search engine. While the creaky library Wi-Fi slowly loaded the results, the student at the other end of the table got up and left, although I was so focused on scanning the search results I barely noticed. The third one caught my eye. I clicked it, and a photograph appeared: smiling out at me was the familiar face of a pretty blonde-haired girl. A gap between her front teeth, a dimple at the right-hand corner of her mouth, large eyes, thick lashes. A face that radiated youth and a zest for life. A face totally at odds with the headline of the article.

STUDENT, 22, DIES IN FIRE AT UNIVERSITY BUILDING

Amelia Victoria Wallingford (b.1960), daughter of the Home Secretary, lost her life in a blaze that broke out last Friday at Trinity College, Cambridge. The circumstances that led to this tragic incident are still unclear. According to a spokeswoman from the University Council, an investigation has been launched in cooperation with the police and fire services. At this time, the authorities have not yet ruled out arson. Wallingford was in her second year studying Social and Political Sciences, and volunteered—

I broke off at the sound of a thud somewhere behind me.

Whirling round, I stared along the serried rows of shelves that yawned before me. The lamps above the stacks were flickering, too, and some had gone out altogether. The gloom thickened as the shelves receded, a colourless labyrinth of interweaving spines and wooden shelving. There was no one to be seen.

Glancing at my watch, I realised the library would be closing soon. Returning my attention to the search results, I scanned the first three pages. Article after article about Amelia's swimming competitions, public appearances with her father and her volunteer work at a local animal shelter. The face in the pictures was always the same. So was the name itself. Except – it wasn't the same as on the bench. Not quite. The second middle name, Heaven, appeared nowhere else, not even in her official obituary.

My heart began to thud, as if it sensed this tiny detail might mean something, even if my rational mind didn't understand what. I hunched so far forward that the tip of my nose was almost touching the paper. The faces told me nothing, yet somehow they jogged a memory. I wasn't sure what it was, but something about them was eerily familiar. The proud look in their eyes, the superior smiles, the upright bearing, and above all the way they seemed to make up a complete picture, even though they were barely touching one another, if at all. Their whole demeanour reminded me irresistibly of Ashton and his friends.

Again, I examined the photograph, pausing over the boy in the middle. Short hair, light eyes, broad shoulders in an elegant jacket. *Cedric Landon Wells*. Something about him annoyed me, but I couldn't put my finger on what it was. Before I could enter his name into the search engine, another thud behind me made me jump.

The bookstacks still seemed deserted, but this time I leapt impulsively to my feet. Grabbing my phone, I looked around carefully before peering down the row of books where the noise had come from. But ... there was no one. All was still and colourless, the only sound the creaking of the shelves. Then, just as I was about to turn away, I saw it. A gap on the shelf nearest the wall. Looking more closely, I realised there were books scattered across the floor in front of it, as if somebody had knocked them off the shelf – which would explain the thump I'd heard.

Approaching slowly, I moved close enough to see what was off about the wall behind it. The white paint was marred with black letters. Letters my brain was loath to arrange into a sentence, even though every single one had been fastidiously drawn.

Memento mori

I didn't have to translate this time. I knew enough Latin to know what it said.

Remember you must die.

Suddenly I was so nauseous that when I swallowed I thought I could taste bile. My rational mind was telling me it was just a bad joke, that it had nothing to do with me, but my heart was hammering so hard that it felt like I was being punched. My thoughts were a welter of bruises, all meaning crumbling away. For a few long seconds I stared at the words, before I reached out to touch the final letter. Even before I looked at my finger, I knew it was streaked with ink. Because it was fresh. Because whoever had written it was still here.

I whipped around, turning in a circle, peering over the edges of the rows of books in the neighbouring stacks and bending down to look underneath. No eyes, no feet, no ... nothing. I was alone. With a deep breath, I straightened my shoulders and put the books back onto the shelf. As if nothing had happened, *because nothing had*.

When I returned to my seat the gong sounded, announcing that the library was closing in ten minutes. I slid my phone into my trouser pocket and began to put the books into a pile. When I got to the yearbook I'd clapped carelessly shut, I hesitated. I threw a quick look over my shoulder, but the coast was clear. Ignoring a twinge of guilt, I tore the page with the photograph out of the book and slipped it into my notebook.

Just as I was about to put the notebook in my bag, I noticed something. The clasp was fastened, although I never closed it myself. The mechanism was so old I was afraid it might break if I tried.

My fingers shook as I opened it gingerly, pulled back the leather flap and ... found myself staring into darkness.

I held my breath. My bag was filled with feathers. Black, gleaming feathers, scattered thinly with a few tiny white dots. My hand shook harder still as I reached for one. It felt real. Real and ... warm. Without stopping to think I pulled out a whole fistful of them and let them flutter onto the table in front of me. The feeling persisted. They were warm. And ... wet?

My eyes shifted from the blackness of the feathers to my hand. My hand, which was smeared red.

Reflexively, I backed away, almost tripping over the chair. My pulse was racing and my feet wanted to do likewise, but I knew it was no use. The blood, the fucking *bird blood*, was already binding itself to my skin.

~

My hand was throbbing as I left the library not long afterwards. I wrapped my fingers more tightly around the strap of my bag, not wanting to look at them, although I'd scrubbed them in the toilets until all trace of blood was gone. Yet I felt as though it had leached into my skin. Just as I felt like the feathers in my bag were stones. The weight of them bit into my shoulder, urging me to stop at every bin and dump them. I didn't. I mustn't. Not until I'd decided what to do with them.

My breath swirled like mist before my face as I walked through the college. The tip of my nose shimmered bluish at the edge of my vision, my fingers tingled, and I could no longer even feel my toes. Somehow, out of nowhere, *all* of my sensations had been muffled. My thoughts, like my body, felt wrapped in cotton wool. Maybe because every fibre of me was refusing to confront the sharp-edged events of the past thirty minutes.

Reaching a lamppost, I stopped. I tilted back my head and took a deep breath, as the words ran again through my mind. Garish and flickering, a neon sign in my own personal darkness. *Memento mori*. I knew the phrase was supposed to be a reminder – appreciate your life – but scrawled on the library wall like that, it felt more like a warning. A threat. Especially since the person who wrote it immediately went and stuffed a whole load of bloodied feathers into my bag.

I wanted to tell myself there was no connection, but how could I? I *knew* it was the same person. I *knew* it was no accident, that whoever it was had intended them for my bag. For me. Just as I *knew*, without even checking, that the feathers had belonged to a starling. A starling that was now most likely dead.

Memento mori.

I squeezed my eyes shut until the letters crumbled away and focused on the key points. The most important questions were: who? And why? For the first question, there were three names that sprang to mind. Three people who knew I had taken an interest in them, who had made it clear to me in various ways that I shouldn't have: Ashton, Victor, Blake. The why was obvious. They wanted to let me know I was on their radar. Presumably the whole thing was meant to frighten me – the only problem was, it lit a fire in me instead. If I'd had any last shred of doubt that the society existed, it was gone now.

It was so funny: in an attempt to stop me learning more about them, they'd given me my first piece of conclusive proof. There could be no other explanation for why they'd given me starling feathers, specifically, when I hadn't mentioned the League to any of them.

I wasn't sure what to make of it. That they underestimated me, and didn't think I would put two and two together? Or that they overestimated themselves, to the point where they didn't care if I did? Well, probably it didn't matter either way. Even if they had guessed at my suspicions—what could they do about it? Secret society or not, at the end of the day it was just a bunch of rich kids. If the worst they could do was put feathers in my bag, I could handle that.

Still, my heart wouldn't stop racing as I made my way through the grounds. I felt alone and unprotected, and I didn't like it. I wanted to talk to someone about it – I *had* to. Quickly making up my mind, I grabbed my phone out of my coat pocket. After our conversation earlier, Davie had sent me a photo of a sad-looking face made out of chips, but even that didn't make me smile.

MABEL

We need to talk.

I didn't want to worry Davie unnecessarily, but after what had just happened, part of me sensed his concerns might not be unfounded. The situation was starting to get out of hand, and while retreat wasn't an option, I knew I'd rather take the next steps with someone by my side.

As I turned the corner, I came to an abrupt halt. Blue light flooded my eyes, dazzling me. I found myself staring in bewilderment at a police car parked in the middle of the gravel path outside a building in Clare College, its light flashing across the wall. A handful of people were huddled behind a cordon, watching the officers positioned outside the door.

I approached a woman standing a little way off, under a beech tree. Despite her puffer jacket, she was shivering so badly that her teeth chattered.

'What happened?'

She looked at me glassy-eyed, then back at the building. Her gaze drifted upward to the roof, twenty-five feet or so above the ground. 'Somebody jumped,' she whispered, as if the words would only become real if she said them too loudly. 'They just took her away.'

'What? Who?' I stared back in horror at the area beyond the police tape. In the lamplit gloom, there was nothing to be seen. Only cold, grey, unforgiving stone. My stomach knotted.

The girl next to me snivelled, hugging herself more tightly. 'A student ... June Owens. I was in a few lectures with her, she's always so sweet and funny. I ... I can't believe she did this.'

The name rang a bell in my mind, but I couldn't follow the sound into the recesses of my memory. The whole situation was just too overwhelming. 'Are they sure she definitely jumped? Maybe she fell, and it was an accident.'

She shook her head, pointing at two whey-faced girls who

were standing by the police car, speaking to an officer. 'One of them lives next door to me. She called me after it happened. She and her friend, they saw it. They found June up there and tried to talk her down but she just—' She broke off, pressing a hand to her mouth in a dry sob.

'Is she...' My voice trailed away. I couldn't bring myself to say the word, or even think it.

'There was so much blood,' she murmured. 'And ... the ambulance took her but they didn't turn the siren on, or the lights. That means...'

That meant she was already dead.

We were silent, suspended in a moment flooded with artificial light yet still so dark. With every second I stared at the ground, I felt colder. Dark stone made darker with blood. Like my hand, just a few minutes ago.

I dug my fingernails into my palm, trying to push the thought to the back of my mind. But just as I was about to lock it away in a drawer in my head, another thought slipped out.

Or not a thought, but a memory.

Victor, on the bridge. *Doesn't matter. My June girl is waiting for me.*

It's a coincidence, a coincidence, a coincidence. The voice inside my head nearly tripped over itself trying to think the words so quickly that there was no room for doubt to creep in. Still, I reached automatically for my phone and typed the name 'June Owens' into the search engine.

The third hit was an article on the Clare College Choir. According to the caption underneath the photograph, June was in the front row: a pretty girl witih honey-blonde hair and friendly eyes. A pretty girl who looked familiar. Because I'd seen her before.

That night at Clare Bridge, when she'd gone swimming in her underwear in the Cam. I remembered it vividly, as if my brain had deliberately registered each and every nuance, even

119

then. It wasn't really about June, it was the person at her side. The person you *sensed* was trouble even if he didn't look it: Victor.

My June girl is waiting for me, those were his words. And now this same girl had jumped off the roof of a building and ... died?

It's a coincidence, a coincidence, a ... the voice in my mind was fading with every word, because the feeling inside me was just so loud. So indescribably loud that I felt like pressing my hands over my ears. Or my heart, which was pumping so hard I was dizzy.

I barely noticed when the girl peeled away from the tree and went over to her friend, who was now standing forlornly by the cordon.

With an effort, I pulled myself together. Before I turned away I took a photo of the scene – blue, glaring light and red tape flapping in the wind – and sent it to Davie, accompanied by another curt message.

MABEL

We seriously need to talk.

CHAPTER 10

CLIFF

Nowhere were the differences between myself and Ashton more obvious than at the pub. Every time I stepped into the airless fug, the dim light and babble of voices, it was brought home to me anew. To me, they meant constant sensory overload and ever-ratcheting tension. To Ashton, they were paradise. People at pubs were generally in high spirits, and more open than usual. The alcohol did the rest.

I found Ashton at his favourite spot: at the bar, so that people were constantly having to edge past him. He had a drink in front of him, probably an Old Fashioned, his usual. I still found Ashton's sense of humour baffling occasionally, even after all this time.

'What are you doing here?' he asked, surprised, as I jostled my way towards him. 'When was the last time I saw you at a pub? Must have been in another life.'

I didn't take the bait, but sat down on the stool beside him. 'Norah told me you'd be here. I wanted to talk to you.' I waited until the man next to us had been handed two pints of beer by the barman. 'I just heard,' I went on. 'It's true, isn't it? That girl ... June Owens, she's dead.'

Ashton sighed and sipped his drink. Instantly his lips twisted a little. Definitely an Old Fashioned. 'Yes.'

The word dropped into the pit in my stomach. When I'd first overheard someone talking about what happened, I'd thought nothing of it. Until they mentioned her name. The name I'd last heard from Victor, moments after we stopped him following her to her room. And not long afterwards, she jumped off a roof. This was no tragic accident, as most people assumed. This was the repetition of a story. *Our* story.

'You know what this means. Victor—' I broke off as the barman appeared in front of me with an enquiring look. Reluctantly, I ordered a whisky and waited until he set the glass in front of me and walked away.

'I've already had a word with him. He says he had nothing to do with it,' Ashton said, before I could go on. 'Not directly, anyway. He overestimated himself – well, her. It was an accident.'

'And you believe him?'

'Does it matter? She's dead, either way.'

'It matters because he isn't going to stop. You know him. He only followed the rule in the first place because he thought there'd be consequences. If he gets away with it ... the whole thing's going to happen all over again.'

Ashton was watching a woman standing at the bar. 'Would that really be so terrible?' He slid his hand casually across the wooden countertop so that it brushed her forearm. She didn't notice, but that only made me all the more aware of it.

I shifted away instinctively, closer to the cool brick wall. 'Are you serious?'

'I'm just saying.' He broke contact and turned back to me. 'We only stopped to give the rumours some time to die down. But it's been long enough. We can allow ourselves to bend the rules for a while. Have a bit of fun. It'll do us good.'

'You know better than anybody how bad it can get when you bend the rules a bit too far. Do I need to say her name?'

A hard line etched itself around his mouth. 'Drop it. Don't you dare ... just don't start.' He finished his drink in two gulps and signalled the barman to bring him another.

'You know I'm right,' I persisted, even though I was aware how thin the ice was when it came to this particular topic. And if we fell through ... that wasn't going to end well. For either of us. 'We need to bring Victor to heel.'

Ashton rolled his eyes but didn't argue, and I knew him well enough to realise that in itself was a win. 'Speaking of: how's it going with your little protégé?' he asked instead, after he'd been handed a fresh glass.

Now it was my turn to reach for my drink to avoid meeting his eye. 'Fine. I've got it under control.'

'And by *it* do you mean you or her?'

I was clenching my jaw so hard my teeth grated. 'Both.'

'Hmm.' Ashton rested his head in his hand and regarded me thoughtfully. 'Then why did Victor tell me she's been asking an awful lot of questions? And why did he see her hanging around in the library the other day, poking through the university and city archives?'

I closed my eyes. *Damn it, Mabel.* 'She's on a full bursary,' I said after a pause that was a little too long. 'She's always at the library. And she's ... just generally interested in things.'

Ashton contemplated me. I knew he was absorbing every single detail: every shade of blue in the circles under my eyes, every fine line drawn by the tension of the last few months, every miniscule imperfection in my skin. I cupped my glass in both hands so he couldn't touch them and feel how cold they still were. 'Did you tell her anything I ought to know about?'

'Are you fucking joking? How naïve do you think I am?' Of all the mistakes I'd made with Mabel, that wasn't one of them. It would be not only my undoing but hers as well.

'I think you're out of practice. And we both know it can be extremely intoxicating if you've been abstinent for a while—'

'I haven't said anything,' I interrupted him brusquely. 'To her, or anybody else, for that matter. What makes you think I have?'

He threw out his arms, and his hand brushed the waist of a man walking past. Ashton shut his eyes, but I knew his pupils were dilating. 'Just a hunch,' he said, unruffled, and folded his arms again. 'Vic told me what books she was looking at. We need to keep an eye on where that's leading. Perhaps you should be showing her a little more affection.'

'Right, like you're doing with her friend?'

'At least my moth is behaving exactly as she's supposed to.'

We were silent as the barman removed a few bottles from the shelf in front of us. 'One Hundred Years' by The Cure was playing in the background, a song that took me back – to a time when I would have agreed with him unhesitatingly. I couldn't do that anymore, but then again, I couldn't bring myself to contradict him either.

'Why was Victor spying on Mabel in the first place?'

Ashton chuckled. 'Don't worry, he's been told to keep his hands to himself. But you know Vic. Once he's caught the scent, it's impossible to call him off.'

'What scent would that be?' I tried to make my voice sound annoyed, but even I could hear the note of anxiety. As stubborn as Mabel was, if Victor set his sights on her, she had no chance of escaping him. Nobody did.

'You know as well as I do. She just has a certain something.' Ashton shrugged, as if to say it wasn't important.

I knew Mabel was a thorn in his side, but I also knew he didn't take her very seriously. Why should he? We always won out in the end. As I thought about the reality of what this would mean for her, I felt an overwhelming sense of loss.

I didn't notice Ashton's hand until it was touching the one

I'd rested on the bar. He turned it over and pressed two fingers to the vein in my wrist. I could see the accusation in his frown, but instead of saying it out loud he let me go and said, 'She likes you.'

I laughed. False and cold, splinters of ice in my mouth and chest. 'She doesn't know me.'

'Of course not. But she likes what she thinks she sees in you. If I've sensed it, then so have you.' He gave me a knowing smile, and of course he was right. I had sensed it: a flicker, a sliver of a crack in the door, a glimpse of something extraordinarily alluring – something I desperately needed to keep at arm's length. 'You've tormented yourself for long enough. Come home, why don't you?'

Ashton's voice was unusually gentle, and the shift hit me like a ton of bricks. Conscience pricking, I shut my eyes. 'I never left.'

'You left a long time ago.' He would never say it, but I knew exactly what moment he was thinking about. It was the moment when we'd all left, in our different ways. Then, knocking back his drink in one gulp, he rose to his feet and placed both hands on my shoulders, which I'd hunched slightly. 'You know it, and I know it. But we also both know that we'll all wait for you. As long as you need. Just ... try and make a bit of an effort, okay?'

He waited for my nod before picking up his coat and heading for the exit, without paying. That was Ashton: he came and went as he pleased, but he was right about one thing. Unlike me, he hadn't checked out.

I rubbed the heel of my hand over my eyes, which throbbed dryly, then reached for my phone. Social media always made me feel a stab of compassion. It was proof of a universal human urge, one which no one wanted to admit: they were desperate to be seen – mostly not for who they truly were, of course, but who they wanted to be. For someone like me, who'd been working for years to hide exactly that, none of the platforms held much interest. I maintained my profile as diligently as was expected of me, uploading the occasional photo from a high-profile event or sharing a post about the Ames family's foundation, but that was all. If I ever did log on voluntarily, it was always using my second account, under a fictional name.

Mabel's feed felt like it reflected real life. Unfiltered, unvarnished, raw and ... her. There were photos of yellowing pages on her desk, of coffee mugs smeared with lipstick, and a collection of the lipsticks themselves – Holy Sinner, Darkest Dream, Lullaby Heart – of curtains flecked with gold in the morning light, of library windows beaded with drops of rain, of Zoe and Mabel eating waffles, walking through colleges, boots kicking through the autumn leaves, sitting side by side in one of the tiny student rooms I'd shunned for years. Every now and then, another face would appear: a man with dark hair, who had a way of looking into the camera that betrayed more about his feelings for the photographer than I wanted to know.

When I got to the most recent post, I paused. Mabel, underneath an ivy-clad archway at Trinity Hall. The tattered coat, the bulging bag she never closed, the plaid scarf pulled up to the tip of her nose. You could see almost nothing of her face, but her eyes alone made it impossible for me to look away. So there I sat, gazing at the photograph of this woman, facing up to a truth I'd been fighting for days, wishing I could rip it out of my head and – most crucially of all – out of my heart.

I felt drawn to her. Not to her eyes, not to her face itself or her body. I felt drawn to the expression in her copper-brown irises. To the furrow that appeared on her brow when she thought no one was looking, to the way she lifted her chin even when I could sense her heart racing, to the intelligence in her questions and the close attention she paid the answers. I knew so little about her, but I felt her *so strongly*. And it was wrong, so terribly wrong that I couldn't bear to look at her. Not even the version of her in a photograph.

I flipped the phone screen-down and bolted my whisky, which seared my gullet and softened my thoughts. It didn't help. I felt miserable and sordid. Like I was peering furtively through a window into a life that was unattainable. Because it was – *she* was. For so many reasons. Perhaps it was time to remind myself of that.

I reached impetuously for my phone and typed in a different name. If Piper had known who was behind my user name she would have blocked me immediately, but this way I could check in on her feed from time to time, scrolling through pictures that were mostly of her own features. Black hair, fern-green eyes, lips curled into a laugh, and a flash of sorrow in her eyes that bored through in every image, at odds with her expression.

My focus shifted, and I found myself looking instead at the face reflected in the screen. The face that was responsible for the grief at Piper's core. *Think it*, I ordered myself, taking a deep breath. *My face.*

That was what I was. Who I was. A human unworthy of the word. Because I was a monster. What I'd said to Ashton was true: Mabel didn't know me. She knew nothing about Blake Ames, nothing about me. If she had, she would have given anything to forget it. Like Piper, like Selma, like Rose. Like all the women whose names I couldn't remember, yet who were the first thing I saw when I closed my eyes at night.

Exhausted, I locked the screen and reached for my wallet. After I'd paid I left the pub. It was late evening, after eleven, and a fine mist hovered above the tarmac and below the lanterns' heavy heads. Their light danced hazily with the mizzle underneath.

I hadn't gone far when my phone buzzed. Instantly I opened the message. Every time Aspen texted me, I was afraid something might have happened.

ASPEN

Tell me you're coming home for the gala!

It took a minute to click. The invitation to the family party had arrived weeks ago, but like most of those messages, I'd quickly pushed it to the back of my mind.

BLAKE

Don't know yet if I can make it. Pretty busy with uni right now.

Aspen came back online straight away and started typing.

ASPEN

Blaaaake, don't leave me hanging. These people are so fucking boring, I need my big brother.

A heavy smile crept across my lips. Saying no to Aspen was next to impossible, so I hardly ever did. And she knew it. Still, with everything going on, I didn't like the idea of leaving Cambridge for a whole weekend. On the other hand, maybe it was time. I really needed to speak to Brice about the equity fund – Henry had been breathing down my neck for weeks. Plus I wanted to check in on Aspen, make sure she was okay. As okay as a fifteen-year-old girl could be when her parents were never home, palming off their daughter onto a succession of housekeepers and private tutors.

BLAKE

Fine. I'll be there.

She answered with a serious of emojis, half of which I didn't understand. Even so, as I slid my phone back into my coat pocket, I felt a little like a weight had been lifted. The moments spent with Aspen were the ones when I hated myself a bit less.

I turned a corner onto a street that in daytime was always

heaving. Cafés alternated with signs for antiques shops and booksellers. By now, however, it was as good as deserted. I saw only a young man leaning against a brick wall, cupping one hand over the cigarette in his mouth as he tried to light it with the other.

I recognised the type before the face. Matthew Bassett exuded the same aura as the people I'd been training myself to spot for years: rich, educated, attractive men who had the world at their feet merely by virtue of the family name. Men so convinced of their own innate superiority that they saw only what they wanted, and took it without regard for anyone else. Selfish, obnoxious, amoral bastards. Blake Ames was a man like that – *I* was a man like that. So I recognised it immediately when I saw it it in others.

I'd seen it all, the moment I first laid eyes on him. Even in the split second before he pushed Mabel. At the memory of it, I inhaled sharply. Matthew, hearing me, turned in my direction. He lowered his hands, removing the cigarette from his lips. 'Can I help you?'

I threw a glance over my shoulder. Over the past two weeks I'd tried, on and off, to catch Matthew alone, but he was always with a group of friends. Running into him here, of all places, seemed an absurd coincidence. *Fate is just whatever we make of chance*, as Norah liked to say. In that moment I understood what she meant.

'You're Matthew Bassett, aren't you?' I asked, moving closer.

He frowned and put the cigarette back between his lips. 'And who are you?'

'I'm a friend of Mabel's.' He stared at me blankly as I took another step towards him. 'Mabel Golding.'

'That uppity tart from Ruiz's supervisions?' He laughed and clicked the lighter. It took all my effort not to slap it out of his hand and hold the flame to the ends of his hair.

My knuckles cracked as I balled my hands into fists, yet I

kept my voice controlled. 'I've seen the way you treat her. And I don't like it. So in future I'm going to need you to show a bit more respect – if you come near her at all. Got it?'

'Jesus, take it down a notch. I wouldn't touch her if you paid me.' He grinned. 'Although it would probably do her good to be taught a bit of humility. She really ought to know her place in our world. You understand.' He gave me a wink before taking a drag of his cigarette.

That settled it. It was true: I wasn't a good person. But I was really fucking good at being a bad one. And this was the only way I could use it for Mabel's benefit. I let Matthew exhale his plume of smoke, then I crossed the final distance between us.

'What—' he began, but my hand was already on his throat. In one fluid movement I had him against the brick wall, fingers digging into his skin. I was pushing harder than I needed to, but not half as hard as I wanted. I felt him stagger – not just his body, but what it contained within. The barrier was so thin I didn't even have to hurl myself against it. A nudge was enough to bring it down. That was always the way: the people who tried the hardest to seem loud and strong were the weakest on the inside. They were so ridiculously easy to break.

I should have despised myself for that thought, but instead it brought a grim smile to my lips. 'And now,' I said softly, my lips very close to his ear, 'you're going to listen very carefully.'

CHAPTER 11
MABEL

Davie and I were back in the library, sitting at the desk by the big bay window. The rain was still pelting down outside. A grey veil had hung above the university since yesterday, and as it drifted past it left droplets of rain like fingerprints on the glass. When the downpour began, news had spread across the university as if washed through by the rain itself. *A student jumped off the roof, a student killed herself, a student is dead.* June Owens: the name was reflected in every puddle, beading on the clothes of hurrying students, trailing them like a soundless echo into the colonnades and lecture halls where they sought shelter. June was gone, and that meant she was everywhere.

Even here, in the small room in the library, where we'd been sitting for the last twenty minutes. We'd spoken on the phone yesterday but were only just meeting up now. I knew Davie had been using every spare second to keep digging. The weary, harassed look in his eyes spoke volumes: the news that had brought the university to a grinding halt was spurring Davie on. And judging by the way his gaze kept darting to the folder in front of us, he had found something.

'Okay, what have you got?' I asked at last.

'I don't even know where to start,' he murmured, running a hand over his stubbly beard. 'The photo you found'—he pointed to the torn-out page—'I checked the names.'

Intrigued, I leant in. I'd tried to look them up online as well, but apart from Amelia, my search had turned up nothing. 'Were you able to find an address?'

'Not one that helps us.'

'What do you mean? I thought we were going to try and speak to them?' To find out if that bird brooch was just a fashion accessory or ... something more.

'I'm afraid I'm not spiritual enough to believe a séance will work.' His tone was so dry that it took me a moment to understand what he was saying.

'Hang on ... they're dead? All of them?' The picture was only forty years old. They should have been in their sixties by now.

'Yup. And that's not even the crazy part.' Davie turned the photograph so that I could look at it properly. 'This picture was taken in 1982. Amelia Wallingford, as you know, died in a fire that same year. Arthur O'Brien died three months later, officially of a heart attack, but inside sources say it was an overdose. His dad – some bigwig at the ministry of justice, apparently – hushed it all up. Ellen Meester and Quentin Middleton died in 1985 in a car accident...' Here Davie cast an uncertain look in my direction, but I deliberately did not return it. 'And Cedric Wells killed himself in 1986 after being diagnosed with pancreatic cancer.' He paused, his fingertip resting on Wells's face. The sight of it still gave me an odd feeling. 'You see? Four years after this photo of five young people was taken, all of them were dead.'

'And you think there's a connection to the secret society we suspect they might theoretically have been members of?' There was more than a note of scepticism in my voice. How could there not be: the whole thing was conjecture. If they really were all dead, then that was tragic, but not impossible. People died. Often, they died too young. It didn't necessarily mean there was a conspiracy or some weird cult behind it.

Davie, on the other hand, seemed more convinced than ever. He nodded. 'And it's not a one-off. I've checked every name that's cropped up in connection with the League, and it always leads to an obituary.'

'So you're saying … its members … have a tendency to die?'

Davie reached for the folder lying between us. 'And so does anyone who gets too close to them.'

My stomach twisted. 'How did you get all this information?'

'Change of approach. When you're looking for clues about a secret society, it's obviously going to be pretty slim pickings – assuming they're even remotely good at what they're doing. So I took a closer look at what else was going on during the years when they were supposedly active at a particular university.'

'And?' I watched nervously as he leafed through the documents until he came across a plastic folder. I could see from the page at the top that it contained copies of newspaper articles.

'I found a lot of … weird stuff, especially when I looked a bit further back. It was more than just vandalism, break-ins and illicit parties. I also found an unusually high number of deaths. I mean, sadly, we both know that the suicide rate at elite universities is comparatively high, but these were massive spikes in the statistical curve. So many students either took their own lives or had fatal accidents or went missing.'

He broke off, breathing heavily. By now I was too, as I struggled with the weight of what he was saying. Suddenly, everything seemed to be coming down on top of me, and I was buckling under the strain. 'You're telling me that June wasn't an isolated incident.'

Davie nodded weakly. 'It's the start of a pattern, Mabel. A dangerous one.'

I wrapped my fingers around my forearms. 'But ... how? I mean, there were eyewitnesses who saw that June was alone when she jumped. That she did it deliberately. It wasn't an accident, and nobody made her do it.'

'Just because she wasn't pushed, it doesn't mean that no one made her do it.'

'What are you saying? That the group had something on her?' I was still sounding dubious, although when I thought of Victor, somehow I found the idea much more plausible.

'Or they did something so awful to her that she didn't think she could live with it.'

Neither of us had to say it out loud. There had been three events during freshers' week alone on the topic of sexual assault, and what I'd read over the past few weeks while I was researching the connection between rape and student societies was enough to remind me for the rest of my life why I wanted nothing to do with them. And yet I'd been unable to connect any of it to the League of Starlings. Not at the library and not at their parties. What *might* be their parties.

God, it was all so confusing. My temples were pounding. I pressed a hand to my head and forced myself to concentrate. 'So what now? What are we going to do?' I tried to reach for the file, but Davie jerked it back.

'*We* aren't going to do anything. You promised me you'd drop it if we found something really bad.'

'But we haven't – not yet.'

'A girl who was at the same party as you is dead. How much worse does it need to be?'

'We don't know why she jumped. It might not have anything to do with the League. Victor and the others might not even be in it. We don't know anything.'

'We know they're not hampered by any sense of

responsibility. That they just do whatever the hell they want. We know they fit the profile of the group we've been researching all this time. And we know that somebody put a whole load of blood-drenched feathers into your bag. That's enough for me, Mabel. And for you too – right?'

He tried to move away, but I clasped his hand. 'Listen. If this is all true, then we need to find some evidence. You can't write an article without any proof.'

'Oh yeah, and what exactly did you have in mind?' He was scoffing, but his expression softened as my hand lingered on his.

I wished I hadn't noticed. And I wished I hadn't used it to my advantage, squeezing his hand. 'You talk to June's friends. Find out if anything happened while she was with them.'

'And you?'

I looked down at our hands and thought, as I so often did, of Blake's fingers. Of the way he'd touched me on Great Court – tentatively, almost guiltily. Of the expression on his face, a mix of sorrow, wistfulness and anger. Of his words, which said so much yet were still so enigmatic. Of how I'd felt: wanting to coax everything out of him, not just the truth about the League of Starlings but the truth about him. I had to admit it, if only to myself: even if I accepted that Blake was part of a dangerous secret society, that wasn't the real reason why I couldn't stop thinking about him. I was interested in *him*. In what drove him, in what he was. Under normal circumstances I'd have made up my mind by now to stay away from him. But retreat was not an option. It wasn't just about me – it was about Zoe, and everybody else in their orbit who didn't know what they might be capable of.

I looked resolutely at Davie. 'I'm going to finish what I've started.'

∾

Blake Ames lived in a peaceful area not far from the town centre. Roughly twenty minutes' walk from Trinity College, his flat was situated above a café in a red-brick building covered in wisteria. Davie had found me the address. He wasn't happy about it, but he'd done it so quickly that I decided not to ask how. Part of me was pretty sure that Davie's methods weren't always a hundred per cent legal.

Along the way, I stopped at Clare College to see June's memorial. The photo pinned up next to the door was a close-up of her face – pretty, smiling, full of life. The image persisted in my mind long after I'd left the college behind me, a faint outline at the edges of my field of vision that I couldn't blink away. Especially not once I reached Blake's flat. The front door was open, even though it couldn't be more than about five degrees.

I'd been wondering as I walked where I'd be most likely to find Blake on a Saturday, but I'd got no further than the college or the vaulted nave of a church. Part of me couldn't imagine him existing outside the places where we'd already met. As if I'd made him up. That would at least be an acceptable excuse for why I kept thinking about him: because he was at home in my head.

Forcing the thought aside, I went upstairs and rang the bell. A few seconds passed before I heard footsteps on the other side of the door. A moment later it opened, and there he stood.

Something was different. His dark hair was wet, combed back from his forehead as if he'd just showered. Yet it also seemed thicker than I'd ever seen it before. His cheeks were unusually rosy, the dark circles under his eyes less pronounced. And even in the rich brown of his irises, I thought I saw a subtle sheen, as if he'd slept properly for the first night in weeks. His eyes widened slightly when he saw me.

'You look different. Sort of ... healthier.'

At the sound of my voice, he blinked. Almost like it had suddenly dawned on him that I was really there. For a split second I wondered whether he, too, thought I might be a figment of the imagination.

'How do you know where I live?'

I grinned. 'You said it yourself. I have a knack for showing up where I'm not wanted.'

He frowned, opening the door a little wider as if to let me in. But when he realised what he was doing he pulled it back again, so that I couldn't see anything of the flat behind him. 'What do you want?'

'To ask you if you have time for a walk with me. And these.' I held up a cardboard tray with two cups and a bag.

Davie had tried persuading me to wait until the next time I was invited to one of their parties. But every minute I sat around doing nothing felt dangerously negligent. I had to speak to someone *now*. And Blake seemed like the safest choice. It was just unfortunate that my heart kept beating faster and more wildly the longer he looked at me.

'Come on.' I tapped the brim of my black cap, which had belonged to my mother. 'I'll leave this on so that no one will recognise me. That way you don't have to feel ashamed to be seen with me.'

The teasing tone couldn't hide the crack in my voice. As comfortable as I felt at the university, I knew I didn't really fit in. I studied too much and partied too little, I took things too seriously and didn't bother pretending to find things funny when they weren't. I wore my ladder-ridden tights like armour, yet I couldn't lie to myself: there were times when people's pointed words cut straight through them. I didn't mind being an outsider, not with most people. But Blake... I hated to admit it, but with him, I evidently did mind.

He shook his head, drops of water pattering onto the collar of his russet jumper. 'There's nothing to be ashamed of.'

I felt myself grow hot, and bit my cheek trying not to smile. 'Tell that to your face. You don't look too keen.' My gaze slid to the neckline of his jumper, but he moved his hand to cover the bare skin below his collarbone. Yet trying to hide it only served to make the presence of the tattoo more obvious, bringing me back into the moment. To the reason why I was here.

Blake leant against the doorframe. 'I thought we'd established that this wasn't a good idea.'

'Because you're not a good person, yeah, I recall. So that's a no?'

He hesitated, then his face sealed itself again into a smooth, cool mask. 'It is.'

'Fine.' Tucking the bag under my arm, I reached into my coat pocket. 'Then could you tell me where to find Ashton? I need to thank him.'

'What...'

He trailed off as I drew out my hand. I was holding a two-inch black feather, which I twirled in the air before his face. 'Pretty, isn't it? I'm fairly sure it's from a starling. Impressive birds, honestly. They're more mysterious than you'd think at first glance.' I gave a guileless smile, but I knew he could hear the provocative note in my voice.

For a few seconds, I was sure he was about to slam the door in my face, but he simply shut his eyes for a moment. Then, in one fluid movement, he grabbed his jacket and scarf from a peg by the door and stepped outside. 'Let's go, Pica.'

～

As we left the town centre behind us, we drank our lukewarm coffee in silence. The November light was growing softer and brighter as the day went on, its silvery shimmer washing over us with ever-greater intensity. Every now and then, my eyes darted to Blake: the open coat, the dark brown woollen scarf around his neck, the quiet vigilance in his gaze as it ceaselessly scanned the world around him. I knew I was under his watch as well, but he didn't actually look at me until I held out the bag. He reached in and took out a pastry without hesitation.

I nibbled the edge of a cinnamon roll as I watched him take a cautious bite of his own pastry, then his mouth twisted.

'Not great?'

'I don't like raisins.'

'Then why did you take the pain aux raisins?'

Blake examined it wistfully. 'Because I want to like them.'

I couldn't help laughing. 'You're one of a kind, you know that?'

A faint grin flitted across his face, just as mournful as the rest of him. 'I wish. But I'm afraid appearances can be deceiving.'

I could only stare at him. He was the strangest person I'd ever met, but perhaps because of that ... the most intriguing. My gaze wandered down his arm, snagging on his wrist. I had to take a second look to be sure I wasn't mistaken.

'Your watch. It's stopped, hasn't it?'

Immediately Blake grabbed his sleeve and tugged it down over the dial. 'Yeah, it stopped working ages ago.'

I wanted to ask why someone with his bank balance didn't buy a new one or get it repaired, but he was obviously uncomfortable, so I didn't push. 'Don't worry, I wasn't planning to nick it,' I teased. 'You can call me Pica if you want, but I'm not that much of a magpie.'

It hadn't taken me long to find that *pica* was the Latin name for the common magpie – and even less to remember that he'd asked me the night we met if I was planning on stealing anything.

Blake said nothing, but I saw a smile of approval creep into the corners of his mouth.

We'd been walking along the Cam for a while, and as we reached a bend, the path led us onto Stourbridge Common, one of Cambridge's oases, where the noisy city seemed further away than it really was. I moved to let Blake walk nearest the river, while I kept to his right.

'Why are you afraid of the water?' Seeing my blank look, he smiled. 'You're being careful not to walk right by the bank. Either you're planning to push me in or you're scared of falling in yourself.'

I hesitated, but steeled myself. Zoe had already told this part of my story to Ashton anyway. Plus, if you wanted someone to be honest with you, you generally had to give them something of yourself first. Even if it was the kind of truth you'd prefer to keep under lock and key, the kind of truth that let slip too much. Talking about what you'd been through always meant revealing who you were. In the end, a personality was nothing but a pane of glass smudged with the fingerprints of experience – and this particular smudge was the size of a hand, placed directly over my heart. 'When I was seven years old, my cousin and I were playing hide and seek, and I climbed into a boat. It came unmoored somehow and drifted away from the shore. I was in there for hours before they found me, and by then it was the middle of the night.'

'Did anything happen to you?'

I shook my head. 'I was a bit dehydrated, that's all. But all those hours by myself, nothing but black, unfathomable water all around me ... it felt like something was looming out of it. There was no way out, you know? No escape from what was closing in. There was this sense of ... being trapped. Powerless against the universe. It made me realise it's impossible to ever fully be in control.'

'So that's why you're always trying to control everything.' It didn't sound like a question, more like an answer to something he'd been wondering for some time.

I wanted to contradict him, but suddenly my therapist's voice popped into my head. *Emotions can never be fully controlled, and that's okay*, she'd said when I couldn't stop crying after my mother died. I cried at the supermarket, on the bus, at school. In ordinary, everyday moments it would hit me out of nowhere: nothing was ordinary anymore, because the core of my everyday life was gone. Without it, you lost your balance. I'd lost it – I'd lost myself. And no matter what my therapist said, it *wasn't* okay. It was awful. It ripped the ground out from beneath my feet and the sky from my mind. No down, no up: only a terrible nothingness, and I fell and fell. So I tried to find a new midpoint. A core made up of routine and security, something to brace myself against, something unconditional.

I found it in books, which allowed me to concentrate on nothing but concentrating. Except for my aunt and my cousin, I didn't let anyone get close enough to be a supporting column in my life, let alone the core. Until I got to Cambridge, and on the very first night this girl came knocking at my door, walked in unasked and sat down on my bed to share a bag of wine gums. Zoe came, and Zoe stayed, and ever since then Zoe has been ... present, in a way I haven't allowed anyone to be in a very long time. She was never a question mark. From the very beginning, she was an exclamation mark, and I never doubted her. She was a mistake I made yet never regretted.

'Yeah, I suppose I tend to stay furthest away from things I have the least control over,' I replied hesitantly. *From people like you, for instance*, I added in my mind. *And yet – here I am.* 'How about you?' I asked, trying to shrug it off. I was only here for research purposes. For Zoe. 'What are you scared of?'

He inspected the pain aux raisins in his hand, tore off a corner and crumbled it between his fingers. I hadn't noticed the ducks in the steel-blue water before he tossed the crumbs to them and they came swimming over. 'I haven't felt fear for a long time.'

It was strange: Blake kept saying things that would have sounded self-aggrandising from anybody else, but coming from him they only felt resigned and weary. Like he was reciting the lines of a role he'd memorised but never wanted or understood.

'You're not afraid of anything?'

'If you're afraid, it means you have something to lose. That you have an attachment to something you want to keep. And I haven't had that for a long time, really.'

We walked on, the beech trees casting dappled shadows across his face. More dark than light, yet I couldn't look away. 'You shouldn't think like that.'

He smiled dully. 'Because I'm still so young, you mean?'

'It's got nothing to do with age. You're alive. And life is ... beautiful. Not always, not every aspect of it. But there are so many things worth giving your heart to – because they make everything easier.'

Blake paused and squatted down. Using two fingers he picked up a gleaming blue beetle in the middle of the path. It was a small gesture, but it stirred something warm in me that I struggled to subdue. Blake put it back down in the grass a little further away, and looked at me. 'What things?'

I didn't have to think about it, because I'd asked myself that question so many times before. For a year after Mum died, my aunt had prompted me every single night: *Come on, let's think of something that makes enduring all this worth it.* It took a while, but with every passing day, more things had come to mind. 'The low light at the library, when everything is golden and the dust is settling across the books. The smell of rain on asphalt. The taste of chocolate cake from Bridget's Bakery.' I had to smile. 'Someone you love, laughing. The feel of lipstick on your lips, and when I see myself wearing it and I feel so ... real. In such an uncomplicated way, because I can feel how present I am. Those are a few of my things. Things that are worth it, always.'

Blake was still crouching in front of me. His coat was trailing in the dew-damp grass, his eyes on mine. He didn't move, but I thought I could see the thoughts racing across his face. Or ... the emotions.

I touched a hand to my temple, feeling awkward. 'What?'

'Nothing. Just ... your Instagram bio, you talk about "Mabel's Mirror". I get it now.'

I froze. 'You found my IG?'

The corners of his mouth lifted as he stood up and walked past me.

'Are you stalking me?' I followed him, unsure whether it bothered me or if it somehow made me feel good.

'I'm sorry, who showed up at whose door today?'

Point to Blake.

I reached into my coat pocket until my fingers found the metal case. I hesitated briefly, then took it out. The gold glinted in the hazy sunlight. I ran my fingers over the petals engraved on the round lid, then clicked it open. My eyes looked back at me – darker than usual, as always when a memory of Mum caught me off-guard. Funny how thinking of the brightest person in your life can feel so dark, once they've left you for good. Like the loss of them takes all the light with it.

'This is the real Mabel's mirror,' I explained to Blake, holding out the pocket mirror. 'It belonged to my mother. She always kept it with her. I tell myself she can see what I'm seeing when I look into it. Same reason I have the Instagram, too. It feels like a way of staying in contact with her. With the memory of her. Collecting moments like that for her keeps it strong. Crazy, I know.' My smile felt sadder and more honest than I liked. 'People do funny things when they miss someone.'

'Yeah.' Blake was looking into the mirror, and a gloomy look crossed his face. 'The best things and the worst things,' he added, then snapped it shut before returning it to me. 'But this is one of the best.'

Our fingers brushed for a few seconds too long as I took the small object from his palm. I felt hot. It wasn't the astonishing warmth of his skin, it was the sensation of his touch. I was tempted to ask if he was missing someone too, when I realised we'd arrived. *At last*, I wanted to think, but I couldn't ignore a pang of disappointment. I knew the conversation would be considerably more tense from this point on. Still, I walked purposefully up to the benches overlooking the water and sat down on one. The dark wood was weathered, the ribs pressing roughly into my back. I waited until Blake had sat down beside me, then I turned to him. 'Can I ask *you* a question now?'

'Sure. As long as you don't expect me to give you an honest answer. I'm not going to tell you anything personal while you're recording me.'

His voice was impassive, but it felt like he'd punched me in the face. A surge of heat welled up in my body as I avoided his amused stare. 'I ... you noticed that?'

'Uh-huh.' He dipped the pain aux raisins into what remained of his coffee, although it must have long since gone cold. 'I saw your phone poking out a bit when you took out the feather, and I just had a hunch...'

I groped instinctively for the phone in my coat pocket. 'But ... then why did you come with me?'

His expression grew softer, less wary. As if he were deliberately lowering his guard to get the next words out. 'As long as you're here with me, at least I know you're not getting into trouble elsewhere.'

More heat rushed humiliatingly to my cheeks. Clearing my throat, I took out my phone and ended the recording. 'Fine. Just you and me, then. Can I ask you something?'

He sighed. 'I'm starting to realise how difficult it is to talk you out of doing anything.'

'Amelia Victoria Heaven Wallingford.'

I tried to read the shift in his expression, but there wasn't one. He didn't even blink, only gazed at me blankly. 'That's a name, not a question.'

'Does it mean anything to you?'

He raised his thumb to the corner of his mouth and brushed away a few crumbs. 'Should it?'

Slowly, I shifted aside to reveal the golden plaque. I tapped it, not taking my eyes off Blake. 'We're sitting on a bench dedicated to her memory.'

Blake didn't look, and in that moment it dawned on me that he'd known all along. He'd known where I was headed the minute we set foot on Stourbridge Common. I'd thought coming here would provoke a reaction, but now I realised that was never going to happen. Still, the lack of a reaction had told me a lot. It was obvious he knew this bench. Which meant he also knew the name.

'And that's a coincidence, or...?' he asked, with just the right trace of boredom and irritation. He was right: he was a very good liar.

'What makes you think it *isn't* a coincidence?'

He rested his elbow on the back of the bench, so that his jacket was covering the plaque. 'You shouldn't play games, Mabel. You don't have a good enough poker face.'

'All right, then I'll be frank.' I straighened my shoulders, my pulse quickening. 'As I'm sure you're aware, there are quite a few student societies at Cambridge.'

'Of course. They make no secret of their existence.'

'Some do.'

'Where are you going with this?'

Instead of answering, I reached into my coat and took out a feather, spinning it again between my fingers.

He frowned. 'I don't get—'

'You shouldn't be playing games either, Blake,' I interrupted calmly. 'You might have a decent poker face, but I can still read you like a book.'

We held each other's gaze in silence. A punt glided past, the water lapping with a soft purl against the bank. Yet the moment felt calm: calm and intense, like the eyes he had fixed on mine. At long last he raised his hand and took the feather. 'Where did you get this?'

'Somebody stuffed it into my bag the other day when I was in the library. Quite a lot of them, actually. And I'm afraid the bird that supplied them must be dead.'

Again he frowned, but this time it looked sincere. *You can't be certain*, I thought. It was possible he *had* known about the feathers – it may even have been him who planted them in my bag. If I accepted the fact that he was a good liar, I also had to work on the assumption that I could never be sure if he was telling me the truth. Yet for some reason I still didn't think his expression was calculated. It looked more like ... genuine concern. 'Somebody put bloody feathers into your bag,' he muttered, running his fingers over the red-flecked plume.

'That doesn't sound like a question. Which makes me think you know who it was.' His lips narrowed, but I waved a hand. 'I can work it out for myself. What I don't understand is why. What are you all so afraid of?'

He lowered his hand, which was clenched around the feather. '*Us?*'

For a moment I hesitated, then I cast all doubt to the winds. My mother taught me early on in life that the clarity of the answer you receive depends entirely on the question. *You have to know what you want. Direct question, direct answer.* 'I know you're part of it. The society that calls itself the League of Starlings.'

Blake's expression was once again so shuttered that I wondered how much practice he'd had putting on a mask. There was no crack, no gap, however small, through which I could catch a glimpse of his thoughts or feelings.

'When did it happen?' was all he asked.

'Three days ago.'

'And it didn't scare you off?'

'Far from it. If they're going on the attack like that, it means they've got something to defend.' I cocked my head. 'You're not denying it. It's true, then.'

'You're going to believe whatever you want either way, aren't you?'

I snorted. 'You think this is what I want? My best friend has fallen into the clutches of some cult that's doing God knows what to her. I'm getting more worried about her by the day. I'm not you, Blake. I'm fucking *terrified*.'

He eyed me doubtfully. 'You're scared for Zoe, but not for yourself, even though you're the one with the bag full of bloody feathers?'

'That's called love. Ever heard of it?'

'Of course I have. Believe it or not, there are people I ... *love*.'

'Who, Ashton? I thought he wasn't a good person either.'

Blake opened his hand, examining the feather in his palm. 'He doesn't have to be a good person to be *my* person. For all his faults, he's still my best friend.' Slowly, he raised his eyes. 'Look, keep this stuff to yourself, all right? If rumours start to get out, not everybody is going to take it as calmly as I am.'

'So you're not planning on telling them. Because you don't want to alarm them or because you're trying to protect me?' My voice had grown quieter, my heart louder. I was drifting off topic, asking questions about what I *wanted* to know rather than what I needed to.

His eyes smiled, but his mouth remained a straight line. 'Which answer would frighten you more?'

'I'm not frightened of you. I told you that before.'

The smile deepened, nestling into the dimples at the corners of his mouth. 'Which is precisely why you're so dangerous, Mabel.'

'No more dangerous than you, Blake.'

A strange look crossed his face. Drawing back, he looked at the water. 'Don't call me that, okay?'

'You prefer Cliff?'

'Yes.' He smiled sadly, almost hauntedly. 'And no.'

'You're a mystery to me,' I said flatly.

He laughed, only briefly, but the sound slipped deep into the crannies of my memory – it was so warm, so soft, so at odds with how serious he always seemed.

'Good. Because you're a mystery to me too.'

We fell silent for a moment, while I tried to organise my thoughts. Blake hadn't confirmed the existence of the League, but nor had he denied it. That might mean it was real – or simply that he wanted me to stop digging before I got to the actual truth. Or, of course, that he didn't care either way. I was still none the wiser, and it was frustrating. Talking to Blake was like reading an old book, a classic I didn't fully comprehend. I understood the words, but I couldn't see through all the layers of interpretation to reach the meaning at its core.

'Maybe I should just start calling you Heathcliff,' I muttered, vaguely annoyed.

'From *Wuthering Heights*? Hardly the most likeable character.'

'He's the archetype of the tortured hero, often a loner born into wealth. Usually hiding a dark secret. Ruthless, too.'

Blake raised his eyebrows sceptically. 'Are you trying to tell me something?'

'June Owens,' I replied, making a sudden decision. I had come to him for answers: I wasn't going to leave empty-handed. 'I know she was at your parties, I saw her. With Victor.'

Blake's face tensed. 'What are you insinuating? That he pushed her off the roof?'

'No. As far as I know, she was up there alone. But that doesn't mean he wasn't involved. That ... *you* weren't involved.'

My heart felt empty. The words, too, somehow. Blake's expression hollowed them out until they fluttered thinly in the air between us. 'If you really believe that,' he said emotionlessly, 'then why are you here?'

I could have dodged the question, but his gaze bored so deep that it cut partway through the layers of distance and defiance I'd built up over the last few years. 'Because I don't think you're like your friends. You're not as indifferent as they are, you ... care about other people.'

'You're wrong. And in any case ... they're my family.' He made to stand up, but I grabbed him. His pulse was strong, his skin still warmer than I'd have expected in this cold.

'You can love something, you can cherish it, and it can still be bad for you. That goes for people just as much as for the life you lead.'

Blake closed his eyes, pinching the bridge of his nose between his thumb and forefinger. When he met my gaze again, he seemed earnest. Genuine. 'Victor didn't rape June, if that's what you're thinking. He never slept with her or pressured her into doing anything like that.'

I swallowed. 'Can you promise me that?'

'Yes.' Blake hesitated, then took my hand off his arm. 'Victor isn't always easy, but he's not that much of a ... monster.' For a few seconds his eyes rested on his fingers, which had closed around mine. Then, as if seeing something I had missed, his cheeks blanched. He let me go and jerked his hand back, shifting slightly to the right, away from me.

Confused and embarrassed, I tucked my hand under my thigh so he wouldn't see it trembling. 'Okay, I believe you. But I still think there's more you're not willing to tell me. Or twitter at me.' I gestured to the feather he had slid into a groove in the wood.

Blake sighed. It was astonishing how quickly he regained his composure – the colour was even coming back into his cheeks. 'If this society you're talking about really does exist, and if we're members of it – and I'm saying *if* – then there's nothing very special about that. Societies exist so people can network.

You build a community, put people in touch, help each other out. That's all.'

'There's just one problem,' I replied with a sardonic smile. 'Normally, clubs like that do everything they can to make sure they stick in people's minds. You, on the other hand, try to keep it quiet. And having met a couple of your friends, I'm pretty sure that modesty isn't the reason why.'

Instead of replying, Blake got to his feet with a regretful nod. 'I have to go now. You know, feed a few birds.'

I wanted to be stubborn, to keep pushing, but I couldn't help laughing. 'Wait, don't tell me that was an actual joke! I think you're getting soft.'

Blake rolled his eyes, but there it was again, the gentle smile that softened his features. He reached out and touched the brim of my cap, nudging it back so that we could see more of each other's faces.

The smile dropped from my mouth, and Blake's eyes leapt straight to it. My lipstick was a pastel red called Cloudy Mind. My own mind felt cloudy, too, as he stroked his thumb over my cheekbone.

'Next time don't wear the cap,' he said in a low voice, barely audible. 'I like seeing you properly.'

'My face, you mean?'

'No. I mean ... you.'

I wanted to smile so badly that I had to bite my lip. 'Okay, *now* you're flirting with me.'

'Maybe.' He drew his hand back and looked at it again, as if realising how contemptible everything about the situation was.

'But you don't want to be,' I realised gradually. 'So ... what am I, like an inverse pain aux raisins?'

'What?'

'Something you might sort of like a teeny bit but wish you didn't?'

He smiled, a proper one this time, then turned on his heel

and walked back to the path. Reaching it, he turned around again and recited a string of numbers.

I frowned, baffled. 'What's that?'

'My number. Put it in your phone – then next time you have a question, you won't have to randomly show up at my house.'

I tapped the brim of my cap. 'And you say you're not a nice person, Heathcliff.'

I saw the words repeated in his eyes: *You're wrong*. But he didn't say them out loud, he only turned and walked off down the path. And although he hadn't told me much – most of it I'd inferred from what he *hadn't* said – I sensed something had changed. Maybe not for my research. But for me. For him and me. For an us that wasn't real and never could be.

CHAPTER 12
MABEL

It was past eight o'clock when I left the Wren Library. Trinity College lay before me, dimly lit and almost deserted. I adjusted my scarf more tightly around my head, having forgotten my hat. And my gloves, I realised, with a muttered swearword as I rummaged for them. I'd spent the last few hours sitting by a draughty window, and my fingers felt numb.

I was supposed to be doing a big presentation in one of my supervisions just before Christmas, but over the past few weeks it had taken a back seat. All the extra bird-related research was coming back to haunt me now, and I had to force myself to focus on my academic studies for a while. I'd been finding it more and more difficult in the two weeks since June's death.

Talk had died down, especially now that the administration and the police were both referring to it as a definite suicide. The college buildings were plastered with reminders of the university counselling service, and everybody seemed to consider the matter settled. At least, almost everybody. I would have preferred to concentrate on what happened to June, but I knew if I started slacking, then I could kiss goodbye to my bursary, and that would put an end to my little side-project altogether. At least Davie was still on it, and he was continually reassuring me that he'd keep me in the loop if he found anything interesting. The thought made me reach for my phone to check my messages. He hadn't texted, but Zoe had.

ZOE

Did you leave a bar of chocolate on my bed?

The light under the colonnade was as dim as it had been in the stacks, and the dazzle of the display made my eyes sting. I stopped to type a reply.

MABEL

There wasn't any room left on your desk. You should tidy up a bit.

After I hit send I waited uneasily. Zoe was still online, but she wasn't typing. In the past she'd never minded if I used the spare key to her room while she was out, but lately things had been a bit awkward between us, and I wasn't sure she'd be okay with it. I hated that. Uncertainty had never been part of our friendship before. We'd been so open with each other from the start, so honest and ... secure, and that was always what I'd valued the most. Tentatively, I followed up with another message.

MABEL

Dumb idea?

This time she answered straight away.

ZOE

No, lovely idea. Thank you.

I exhaled, relieved, and walked on.

> **MABEL**
>
> I'm on my way home. Want to hang out tonight? I could pick up some chips.

> **ZOE**
>
> I've already eaten.

> **MABEL**
>
> Then I'll grab some and you can just eat however many you want. Deal?

Again, hesitation. I could picture her eyes darting back and forth between the bar of chocolate and the phone. I chewed my bottom lip until at last an answer came.

> **ZOE**
>
> Deal. But only if you agree to watch Romeo & Juliet with me. I feel like drooling over Leo tonight.

I sent her a groaning-face emoji then typed again, *Deal*. The truth was I would have done pretty much anything to get her near those chips. If it also involved her drooling over someone who wasn't Ashton, then so much the better.

Zoe had been at her parents' place over the weekend, and as always when she got back, she seemed a bit down. She never talked much about her visits home, but I was always keenly aware of the changes in her behaviour. The way it took her longer in the mornings to get ready because she kept changing her outfit. The way she swapped pasta for a salad more often than usual, or nibbled on apple slices during movie night when normally she'd have eaten half a bar of chocolate. The self-critical frown whenever she caught sight of herself in the mirror. The tears that welled up in her eyes when she was handed back an essay with a slightly lower mark than usual. How sensitive she was to any form of rejection, as if me asking to reschedule a coffee meant I was getting fed up with her.

I wondered how they could have given birth to such a kind, fun-loving person, only to sap her of those very qualities on every visit. Because that was what they did – even if I didn't know exactly how.

I'd only met them once, when Zoe invited me home over Easter. At first glance, the Haywoods seemed like a picture-perfect family: the successful husband and wife, married for thirty years, living in an enormous house with a pool and a home cinema on the outskirts of London. Three children, all grown up, gorgeous and well educated. Zoe's older siblings were twenty-seven-year-old twins. Her brother had studied medicine and was now a consultant working in the NHS. Her sister had studied psychology, like their dad, but did a bit of modelling on the side and was engaged to the heir of a major fashion company. Zoe was the baby of the family, and was still treated that way, as I realised when I heard them calling her Zazu after the bird in *The Lion King*, Zoe's favourite film as a child. Although they had all been immaculately pleasant and courteous, I'd sensed how unnaturally tense Zoe was around them.

When I'd tried to gently probe and find out what the problem was, she always downplayed it. Sometimes I wondered if she thought she wasn't allowed to complain about her family in front of me because, unlike me, she still had one. I'd gladly have told her that wasn't true, but I didn't want to twist her arm. All I could do was be there for her, time after time, until the influence of her family gradually waned and she came back to herself. Normally it didn't take long enough to seriously worry me, but this time I was afraid her recent low mood would make things worse.

Thankfully, I hadn't seen anything of Ashton for about a week and a half. I didn't ask if they were still seeing each other, and she didn't mention it. It had also been about ten days since I'd spoken to Blake, and four since I'd bitten the bullet and texted him. I'd regretted it every minute since hitting send, because he still hadn't replied. I wasn't surprised, but I was hurt. Which was maybe the worst part of the whole thing. He was allowed to annoy me – after all, Blake was the most reliable source I had – but never to *hurt* me. Getting hurt was a reflex of the heart, not of the head.

I slid my phone into my coat pocket, about to step out into another courtyard. It was bare except for an empty fountain. For a split second I didn't notice the person sitting on the lip, but as soon as I caught sight of him I stopped dead under the covered archway. My heart began to pound before my mind caught up.

Victor's hair was tied back in a bun, as always, a few stray wisps framing his strikingly ruddy cheeks. Maybe it was the light from the sky or the lamppost next to him, but I'd have bet money he was burning hot. For one thing, he'd taken off his jacket and draped it next to him.

I drew back into the shadows, just far enough so that I could still see his companion. On the edge of the fountain next to Victor, sat a young man with blond hair and softly chiselled features. It took me a moment to pinpoint where I knew him from: he was one of the people who'd paid me so much unwanted attention at the first party. What had Victor called him? Jake? *Jack*, my brain corrected automatically.

Only then did I notice the woman sitting next to him. Her hair gleamed gold in the light as her laughter wafted over to me. At least until Jack sighed irritably. 'You're getting on my nerves, Paulina.'

My mouth twisted, but she seemed more bewildered than annoyed. She got up uncertainly from the stone rim and took a step back. 'Should I go?'

Jack reached out a hand and twirled a lock of her barley-blonde hair between his fingers, taking a drag of his cigarette. 'Ah, but you'll be back. You always come back, no matter how badly I treat you, don't you?'

Paulina shook her head vigorously. 'You don't treat me badly.'

'Oh yes, I do.' Jack blew the plume of smoke directly into her face. I didn't need to see anything else to know he was right. 'You just forget about it, because I want you to. I've got no choice, unless I want you to go blabbing about us. It's a vicious cycle.'

I froze. His words were so bizarre that I felt almost certain he was drunk. Yet it didn't seem that way from his gestures and demeanour – they were too controlled. He knew what he was doing and he believed what he was saying.

Victor coughed. 'Then break it.'

Jack let go of Paulina and turned to look at him. 'And how exactly am I supposed to do that, Vic?'

'You know how. The same way I got rid of June.'

My heart stopped. I let out a gasp, barely clapping my hand to my mouth in time. I drew hastily back, further into the recesses of the stone. I could still hear their voices clearly, perhaps because their words were so brutal that they simply tore through the other sounds.

'You told Ashton it was an accident.'

Victor sniggered audibly. 'I tell Ashton a lot of things that are only half true. After all, we have to assume he's passing them on.'

'So you made her do it? On purpose?'

Take out your phone and record them. It was the only thought in my head. But I knew I was too far away for my phone to pick up their voices properly, and I could barely bring myself to move a muscle. I leant timidly forwards, just in time to see Victor shrug. 'I just wanted her gone. She chose the ... simplest way to comply with that request. And what happened? *Absolutely nothing.* No idea why everyone's getting their knickers in such a twist. How would they ever prove it?'

'You know we've had some pretty close calls in the past. Which is why we all agreed not to attract that kind of attention.'

'*Agreed?*' Victor got to his feet with a snort. 'Nobody asked me. It's orders from above. But they're not the ones who have to sit around twiddling their thumbs in this shithole of a university, surrounded by a load of slack-jawed idiots.' He jerked his thumb contemptuously towards Paulina, who was standing between them wide-eyed.

Jack followed the gesture, surveying his companion. 'I don't know, mate. If they find out—'

'They won't,' Victor interrupted impatiently. 'It's only you and me here.'

'And me.' Paulina smiled uncertainly. Her fingers were curled into the hem of her thick velvet jacket, her eyes on Jack's face. I couldn't understand why she didn't just leave. Why she was looking at Jack as if he was the only place in the world where she belonged.

'That's right, sweetheart.' Victor stroked her head. It could have seemed affectionate, but for some reason it looked like he was petting a dog. 'And that's the problem.' He took a step towards Jack, who looked up. 'Come on. I know you want to. How long has it been since you took as much as you wanted? We've been leashed for far too long. It's against our nature. Just think about how powerful we are – what's the use of all that power if you never get to enjoy it?'

'Ashton...' Jack began hesitantly.

Victor threw back his head and groaned. 'Ashton isn't here. Neither are Norah or Blake – which means there's nobody to tell him.' I flinched inwardly at the sound of his name, but I still couldn't move or string together a coherent thought from the jumble of information. 'I'm sick of Ash acting like some fucking prince, bossing us around like his own personal court.'

'I mean, he sort of is, isn't he? A prince.'

'Well right now he isn't here at all. So. What's it going to be?'

Jack's eyes darted between the mute, almost absent-seeming Paulina and his friend. He ran his hand several times through his cropped hair, as if trying to organise the thoughts underneath his skull.

Victor took a step back, raising his hands. 'Or are you scared? You think maybe you're too out of practice?'

'I can see what you're trying to do. I'm a psychology student, remember?' Jack rolled his eyes, but even so, he sat up a little straighter.

Victor had noticed it too: he was smirking triumphantly. 'So, is it working?'

'Unfortunately, yes.' Jack sighed deeply, stubbing out his cigarette on the stone edge, where he simply left it. 'Fine. Paulina, my love – come here.' He drew her closer by the wrists, pulling her in between his legs.

Immediately she clasped his hips, beaming at him. 'Hi.'

Jack smiled, but even at this distance I could see the watchful look in his eyes. He brushed the hair back from her forehead, then cupped her face in both hands, looking steadily into her eyes. 'You like me, don't you?'

She nodded hastily, a little too eagerly. 'Of course.'

'Then just think about how much, okay?' He leant in until the tip of his nose grazed hers. 'Will you do that for me?'

'Of course,' she breathed, closing her eyes.

I tensed, ready to come out of the shadows if he grabbed hold of her. But he didn't. At least, not really. He merely circled his thumbs gently over her cheeks before lowering his hands – to her throat.

And there they stood, motionless, both with eyes closed. After a few seconds Paulina's body appeared to soften. She shifted closer to Jack, wrapped both arms around his hips and sighed gently. He smiled without opening his eyes. Victor was slowly stepping back, arms folded, a broad grin on his face that felt more menacing to me than anything else about the situation. I didn't understand what was happening, and I wasn't sure if I should do something – and if so, what. Jack's hands were still resting on her throat, but there was nothing rough about the way he was touching her, and meanwhile Paulina kept clutching ever more determinedly at his hips. It didn't look like he was hurting her. Far from it. In the flat light of the lamp, I could see her face growing more peaceful and relaxed with every passing second. She sighed again, longer this time, deeper.

Jack blinked and rested his forehead against hers. 'God,' he murmured, languidly, almost dazedly, and pressed a kiss to her cheek. 'I'd forgotten how good that feels.' His voice seemed to vibrate with satisfaction, a pulse that spread into his body. Although the colour had risen to his face, he seemed to be quivering. I felt sick, my fingers boring into the stone in front of me.

'Do it now,' Victor ordered softly.

Jack hesitated a final time, then once again he took Paulina's face in his hands. He rested the tip of his nose against hers, then put his mouth very close to her ear.

My hands were clenching so hard that I tore a nail. A keen stab of pain ran up my finger, but I barely noticed it. My body was on high alert, my heart thumping rapidly. Every fibre of me was ready to step in the moment something happened.

But … nothing did. I could see his lips move, but I couldn't hear what he said. Paulina leant quietly against his chest until he pulled away. Again he pressed a kiss to her cheek and pushed her back. 'Will you do that for me?' he asked mildly. She nodded, much more weakly now, but didn't move. Jack raised his eyebrows and shooed her with his hands. 'All right then, go.'

Paulina wavered briefly, then nodded again and turned around. Her body stumbled over the first few steps, but then she pulled herself up and walked slowly away. Out of the courtyard, towards the main college gates.

Jack watched her go, brow furrowed. 'Do you think it worked?'

'Guess we'll find out tomorrow morning.' Victor grinned and clapped him on the shoulder, but instantly jerked back. 'Holy shit.' He flapped his hand, laughing, as if he'd burnt himself. 'Come on, let's get out of here, make sure we go somewhere people can see us. Just to be on the safe side.'

I waited until the two of them were out of sight before following in the direction Paulina had gone. Part of me wanted to shadow Victor and Jack, try to hear more, but I sensed Paulina was more important. Whatever had passed between her and Jack, it seemed like she was under some sort of … influence. I couldn't let her be alone in that state.

Every step I took without finding her made me more nervous. It wasn't until I walked through a covered passageway and emerged not far from one of the bridges that I spotted a figure some distance ahead of me, standing by the balustrade. The blonde hair fluttering in the wind was unmistakeably Paulina's. I breathed a sigh of relief and set off in her direction, until suddenly I went rigid.

She wasn't standing by the balustrade – she was standing on it. For a moment, the sight of it crossed wires with a memory: that night on the bridge, weeks ago, when Victor got up onto the balustrade and said, *People like us don't have bad luck*.

Even at the time, it had struck me he was right. People like him *brought* bad luck instead. The sight of Paulina now felt like confirmation.

My heart was beating in my throat as I moved warily towards her. Gravel crunched under my shoes, but Paulina didn't turn around. Her eyes were fixed on the water flowing some yards below us: black, flecked with silver light reflected from the stars and the lampposts dotted few and far between along the riverside. By the time she noticed me, I was barely three steps distant. Her eyes were narrow, somehow vacant, as if she was looking straight through me.

'Hey,' I said cautiously, holding up my hands. Trying to stay calm, although what I really wanted to do was lunge and grab her. 'You're Paulina, right? I'm Mabel.' Putting my hand on the balustrade, I took a step towards her, but she flinched. Instantly, I froze, forcing a smile to my lips. 'Paulina, maybe you could come down here, eh?'

She stared at me blankly. Her fingers had curled again around the hem of her jacket, but I saw now they had a bluish sheen. Like her face. I didn't have to touch her to know how profoundly cold she was.

'I can't.' She looked down. 'I have to.'

'You don't *have* to. Listen to me. Whatever they did or said, we'll figure it out. You're not alone, okay? I'll help you.'

Her eyes sank again to the jet-black face of the Cam. The more she stared, the more its darkness carved itself into her face. 'I'm so tired.'

I'd never felt so overwhelmed in all my life. Countless options raced through my head, but all of them felt like mistakes. I wanted to reason with her, to call the police, to dart forward and try to drag her back. I wanted to do something, but I didn't know what. Not what was wrong with her, not what Jack had said, not how to stop her from jumping. I just knew I had to *try*. Because I absolutely could not let this happen. The bridge wasn't all that high and the Cam wasn't all that deep, but it was late November, it was the middle of the night, and Paulina was obviously in bad shape.

I took another step towards her, arm outstretched. 'Give me your hand, okay?'

She shuffled away from me, her shoes grinding on the balustrade, her body swaying. Her eyes wouldn't quite meet mine, glassy and empty. 'I have to go.'

Before I could so much as think a single word, it happened. Paulina was still looking in my direction when she took a step forward.

She didn't scream, and nor did I. There was only the wind wrenching at my hair, my heart skipping two beats, and then the sound of water parting.

I stood at the balustrade as the surface levelled and grew sleek again. A slight ripple, an indignant glint. Nothing more. With every second that I couldn't see Paulina, my stomach knotted more tightly. I had to do something – right now. It would take me minutes to climb down to the bank, and much longer for an ambulance to arrive. Time I was pretty sure she didn't have.

I was still staring at the river. The water was dark, opaque, and I knew it would be freezing cold. Just looking at it took the breath from my lungs. Paulina was wrong: she didn't have to do this. But I did. If I didn't act, no one would. If the worst came to the worst, she would drown. And as much as I didn't want to jump, I was even more reluctant to watch her die.

Tearing my bag and coat resolutely off my shoulders, I kicked off my shoes and pulled my heavy woollen jumper over my head. I tossed everything onto the ground then climbed up onto the balustrade. My body was shaking, gooseflesh rising on my bare arms. My breath danced hazily before my face, and my vision swam as I looked down. I felt a surge of dizziness, which I forced back down with all the strength I had.

Don't think, just act.

I unclamped my fingers from the balustrade and stood up. The stone bored through my socks, and I gasped as the wind tore at my ankles.

Don't think, just act.

Gritting my teeth, I took a tiny step towards the edge. My pulse was hammering in my ears, and I heard the rushing of my blood but nothing else. Except, very faintly, I thought I heard someone calling my name – but it was too late for that. Pushing hesitation aside, I took a deep breath and jumped off from the bridge with all my might. Leaping into nothingness.

The water was concrete. Or so it felt, when my body hit the surface. A hot, stabbing pain shot through my body as the icy water surged around me. For a brief moment, everything was gone: my breath froze, my heart stopped, my mind crumbled away. I was nothing but this throbbing, all-consuming pain, which took me in its terrible hand and squeezed. I was sinking into the black – into the Cam and into my own inner darkness. I was seven again, reliving everything: the powerlessness, the helplessness, the realisation that life's worst cruelties could be neither controlled nor prevented. I was defenceless, and the thought almost made me pass out.

Three … four seconds it lasted, then my head broke the surface and I came to my senses. I coughed, spat, gasped. Perhaps I screamed. It barely registered, because all I could think about, all that mattered, was Paulina.

I shoved the hair roughly back from my face, keeping myself above water with the other hand. The Cam wasn't deep, but I couldn't touch the bottom, and swimming had never been my strong suit. I whipped around frantically. The banks blurred into a veil of different greys. Lone daubs of light and shadow, lanterns and willow trees. Nothing else. The water itself spread before me like a black cloth, pressing itself over my eyes as it closed again and again over my head. The muscles in my arm were weak, the cold a relentless gnawing presence. I shivered, coughed, called Paulina's name. My cry was barely more than a croak, trickling away immediately into the depths around me. I swam desperately, my eyes searching for her body.

Just as I was about to dive down, I noticed a pale flash a few yards away, right underneath the bridge. My heart squeezed painfully as I recognised the blonde hair.

I swam towards Paulina, swallowing riverwater as I went.

I could no longer feel my hands, but I was still able to grip her body and turn her over. Her face glowed wanly in the darkness. Closed eyes, open lips, a bluish filter over her skin. I tried to say her name, but my voice was drowned in another swell of water. Her weight was pulling me under – I could feel the depths tugging at my feet. I tried desperately to keep a grip on the stone pillar, but my fingers only scrabbled hopelessly. My elbows kept knocking against it, and another nail tore. Even the pain was dark and soft. I barely felt it. All I felt was that I wouldn't be able to keep this up much longer. I wasn't a good swimmer at the best of times – I'd never make it to the bank with another person in tow. I dived under again, using all my strength to keep her above the surface. But just when I thought I couldn't hold her weight anymore, it lifted.

A second later, a hand closed around my upper arm, dragging me up far enough to take a breath. I was still clutching Paulina's shoulders.

'I've got her, let go.'

The voice was very close to me, but I couldn't see where it was coming from because the water had set my retinas on fire. Everything clouded, and I sank again. The grip tightened. 'Mabel, let go!'

I blinked until the silhouette next to me finally came into focus. Blake had one arm wrapped around Paulina's upper body, while with the other he was supporting me. I didn't understand how he was staying above water, but I forced myself to let go of Paulina so he could relax his grip on me.

'Can you make it out on your own?'

I nodded, coughed, urged my muscles to obey. Blake hauled her lifeless body through the water, taking the shortest route to the bank, and dragged her up onto the grass. My fingers slipped on the edge several times, but I managed at last to pull myself out as well. For a few moments I stayed crouching on the grass, until my breathing had begun to even out. Until then I didn't want to risk standing up.

Blake was sitting a few feet away, next to Paulina's slumped body. Beside him was a pile of fabric: it had to be his coat and jumper. He was wearing only trousers and a shirt, both sodden and clinging to his skin. He stared at me anxiously. 'Are you okay?'

I nodded. My limbs were dead weight, my insides on fire. I was so nauseous I thought I was going to throw up, and I had the vague sense of blood trickling down my elbow. But none of that mattered. 'What about her?' I panted. Blake had rolled Paulina on to her side, and his fingers were resting on her throat. Like Jack's had been, but different. He didn't seem threatening, just worried. Or was that wishful thinking?

'Her pulse is faint, but it's steady. She's alive.'

'Then call an ambulance.' My teeth were chattering, and I rubbed my arms. I waited impatiently for him to take his phone out of his coat, but he didn't move. His eyes were on Paulina's throat, as if sensing something that had stopped him in his tracks. I watched disbelief cross his face, closely followed by anger and ... fear. 'Blake,' I hissed, then louder, and unable to explain why: '*Cliff!*'

He jumped, and I saw in his eyes a look I'd never expected to see: helplessness.

'Either call an ambulance or give me your phone so I can do it, right now!' I commanded as forcefully as I could, although I had no more control over my vocal cords than the rest of my body.

The seconds he stared at me felt like I was crashing through the water's surface all over again. My breath caught, my heart clenched. His hesitation was such a slap to the face that I felt the tears well up. Just as I was reaching for his coat, he stirred, the blank mask dropping across his face as he took out his phone.

We sat there as we waited for the ambulance. Blake fetched my things so I could put on my coat. He draped his over Paulina, but a moment later his hand was at her throat again, and he left it there a long time. I wasn't quite sure why: to make sure her pulse was holding steady, or ... to check for something else. Jack's touch, perhaps, although that made no sense. None of it made any sense.

Perhaps I didn't even want to know what Blake as thinking or doing. Because although we were sitting so close that I could feel his warmth, I felt for the first time in those long minutes like I was seeing him the way I should have from the start: as a stranger.

CHAPTER 13
MABEL

I fidgeted restlessly in my seat. The voice of the professor, leaning against her desk at the front of the room, was so tightly interwoven with those of my fellow students that my ears felt blocked. No matter how hard I tried to pay attention, I'd barely heard anything of the seminar. Even Zoe, sitting next to me, seemed more on the ball than I was.

Ever since last night, my mind had been on other things – on the bridge, and the girl I'd pulled out of the water with Blake's help. The paramedics had taken her away in an ambulance, assuring us her condition was stable, but the sick feeling in the pit of my stomach remained. I'd wanted to go to the hospital that same night, but they wouldn't have told me anything – after all, I wasn't family – and besides, I wasn't really in any fit shape myself.

My body had been so cold that I couldn't feel much. The river water had gnawed away at my muscles, and my thoughts were consumed with worry and confusion about Paulina and what had happened. Blake had walked me to my staircase, and when I nudged the curtain aside in my room, I saw he was still standing in the court outside, a dark outline that stirred up starkly conflicting emotions. Emotions I'd been ignoring ever since, almost as diligently as I'd been ignoring the one thing I was actually supposed to be concentrating on: my academic work.

With a furtive glance at the professor, I reached again for my phone. There were several texts from Davie, responding to a voice note I'd left him this morning, but that was all. I'd asked the hospital to get Paulina to call me the minute she was awake and up to it. That was almost five hours ago now.

Just as I was about to put the phone away, the screen lit up. One glance at the unknown number, and my pulse quickened. I hesitated briefly, knowing the professor hated it when students left the room in the middle of a seminar. Only a second or two, then I stood up with an apologetic gesture. I'd never have believed it, but this was more important than university.

As soon as I was outside, I took the call. There was a moment's silence, then someone cleared their throat at the other end of the line. 'Hey, I ... so I don't think we've actually ever met. This is Paulina. Paulina Gallagher.'

I breathed a sigh of relief. 'Hey. So ... how are you feeling? Are you still in hospital?'

'I'm all right, just a bit of hypothermia and some bruises. They're keeping me in for a few more days, but the doctor says I'll be fine. I was lucky, and she told me that's partly down to you. You were there yesterday when I...' she trailed off, cleared her throat again. 'She said you helped me.'

'It wasn't just me, but ... yeah. I saw you jump,' I explained in a low voice, retreating around the corner to stand in a large bay window. The corridor was empty. I could hear the muffled babble of voices behind a couple of doors, but otherwise there was only heavy breathing and rustling down the line, as if Paulina were fretfully smoothing her sheets.

'Yeah, they said that too, but I don't understand why I did it. I don't ... I don't want to die.'

169

For a moment I hesitated. I didn't want to overwhelm Paulina, but it was probably best to talk to her while the memory was still as fresh as possible. 'I think someone made you do it. Just before it happened, I saw you: you and Jack. He said something to you, and straight after that you ... ran to the bridge.'

'That's not possible. Jack would never hurt me.'

At least she still knew who he was. 'Have you known each other long?'

'A couple of weeks. I met him at a university event. We got on well, exchanged numbers, went out a couple of times. He even took me to meet his friends.'

I tried to recall if I'd ever seen her before, but I was always too focused on Ashton and his friends to notice anybody else. 'Did anything ever strike you as, I don't know, a bit weird?'

'No, not really. Just ... afterwards, I felt a bit funny sometimes. Like, I'd be drinking a normal amount, not too much or anything, but I was just constantly knackered, like I had the worst hangover of all time. I even blacked out once or twice, and I never do that.'

'And Jack? Did he ever bother you, put any pressure on you?'

Paulina didn't hesitate. 'No. I mean, we kissed, but that's as far as it went. I wanted to, though – *want* to. I like him. I ... I'd do anything for him.'

I felt goosebumps rise on my skin. Not because of the words themselves, but because of the way she said them. I heard it every time Zoe talked about Ashton: the unconcealed devotion and admiration that smoothed the edges off every syllable. 'Do you remember what happened yesterday?' I persisted hoarsely. 'Did he tell you to do it?'

'No, that would be... No. All I remember is that I bumped into him in the courtyard and asked if he wanted to hang out. He was being sort of grumpy, but he wouldn't tell me why.

There was another guy with him, a friend of his, one of that group he's always hanging out with.'

'Victor.'

'Yeah. We were chatting, and ... it was nice. I always feel so warm when I'm with Jack. Everything feels so much lighter and more bearable.' Her voice was softening. I could almost see her smiling dreamily. Until she coughed again. 'Anyway, and then ... I don't know, it's all a blur.' She broke off and took several gulps of air, as if trying to breathe the memories in.

'It's all right,' I said, as gently as I could, although I wished she could remember more. I'd heard enough of Victor and Jack's conversation to be convinced, but I hadn't recorded it, and whatever Jack had said to her, only the two of them knew what it was. She was the only person who could report him to the police. Him and his friends. I closed my eyes as instantly another face crossed my mind. *Not now.*

'Do you think he'll come to visit me?'

It took me a moment to realise who she was talking about. I frowned, exasperated. Apart from the fact that Jack was obviously involved in what had happened to her, I'd seen how he treated her. How could she have forgotten? 'Do you want him to?'

'I shouldn't, should I?' She was still trying to sound upbeat, until she suddenly started sobbing, so heart-rendingly that I felt the tears well up in my own eyes. 'Then why do I feel like I'll fall apart if I don't get to see him again? I feel so empty inside. Like I've already ... disappeared.'

∾

My professor was leaving the room as I came back. She gave me a nod, eyebrows raised, but not even her disapproval upset me. How could it, after everything that had happened?

Zoe was sliding her folder into her bag, while the others

drifted one by one out of the room. 'Everything okay?' she asked.

'I spoke to Paulina on the phone.'

'Poor girl, I really hope she gets the help she needs.' Zoe pulled a sympathetic face. I'd given her a quick run-down of the incident over breakfast. Specifically, I'd censored everything except for the fact that I'd found Paulina on the bridge and then jumped in after her to rescue her. I didn't know how to tell Zoe the rest without risking an argument.

I shoved my things distractedly into my bag. 'She says she wasn't trying to kill herself. She doesn't know why she did it.' I darted Zoe an uncertain glance. I knew it was unwise, but I couldn't hold it in. 'She went out with Jack a couple of times. He's one of Ashton's friends.'

Zoe had been combing her fingers through her hair, but now she froze and narrowed her eyes ominously. 'Mabel—'

'No, listen,' I interrupted, taking a step closer. 'She was at their parties too, and the way she talks about Jack is exactly the same way you talk about Ashton.'

Zoe crossed her arms and leant back against the table. 'So what? Being in love isn't a disease.'

I knew it was the worst possible reaction, but I couldn't help myself: I snorted derisively. Not that I disapproved of the sentiment: I was just appalled at the person she had chosen to fall in love with. And because I was so sure he didn't share her feelings. 'That's not love, it's ... I don't know, an addiction. Something unhealthy, at any rate. He's just using you – he doesn't actually care about you at all. Like Jack doesn't care about Paulina.'

Zoe blinked, wounded. 'Wow, thanks.'

'It's got nothing to do with you, it's not your fault,' I added hurriedly. 'But those people are dangerous. And they've been dangerous for a really long time.'

'What are you talking about?'

'I'm talking about the League of Starlings,' I blurted. I could almost see Davie face-palming, but I pressed on, ignoring my guilty conscience. I *had* to tell Zoe. After everything that had happened to June and Paulina, I had to make sure she learnt the truth. Or at least the part I knew. 'It's the name of a secret society that Ashton and the others are members of. It's been around for more than a century, and it's been linked since the very beginning to dozens of crimes and ... deaths.'

'Deaths?' Zoe stared at me, baffled. Clearly Ashton hadn't mentioned anything about it.

'Yes. People who cross paths with them die, Zoe. Like June. Like Paulina, if Blake and I hadn't been there.'

'Blake?' She shook her head, visibly torn between perplexity, mirth and annoyance. 'Ashton's best friend, who according to you must be part of all this too? What reason would he have to save Paulina's life if they're trying to kill her?'

She had a point. One that left me stumped. I kneaded my temples, frustrated. 'I ... have no idea. He's different, somehow.'

Zoe laughed hollowly. 'Oh, right, so the guy you like is *different*, but the one I happen to be in love with – a guy I feel really good about, for basically the first time ever – is a serial killer?'

'I know how it sounds.'

She smiled bitterly and pushed away from the table, tying her scarf around her neck. 'It sounds like you think I'm a terrible judge of character without a single ounce of common sense.'

'That's not true,' I replied firmly. 'But Davie's been gathering evidence about them, he—'

'Davie's been roped in too? Hang on, is this what you've been doing for the last few weeks when you were supposedly revising?'

I could see her vexation giving way to another emotion: hurt. There was nothing Zoe hated more than being left out.

'We weren't trying to hide anything from you, we're just worried about you.'

She threw back her head with a groan. 'I can't listen to any more of this. How many times do I have to say it?' She looked at me. 'Ashton is just a nice, normal guy. He's not in any sort of creepy cult, he and his friends aren't criminals, and what happened to June and Paulina is tragic but it *isn't* their fault. Okay?'

I could only stare at her. Her face was set. I could see she had made up her mind that Ashton deserved her loyalty, which was very obviously *not* okay. But how was I supposed to explain it to her when Davie and I were still trying to figure things out ourselves? 'Zoe, please. I'm just asking you—'

She reached for her bag and slung it over her shoulder. 'No, Mabel. I'm asking *you*. Don't ruin our friendship because you're paranoid.' She stepped towards me and took my hands. Her fingers were warm and soft, and I could smell the peach-scented cream I'd bought her for her birthday. 'I love you, but this needs to stop now. I just want to be happy. Why can't you let me?'

'Of course I want you to be happy,' I replied incredulously. 'But—'

'No buts. Trust me. I know what I'm doing, okay?'

She beamed at me, her smile so endearing and so confident that my objections melted away. Not that they'd disappeared – I just couldn't risk saying them out loud. I didn't want *Zoe* gone as well. So I forced myself to nod. 'Okay.'

Zoe squeezed my hands one final time before she let them go. 'Thank you. Anyway, I'd better head off, I've been invited for dinner.'

Something about the way she said it put me even more on edge. 'With Ashton?'

Zoe paused in the doorway and turned back to me, a

mixture of resignation and warning in her eyes. 'We haven't seen each other for more than a week.'

I bit my lip, but the words forced their way out regardless. 'And you haven't noticed how much ... better you've been feeling?'

The sigh she let out didn't sound especially annoyed, probably because she was already thinking about their date tonight. Her face was aglow with the tenderness that only Ashton could bring.

'Maybe you should let me decide that for myself.' And she slipped out through the doorway with a wave, not giving me the chance to reply.

Not that it mattered. It was obvious by now that it would take a lot more to keep Zoe and Ashton apart. So that was what I needed. More.

CHAPTER 14
CLIFF

O ut of all the universities I knew, Cambridge was the one with the most human soul. Not so much because of what it was, but because of the act it put on. It did everything it could to hide its flaws. All the grand dinners, the parties, the events, always filled with the same gowns, the same recitations. The gilded halls that made even the cafeterias look like ballrooms, the glorious libraries, the brand names paraded across campus on clothes and watches ... the glitz, the beauty, the tradition: it was all a front. A carefully tended face that hid a crumbling soul.

If you were word-associating 'elite university', 'inequality' would spring to mind pretty quickly. At Cambridge, it began with which students were selected – most of them from private schools – and from there it crept into every cell of the university organism. Strictly speaking, it wasn't my problem: after all, I was a shining example of how well the system could treat a person with the right name and the right face. It's easy to shrug off injustices when they benefit you. Yet, as perfectly as I fit in, I felt like an error. Maybe it wasn't so much the university's issue as mine. The cause was obvious: Cambridge and I were just too alike.

I barged past a few people standing outside the building where my last lecture had been held. A few of them I knew, but I made no effort to stop. Ashton liked to say I had to work on my approachability, but I could rarely bring myself to make small talk. Especially now, when there was only one topic on everybody's lips. And on my mind.

It had only been two days since Paulina had jumped off the bridge, but already the whole town was enmeshed in a web of half-truths and rumours. You were caught in it wherever you went. People were naturally drawing parallels between June's death and Paulina's accident, and some were even calling it a suicide club, which was not merely tasteless but dangerous. Especially for us.

Two days, but they felt like an eternity all of their own. Days spent talking to the others about what to do next. Days of fighting bitterly with Victor and Jack, until Ashton threw me out of my apartment. Days of visiting the hospital to check on Paulina – knowing it was out of my hands whether she would ever come home. Days when I wished I could simply disappear, although I knew that wasn't possible. They wouldn't let me. And even if they had, I would never be able to do it. Because what I'd mostly been doing for the last two days was scrolling down to Mabel's number on my phone, ready to delete it, only to end up almost calling it every single time.

I tussled with myself for nearly forty-eight hours before I finally gave in. There was no other way to explain why I was heading straight towards the Trinity Hall library. I'd been keeping an eye on Matthew Bassett's Instagram account for weeks, and when I watched his story just now I immediately noticed the pocket mirror on the table in front of him. If he was at the library with Mabel, it most likely meant they were working on a project together, but I knew I would be unable to concentrate until I'd made sure this encounter went better than the last one.

It wasn't long before I reached the main reading room. Wooden tables were arranged in front of the floor-to-ceiling shelves, a few small groups of students seated around them. I hadn't even begun to look for Mabel before Matthew came walking towards me. Rucksack over his shoulder, phone in his hand, his eyes fixed vacantly ahead. He went straight past me without a glance.

I had to hold back a smile. It had been at least two weeks since I'd spoken to him, but during that time I'd brushed past him casually on a couple of occasions – just enough contact to make sure everyone was happy. Ashton, because he could sense I was feeling better, Mabel, because Matthew was leaving her alone, and me, because it was one less thing to worry about, at least.

I turned away, scanning for Mabel. She was just slipping between two bookshelves, a stack of books clutched to her chest. I knew I should walk away, but I followed her instead. She was smoothing the dog-eared corner of a page when I found her. Immediately, she looked up. A string of conflicting emotions chased across her face, then she shut the book and gave me a terse nod.

Just go, I thought to myself, but taking a step towards her. 'I just saw your supervision buddy. How are things going with him?'

She frowned. 'Better. He's been remarkably chill ever since he almost killed me.'

'Glad to hear it. And if you do have any problems – and I know you don't want to hear this, because you can handle yourself just fine but ... you've got my number.'

'You know, I'm not sure I do, actually.' She turned her back on me, sliding two books back onto the shelf with so much force that I could barely hear the next few words. 'I messaged you.'

'I know.' Six days ago, to be precise. I'd been sitting on the cramped balcony of my flat, watching fresh pastries be delivered to the café below, when my phone lit up. Four little words: *I am Heathcliff, right?*

I'd got the reference to *Wuthering Heights*, and I knew this was Mabel's way of taking a tentative step towards me. It felt like she was nudging ajar a door that had been unlatched ever since our walk – or maybe even before then. All I had to do to open it was give it a gentle tug. Instead, I'd backed away.

'You didn't text back.' She stroked the spines of the books in front of her, avoiding having to look at me. She tried so hard to seem unaffected by other people, yet I could tell she was hurt. She couldn't know that what she saw as rejection was ultimately the kindest thing I could do for her. And now here I was, ruining it all again.

'I did. Plenty of times. I just didn't hit send.' I gave a half-hearted smile. 'And after what happened the other day, I wasn't sure you were still talking to me.'

'Yeah, I ... I wasn't sure either.' She turned to face me, resting her back against the shelves. 'That night, by the river ... you were hesitant to call an ambulance.'

I could have denied it, but what for? Somehow she was able see straight through my lies, even the ones I'd told so often that I almost believed them myself. 'I didn't want her to die.' That was part of the truth, the bit I liked the most. But Mabel, of course, heard the ugly part too.

'Right, but you also didn't want her telling anybody how she nearly ended up dead. How your friend drugged her up to the eyeballs with God knows what until she was so confused and distraught that she thought she had to do it.'

'You don't know what you're talking about.'

'And you won't explain it to me – we're going in circles here, *Blake*.' She smiled grimly. 'I spoke to Paulina on the phone the next morning. She remembered being with Jack and Victor just beforehand, but when I tried to talk to her again today, it was like her memory had been completely ... erased. She told the police she didn't even know how she got to the bridge. Whatever you and your friends did, it was enough to intimidate her. She acted like she didn't even know who I was.' Her voice broke, as if she was admitting some kind of failure.

I wanted to tell her it wasn't true. That it wasn't an act: Paulina genuinely had forgotten everything, including Mabel. Instead, I shrugged. 'Take it as a sign.' *A sign you can't save her.*

She narrowed her eyes. 'To give up? You really think that's an option? I mean, can't you understand why I'm so worried?'

'You're worried about Zoe, I know.'

'And about you.'

'About me?'

Mabel glanced at a girl who was standing nearby, examining the spines of the books. A moment later, she grabbed my forearm and pulled me down the walkway and around a corner. Only once we were at the end of a new row of shelving, directly by an almost full-length window, did she let me go. 'It's not just the outsiders you invite to your get-togethers who have a tendency to meet with little accidents.' She paused, watching my face alertly.

Again, I didn't deny it. By now I knew her too well to bother trying. Mabel wasn't just clever, she was also remarkably intuitive. Whatever I said, she drew her own conclusions, and given everything she'd already discovered about the League of Starlings, I wasn't surprised by what those were. If she hadn't already been suspicious, the feathers in her bag were the final nail in the coffin. Lying wasn't going to help.

I hadn't told Ashton what she'd said to me. Or where she'd taken me when we last met. It was a place I hadn't been since we arrived in Cambridge, although it was never far from my mind. In the end, all roads led back to *her*. To Heaven, whose memory had become our personal hell.

'It's the members themselves,' Mabel added in a low voice, jolting me back into the moment. 'And that means ... I have to worry about you, too.'

The words stirred an odd feeling in my chest. It had been a long time since anybody had shown me genuine concern. With Ashton and the others, there was always a trace of irritation and impatience, because they knew ultimately that nothing bad was going to happen to me. They wouldn't let it. And everybody else ... well, I hadn't given the people around me much reason to show me real concern in a very long time.

'Why?' I asked softly.

Mabel leant against the window. The light fringed her silhouette, but she was still staring at me intently. 'Because I don't want anything to happen to you. I wouldn't want you to ... disappear.'

My heart dropped, and so did my gaze. Straight to her mouth, which looked a little darker than before. I wondered what this shade of red was called. *Saddest Truth*, perhaps. At that moment it was the only thing running through my head, because this was mine: 'You should be wishing I would.' And, sadder still, but impossible to say: *There's nothing you can do to stop it anyway*.

Mabel rolled her eyes, as she always did when I said something that would have scared off anybody with a semi-functional instinct for self-preservation. 'I've never been good at following pseudo-dramatic orders. Thought you'd have figured that out by now.'

'You don't have to worry about me. Whatever happens to me, I deserve it.'

Mabel came closer. 'That's bullshit. There are a lot of things in life that aren't up to us. But we can still decide where we go next. Whatever family or cult you belong to, it doesn't justify your passivity. And whatever you've done, it's no excuse for what you do now. You get up every day and decide what kind of person you want to be. Responsibilities don't just go away because you've ignored them in the past.'

The words were spoken so forcefully that somebody on the other side of the shelves hissed a *shh*, but Mabel seemed not to notice. Her whole focus was on me. Her eyes were bright, her cheeks glowing. All I could think was how beautiful she was. Not just visually, but simply for what she was. She was so ... real. Every word she said reflected her inner self – Mabel's mirror, through and through.

She was right, of course. But what she didn't know was that the decisions weren't mine to make: I wasn't a bird, free to fly, I was a goldfish in a bowl. The minute I thought I'd broken out, another one came down over my head. The parallel was almost ludicrous: Mabel was afraid of not being in control. She'd be scared to death if she had to spend a day in my life.

'You're an old soul, Mabel,' I said, hoping my voice sounded only half as heavy with affection as I felt at that moment.

She blew a few strands of her fringe aside. 'Thanks a lot.'

My phone vibrated in my coat pocket, and I pressed my hand over it. I knew without looking who it was. Patience wasn't Ashton's strong suit. 'I have to go.'

'Okay, but ... are you coming to the memorial service they're doing for June tomorrow?' Her tone hovered somewhere between provocation, uncertainty and embarrassment. I wished I couldn't read her so well. She wanted me to be there, for two reasons: to see how I'd behave, and to see ... me. I wasn't sure if that last part made me want to go or made me want to give it an even wider berth, but in any case, I didn't have a choice.

'No, I can't. I'm going home, to a gala. I promised my sister.'

'You have a sister?'

'Her name is Aspen. She's fifteen.'

Mabel's lips twisted sympathetically. 'Terrible age.'

'I think she's getting on all right. She's very stubborn, and very much herself.' A note of pride drew the corners of my tense mouth upwards, although it wasn't mine to feel. 'Which I guess is why I can never say no when she demands to see her brother.'

'Hmm.' Mabel regarded me thoughtfully. She wrinkled her nose, making her freckles dance and my heart skip. I almost never mentioned Aspen in front of other people because I always felt bad. Like I was using her to seem more genuine.

'It takes a truly strong person to ask for help,' Mabel said in a mock-supportive voice.

'Who said that?'

'I did. Think it over.' She grinned pointedly. 'And ... have fun, I guess.'

'Unlikely. Visiting the family usually feels more like a business meeting.' *In the most literal sense*, I thought bitterly. I tried to put the thought at the back of my mind, and it must have taken my common sense with it, because I slowly raised my hand to touch her throat. Just to feel her pulse. Just to make sure no one else had done it. Just to rest it there two seconds too long. To feel her, her skin, her warmth, her presence – before I took back my fingers, loathing the heat that welled up inside me, even though I hadn't done anything. 'Be careful, Pica.'

'Don't worry, I've been reading all about bird flu.' She gave a taunting smile, but again I saw the telltale flush along her cheekbones.

Truly, she was *so beautiful*. So beautiful that I turned away without a word. I'd always had a weakness for bodies that were an unfiltered mirror of emotion.

As I reached the end of the shelving, her voice held me back. 'Heathcliff?'

I turned, waiting. The contours of her silhouette were vague in the light of the window, but still, I felt I could drink in every single detail of her.

'If you text me'—she was still smiling, more genuinely now, more softly, yet more beautifully—'I'll answer.'

~

Ashton was waiting for me on the bridge. He was sitting on the balustrade, his legs dangling above the November-grey water of the Cam. His coat was draped over one of the stone spheres, his curls tousled by the wind. He swore repeatedly as he tried to light the cigarette in his mouth.

I leant my back against the stone, not bothering to greet him, and eyed the spot a few yards down where I had stood two days earlier. If it hadn't been for Mabel, there'd be flowers there now, underneath a grainy photo of Paulina. I didn't need one to picture her face, and I wasn't sure what it made me feel. Guilt, regret, jitters, tension? Perhaps all four.

Ashton and the others knew only that someone had dragged Paulina out of the river, but not that Mabel was involved. Or me. And I was going to make sure it stayed that way.

Ashton had successfully lit his cigarette, and he took a long drag before he looked at me. 'Calmed down yet?'

I didn't respond. It had been a long time since Ashton and I had fought like that. For ages now I'd deliberately kept out of things, trying to avoid these situations. You couldn't have a difference of opinion with someone who didn't *have* opinions. I could tell he was equal parts confused, relieved and annoyed that I had chosen this particular moment to stick my oar in.

What's your problem? he had shouted yesterday, as he shoved me out of the front hall. My knuckles throbbed from the blow to Victor's chin, my temples with the onset of a migraine, and the rest of me with ... everything. There was no answer he or I would understand, so I simply turned on my heel and left.

'How did the conversation go?' I asked.

'Shit. Our dear leader is a little on edge, given the latest turn of events.' Ashton coughed into the back of his hand. 'He said this is beginning to feel eerily familiar, and he isn't happy with how the last time turned out.'

'Well he's not wrong, is he?' I tilted back my head, looking up at the sky above. No clouds, only delicate streaks of cold and a gathering dusk. On the news they'd said a meteor shower was on its way. It made my heart flutter to hear it. 'Do you think about her much?'

Even without looking at him, I knew he'd tensed up. 'Why? Are you getting sentimental?'

'Maybe.' I smiled weakly. 'I miss her. I think about her a lot. Every day, actually.'

'Yeah, well, that's not going to bring her back,' he replied, so gruffly that I didn't respond. Ashton defended his boundaries firmly, and he'd walled off this topic years ago. The slightest mention of it and I could see him fighting not to leave. Or to throw me off the bridge.

'What's happening with Paulina?' I asked evasively. After all, she was the reason why Ashton had been called in for a chat at the vice-chancellor's office. Paulina and June, two names, two people, two mistakes, which naturally hadn't gone unnoticed.

Ashton put one foot up onto the balustrade and leant back against the finial. 'I can't believe you go to the effort of remembering those names.'

'Not all of them, Ash. Just the ones who end up in hospital because of us. It's a matter of respect.'

He tapped the ash off his cigarette on the stone next to him. 'Brooks sees it the same way we do. There are only two options.'

'Then we'll take them, and be done with it. We'll just leave her in peace,' I suggested, careful to sound calm. 'I went to see her after you took care of it. She's strong, but not *that* strong. Even if she recovers, she's no threat.'

Ashton was spinning a lock of his hair between two fingers.

I knew he kept toying with the idea of chopping them all off. But no matter what he said, there were rules by which even he abided. Especially because he was checked more often than the rest of us. There were advantages and disadvantages to being so close to Henry. 'There will always be a slight risk that she'll remember.'

'Then we'll keep an eye on her.'

'Because we've got nothing better to do?'

'All right, then what do you suggest?'

He regarded me soberly. 'You know what.'

Of course. The simplest thing, the most obvious, the right thing to do for us, although it hadn't felt right to me for a very long time.

'Then why haven't you already done it?'

Ashton sighed and jumped down next to me. He picked up his coat and shrugged it on over his green pullover, although his skin glowed rosy pink despite the cold. 'Because that's the one rule I never break without permission, my dear. I prefer to keep the family peace. An angry Henry isn't something I take lightly.'

He patted my shoulder, but I didn't fail to notice the way his hand brushed searchingly over my bare neck before he let me go. I was so relieved by the satisfied look in his eye that I exhaled a little too loudly. What Henry was to Ashton, Ashton was to me.

'Which is precisely why Brooks and I have decided to tell him. Let's let them decide how to solve the problem.'

I froze, my short-lived calm washed away by a rush of panic. I stared dumbfounded at Ashton, who was already walking off towards the college. 'But then they might just show up here.'

He turned to me, kept walking backwards. 'Then so be it. You'll survive a few days in a student room, for appearances' sake. After all, isn't that what we do best?' He threw out his arms, grinning. 'We are the perfect illusion.'

He strode off before I had the chance to respond, although in any case there was nothing to be said. Again, I wanted to deny it, but no matter how many lies I told, that particular truth wasn't one I could hide from myself.

CHAPTER 15
MABEL

'Do you think my sister would like a clothes steamer?' Zoe sucked her bottom lip sceptically between her teeth, scrolling on her phone.

It was the first of December, and Zoe was spending most of her free time hunting for the perfect Christmas presents for her family. I was more than happy to talk her out of buying one for me.

'I don't know Lydia well enough to say, I'm afraid. But isn't her fiancé a millionaire? Why are you even giving her anything?'

'Buying someone a present isn't about whether they can afford it themselves. It's about showing each other you've made an effort.' Zoe put the phone away and linked her arm through mine as we strolled through a courtyard in our college, following the path between two patches of grass. 'So what are you doing for Christmas this year?'

I gave an inner sigh. I knew she wasn't going to like what I said next. 'Clara called me yesterday. She and Timothy are going up to Aberdeen to visit my uncle's parents. They want me to come, but I'd rather stay here.'

Zoe ground to such an abrupt halt that I was forced to stop

too, although we were in the middle of the path. She stared at me in horror. 'Nobody stays here over Christmas! I can't allow it. Come to mine. I'm sure my mother won't mind, she adores you.'

'That's sweet, but I've got a lot of work to catch up on. Anyway, Christmas isn't exactly my favourite holiday.' I forced a smile to my lips, but even I could tell I wasn't pulling it off.

'I know, but that's the thing.' She surveyed me, dissatisfied. 'At least promise me you'll call if you get lonely, okay?'

'Sure thing.' I got her moving again with a gentle tug. 'I'm glad you're back.'

'Yeah, me too. I've missed you.'

'So you're not angry anymore?' Ever since our last conversation, when I'd told her about the League, we'd avoided any mention of Ashton. I kept an eye on her, but apart from the fact that she was always yawning, she seemed in pretty good shape.

She sighed. 'I've decided to take it as a compliment that you're always worrying about me. I mean, you're a Scorpio.'

I pulled a face, amused. Zoe's fascination with the cosmic influences of the universe was a perpetual mystery to me. 'What's it got to do with my star sign?'

'Scorpios only sting people when they or someone they love is threatened.' She poked me in the hip. 'The fact that you think all that stuff about Ashton just means you love me. Anyway, you know I'm a classic Sagittarius. Tolerance is my middle name.'

I couldn't help laughing as we passed through an archway, leaving Trinity Hall. 'I never thought I'd say this, but I've even missed all your creepy superstitions.'

'Watch it, Golding – there are limits to even my tolerance!' She jabbed me again in the ribs, only to pull me in even closer. 'And now let's not keep Davie waiting any longer. As a career-focused Capricorn, he has a dangerously solitary streak.'

The first thing I saw as we turned the corner was the blue

light. I stopped short and grabbed Zoe's arm. *It's happened again* – the words shot through my head. The thought was dark and viscous, oozing through my whole body, until I realised a moment later that the light wasn't coming from a police car. It was the fire department. The vehicle was parked immediately outside the building where Zoe and I were headed. Rapidly, I scanned the façade, but I couldn't see anything out of the ordinary.

Zoe, too, was staring in alarm. She flagged down a passing student. 'Do you know what they're doing here?'

'Somebody said there was a fire. But they put it out before the firefighters got here. No big deal.' And he walked off with a shrug.

Zoe and I wavered for a moment, then, tightening my grip, I got her moving. 'Come on.'

Nobody stopped us as we opened the door and entered the building, and as yet things still seemed normal. No ash, no smoke, no skittish university employees. Something about the stilted silence made my heart beat faster. With every step we took through the narrowing, lightless, ever-more-deserted corridors, my misgivings grew, and by the time we reached the editorial offices of the *Blue News*, dread had gathered in my mind like a pitch-dark cloud, giving my thoughts no room to breathe.

I knew it. I knew it before I let go of Zoe, flung the door open and saw it for myself. Although the windows were wide open, the room smelt not of late autumn but of ... smoke. Zoe coughed and stopped in the doorway, while I walked inside as if in a trance. The guy had been right: the fire must have been small. The desks at the front appeared untouched: the usual warren of overflowing filing cabinets, mountains of paper, supplies of sweets, paperclips and notepads, as well as ancient laptops and personal belongings, like wizened potted plants and forgotten mugs of coffee.

The only evidence of the fire was on the desk at the very back, by the window. It gave off an unpleasantly acrid stench, and the tabletop was covered in a layer of black ash. Directly in front of it stood the only person in the whole room.

'Davie, what happened here?'

When he looked up, his face was as sombre as I'd ever seen it. 'Isn't it obvious?'

Zoe followed me inside. She was clasping her beige scarf to her nose and mouth, muffling her voice. 'Did something short-circuit? Jesus, I've been telling you for months that the wiring at this university is the worst.'

'It wasn't the wiring.' With a distracted gesture, Davie slid shut one of the drawers in the filing cabinet next to the desk. All of them had been pried open, leaving them slightly dented, as if they'd been forced. And they were empty. I didn't have to ask to know that all the documents Davie had kept in them were now on the table in a heap of ash.

'The firefighters thought it might be arson. As if that wasn't obvious the minute I walked in here and found my desk on fire. They must have only just left – I put out the fire before the flames could spread. One bit of luck, I suppose, under the circumstances.'

My heart dropped into the pit of my stomach, thudding so violently that I pressed a hand to my belly. 'They set fire to your desk, nobody else's?'

Davie smiled grimly, picking up a picture frame that had fallen over on the charred tabletop. 'Yup.'

'And...' My voice broke as my eyes darted to Zoe, who was looking back and forth from one of us to the other, confused.

Davie understood me regardless. His expression hardened. Scooping up a handful of ash, he let it trickle back down onto the wood. 'Yes.'

I dropped the bag containing our lunches onto one of the

book trolleys. I felt so sick I couldn't imagine keeping anything down.

The fire had destroyed all Davie's research into his latest case. *Our* case. This was no random act of vandalism: this was the targeted eradication of all the evidence we'd collected on the League over the past weeks. It was obvious who was behind it. The only question was ... how? How had they found out? I'd told no one. I hadn't mentioned it to anybody that... The thought crumpled under the impact of the memory. Guilt pinched at my eyelids, closing my eyes. 'Please, no.'

'What?' asked Zoe, bewildered. 'What are you talking about?'

'Zoe.' I turned to her with an urgent look. And beseechingly, perhaps, because I really, really wanted her to say no to the next question. I wanted so badly to be wrong. 'What I told you the other day about Ashton. About the secret society. You didn't mention it to anybody else, did you?'

Slowly she lowered the hand clutching the scarf. The way her face shuttered itself told me everything. Remorse, coupled with uncertainty and mistrust. 'Why?'

Davie swore, then a moment later slammed a kick into the filing cabinet. Zoe jumped, and I tried not to cry with frustration and despair.

Crinkling the tip of her nose, she tucked her hair behind her ear. 'I mean ... last time I met up with Ashton he asked me why you and I weren't hanging out as much these days. I didn't want to lie. And ... they're just rumours. He deserves a chance to defend himself. And he did. He laughed and said the whole thing's absurd, that you have a vivid imagination, and that he's flattered you find him and his friends so mysterious, but...'

Neither Davie nor I were really listening. We just looked at each other, resigned and nervous, because we had both realised what was happening. One, that Ashton and his friends were definitely members of the League of Starlings. And two, that they knew now we were on to them.

'I'm sorry,' I said, meaning it. This wasn't Zoe's fault, it was mine. Davie had cautioned me against telling her the truth, but I did it anyway. I had wanted to be honest with her, because that was what she'd taught me: when you like someone, you tell them the truth. The only problem was that I'd underestimated how much Zoe liked *Ashton*.

Davie rubbed his head. 'It's fine.'

Again, Zoe's baffled eyes flitted between us. She was so trusting that it took her a visible effort to put two and two together. Once she had, she gasped. 'Wait, are you guys saying Ashton did this?'

Davie gave a hoarse laugh. 'Zoe, wake up! He isn't who you think he is.'

Zoe gripped the strap of her bag. 'You don't know him!'

I wanted to say something to defuse the situation, but Davie got there first. There were deep cracks in his normally calm and patient façade, and shining through were the strain, disbelief and rage he was feeling.

'Jesus fucking Christ, Zoe, can you really be *that* naïve? I know more about him than you do. And I could have proven it to you if your psycho boyfriend hadn't burnt all the evidence!'

I understood why he was so angry. The outburst wasn't really aimed at Zoe, it was more the fact that months of research had been destroyed with the flick of a lighter. This was his way of coping. Words instead of plates, Zoe's face instead of walls. Still, I wished he wouldn't. Zoe would never listen to us if we went about it like that. If she felt like we were attacking someone she cared about, she'd shut down. Her loyalty was unshakeable – nobody knew that better than me.

'Davie,' I began, but he cut me short.

'What, Mabel? If she'd kept her mouth shut, we wouldn't be back to square one right now!'

'You know it wasn't on purpose. Zoe's just a bit—'

'A bit what? *Stupid?*'

'Zoe...' My voice trailed off. Not because I'd been about to say it – I'd never call her or anybody else *stupid* – but I couldn't think of a word she would prefer to hear. The fact was, Zoe's optimism and her unalterable faith in people did make her a little bit naïve. It wasn't wrong, wanting to believe in goodness, but it was dangerous to be gullible. I knew, however, that she wouldn't take that word as a sign of concern and love, but as derogatory.

Zoe smiled bitterly. 'Fine. I know you both think you're more intelligent than me. And you probably are, but that doesn't make it okay to look down your noses at me! I'm not going to let myself be patronised or manipulated, and I certainly won't be insulted. Even by you.'

'Zoe, please, you know we don't—' I took a step towards her, but she raised her hand and flinched back.

'Just leave me alone. And Ashton. Okay?' She turned on her heel and threw the door open, slamming it so hard behind her that a swirl of ash went eddying out of the window.

Davie watched the dust settle with a sigh. 'What a fucking shitshow.'

I couldn't disagree. Dumping my bag wearily onto a desk, I walked over to him. 'Come on, let's clean up this mess.'

~

We spent the rest of the day at a café, mostly in silence, because words seemed futile. I tried to hide it from Davie, but I was feeling as discouraged as he was.

Back in my room, I sat down at my desk and tried to prepare for my supervision the next day. It was nearly two when my phone lit up beside me.

It was absurd: I had only to read the name and my heart began to race.

HEATHCLIFF

Are you okay?

I read the question several times, trying to work out how it made me feel. Warm, because he was thinking about me in the middle of the night? Relieved, because despite what his friends had done today – and he must know about it – he wasn't distancing himself? Or angry, because 'his friends' included him, and I couldn't be sure he didn't have something to do with it? I looked again at the name I'd saved him under. Heathcliff, instead of Blake. What I wanted to see, instead of what he kept showing me: he was one of them.

PICA

Did you know they were planning to burn Davie's research?

I drew my feet up onto the chair and hugged my knees, waiting for him to reply. He was online, but he wasn't typing. Maybe three minutes, then two words came back.

HEATHCLIFF

Mabel, please.

Rage flared, smothering all gentler emotions. I hammered fiercely at the keypad.

PICA

???

This time he began typing immediately.

HEATHCLIFF

You know I'm not going to answer that.

Of course I knew. It didn't mean he was involved, or that

he'd known about it in advance. But it did mean he wouldn't say anything to incriminate his friends. He would always keep his mouth shut to protect them. After all, he'd been doing exactly that for weeks: being evasive, saying only as much as he wanted to. And it wasn't enough. I wouldn't let it be enough. I couldn't give up now, just because gathering information was becoming less important to me than what I felt when we were together. The curiosity, the fascination, that warm sense of being seen. Of being understood. Ultimately, none of it meant anything, because it didn't matter who Blake *could* be, or who he might have been without his friends. It only mattered what he was now. Someone who was allowing all this to happen around him. Someone who wasn't helping me. Someone I couldn't allow myself to like, if I wanted to still like myself.

My lip quivered, but I didn't hesitate.

PICA

> Then don't bother to text me back. You were right. It's better if we just drop the whole thing.

Immediately, Blake began to type. He paused, began again, paused again. For nearly five minutes I stared at the screen — eyes throbbing, heart pounding. It skipped two beats when the answer came.

HEATHCLIFF

> Just leave it alone, Pica.

I smiled bitterly, and the movement tipped the first tear down my cheek.

PICA

> Not your problem, Blake.

I knew using that name would have more impact than blocking him. He knew it too. And he stopped responding. I should have been relieved, but instead I ended up sobbing at my desk at two in the morning, surrounded by a jumble of papers scrawled with notes for essays I should have finished ages ago, photos of me and my best friend, who wasn't talking to me, the golden glow of my desk lamp, and the grey curtains, shadow weaving into nightmare in their folds. And running through my mind was a single line, the last thing I'd read before I shoved the book to the far corner of my shelf. *It is a long fight; I wish it were over!*

I wished it too, I truly did. The only trouble was ... I sensed the fight had only just begun. Yet I wasn't crying because I was afraid of what lay ahead. I was crying because it struck me that some things ended before they'd even had a chance to start. And that it was funny how an end without a beginning could hurt this much.

CHAPTER 16
MABEL

I eyed my reflection sceptically in the gold-framed floor-to-ceiling mirror, which hung in the front hall next to the coat rack. My black velvet dress had puff sleeves and buttons down the front, and was gathered at the waist in a way that made the skirt swing with every step. It was so tight that each breath was slightly painful. This was mainly because I'd had it for three years, but unfortunately it was the only dress in my wardrobe that could conceivably pass as fashionable.

I could have borrowed one from Zoe, but then I'd have to talk to her. Since the argument more than two weeks ago, she'd responded in monosyllables to my attempts at conversation. I barely saw her outside of lectures and seminars, but I got the sense she only went out to see Ashton, and apart from that, she hardly left her room. Which was making me uneasier by the day.

Last year Zoe had dragged me to pretty much every Christmas party the university had to offer. We'd gone to half a dozen champagne receptions at faculties that had nothing to do with us, to carolling singalongs with at least as many choirs, to various university-club drinks. I'd only tagged along for her sake, knowing there'd be no other reason for me to go next year, either. But now here I was, on the Friday before the Christmas break, going to the History Faculty's drinks reception at Trinity College.

I took Mum's compact mirror out of my bag and examined my face: the pearl-studded hair clip that pinned back my fringe, my unmade-up eyes, my scarlet mouth. *Bravest Heart* it said on the tube in my handbag – a promise yet to be fulfilled. I didn't feel brave, I felt out of place. Not just because I knew no one at the History Faculty, but because I was going alone. Without Zoe, who was probably in her room, waiting for a text from Ashton. Without Davie, because he'd gone home early to celebrate his mother's sixtieth birthday.

We'd spoken on the phone after he got an email from uni, telling him the arson case had officially been closed. *No evidence, no lines of inquiry, no significant damage*, Davie had quoted, morose. *I guess that translates as: no interest in helping me or the newspaper.*

Ever since the fire, he'd been in such a foul mood that I couldn't bring myself to tell him what I was planning. In any case, it might be a dead end. But Davie had taught me that sometimes, if you wanted to get to the heart of truth, you had to take the long way round, so over the last few days I'd been chasing down a few more obscure references to the League of Starlings. Passages in the university archives that mentioned rites, but offered no additional detail. Articles that described incidents I guessed were connected to the group, based on our previous research, but which weren't linked to a specific name. The more I read, the more jarring I found some of these gaps, especially as the man who had worked on many of the publications was a well-known expert on the history of British universities in general and of Cambridge in particular. He had written essays on pretty much every student society in the country – but not a word about the League of Starlings. It might be a coincidence, but I no longer believed in those.

Nor did I believe it was a coincidence that Professor Garrett Edwards was retiring at the end of this term as a professor of history – at Trinity College, no less. It was no accident. It was a lead, and I had to follow it. Even if that meant squeezing myself into a too-tight dress and crashing a party, all by myself, full of people I didn't know.

One last look in the mirror, a half-hearted smile, then I straightened my shoulders and strode off down the corridor.

The building was used mainly for official events. On the top floor were offices belonging to a few professors and administrators. The corridor on the ground floor was laid with reddish floorboards, the walls hung with watercolours depicting Cambridge throughout the centuries. I was about to turn left, following the babble of piano music, clinking glasses and voices, when I caught a glimpse of a shadow through a crack in the door on my right.

Impulsively, I went over and pushed it open. These walls, too, were hung with works of art, mostly portraits in muted earth tones. A man stood in front of the painting of a woman; she had black curls, deep brown eyes and a face at once young and old, her expression grave in a way that spoke of life experience.

Shaped by memory, I thought, examining her painted features, but the phrase ran through my head a second time when the man turned around, still evidently absorbed in contemplation.

As he gazed at me, the look of rapture faded, and the soft lines around his mouth hardened. 'Can I help you?' He couldn't have been much beyond his late thirties, but the way he fixed me with his unnaturally bright blue eyes reminded me of the disapproving glare of an old man.

Hesitantly, I forced myself to shake my head. 'No, I was just looking for—'

'I doubt you'll find it in here,' he interrupted, smoothing his dark grey jacket with his hand. His fingers were adorned with numerous rings, and on his lapel was a pin with a symbol I couldn't quite make out. 'This area of the building is off-limits to ... the general public.' It was obvious from the way he looked at me what he was really thinking: *to plebs like you*.

A few words left unsaid, and my timidity vanished. I beamed an exaggeratedly friendly smile. 'Then you should have put up a sign. Otherwise, this is a public building, and as far as I know, there's nothing in the university statutes about having to prove your annual salary before you earn the right to set foot in it.'

He frowned, then there was the sound of footsteps behind him. A door opened, and someone entered the room. 'Henry, Brooks is here, we—' Ashton stopped abruptly when he saw me. A look of unease flitted across his face, then he smoothed it, erasing all trace of emotion. There was not the slightest sign of recognition. 'Are you coming? Then we can get started.'

He seemed unusually stiff. It wasn't just his face, it was the way he held his shoulders in his elegant black suit, the way he clasped his hands behind his back. There was no glimmer of his usual cocktail of self-assurance, mockery and poise. Beneath the thin veneer of confidence, he looked like a dog expecting a kick.

The other man nodded and turned towards him, not dignifying me with a second glance. Ashton, however, stared after me as I left the room, the feel of his eyes on my back as unmistakeable as the nagging voice telling me this moment meant something. As if the scene were somehow coded in a way I couldn't crack. Not yet.

There were about fifty people gathered in the room where the party was being held. Flowing dresses made of glittering fabrics, expensive-looking suits, countless perfumes and vocal registers intermingled, green floral arrangements on side tables, candles on the mantelpiece. The distinctive waft of money, mulled wine and spruce: the scent of Christmas at Cambridge.

I tugged at my neckline, wishing I could undo a button so I could take a proper breath. Instead, I accepted a glass of mulled wine and meandered through the room. I had examined the photos of Professor Edwards again before I set off, but now I couldn't see him anywhere. Frustrated, I stopped at a table and scanned my environment, until a restless alarm began to prickle at the nape of my neck. I glanced around discreetly, my eyes wandering across the crowd, but I didn't recognise any of the faces. The light was too dim, the room too full, my heart too nervous. It was thudding so hard it made my vision swim, and I narrowed my eyes repeatedly before I turned back and set the nearly full glass on the table.

When I looked back up, I saw a man standing by the fireplace, a plate of mince pies and a glass of mulled wine on the tall table in front of him.

Wiping my fingers on my dress, I pulled back my shoulders and made my way towards him. 'Excuse me,' I said, making an effort to sound friendly, as I came to stand opposite him at the table. 'My name is Mabel Golding. You're Professor Edwards, aren't you?' He nodded with his mouth full, and I gave a relieved smile. 'You're retiring in the new year, is that right?'

'That's right,' he said, swallowing, and held out his free hand. 'This is my last soirée as a professor. Were you one of my students?'

'No, but I'm really interested in history,' I replied, as I took back my hand. 'Including university history. Your name kept cropping up in the articles I was reading.'

'Which articles?'

'The ones about student societies.'

'Oh, yes.' He chuckled and hacked off another bite of mince

pie, spearing it on his fork. 'I've written quite a few of those over the years. Anything particularly catch your eye?'

'Well, it was more something you didn't explicitly mention, I suppose. Something I ... read between the lines. It was about the League of Starlings.'

He froze mid-movement, the fork suspended in the air. A second later, he darted a look first over his own shoulder and then over mine. 'You shouldn't say that name so loud,' he muttered under his breath. 'Especially not in a place like this.'

I was so deeply relieved I almost sighed. 'So you've heard of them before?'

Professor Edwards regarded me warily before setting his fork down on his plate and brushing off his hand on his jacket. 'Come on, let's nip next door for a minute.'

Nobody paid us any heed as we left the room, passing through the hall to one with a bar, where a man behind it was polishing glasses. The music from the other room was audible here, too, but otherwise there was nothing but the snow gusting against the windowpanes.

We made for a table by the window, and immediately he clutched at it with both hands, as if the mere mention of the society had made him dizzy. 'Where did you hear about them?'

'I think they're back. Here. At Cambridge.' I did my best to keep my voice low, like his, but I was so excited it was hard to stay controlled.

He threw another apprehensive glance over his shoulder, but other than the barman, who showed no interest in us, and a handful of people chatting in the corridor outside, we were alone.

'June Owens and Paulina Gallagher,' he replied, as if that was an answer.

And in a way, it was. 'It's a pattern, isn't it?'

He took a handkerchief from his jacket pocket and dabbed his mouth, but still I saw his lips twist. 'Listen. There's a reason

203

why I never named them outright. A reason why I kept my research unofficial.'

'You're frightened.' It wasn't an entirely new thought – it had crossed my mind as I considered the reasons why someone would deliberately withhold information. But even so, I was surprised. This was a grown man, a famous name in his field, wealthy, educated, influential. Why would someone like him be afraid of a few students?

He lowered the handkerchief, fingers trembling, and gave a strained smile. 'Because I've got common sense.'

'Okay, but I'm scared, too. My best friend has got herself mixed up with them, and I don't want her to be the next to—' I broke off, my throat so constricted that I couldn't get the words out. 'I have to figure out what's going on. I have to stop them.'

His features softened with compassion. 'You can't fight a forest fire with a watering can.'

'I'll call in a water-bomber if I have to.' I took a deep breath and leant in closer. 'Please. Just tell me what you know. I promise I'll never mention your name. Whatever you tell me, it stays between us.'

He was silent. A woman next door gave a shrill laugh, and the barman landed a glass onto the countertop with a clunk. I didn't even dare to blink. This was my only promising lead after a string of failures, my last chance this year to find out something that might give me hope that the next one would be better.

At long last, the professor sighed and tucked the handkerchief back into his jacket pocket. 'Very well, but ... if you want to know what I've discovered over the years, you'll have to keep an open mind. My research has taken me in a somewhat unorthodox direction.'

'How do you mean?'

He slid his thin wire-framed spectacles down his nose a

little, peering at me over the top. 'Are you a spiritual person, Miss Golding?'

I frowned, puzzled. 'My best friend reads me my horoscope a lot, does that count?'

'Not quite the direction I mean.' He smiled, although there was a deep, almost hypnotic gravity in his eyes. I couldn't look away. 'There are legends, you know, legends that involve this university. Myths circulating about it and its members.'

I found myself blinking several times before I understood what he was hinting at. 'And by myths you mean ... something supernatural?' The word sounded as incredulous as I felt, and perhaps even a little mocking.

He was unperturbed. 'Well, that depends on your definition. Science tends to be a little rigid when it comes to what's considered natural. I personally believe that there is far more in this universe than we can explain by means of logic and reason.'

'Like what?'

He folded his hands on the table, twisting the wedding ring on his finger with intense focus. 'Like what... Well, let's imagine we have a student society. Its existence has never officially been proven, but clues keep popping up all over the place. Have been for more than a century, actually, at various universities across the country. And not only that. When we look at some of the most influential areas of our society, we find that certain positions – *powerful* positions – are repeatedly linked to this society. We're talking influential ministers, successful business moguls, prominent lobbyists, developers, visionaries. What would you say if I told you that, sooner or later, these people always seem to vanish from the surface of the Earth, and always in the same way?'

I swallowed hard, my whole heart in my mouth, thudding, thudding, thudding. 'They die?'

Professor Edwards tilted his head slowly from side to side. 'That's one possible interpretation.'

'What—'

'Garrett!' The voice was so abrupt that it made me jump. A woman in her sixties was standing in the doorway, waving in our direction. Judging by her flushed cheeks, she was several glasses deep into the mulled wine. *Go to a Christmas party and you'll realise professors aren't God almighty, they're just people too*, as Zoe liked to say. 'So here's where you're hiding, we've been looking for you! Come on, I need your help in an argument I'm having with Thomas.'

'Just a minute.' He smiled until she had gone away again, then gave me a nod. 'Please excuse me. This isn't the right place for this conversation anyway. I'm going to London tomorrow morning, but I'll be back in mid-January for a couple of days to clear out my office. Make an appointment through the faculty admin.' He hesitated, then leant in towards me. 'And don't mention this to anybody. It's in both our interests.'

All I could do was nod and say thank you. My mind was in a whirl, and the only word I could latch on to properly was *supernatural*.

If I told Davie, he'd never be able to stop laughing. And it *was* ridiculous, really, even to consider the idea. The group was strange, sure, but they were just people. Students with too much money and influence, too easily bored. A dangerous mix, but hardly worthy of a fairy tale. What was Professor Edwards trying to imply? That a bunch of snobs were going around sacrificing people in tribute to some ancient god?

I shook my head, turning away from the table as the professor reached the door. My eyes went instinctively to the person standing on the opposite side of the corridor. Just outside the door I'd opened earlier.

Between Blake and myself were yards of air, dim, reddish light and several people chatting in the hallway, yet I knew we were looking straight at each other. I stiffened, seeing his eyes drift left – to where Professor Edwards must be standing. I didn't need to see Blake clearly to know he'd recognised him. To know he knew.

My lungs tightened, making it hard to breathe. The weight of the moment flooded through me like tar, and I couldn't fight my way through. Before Blake could look back at me, I ducked left and opened the second door out of the room. I found myself in a narrow passage, where some steps led upwards. I didn't stop to think, just grabbed the banister as quickly as I could and hurried up the wooden staircase, my heart clattering almost as loudly as my feet. I'd just reached the first-floor landing when I distinctly heard a creak from below. I knew what door it was, of course – I knew who'd opened it and who was coming up the stairs behind me. With a calm but determined tread that only spurred me on.

I reached the top floor: a deserted corridor, old-fashioned lamps at head height, tapestries adorned with floral patterns, several closed doors covered in ornate carvings, and a single window at the far end. No more stairs, no obvious exits, no way out.

Before I could rattle a handle or reach for my hairpin, I heard him behind me. Then, a moment later, his voice: cool, tense, furious. 'I know this building better than you do. So stay put.'

Heat rushed through my muscles, and I whirled around. 'I bet you do. Is the society meeting here tonight? What's for dinner? Roast starling?'

Blake neared me slowly. It only struck me now that he was wearing a suit. Shirt, trousers and jacket all in the same deep black. As black as the look on his face as he stopped a few feet away from me. His eyes slid briefly over my body, then locked onto mine. 'What the hell are you doing here?'

I gazed up at him innocently. 'What does it look like? I'm networking, getting drunk at the university's expense, getting into the Christmas spirit. The usual.'

'Don't give me that. I know exactly who he is.'

'I have no idea what you're on about.' I planted a hand on my hip so he wouldn't see it shaking. I felt like I'd been caught red-handed, although I wasn't sure at what. Professor Edwards hadn't told me anything new, and his hints had been so odd that I thought probably they'd just made me more confused. There was no reason for Blake to be so upset, unless ... he knew the professor could tell me something that would get him and his friends into trouble.

Before I could follow that line of thought any further, he took another step towards me. I saw the strain in his face, all softness gone. Harsh notches in the muscles of his cheek, his mouth a line that ironed out every dimple, the crease between his brows unusually deep. 'I told you to leave it alone.'

'And I told you it's none of your business. I'm not your problem!'

I tried to stalk past him, but he grabbed me and pulled me in tight, so forcefully that I stumbled and fell into him. For a moment I was distracted by the nearness of his face to mine. There were delicate flecks over the bridge of his nose. Tiny moles, too dark to be freckles. Not something left by the sun. *Moonspots*, I thought, and I felt they suited him much better.

'Oh yes, you are,' he said grimly. 'You've been my problem ever since I found you in that goddamn library. You are my problem, Mabel, mine and mine alone, and you're getting less and less solvable the more I see you.'

I could have laughed. 'Don't you dare! Don't act like you give two shits about me. If I meant anything to you at all, you'd talk to me.'

I tried to pull away. Maybe a little half-heartedly, because distance wasn't really what I wanted. What I really wanted was for him to pull me close, I wanted to tear off his black shirt and lay my fingers on his tattoo, I wanted to clasp his face and make him look at me until I could see inside, until I finally, finally understood him. He made me angry, he frustrated me, he messed with my head like no one else. And I hated it. I hated that I had to think about him all the time, that even now I was thinking how good he smelt and how close he was and how it wasn't close enough. How *none* of it was enough.

'You'd help me keep Zoe away from Ashton, and you wouldn't let your friends burn Davie's research! You wouldn't let them threaten me or—'

'Why won't you understand that all that stuff is out of my control?' he broke in. I tried to jab my knee in between his legs, but he threw me up against the wall behind me. 'That the only way to protect you is to try and make sure you stay away from us – from *me*? And I am trying. I've been trying for weeks, but you make it so goddamn difficult!'

There was such a note of desperation in the last word that I swallowed. My movements went limp, my body slackening against the wall. My head fell back against the midnight-blue velvet of a tapestry as my eyes sank into his. His gaze, turbulent and angry, but at the same time worried, helpless and ... yearning.

At that moment I understood: he was feeling everything that I felt. Which, suddenly, left me with only one reply.

'Then don't,' I said calmly, although the fierce hammering of my heart was almost unbearable. Surely he must be able to feel it – his fingers rested on the arteries in my wrists as he pressed my hands against the wall.

'What?' He relaxed his grip, but didn't pull away. A few locks of hair hung loose over his forehead, his cheeks were red, his eyes leapt from my eyes to my mouth and back. Not to my neck, as they had so many times before. Only to my lips, which were trembling slightly. And this tiny detail told me that he'd known for a while: the answer to his question was one he kept hidden in himself, one he was reluctant to admit.

'Don't try to protect me. Don't try to stay away. That's not what I want from you.'

He let go of my wrists, running his fingers lightly down my arms to the sleeves of my dress, then he planted his hands on the wall behind me. 'What do you want, then?'

Something in his voice pleaded with me to say it out loud, while something behind it begged me not to. Despair and desire in one, in all of him in that moment: his body, so close to mine, his furrowed brow, his heart, which beat faster as I rested my hand on his chest.

This is madness. The thought raced through my mind, but it crumbled under its own weight until there were only fragments. Only one piece of solid ground.

I ran my hand slowly up the buttons of his shirt until I reached his throat and then his face. His skin was cooler than before, but warm enough to make me shudder a little. Blake closed his eyes as I stroked the scar on his temple.

'I'm about to kiss you,' I whispered. 'If you want to spread your wings and fly away, now's your chance.'

'Be quiet.' The corners of his mouth twitched, and he put his hand on my neck. Fingers resting on my vertebrae, breath on my lips, *so* warm. 'And ... close your eyes,' he murmured.

I searched for his gaze, confused, but his eyes were still closed. 'Why?'

He shook his head. 'Can't you just do what I ask you to, for once?'

I should have said no, I should have pushed him away, turned around and left. I should have done anything, absolutely anything, except close my eyes. The problem was, it was all I wanted to do. The truth was that I'd wanted to kiss Blake Ames ever since I met him that first night at the library.

I'd convinced myself he was part of a puzzle I wanted to solve, because I loved solving puzzles. But in this moment I realised it had never been about that. I didn't need to fully work him out to feel like I understood him. Or to want him.

I stroked one hand languidly down his cheek until it came to rest at his throat. Rising up onto my toes, I leant forward until the tip of my nose was touching his face. Taking a deep breath, I inhaled his perfume, a distinctive scent that reminded me of woody oud and rich lavender, perhaps a trace of cinnamon.

I thought, *Blake*. Thought, *Cliff*. Thought, *Heathcliff*.

I thought nothing as he cupped my face in his hands and turned it gently to the side, just far enough that I felt his lips on mine. He paused, I held my breath. And then we gave in to it.

As I shifted towards him, he gathered me close. We kissed each other at the same moment, warily and yet with such ... certainty.

Nothing hesitant, nothing tentative, only his lips on mine, and my beating heart, which sank through my chest to between my legs. A kiss in the blink of an eye – and everything inside me throbbed.

I grabbed the collar of his shirt and held it tightly as he pushed me once more against the wall. My dress rasped between my shoulder blades. I still couldn't breathe in it, and I wished he'd unbutton it.

It wasn't raw desire I felt but something softer, more innocent, yet at the same time more intense. The kiss was scraping at the core of something I thought I'd recognised in Blake from the moment we first met. And I wanted, at last, to reach it. I wanted to crack through every false shell until there was only us. No more fabric, no lies, no secrets, no one else, no other influences. Just us.

But Blake's hands were still on my face, his thumbs tracing soft circles on my cheeks. There was only his knee, pushing between my legs as he kissed me more deeply, more urgently. His lips were warm and a little rough, like the sound that came out of my mouth as I felt the pressure of him through the layers of cloth. Oh God, it really *was* madness, but I loved it.

It sent a jolt through Blake. He broke away from the kiss and rested his forehead against mine, breathing heavily. His breath was hot on my face, which was already burning. I didn't dare to move, not even to blink. 'Why can't I look at you when we kiss?' I whispered, my voice brittle.

'If you need your eyes to see me in a kiss like that, then something is wrong,' he answered, just as softly. I wasn't sure I understood the words, but I thought I grasped the emotion behind them.

Because I did see him. In that warm, dark moment, he was the only thing I saw. And for the first time since I'd known him, I found nothing conflicted there. No mismatch between his expression and his words, no gulf between the glittering perfection of his friends and the broken way he viewed the world, as if he were alone in it. He wasn't perfect, and nor was I, but he was whole. Wholly himself.

For seconds we stood before each other in silence. The wind whistling through the window, the music spilling through the floorboards from below, the noisy world snatching out at us on all sides. Yet in that moment, it couldn't reach.

'This is you drawing back the curtain, isn't it?' I whispered.

'Yes.' He smiled audibly.

'Is it real, or is it an illusion?'

'It's all too real with you, Pica,' he murmured into my mouth. 'That's the whole goddamn problem.'

I was about to say something, but his lips were on mine again. And kissing him was more enjoyable than asking questions he wouldn't answer anyway. So I put my hands on his neck and sighed into his mouth as he buried his fingers in my hair and tilted my head back a little.

'Blake.'

The voice reached my ears as if through cotton wool. Or through velvet, because everything about me and in me felt that way: like dark, soft, protective velvet. The world bounced off me, until that little word, that *name*, bristling with thorns, slipped through and tore the shell of the moment apart.

Blake switched more quickly than I did. First he stopped mid-kiss, then released me with a jerk and backed away.

I blinked, my eyes adjusting to the dim light in the corridor.

The silhouette a few yards away came only reluctantly into focus. Norah was wearing an evening gown: pale blue satin that accentuated her slim figure and made her hair look even redder. It might have made her look gentle, but the way she stared at us was sharp-edged. She was ... appalled.

'Henry's gone, but the others are looking for you. And Ashton is'—her eyes flicked in my direction, and she lowered her voice—'Ashton. We should go before he comes up here and...'

This time she looked at me without seeing at me. My face was tingling, my tongue too. Blake had been right. I'd been able to see him without opening my eyes. And now I could sense him even though he wasn't touching me. He took a step forward, between Norah and me. 'At the other end of the hall there's a second flight of stairs. Take that, grab your jacket and go home,' he told me.

His voice was still a little breathless, but his body was well under control now. He swept the hair back from his brow and adjusted the collar of his shirt, as if by doing so he could cast off all memory of the kiss – and of me. Yet I saw a smear of my lipstick on his mouth, and – much more important – still felt the touch of his hands. And I knew it was the same for him. I just knew.

'I—' I began, confused, but then he turned to me.

'Please.' His voice was so earnest, so deep and strained, that it almost made me flinch. 'Go home.'

I moved unwillingly away from the wall, smoothing my dress. 'Fine. But that's the second time you've asked me to do something and I've said yes. You owe me.'

'*Blake.*' Norah snarled his name. His shoulders tensed, but he didn't take his eyes off me as I took the first step past him.

'You'll text me?' I asked, so quietly I could barely hear the words myself. But I could taste them – especially the bittersweet trace of hope.

A pained look crossed his face. He made no answer, just moved his lips soundlessly, shaping one word: *go*.

So I went. Past Norah, who turned her head as if she couldn't bear to look at me. Down the corridor and around the corner, until I found the narrow stairs that led directly to the front hall.

I saw no one on the way back to my room. The college was invisible beneath a thin quilt of snow. It crunched under my feet with every step, still drifting down from above. Despite the cold, I was blazing hot. My mind should have been thrumming with questions, but I felt a throbbing only in my mouth and heart, in a way that made me feel like I'd found an answer today, after all – an answer to a question I hadn't yet dared to ask.

CHAPTER 17
CLIFF

Not until Mabel's footsteps had died away behind me did I let myself breathe and face up to what had just happened. I wished I could think of it in such passive terms, but of course I knew better. None of it had just *happened*: I'd wanted it, done it, loved it.

'I...' My voice petered out as I heard the noises on the main staircase. Besides, there was no good way to finish that sentence. No logical explanation for how I'd let this happen.

Norah's lips were tight, and a moment later, Ashton appeared in the hall. 'What are you two doing up here?'

I shook my head, looking at Norah. For a while now we'd been closer than she was with Ashton, but I knew how hard it was to hide anything from him. Still, she shrugged without hesitation. 'Nothing. I just told him we were leaving.'

'Mmm.' Ashton looked from one of us to the other. He was usually able to sense when there was something going on under the surface, but he couldn't possibly know what it was we were keeping from him, could he? It was absurd. 'Your moth's here,' he said at last, so abruptly that I almost jumped.

I pulled myself together. 'Yes, I saw her too. She's getting a little clingy these days. I sent her away.'

Ashton came closer to me. 'Vic saw her at the party downstairs with that professor. Coincidence, is it?'

Over his shoulder I saw Norah gesture to her mouth, and reflexively I wiped the back of my hand over my lips. I didn't have to look to know there was make-up on them. *Strongest Temptation* was what I'd just been feeling – *Biggest Fear* was what I felt now.

'What else could it be?' I said, after a pause a fraction too long.

Ashton came to a halt in front of me, studying me closely. Ever since Zoe had told him about the little research project Mabel and her friend were doing, he'd been even more on edge about her. I had to promise him again that I'd take care of it. If he knew what had just happened, he wouldn't have hesitated to take matters into his own hands.

My pulse was beating so hard I could feel the very core of my body quivering. Ashton's eyes wandered to it, then he shook his head. 'You know what?' He drew back with a grim smile. 'Not my problem, not today. I can't deal with that shit on top of everything else.'

He ran a hand over his face, but the weary look remained. I felt my guard come down a little, transforming into an emotion I rarely felt for Ashton. Only in those moments when I saw cracks in his invulnerable façade. Most of the time it was one particular person who made them appear. Henry's words were fists, his glances well-aimed kicks, and Ashton was his favourite punching bag.

'You know he doesn't mean it like that,' I said softly.

Ashton snorted. 'What? That he's ashamed of me? That I'm a crushing disappointment? Yes he does. And he's right. Because everybody around here does whatever they want, and because every lapse makes me look bad.'

'You seemed quite happy to bend the rules yourself the other day,' I reminded him, although Norah's expression warned me I was on thin ice.

'Yeah, well if I did, I wouldn't let myself get caught,' he hissed. 'From now on, we make no more mistakes, got it?'

'So we'll leave Paulina alone?'

'You heard me. We can't afford to draw any more attention to ourselves right now. We'll keep an eye on her, but as long as she doesn't go blabbing...' He shrugged.

I nodded slowly. It was exactly the answer I'd been hoping for, although I wondered why Henry had gone to the effort of coming all this way. Well. The reason was probably standing right in front of me, tense and rigid, as if in pain. He'd never admit it, but I could tell that Henry's dressing down had got to him. He was suffering. And no matter how angry I'd been with Ashton lately, I hated to see it.

'He doesn't mean it, Ash,' I repeated, more gently.

Ashton briefly closed his eyes, then he forced a grin. 'Doesn't matter. I feel like getting hammered. Let's go down the pub, or a club, maybe.'

I relaxed. It was selfish, but when Ashton was in this mood I preferred the thought of him in a crowd than near one person in particular. 'Sure. You round up the others and we'll meet you outside.'

As soon as his footsteps had receded down the stairs, I turned to Norah. She hadn't moved a muscle throughout the whole conversation, her gaze burning into mine. I didn't bother to start explaining. I knew her well enough to be sure she'd always share her loudest thoughts with me. And this one was shrieking so deafeningly that I could hear it even before she opened her mouth.

'Just clarify for me: which of you is the moth and which is the light?'

I rolled my eyes and went over to the window, knowing my

217

face couldn't keep up the lie much longer. 'I just got carried away for a minute. It happens, you know that.'

'Not to you. You *always* keep that stuff separate. And something tells me you still are.' She had followed me, her nearness a shimmer behind me. 'So, if I'm right, then what I just saw is the *only* way you touch her. Correct?'

My eyes fell on the back of my hand. On the streaks of red lipstick, reminding me of red-smeared blood. I wiped them roughly, until the skin was on fire. 'There's nothing wrong with that.' I wanted so badly to believe it.

'Of course not.' Her voice softened. 'We all have needs, we're people too. It's just ... how long has it been since you allowed that kind of contact?'

A long time. A very long time. So long that I could barely remember their names, let alone their faces. I could count on one hand the women I'd slept with in the last few years. On one finger, those I'd slept with more than once. It wasn't that I'd never wanted to, but the self-loathing afterwards had always outweighed the satisfaction. Lately, there had been another reason, too, why being with a woman felt impossible. I'd thought it wasn't worth it. That I could rise above it, the same way I'd risen above my strongest urges. Only, with Mabel, it hadn't felt like an urge. That was the thing: getting closer to her didn't feel like a choice, it felt inevitable. What had just happened wasn't a carefully considered decision, it was a surrendering to emotions that had been building up for weeks.

'What do you want, Norah?' We didn't have much time before Ashton lost patience, and I didn't want to have this conversation anyway. I didn't want to hear what Norah thought, because I already knew the gist of it. I wasn't just thinking it, I felt it too: it's always the happiest moments that leave the bitterest aftertaste of guilt and regret.

I felt constantly guilty, but especially now. So why couldn't I bring myself to regret the kiss? Why couldn't I regret anything when it came to Mabel? How could I know it was wrong, yet still not want to stop? And how could I not even hate myself for it? Maybe because, for the first time in an age, I felt like she saw someone in me who deserved more than that? Who *was* more than that? Who might be exactly the person I so badly wanted to be?

'I'm just trying to understand you.' Norah laid a hand on my back until I turned to face her. There was worry in her eyes, and maybe even grief. 'What are you doing?'

I have no idea, I thought, but couldn't bring myself to say it. I couldn't even look at Norah. Her expression of confusion, anxiety and horror was too much. Too much of what I'd been trying to block out for weeks. Because she was right, of course. Mabel wasn't the moth. Mabel was the light, the light I couldn't resist, and which would burn me, in the end. And yet she was the one who would ultimately lose her wings, who would lose *everything*, if I allowed that kind of closeness.

'Oh, Cliff,' Norah sighed, in the sad way she always said that name. She only did it when the others weren't around. My favourite defiance of the rules, and one that always made me close my eyes, just briefly, and remember. What I'd once been, what I'd so dearly like to be, what I could never be again.

'If it's her face you like, maybe we can find a solution. You know they make exceptions sometimes.'

I raised my eyes, confused. 'Her face?'

'She's pretty,' she said matter-of-factly. We both knew how ephemeral that was. 'She has thoughtful eyes. I know you like that.'

I gave a hoarse laugh. 'I don't care about her face, Norah.' I turned away abruptly, steadying myself on the windowsill. Outside, the college was sinking into a deep blue, my reflection glimmering as palely as the thin blanket of snow on the asphalt.

Norah was silent for a moment, then she took a deep breath. 'Well, that's inconvenient.'

'I know.' Inconvenient, impossible, unforgiveable.

I turned back to her. Arms crossed, I leant against the window frame and glanced down the corridor. Everything felt alien. This place, these people. They were my only family, my whole life. Yet I couldn't deny it any longer: I was rediscovering a long-lost part of myself, and I sensed that it would mean losing something else, something essential, and final.

'Don't tell Ashton. Please.'

'Don't worry.' She smiled feebly. 'But you know him. He'll sniff it out. And even if he doesn't ... there's no way this ends well. You know that, right?'

'Of course I do. No chance of that for any of us, is there?'

For us, there was no way out. None. No escape, no end. It all went simply on and on, just as it had begun, long ago. With the people who had begun it. With us. Any other contact was fleeting and insignificant: that was a fact we had to accept. And yet here I was, thinking about a woman who was already slipping away from me with every breath. And I'd never even let myself hold on to her as tightly as I wished I could.

'*Life breaks everybody. But it breaks us a little harder. Just got to make the best of it.*' Norah's voice cracked with the sound of tears through her smile. 'You remember how she always used to say that?'

I had to smile myself. 'As if any of us could ever forget.' Although the words always set off a dull pressure in my chest, I loved to hear them. As long as it hurt to remember, the emotion was still real. And we owed her that much. We'd promised her. *A real life.* I thought about it often, but lately I'd been wondering more and more if perhaps we'd had a different understanding of what that meant. Because the most real moments I'd had in a long time had been with Mabel, even though she could never be part of my life – *our* life.

Norah nodded thoughtfully. She reached for the watch on my wrist, with its unmoving hands. 'You know, sometimes I think Ashton's whole personality is shaped by how much he misses her.'

'We all miss her. Just in different ways. Some of us more problematically than others.' I thought of the gold chain in Ashton's wallet, threaded with two rings, which I only knew existed because it had once fallen out while he was paying for something. I hadn't mentioned it, and forbade myself to tell Norah. If he'd kept them all this time, it had to mean that, somehow, he was still the same. I clung to that, whenever I felt like I no longer recognised him. Grief had many faces. The one Ashton wore was among its ugliest. But that didn't mean the emotion behind it wasn't beautiful. Love wasn't always easy. If anyone knew that, it was us. All of us.

I shook my head, thinking of the fourth person included in that *us*. 'Speaking of, have you heard anything from Nox lately?'

Norah's lips pursed into a thin line, as they always did when she heard that name. Sometimes it felt convulsive, like she was having to tamp down her spontaneous reaction. 'Not since Canterbury.'

'I assumed he'd jump at the chance to tag along with Henry.'

'I didn't.' She fiddled with the neckline of her dress. It was violet, the same shade as her eyes. Nox's favourite colour. Although I couldn't remember now which of those two things had come first. In any case, it told me that part of Norah had been expecting him to show up, too. 'If he has his way, I doubt we'll be seeing each other anytime soon.'

'You were the one who split up with him, Norah.'

'Splitting up with someone who's already checked out isn't really ending things. It's accepting that it's already ended.' She shrugged, as if to shake off the weight of the memory. For years I had seen it grow heavier day by day. Her eyes drifted past me, and I watched them meet those of her reflection in the windowpane. The shadows smudged the violet of her eyes into a pale grey. 'Strange, isn't it?' she murmured. 'When we lost her – she took so much with her.'

'I think it just made us more aware of what we actually have. What we ... are. Losing her tore off a mask we didn't even know was there.'

She smiled and laid a hand on my forearm. 'I thought we were losing you too, Cliff. Truly. But for a while now ... ever since Mabel, it feels like you're coming back to us a little.'

What she said was so true it ached, in a way that made me dig my fingernails into my palms until it hurt. Physical pain was more bearable. *Anything* was more bearable. 'Yes, but it doesn't matter,' I snarled bitterly. 'We all know how this is going to end.'

'Still, I'm happy for you. It's good to be reminded every now and then why we're all doing this, isn't it? It's no less precious just because it can't last. There's no point living a life like this if you're dead inside.'

At least if you're already dead inside, you don't feel like you're still dying, I thought, but I didn't say it out loud. It wouldn't help. Besides, I'd known from the start what I was getting into. I had seen the light, and knew what it would cost me to reach my fingers towards it. Getting them burnt was just part of the deal, one I was willing to accept because I'd been so cold so long, and because Mabel and her radiance were the first in many years to hold such allure. Perhaps the first of all. I'd never felt anything like it, which was fascinating and soothing and beautiful and ... deadly. For the both of us.

'The pain will fade. It always does, you know that.' Norah leant her head against me, her hair tickling my chin, her words in her eyes. 'In the end, all we have is each other.'

I didn't answer, only stood, breathing, trying merely to exist and not to be. I'd been doing it more and more these days. Yet I couldn't ignore what, deep down, I had already realised: I didn't need to have Mabel to know I was going to lose her. To know that she was already losing something herself. Much more than she could possibly know. If I'd been stronger, if I'd been better, I would have protected her. I would have kept my distance. But I wasn't strong or good, I was exhausted, and at the same time strangely elated. As if being near Mabel had dug a hole at the very core of me. It had been so hardened for so long I'd thought that was impossible, yet there it was: a chamber softly scratched out at my centre, and I felt her in it. Suddenly, somehow, I felt many things. It hurt, but the hurt was what made it good. After all, what was a wound, if not a sign you were alive?

I knew that every second I allowed myself to feel this way would only make the end feel even worse. But in that moment, I didn't care. I didn't want to let it go yet. I didn't want to let *her* go yet.

What did that make me? A fool, a monster, or a human being? Perhaps it didn't matter much, because in the end, it all came to the same thing. For someone like me, living always tasted like dying. And finding something always tasted like losing it again, in the cruellest possible way.

CHAPTER 18
MABEL

Christmas came, and the people around me went. The colleges were emptier each day, the snow falling more thickly. When I left my staircase in the morning, my footprints were the first to break through the white. When I returned from the library in the evening, they had been swept away as if they were never there. As if I were never there.

That wasn't the only thing that made me feel like a ghost. I was only sporadically in touch with other people: Clara called a few times, Davie sent me snaps of the family dogs wearing reindeer antlers, Zoe ignored my texts, and Blake ... Blake didn't communicate at all.

I didn't text him either, just stared again and again at the open chat, wondering what it was that held him back. The kiss, or everything else. Me, or all the stuff about the professor, Ashton, his friends, his ... society. What was the mistake, the big, glaring error always stirring at the back of my mind when I thought about that night?

I should have been relieved that he made no attempt to pick up what Norah had interrupted. Yet I felt a pang of disappointment every time I took out my phone to find no new messages from him. Like on Christmas Eve, when I got back to my room around six. Flecks of snow were melting on my coat, my hair was damp, and the tip of my nose began to tingle unpleasantly as soon as the heated air began to gnaw at its chilly armour.

I rubbed it with the ball of my hand as I checked my phone again, so that I didn't notice the box ouside my door until I nearly tripped over it – even though it was wider than me and as tall as my chest. I looked for the sender's name, confused, but all I could see on the lid was my own name. That and the outline of a ... bird. For a moment I thought it was a starling, but then I realised there wasn't a twig held in its beak but a beaded necklace. So, a magpie. Suddenly I knew who'd left me the box.

I glanced around, but saw no one. Everyone else on my staircase had gone home. I was alone with a box so large it was a struggle to manoeuvre it over my doorstep. Something inside it rustled as I put it next to my bed. I stared at it uncertaintly, taking out my phone again and opening the chat with Blake.

PICA

> Have you ever seen the movie Seven with Brad Pitt?

As soon as I'd sent the message, he came online. Immediately, he started typing.

HEATHCLIFF

> I promise you, I didn't leave a severed head on your doorstep.

PICA

> If the size of the box is anything to go by, it's not severed.

HEATHCLIFF

> Just open it, Pica.

I bit my lower lip to hold back a smile. I put the phone down without answering, slung my damp coat onto the bed and picked up some scissors from my desk. Even before I'd opened the lid, I could smell what it was. I caught a tart waft of pine needles and resin, and moments later, the first prickly branch came poking out. A tree, its spreading branches already decorated. Stars made of gold and silver-laquered glass, hand-painted baubles, ornaments made of crystal and straw.

My heart grew heavy and warm. My knees felt weak, and I sat down on the edge of the bed. Mum and I had always chosen our tree together, decorated it, drank our mugs of caramel hot chocolate beside it. After she was gone, somehow I'd associated Christmas trees with everything I'd lost. But to be gifted one – by someone who didn't even know what it meant to me – made me feel for the first time in six years like I could begin to think about what I'd had. What I'd always been grateful for at Christmas.

Giving in to a sudden impulse, I called Blake. He picked up in seconds. 'You got me a Christmas tree?'

'Mmm.' I heard him take a few steps, then a door swung shut. 'You like it or you don't like it?'

'I...' I stood back up, moved closer to the present. The worst thing was probably how much I *did* like it. I didn't want to be so moved. I didn't want it to take my breath away. 'How did you even know I was still here?'

'I saw Zoe with Ashton the other day, and we had a brief chat. She told me you were staying in college over the break, seemed a bit worried about it. She said Christmas isn't an easy time for you.'

The soft feeling in me deepened. 'My mother got into an accident around this time of year. Stuff's just been a bit ... difficult, since then.'

'I understand. Should I not have?'

'No, it's fine.' Gently I reached out and stroked a branch.

'Sounds like you've talked to Zoe more than I have lately. She didn't even say goodbye before she left.' I fell silent briefly, running my fingertips over a scratch on a silver glass star. 'Nor did you.'

'I know.' Something crunched, and in the distance I heard the rustling of leaves. I pictured him standing in the snowy driveway of some big house, and wondered why even in my imagination he seemed out of place there. 'I was worried you might be regretting what happened at the Christmas party.'

It wasn't a question, and yet it was. And I was still me: not a good liar. 'I don't regret it. I probably should, but I don't. What about you?'

He laughed a little breathlessly. Maybe he was just cold, maybe he was relieved. 'I got you a Christmas tree. What does that tell you?'

I forced myself to sound casual. 'Guess it could be a thank-you present, because the kiss was so incredible.'

'No comment.' I could tell he was still smiling. 'But no, that wasn't how I meant it.'

'How, then?'

'As ... a suggestion. What if we gave each other a Christmas present this year?'

'If it was anybody else, I'd say you were about to make me an indecent proposal,' I said dryly, although my body flooded with a treacherous heat.

'Don't worry, I just mean ... a break. From everything around us. Just until the end of the year – maybe we can pretend that things aren't quite as complicated as they are.'

The last trace of a smile faded. I rolled a little ball of resin between my fingers. The tree was wounded, and so were we. All of this – the kiss, the conversation, each spark of intimacy between us – it all felt good, strong. But it wasn't. Whatever this thing was between us, whatever it might become if we let it, it was doomed to fail. The strangeness of our first meeting, my determination to thwart his friends, the enmity they felt towards me in return: all of it tore an open wound in what we were. We would never be undamaged. We would never work. We would never be ... right.

'As impossible, you mean,' I whispered.

'Yes.' His smile was sounding sadder now. 'What do you think?'

He knew all the objections as well as I did, but for some reason they didn't seem to bother him enough to make what seemed like the obvious right choice. Perhaps because, like me, he'd sensed that keeping our distance didn't feel right, either. If all you have are wrong choices, maybe you just have to pick your poison. And Blake and I – we felt like the best kind of wrong I could imagine.

'It wouldn't be Christmas without miracles,' I answered, pushing all my doubts aside with an effort of will. 'Or without a tree.' Carefully, I took a woven heart into my palm. 'You didn't have to do this.'

'I know. But the thought of you spending Christmas all alone in your room was hard enough already.'

Suddenly I was glad we were only speaking on the phone, and that he couldn't see me. By now my face was so hot that the reflection in the star was flushed red. 'These ornaments are really pretty,' I said, trying to deflect.

'Most of them are heirlooms, so some are a bit dinged-up.'

I jerked my hand back. It was just like when he told me the books in the small library were first editions. 'You're giving me a tree decorated with *heirlooms*?' I knew from what Davie had told me that the Ames family was extremely wealthy. If even one of these baubles cost more than about two quid, he was crazy to let me anywhere near them.

'I guess I am,' he replied calmly. 'Only the magpie is new. It reminded me of you, for obvious reasons.'

It took me a moment to find the bird. It was about the size of a walnut, made of glass in shades of black, white and blue, and so delicately crafted you could make out every single feather. 'It's beautiful.'

'It is.' Another smile. One so soft that it flowed down the telephone line and wrapped itself around me. More heat rushed to my face, until I felt ashamed of myself.

'Heathcliff?' I was smiling. 'Thank you.'

'My pleasure.'

'You're with your family, right? How's it going?'

Again there was the crunch of snow under his feet as he walked on. 'I've only been here a few hours. Aspen and I are alone with the staff – I doubt there'll be much change there within the next few days.'

'Where are your parents?'

He hesitated. 'Busy. Companies like ours don't take holidays.' There was a trace of bitterness in his words. I guessed he was mainly thinking of his sister. Blake's face rarely looked as tender as it had when he was telling me about her. I think that must have been the moment when I finally admitted to myself that I ... liked him. He couldn't be all bad if he loved someone that much.

'I see.' I sat down on the bed with the magpie in my hand. 'Aspen must be pleased to see you.'

He sighed deeply. 'She's made a list of about fifty Christmas movies for us to watch together.'

I grinned. 'Sounds perfect.'

'Are you doing anything except revising?'

The pattern of feathers felt as rough beneath my fingertips as the answer felt on my tongue: 'We'll have to see.'

'Hmm.' He didn't push, which I was grateful for. Just because we were taking a break from the chaos, that didn't mean it had ceased to exist. I'd promised Davie I would keep going, and I fully intended to.

Blake was quiet for a while, his footsteps slowing, his

breathing becoming more laboured. I wanted to tell him to go back inside, that he must be freezing, but then I knew he'd hang up, and ... I didn't want that. 'You should give yourself the day off,' he said at last. 'Do the whole clichéd Christmas thing. Eat roast chestnuts, drink mulled wine, watch *Love Actually*. According to Aspen, it's *the* modern classic of our times.'

'Ah, well if Aspen says so,' I grinned, leaping at the change of topic. 'I might have to give the food a miss, though. The supermarkets are closed by now, and the only snacks I've got here are wasabi nuts.'

'Didn't anybody ever teach you to look under the tree?'

I paused, then bent down to lift the branches. Sure enough, there was a slim box on the cardboard base next to the pot in which the tree was planted. I fished it out and opened the lid. Several paper bags of nuts, the kind you'd buy at Christmas markets, mulled wine, mince pies and cocoa. My throat tightened, my heart trying doggedly to force itself into my throat. I tried to tell myself I was uncomfortable with the gesture because I didn't like presents. But I realised it gave me the same feeling as Zoe's habit of buying clothes in my size and wearing them fitfully for three weeks before acting like she didn't want them anymore. Or Davie's trick of persuading me to eat cake by pretending I was doing him a favour. None of it was about being pitied. It was about being liked, and I wished I handled it better. It was beautiful and awkward at the same time: it showed me what I wanted as well as what I feared.

I rubbed the bridge of my nose, opening my mouth to reply several times. I wanted to say thank you, at least, but all that came out in the end was: 'When are you back?'

Somehow I was sure he knew what I was trying to say. 'Not until the new year. Aspen's going skiing with a schoolfriend and her family. It wouldn't feel right to come back sooner.'

'So that means I won't see you again this year.'

'Well, I wouldn't say that.'

'What does that mean?'

'It means there's ways of seeing someone without literally seeing them. I explained it to you before.' The smile that clung to the words was bathed in the dust of memory. It was red: I felt it settle on my cheeks, warm.

I let myself fall back on the mattress, turning the magpie in the light of the ceiling lamp. The way it twinkled cast patterns on the walls around me. 'So you're suggesting we keep in touch over the holidays? In a totally straightforward, block-out-the-world-around-us kind of way?'

'Yes,' he said simply.

My lip was throbbing, maybe because I was biting it again to keep from smiling. Maybe because my body was thinking about something my conscious mind would never allow. Because if it had, I'd have asked Blake to come straight over. 'Then you have to text me back this time when I message you.'

Before I'd even finished the sentence, my phone vibrated in my hand.

HEATHCLIFF

I will.

This time I allowed myself a smile. It threaded itself so completely into my voice that I barely recognised it. 'Great, then we'll talk soon. And ... merry Christmas, Heathcliff.'

'Merry Christmas to you too, Pica.'

We hung up, and I stayed lying where I was. Sinking into the sheets and the smell of pine and baked goods, a glass magpie in my hand and a warm feeling in my belly. For the first time in years, I believed this really might be it. Maybe not a merry Christmas, exactly, but at least a bearable one.

∼

And it really was. I had been trying for years to cut Mum out of the picture of Christmas I had in my head, but in doing so I'd erased all the magic as well. This year I allowed myself to think about her, and it reminded me of all the things I loved about the season: the stillness that descended over the world, the cosiness of warm socks pulled on after a winter stroll, the taste of shortbread, the spectacle of shop-window displays at dusk. And so I immersed myself in the feeling again: I wandered through the deserted colleges, drank hot chocolate, ate all the sweet treats in the box, watched a dozen Christmas movies, and thought very little about my own life, which was so different from those unspoilt, fairy-light-decked realities that flickered across the screen.

Blake texted me a lot; he sent long messages, he always responded. What happened between us at the Christmas party floated above us like a silk scarf, one that neither of us reached for. Our messages were harmless yet meaningful. Messages while I was studying at the library, when really I should have been ignoring my phone, but was waiting instead for the screen to light up. Messages when I was cooking alone in the evenings in the shared kitchen. Messages as I lay in bed unable to sleep, and we spent hours discussing lines from various books.

People like Heathcliff are idiots, Blake wrote.

Not always, I replied, with a smile I only allowed myself in the solitude of my darkened room.

We were something I didn't understand. I shouldn't have liked him, I should have been afraid of him, and I definitely shouldn't have trusted him. I knew that, but what I *felt* was another matter. I felt myself becoming more relaxed with every sentence, every shared word, every flicker of the screen, every moment spent staring at those three little dots. It was like we'd known each other forever, and so well that I never felt awkward with him. We texted about everything – except what mattered most. Nothing about Ashton or Zoe, nothing about anything connected to them. The period between Christmas and New Year was one long, warmly lit in-between, and it belonged to us. I knew that as soon as the university sprang back to life in the new year, the fragile lull would end. I had let Blake into my life, into my thoughts and my emotions, I had tried to forget he was one of the Starlings, but it was a compromise that couldn't work long-term. And I kept telling myself that was fine.

Together we had found a refuge, burrowing down so deeply that we knew at any moment we could be buried in a landslide. It was only a question of who, out of all the people around us, set it off.

CHAPTER 19
MABEL

My reflection in the windowpane was dotted with white flakes. The snow had thickened just in time for New Year's Eve, and the blanketed asphalt glinted in the orange glow of the last Christmas lights.

Suppressing a yawn, I looked away. By now the nook was empty except for me, because everybody else in the pub was already on their feet, chatting, laughing and counting down the minutes until midnight. Davie had persuaded me to come. I hadn't seen him for weeks, after all, and though the new term was a while off, he'd come back early – I suspected out of pity for me, which I hated. And Zoe. She was spending most of January with her family. Though she had responded curtly with a '*Fine*' when I plucked up the courage to text her to ask how it was going. The fact that she even responded gave me some encouragement, at least, for when she returned.

I clicked again on the chat with Blake, staring in frustration at the single tick next to the question I'd sent him two hours ago, asking what he and Aspen were up to that night.

'Everything okay?'

I hurried to lock the screen, glancing up at Davie with a heavy sense of guilt. He didn't know, of course, that I was in touch with Blake. He would have asked for news about the League, and I would have had to confess – to the both of us – that I hadn't really given it much thought lately.

I pushed out a smile. 'Just a bit tired. I did warn you I wouldn't be the best company today.'

Davie slid into the booth next to me. He was clutching a half-empty red ale, and his cheeks were flushed the same colour as the booze. 'You're always the best company as far as I'm concerned.'

'Just how drunk are you?' The teasing note in my voice wavered as I saw the warmth in his eyes. Like the warmth of his hand, resting only centimetres from mine on the seat. I pulled mine back, reaching for my glass of cider to give myself an alibi.

Davie took a deep breath. 'Mabel, I—'

'Fifteen minutes to go, people!' Cody appeared so suddenly at our table that Davie spilt some of his beer. Blond hair tousled around his face, shirt half open. I'd known him for about a year as Davie's neighbour and colleague at the paper, but I'd never seen him as hammered as he was tonight. He was gazing at us aghast, tapping an imaginary watch on his wrist. 'Chop-chop. Get yourselves some champagne, or at least some nicer glasses for your beers!' Then he was gone, moving on to the next table to make the same announcement.

'I think Cody's forgetting which one of you is the Commander.'

Davie rolled his eyes. 'He's an idiot. But he's right. I'll get us something to toast with.'

'Go for it.' I followed him as he slid out of the booth. 'I need a breath of fresh air. Otherwise I'll be nodding off by midnight.'

Outside, Cambridge seemed nearly lifeless. A few windows were lit, leaking candlelight or the silver speckles of a disco ball, but otherwise there was only the milky brilliance of the lanterns, cast across the snowy tarmac. I tilted back my head, waiting for the December air to finally sweep away the nagging urge to call Blake.

Exasperated, I turned on my heel – but froze when I saw the figure leaning against the building next to the pub. I recognised him even before he broke away from the wall and came slowly towards me. I knew by how it made me feel: surprised and ... relieved.

Blake pushed the snow-laden hair back from his face, giving me a cautious smile. 'Hi.'

I stared, dumbfounded. 'What are you doing here?'

'Aspen left for her friend's a bit early, so I thought I'd come back to college early, too.' Blake stopped two steps away from me, hands hidden in his coat pockets.

I wondered if it was because he was hoping I'd reach out for him. And I did want to: to touch him, hold him ... kiss him. Simply because we'd done it last time, and I couldn't grasp that there could ever be a time I hadn't thought about it.

I folded my hands in front of my stomach, which lurched gently. 'This isn't a coincidence, is it? You knew I was here.'

Blake shrugged, but his eyes never left my face. 'I wanted to see you, at least for a moment, before ... the year ends.'

A lump was forming in my throat. 'You mean, before our deal ends.'

His smile faltered. 'Yes.'

It was absurd how much it stung, even though I knew it was coming. We had only allowed ourselves this shared respite from the world because we'd agreed in advance how it would end. Because we knew there was no other choice. Yet here I was, listening to the muffled roar of laughter and music and voices drifting from the pub, and hearing nothing but the beating of my heart. It thudded slowly, as if it didn't want to let the moment go. As if it didn't want to let *him* go.

I scuffed at the snow with the tip of my shoe. 'So, what is this? A hello or a goodbye?'

'Maybe both.' He took a step towards me, leaving only one between us.

I tried to remind myself it wasn't true. That the gulf between us was much greater. But I couldn't do it. I just couldn't remember the reasons why I shouldn't cross that last half a yard between us. I tried to tell myself it was the cider, but I knew better: it was the last few days. It was seeing Blake now and simply knowing who he was. Not all the subtler shades of him, but the essence. I had discovered my sense of him, and that made it impossible to keep my distance.

Just as I was about to take the final step towards him, the pub door flew open. Cody poked out his head, wearing a small sparkly hat. 'Mabel, three—' He stopped as he caught sight of Blake. 'Oh, a friend of yours?'

I opened my mouth, but Blake beat me to the punch. 'No, I'm nobody. And nobody is leaving now.'

I knew what he was referring to. That night in the chapel, when Norah had walked in on us. Our second little glimpse through the window. I wondered if it had also occurred to Blake that we only pulled back the curtain when we were alone – never in front of other people.

'You don't have to go,' I said, although I knew it made no sense. Even ignoring the fact that the deal was ending, Davie was in the pub, and given his history with the Starlings, I was pretty sure I knew how he'd feel about it. And so did Blake, of course.

'Yes, I do. It's almost midnight.' He took a step forward. I hated knowing that he wasn't walking towards me but past me. 'All the best, Mabel.'

His hand brushed mine, and I grasped it. 'Don't call me that,' I whispered.

He smiled, bending down until his mouth grazed my

temple. Fleetingly, and yet so close that I felt the words on my skin – and somehow, a moment later, beneath it. 'Happy New Year, Pica.'

I sensed them carve themselves into my mind, the memory born even as the moment lingered. 'It was good to *see* you, Heathcliff,' I whispered back, and I watched him as he walked off down the empty, snowy lane until the night had swallowed up his shadow. I wished it would take the strange feeling inside me, too.

Back in the pub, I found Davie at our table. He had two glasses of champagne in front of him, one of them already half empty.

I took my seat next to him with a frown. 'What...' My voice trailed off as I followed his gaze outside. In a flash, all the colour drained from my face. 'I didn't know he was coming. It was a coincidence.' Davie was staring at me so expressionlessly that, reluctantly, I went on. 'I did tell you we knew each other a bit. Because of the research. Like we agreed.'

'The way you looked at him – that's definitely not what we agreed. I would never have allowed that, because that's absolutely the last thing I want.'

The lump in my throat was back, and this time its edges were sharp. I wasn't sure exactly what had put it there. Maybe it was simply the realisation that this conversation would destroy something. 'You don't have to worry about me. I'm being careful.'

'It's not about that.' He ran a hand over his head, resting it on the back of his neck. 'I mean, obviously I'm worried. But ... it's not about that.'

There was something worse than being hurt. Nothing was more awful than knowing you'd hurt someone you loved. Because sometimes, loving someone wasn't enough. Not when it was a different kind of love to what the other person wanted.

'Davie.' I made to reach for his hand, but at the last second I drew back.

He smiled dully. 'I know. I'm an idiot.'

'You're not. It's just ... you're my best—'

'Don't say it, please.'

'But it's true. You know how much you mean to me.'

'Yes, I do. And I know it's enough, but right now it doesn't feel that way.' Gradually he turned his face to mine. The mottled glow of the fairy lights above us was splashed across his features. 'Seeing you with him feels like shit, for several reasons. You know as well as I do, Mabel. Surely it's obvious he can't be a good person if he's mixed up in this crap.'

All around us, people were beginning the countdown, but neither Davie nor I moved. It didn't really matter that the year was ending: we weren't going to leave this behind us. Part of me was afraid we'd never fully shake it off, no matter how much time passed. I understood that Davie wasn't just hurt, he also felt betrayed. And I wished I could explain to him that Blake wasn't part of what we were fighting. But how do you explain something when your only argument is gut feeling?

'And what if there are no good people?' I asked softly. 'Only good or bad decisions?'

Davie sneered. 'Did he tell you that?'

'No. It's just something I've been thinking lately.'

'Maybe it's what you want to believe. You're looking for an excuse to like him,' Davie snapped, reaching for my glass.

I almost snatched it out of his hand. I would have done anything to wash his words away, because I was all too aware of how true they tasted. 'Maybe.' My voice was lost in the din that erupted around us. People laughing, jumbled shouting, hugging. Sparklers fizzed at the edges of my vision, and somebody got up onto a table to sing an off-key rendition of 'Auld Lang Syne'. I hadn't felt this quiet in a long time.

After a while, Davie took my hand. 'Just be careful. This isn't going to end well, and I think you're smart enough to realise that.'

I swallowed. 'Yeah. And I also know that what I see in him doesn't change what I see in *them*. I'm still ready to do whatever it takes to figure out what's going on with the League.'

'Even if you have to betray him to do it?'

As conflicted as my feelings were for Blake, my answer was clear. 'Yes. This is about Zoe. It's about … everything. If we're right, then we can't let them get away with this. Any of them.'

Davie nodded slowly. 'Okay. Good.'

He tried to pull his hand away, but I held on tight. Part of me was scared that if I let go now, I might lose him for good. 'I really am sorry, Davie. I should have said something before, or—'

'It's fine. Don't shut me out, okay? I'll be all right.' He smiled, again pulling back his hand. This time I forced myself to let go. Anything else would have been unfair, and probably no use anyway. If there was one thing I'd learnt, it was that clinging on to something doesn't shield you from loss. Life always has a stronger grip.

'You sure?' I asked uncertainly.

'Absolutely.' He grinned at me over the rim of his glass, the smile a bit more genuine now. 'I'll just focus on how much of a pain in the arse you can be.'

My laugh sounded jarring. 'Right back at you. But maybe I should get going anyway. We'll talk … soon?'

'Sure.' He smiled a little self-consciously, but then shuffled closer and gave me a hug. Brief but tight. 'Happy New Year, Mabel,' he murmured into my ear. 'May it get off to a less shitty start than the way the last one ended.'

The words lingered in my mind as I said my goodbyes and stepped at last into the outside world. The silence of the vacant city settled itself around me, even as a dull echo of the music thudded in my ears, Davie's words ran through my head, and my chest was alive with the emotions Blake's arrival had stirred up.

I couldn't fully agree with what Davie had just said. Yes, the last few months had been extremely stressful and confusing. They'd been frightening in all sorts of different ways. But they had been more than that. *I* had been more. I had felt more than I'd let myself feel in a very long time.

Saying goodbye to Blake had been the only right thing to do. The only logical thing. Whatever this thing was between us, it had no future; it didn't even truly exist in the present. It was just a secret we had shared, a fleeting illusion woven out of possibilities that weren't really possible at all, because our lives were made out of two utterly different fabrics. It would never hold: it would tear the moment we reached for it.

I knew this, and yet I was on the verge of tears. Right here, right now, outside a loud, thumping, brightly lit pub in the middle of a snowstorm on New Year's Eve. It didn't feel like a new beginning to me. More like the end of something that had barely even begun but that I didn't want to lose. It wasn't just about the days we'd shared, it was the moments Blake and I had spent together since the start of term. He had challenged me, irritated me, frustrated me and maddened me and ... touched me. In so many ways. He had made me think and made me feel. Not through what he did but what he was. Through what his nearness brought out in me.

Seeing Blake – *our way* of seeing – was like looking in a mirror. I recognised parts of myself I'd tried for years to keep concealed, even from myself.

Something about him made me feel whole, for the first time in so long. Not because he completed me, but because he reminded me that I was more than I'd allowed myself to be, until now. I liked seeing this reflection of myself. I liked seeing *me*. Especially – and I knew how dangerous it was – with him.

This was my own personal window moment. The truth I couldn't hide from myself, and didn't want to. And no matter what the obstacles might be, I wasn't ready yet to close the curtains.

CHAPTER 20
MABEL

My footfalls echoed in the hall, my heartbeat in my ears. Blake's door at the end of the corridor was ajar. Taking a deep breath, I made my way towards it and knocked on the wood. Before I could enter, I heard an irritable voice from inside: 'Just come in, you always do anyway.'

I felt like turning back. The fact that he'd just buzzed me in downstairs should have alerted me, but it was obvious now he was expecting someone else. And why shouldn't he be? I wasn't even sure myself what I was doing here. This was madness, yet again. What did it say about me that it felt like the only solid ground beneath my feet?

Before I could decide what to do, the door opened. 'I thought you were still in—' Blake froze when he saw me.

I forced a teasing look onto my face. 'I'm so sorry, apparently I'm not who you were expecting.'

'No.' He hesitated, running a hand through his hair. It was still damp with snow, like the scarf hanging from the peg behind him. 'There's really only one person who shows up unannounced at this time of night.'

Suddenly the heat rushed to my face. God, why hadn't that

occurred to me? Strange as Blake might seem to me, he was a twenty-three-year-old man. Obviously he'd have someone for *that*. 'Oh.' I cleared my throat and took a step back. 'It's fine, forget it I—'

'I meant Ashton. He spends the night on the sofa from time to time,' he broke in, unflustered. Still, I saw the tiny smirk, and my cheeks burnt even more fiercely.

'Oh,' I repeated – *very imaginative, Mabel* – and picked at the fluff on my scarf to avoid his eye. 'Do you think he'll come over tonight?'

'No, he's obviously still in Cornwall with the others.'

I nodded slowly. 'Okay.'

The light went out, but neither of us moved. Blake was leaning against the doorframe, I was a few steps away. The darkness soothed my pulse, and I breathed more deeply. This was better. I could see him more clearly in the dark, I could see myself and what was beginning to feel like an us. I could see what had made me come here.

'Why are you here?' he asked, as if he could hear my thoughts. Maybe, just maybe, because they sounded so much like his own.

I stepped forwards. 'Would it be better if I left?'

He opened the door a fraction wider. 'Yes.'

'Do you want me to?'

With only a step or two between us now, I stopped. Waiting for him to make up his mind what to do about this distance. Remove it, reinforce it: an either/or that wasn't mine to decide alone. I had taken the first step, but I wasn't going to chase him. If he turned around, I'd let him go.

But he didn't. He didn't step back either. He raised his hand; I sensed it more than saw it. His fingertips at my throat, my cheek, then his thumb on my lower lip. Everything in me trembled.

He whispered: 'No.'

'I don't want me to go either.' Boldly I took the last step towards him, until the heat of his body was flickering against mine. 'Happy New Year, Heathcliff.'

'Happy New Year, Pica.'

I heard him smile, and then I felt it too, because I rose up on to my tiptoes, cupped his face in my hands and kissed him. Just like that, because this was madness, and it was the only solid ground we had.

Blake didn't hesitate: he returned the kiss, pulling me in close. I stumbled over the doorstep and into something that wrapped me immediately in a warm embrace. Warm and tingling, especially where he touched me. His fingers felt their way under my coat and slid it off my shoulders. It fell onto the parquet as my heart dropped into my stomach, Blake's hand moving to the crook of my neck before he twined his fingers into my hair and pulled my head back. It smarted a little, it hurt in the best way, and I wanted more. I wanted all of it, all of him.

Reaching for the edge of his jumper, I pushed it up until he let go and I could pull it over his head. There was a shirt underneath, too much fabric, but before I could reach for it Blake had clasped my face again and was kissing me. Kissing me more deeply, kissing me more intently, kissing me, kissing me, kissing me until it was all I could think about.

I was vaguely aware of us stumbling down the hallway into a large living room – low lighting, black-and-white photographs on the walls, but I noticed nothing else. In any case, I didn't care where we were, because I couldn't let myself care *who* we were, or I couldn't be fully in the moment. And I wanted to be, because it felt so good. Because nothing bad could be this good. Or so I hoped.

Blake slipped the strap of my dress off my shoulder, running the pads of his fingers down my skin. I shuddered as he rubbed two fingers over the swell of my nipple beneath the lacy fabric of my cami top. It went hard, and so did he – I felt him as I slid my hand from his stomach down over his waistband, then again as he pushed me adamantly up against the wall and pressed himself close to me. Woodchip wallpaper at my back, his body on mine. I couldn't remember the last time being trapped felt so much like the place I wanted to be.

'Blake,' I whispered into his mouth, without reason, because I had nothing to say. All my words had washed away, and all doubt with them. In that moment I knew I could let this happen – that it had to happen.

The second I uttered his name was the second he paused. His fingers stopped at my waist. Slowly he removed them from my body, smoothing the fabric that had ridden up around my hips, then lifting the strap back into place. His breathing seemed controlled as he stepped away slightly. His thumb brushed the corner of my mouth, where there must have been a smudge of lipstick. His lips were smeared too. Silently, I followed his touch with the tip of my tongue. He watched me, blinked, dropped his gaze. Another out-breath, then he raised his head again. 'Hungry?'

I laughed. 'You're offering me something to eat? *Now?*'

He shrugged and walked towards the kitchen counter, which was towards the right-hand side of the room. 'My one a.m. pancakes are legendary.'

Watching him, I shook my head. I knew he was stalling, but as long as he was letting me stall with him, that was fine by me. Wiping my throbbing mouth with the back of my hand, I followed him. 'You're going to have to prove it.'

~

Half an hour later, I was staring at a plate of pancakes that did, indeed, look legendary. They tasted it, too. Melted chocolate chips and blueberries mixed into the batter, the perfect blend of sweet and sour.

'No raisins,' I remarked.

'Nope, not this time. Right now I'm kind of in the mood to just like what I like.' He rubbed chocolate from the corner of my mouth, like he'd done with the lipstick.

We were sitting on the sofa about eight inches apart, but I felt as close to him as ever. My toes were nestled in the woollen socks Blake had given me, and he'd put his jumper back on. I looked around. The sofa separated the kitchen area from the living space. Blake followed my gaze across the grey-painted walls and simple wooden picture frames.

'I like black-and-white photography. Black-and-white films, too,' he explained. 'The world inside them is so tidy. Just light and dark, just good and evil. I find it comforting.'

'But you know, black-and-white scenarios are still made up of shades of grey. There's so much in between.' I hesitated, before setting the plate down on the side table and turning to Blake. 'I've been thinking about it a lot this Christmas. That maybe there's no such thing as good and evil, it's all just different sides. To what we think, what we do, what we are, what we experience, what we feel. Like, for years I've been doing everything I can to just get through Christmas without thinking about my mum. But that meant I lost out on so much more than just the memory of her. Things are never one-hundred-per-cent light or one-hundred-per-cent dark. They're always both, and it just depends what we make of it. How we cope with the bad, if we can turn it into something beautiful.'

'Yeah, I know what you mean. Pain is part of that. Of everything. And just because it hurts to lose something, it doesn't mean you should stop looking for that stuff. Otherwise life is nothing more than a string of days and empty moments. It's easier, but it's less real. Less worth living.' He was studying the hands cupped around his mug of tea, lost in one of the reveries that gave his face that familiar absent look.

'You've lost something, too, haven't you?'

He smiled half-heartedly and put the drink aside. 'A lot, actually. I've lost quite a few people in my life, one way or another. I've come to believe that the more often you experience something like that, the more it changes you.'

'You mean, at some point you start to miss the person you were with them just as much as you miss *them*?'

'Does that sound crazy?'

'God, I don't know. But it sounds like what I'm feeling, even if I've never had the guts to put it into words.' When I missed Mum, I was missing myself, as well. The me who could meet someone and get close to them without thinking about what it would feel like to lose them. The me who didn't base every decision on a sober assessment of the trade-offs. The me who was so much better at living in the moment. I knew I'd never get that me back, but the fact that I was here showed me that at least a part of her was still inside me.

'Listen,' I started hesitantly. 'I was talking to Davie earlier, and he made me realise how crazy this is. You know I'm intending to find out the truth about the Starlings. And I know you won't help me, because it isn't what you want. I should hate you. You should hate me. We should absolutely be trying to get each other out of the picture, but when I'm with you, I don't feel that way.'

His arm edged towards me on the back of the sofa, his fingers brushing my shoulder. 'So what are you thinking?'

Nothing, anymore, was the first answer that popped into my head. But that wasn't true. I was thinking, but on a more intuitive level than usual. My thoughts had moved beyond the purely rational. When it came to Blake, they were a mixture of emotion and instinct. 'About ... how I look at you and feel like I know you. And yeah, I get it – you told me once that you can't know someone you've only just met, and that's true, but ... it still feels that way. It's like I recognise you, like I'm recognising a part of myself at the same time. A part I've lost touch with over the last few years. Ever since Mum died I've been trying not to get so emotionally involved with people. Because if they left, it would be too painful. But then I met Zoe. And Davie. And ... you. I know it doesn't make sense, but I think I'm starting to realise that sometimes it doesn't have to. It is what it is. And I like what this is. Just ... it scares me, too.'

'Why?' His face was still dispassionate, but I saw an impulse stirring underneath. I saw it because I was truly seeing *him*.

'Because this thing we have, it doesn't stand a chance, does it? *We* don't stand a chance.'

'No, we don't.' His fingers stroked my shoulder again, and I leant into his touch. 'But that doesn't change how much I want this. I've always wanted it. From the very first moment. No matter how crazy and hopeless and ... impossible it is.' He smiled sadly. 'Does that scare you even more?'

I shook my head. 'To be honest, I'm glad it's not just me. I guess we're both a little bit irrational, Cliff.'

His smile vanished, and he moved his hand away. 'You shouldn't call me that.'

'The look in your eyes says otherwise. It softens when I do, did you realise that? Like you're remembering something. Something beautiful that's gone now.' I was half-guessing, but even as I spoke, I saw that I was right.

Blake's face grew tense at first, like he was trying to draw the curtains, before remembering that with me he didn't have to. 'You're too observant for your own good.' He ran a finger over the scar on his temple. 'Fine. I don't mind you calling me that, but you mustn't. Because I like it *too much*. And because it will get us both into a lot of trouble.' He broke off, but I knew we were thinking the same thing: we were already in it. And I could think of only one thing that would make it easier.

Without stopping to think, I kissed him again. On the mouth, with everything I had, felt and wanted. He responded without hesitation. Gently he cupped my face, letting his fingers run down my neck, stroking the vertebrae, moving downward until he reached the collar of my dress. He lingered over the zip, I could sense it. The hesitation drifting between us. I wanted to dispel it, but he reached for it instead. Burying his face in my hair, he took a deep breath, then raised his head and looked directly into my eyes. 'We should stop.'

Instantly I took my hands off him. 'Okay, I mean, sure, I didn't mean to...' I faltered, because at that moment he was stroking my cheek with his thumb, his eyes on my mouth. The throbbing in me intensified again, and I shrank back uneasily. 'You can't just look at me like that and think it isn't doing things to me.'

'I'm looking at you like this because you're doing the same things to me. It's just ... we can't.'

'Because you don't want to?' I wasn't trying to persuade him, I just wanted to understand. Not everyone was interested in sex, of course, and I wasn't usually someone who rushed into that stuff. If he didn't want to, that was totally fine. But the mixed signals – he did want to, but somehow he couldn't – was deeply confusing.

He laughed hoarsely. 'That's not the problem, trust me. But I can't. It would be ... you have no idea who I am.'

'I think I have a better idea than you realise,' I countered soberly. 'You're just afraid I'm right about what I see in you. Because it doesn't fit with what the others want to see. What *you* want to see. Or think you have to see.'

Blake had drawn back his hands, gazing at them again as if they were a stranger's. 'Trust me,' he murmured. 'If you knew what these hands had done, you wouldn't want them touching you.'

'That's not true. I've told you before: the mistakes you've made don't define your character.' I bit my lip because it was throbbing again. Because *all* of me was throbbing again.

'Anyway, those hands have already touched me. And I liked it. A lot, actually.' My fingertips stroked his arm as if of their own accord, making the delicate hairs rise. And I loved that. I loved that he responded to me the same way I responded to him.

Blake took a deep breath, the muscles in his arm flexing. Just as I thought he was about to bend down towards me, he pulled back, mouth twisted half in amusement and half in despair. 'I can't.'

Again I took my hands away, the throbbing inside me overwhelmed by a rush of guilt. 'I'm sorry, I don't want to pressure you or—'

'You don't have to apologise,' he interrupted gently. 'Everything we've done, I wanted to do it, and I want more, I really do want *everything*, but ... it's impossible.'

'Okay.' I nodded, adjusting my dress. I still wanted to persuade him to change his mind about himself, but you couldn't really talk about stuff like that. 'Do you mind if I stay? I promise you I'll keep my hands off.'

Blake frowned. 'Even though you can't think of any reason except sex why people would want to spend time together?'

I had to laugh. 'Take it as a compliment.'

'I will.' He stretched his arms towards me so that I could nestle in closer to him. My head sank into the hollow at the base of his throat as my mind drifted.

Outside, I saw the splash of fireworks. Gold, silver, red and blue. I thought of the windows at the chapel, and hoped this glimpse behind the curtain would never be shattered.

Maybe Blake was thinking the same thing, because at some point, when I had almost nodded off, he pulled me in more tightly to his chest. 'Ashton can't find out about this.'

'That we're seeing each other?' I asked drowsily.

'It's more the *way* we're seeing each other. He absolutely cannot find out we've got this close. You promise?'

I raised my head and tried to look serious. 'I won't mention it at our daily coffee catch-ups.'

Blake didn't smile. 'It's not funny, Mabel. He can't find out. None of them can.'

'You're actually scared,' I realised, astonished. 'I thought you weren't afraid of anything.'

'I haven't been, not for a long time,' he said softly. I could feel his heart against my skin, beating rapidly. 'But now you're here, and ... that changes everything.'

Perhaps it was the greatest compliment he could give me. If emotions had shadows, then the shadow of attachment was definitely fear. It clung to its heels and could not be shaken off, ever. Even in moments of brightness, when it was invisible, it was still there. I knew that because I was still as afraid as ever. Not of him, but for him.

'But it doesn't really change anything, does it? You're still you, and I'm still me. We're just not on the same side.'

'I'm on your side. More than you know. But that's exactly why I can't give you what you want.'

I rested my head against him, closed my eyes. I didn't have to look at him to know he wasn't going to change his mind. But nor was I. 'Fine, then that's just how it is: I won't give up, and you won't give in. Right?'

Gently he stroked the back of my head, but his voice was hard and resolute. 'Right.'

So simple, so complicated, so utterly impossible, this thing between us. It changed nothing and it changed everything. Perhaps all that remained to us was this. This moment, in a bubble all our own.

CHAPTER 21
MABEL

I ran a sharp eye over the kitchen counter as I shrugged on my coat. Blake said when I was in his flat I acted like a guest at a holiday rental, because I made a point of leaving it tidy when I was here alone. But he must have known it was my way of saying thank you for letting me come here when I needed a change from the library.

My fingers fumbled for the magpie ornament in my pocket. With a shake of the head, Blake had dismissed my attempt to return the Christmas decorations I took down from the tree last week. *Keep them. They mean nothing to my family, and I'd rather know you had them.* It had sounded like goodbye, like so much of what he said to me. Like the way he looked at me sometimes, too. As if he was trying to commit something to memory. Not what he could see, but the whole moment we shared. The quiet moments when I came to his flat and we ate together and watched old films, talked or simply looked at one another, really *seeing*. When he dropped in at the library and kissed me behind the stacks of dusty books. The smell of paper, the low light, whispers, pounding hearts – that was all. When I saw him walk past my staircase while we were on the phone, and he always refused to come up. I didn't know if he was afraid of bumping into Ashton or Zoe, or if he was just afraid of me. Of forgetting why he couldn't do what we both so obviously wanted to. Whatever it was, it always made him pull away from the kiss just as I was getting so turned on I couldn't think straight. The kind of turned on I would never have allowed if I had a choice, because it made my movements jittery, the reactions of my body treacherous, and turned my words to sighs. It was so at odds with the me I expected of myself: rational, prudent, sensible. But it did fit the me who felt so complete since finding Blake, so much more than I had been before – the person I had been since we'd begun to share these moments, which he gathered up with his eyes as if he knew deep down they were finite. So finite they were more end than beginning.

I pushed the thought to the back of my mind as hard as I could. By now I'd had a lot of practice. Just as I was about to head for the door, I heard someone unlocking it from the outside. A moment later it flew open, and a girl barged into the flat. She couldn't be older than fifteen or sixteen, and she looked so strikingly like Blake that I could only stare at her. Her hair was just as thick and dark, her eyes serious in a way that made her seem older than she was. Classic features, and a piercingly sharp gaze that surveyed me warily.

'Hey. You're Aspen, right? Have you come to see your brother?' Blake hadn't mentioned anything to me, but I knew Aspen had a spare key for emergencies.

'No, I just came to grab my riding helmet, I left it here last time. The driver's waiting downstairs.'

She gave me a curious smile, which softened the edges of her face. 'You're the girl my brother was texting all through Christmas, right? I recognise you, Blake's been stalking you on Instagram.'

'Oh... Uh, yeah, that's me. Mabel.'

'You're in his phone as Pica.'

I bit my cheek, holding back a smile. 'He's in mine as Heathcliff.'

'You guys are weird.' She stared at me again, as if trying to see inside me.

At that moment, I realised she loved Blake as much as he loved her. Which only made the idea sprouting at the back of my mind feel even meaner. Over the past two weeks, Blake and I hadn't talked about the League of Starlings, although I couldn't help thinking about it when we were together. This could be my chance to get more information, something that would make it easier for me to mentally separately them from Blake. I took a tentative step towards Aspen. 'Can I ask you something?'

'Sure.' Aspen unwound the scarf from her neck.

'Do you know Blake's friend Ashton Griffin?'

She paused. 'I know the face, yeah. They've been hanging out for like two years. I don't know how they met, but they were inseparable basically from day one. After he finished school, Blake just kind of bummed around for a couple of years. It wasn't until he met Ashton that he applied to Cambridge.'

I frowned. 'He didn't want to go to university before then?'

Aspen hesitated. Wadding the scarf into a ball, she chucked it onto the sofa then plumped down on the armrest. 'Look, don't judge him, okay? Or me, for telling you, but Blake used to be a massive arsehole.' She pulled a face. 'I mean, he was really horrible. Plus he was a total fuck-up – if it hadn't been for Mum and Dad, he'd definitely have been arrested, like, a lot. Drink-driving, breaking into places with his mates from school, getting into fistfights and...' She trailed off.

I was breathing so haltingly that for a moment I couldn't get the question out. 'And what?'

She was frowning. 'Look ... I shouldn't have told you that ... I mean, if Blake hasn't told you himself... It was wrong of me, to—'

'I'm not judging him,' I jumped in. 'Really, it's not like I thought he was some sort of goody-two-shoes.' I smiled reassuringly.

She nodded. 'I get it. A girl wants the intel on her new man.'

I hesitated, then shrugged.

'Okay, I'm not even supposed to know this, but ... just before he left school, he got into serious trouble. This girl in his class made a complaint against him. She accused Blake of...' She paused, and I suddenly didn't want her to keep going. I didn't want to hear it, think it, feel it: it was like she'd punched me in the face. Or reached directly into my mind, the words planting images there I didn't want to see. 'They tried to hide it from me, but I knew what was going on. Blake didn't take any of it seriously, like usual. So Mum and Dad talked to her. I think they gave her money. And if she took it, that means it wasn't true, right?'

It felt like she was telling me about a stranger. It couldn't possibly be *him*. I'd sensed Blake was keeping secrets, dark secrets, but this ... this was so awful I couldn't square it with the person I knew. It couldn't be. It mustn't.

I forced a reassuring smile to my lips, which quivered traitorously. 'Yeah, absolutely.'

Aspen grinned, relieved. 'Well, either way, he was such a dick. And then he met Ashton and ... I don't know, ever since then he's been a different person. He's the best big brother in the world. Even though he lives really far away he's always there when I need him. He's ... yeah, just different, I guess. A lot better.'

'And you think that's down to Ashton's influence?' I asked without giving away my scepticism. Nothing about the person I knew screamed good influence: that Ashton was conceited, spoilt, smug – that was all.

'No idea. All I know is that Blake came home one morning with a cut on his face – where his scar is now.' Aspen put a finger to her temple. 'And from that moment on, he pretty much did a one-eighty. Sometimes I wonder if maybe he hit his head a bit too hard. But if he did, it was the best thing that ever happened to him.'

'So, what's your read on Ashton?'

Aspen wrinkled the tip of her nose. 'I don't see him much. Mum and Dad don't like him. I don't either, to be honest. He's always nice to me, but he seems so ... fake. I don't know. And one time I heard Dad say that Ashton's father came and talked to him because Ashton had changed since he started hanging round with Blake.'

'He became a better person, too?' I pulled an incredulous face. If this was the new and improved Ashton, then what the hell was he like before?

'No, the opposite. His father said Blake was a bad influence. That he barely recognised his own son anymore. He wanted Dad to make Blake stop seeing Ashton. But I mean, how's it possible that they influenced each other in the opposite direction? Like, Blake got nicer and Ashton got meaner the minute they became friends? It makes no sense, right?'

'No, it doesn't,' I murmured, desperately trying to make something coherent out of all these details. *This is madness*, I thought again, but even that didn't feel quite right anymore. Not if there was any truth to what Aspen had just told me.

'Do you like my brother?'

I blinked, trying to focus on her. The answer came from the gut, not from my rattled mind. 'Yes, I do.'

Aspen smiled, more frankly now. 'He likes you too. You know, ever since Blake had his personality transplant, he's looked so sad a lot of the time. But when he's texting you or stalking your photos, it's gone. That's kind of nice, I think.'

It's possible to be happy and to feel like you're bleeding inside at the same time. I couldn't tell where embarrassment ended and uncertainty began, I only knew that my emotions had bared their fangs and were consuming me, the good and the bad, because I wasn't sure anymore which ones I was more ashamed of.

Before I could say anything else, the alarm rang on my phone. I switched it off and gave Aspen a weak smile. 'I've got to go, but it was really nice to meet you.'

She grinned. 'Good to meet you too, Pica.'

Not until I'd reached the hall downstairs did I check my phone. Blake had texted me a picture of a half-eaten pain aux raisins, but I could hardly bear to look. I clicked away from the thread and opened my chat with Davie. Although I'd texted him hours ago, my message was still unread.

MABEL

> Talking to the professor today. Come meet me afterwards? I need to tell you something.

Lectures had started this term and hit the ground running, but Cambridge itself still felt a little sleepy. At least the sun was shining more often these days, gradually melting the thick carpet of snow that had fallen over Christmas. A few ridges of white still clung to the edges of the pavements, and the barren meadows glinted wetly.

At a few minutes to four o'clock, I entered the building where the professor's office was located. As soon as I'd reached the college, I had decided to put what Aspen had told me out of my mind for the time being. Right now I needed to focus on the conversation ahead: over the last couple of weeks, I'd reread all the professor's articles in preparation. I knew he had answers – I just had to ask the right questions. But I also had to accept that I might not immediately understand them. Whatever it was he'd been trying to tell me at the Christmas party, I was at least willing to hear him out.

I checked the room number I'd been given, along with the confirmation of the appointment. As I put my phone away, I noticed I had several missed calls: not from Davie, as I'd expected, but from his friend Cody. I stared at the notification, brow furrowed, but then dismissed it and went upstairs to the second floor. *First things first*, I told myself.

The door to his office was unlocked. I knocked on the frame and pushed the door open far enough to see into the room. A blockish desk, positioned in front of a window with dark green velvet curtains. Behind it stood a petite woman, gathering pieces of paper into a pile.

I cleared my throat and stepped inside. 'Hi, sorry. I've got a meeting with Professor Edwards.'

She looked up at me, her hands still busy on the desk. Her movements seemed nervous, uncontrolled, her eyes darting from me to the cardboard boxed scattered around the room. I caught glimpses of ring binders, books and desk supplies. The professor must have asked a department secretary to help him pack.

'I'm afraid not,' she said in a hollow voice, tossing a stapler into the box beside her.

Confused, I moved further into the room, stopping next to a round meeting table. 'My name is Mabel Golding, I have an appointment, he—'

'Professor Edwards died last night,' she broke in.

Comprehension descended like icy hands around my throat, squeezing. I clutched the back of a chair reflexively, trying to breathe. To understand. My gaze flitted across the chaos in the room, then back to the secretary. My heart was thudding. 'What happened?'

'They found him in the building next door, in the atrium. It seems he fell from one of the balustrades. The police said they found no evidence of foul play.' Her voice cracked, and she fished a tissue from her trouser pocket to blow her nose. It was only then I realised she wasn't emotionless, she was in shock.

And maybe I was, too. Because I knew what she'd just said but it hadn't sunk in. Although I was aware of what that last sentence implied, I refused to contemplate the thought. I knew the building she was referring to: one of Trinity College's crowning jewels, adorned with intricately carved wooden balustrades that overlooked the foyer below. A foyer paved with cool grey stone slabs. Nobody fell over a chest-high railing by accident. You were either pushed or ... you jumped. *No foul play*. Presumably that meant the police thought it was suicide.

I was gripping the wooden backrest so tightly that a splinter lodged in my skin. I barely noticed it – all I could think about was Professor Edwards's voice that night at the Christmas party. *June Owens and Paulina Gallagher.*

It's a pattern, isn't it? I had said.

It's a pattern. I knew that now, and I felt like throwing up. *June Owens and Paulina Gallagher and Garrett Edwards.* This was no accident, and it certainly wasn't a suicide. It was *them*.

I shook my head vehemently. 'But that's ... no. He was just on the verge of retirement, he—'

'That's all I can tell you,' she interrupted in a wavering voice. Her eyes glistened with tears, her cheeks trembled. 'If you don't mind, I've got a lot to do.'

I was barely aware of the walk back to my room. The faces that passed me blurred into featureless planes of red cheeks and blue-tinged noses, the college to a picture book of winter colours.

I felt numb. How was this possible? How could the only person who might have held some answers die just one day before he was supposed to give them to me? And ... if I was right, and the League really did have something to do with it, did that make it my fault? What if they'd found out he was planning to talk to me? But how could they...

I stopped halfway up the staircase to my room. Of course: someone had known. Blake had seen me with him that night, and he'd admitted quite frankly that he knew who Professor Edwards was. What if he'd told Ashton and the rest? What if they'd decided together to make sure we didn't get another conversation? What if...

He wouldn't do that. The thought pressed itself to the surface of my mind, a beacon of hope I clung to because everything else in my head was so dark.

I knew Blake. Not everything about him, but I knew what kind of person he was. He wasn't like Ashton and the others. He had a good soul.

And if you're wrong about him? the doubting voice inside me whispered as I fumbled for my key with trembling hands. *How can you still believe you really know him after what Aspen told you?*

At long last I fit the key into the lock and turned it. Pressed the heels of my hands against my throbbing eyes. I didn't know if I was about to cry, to laugh in despair, or to curl up on the floor and stay there until it all stopped. Until it wasn't real anymore – because it just couldn't be. I felt too little, I felt too much. This was so crazy.

Resolutely I opened my eyes and took a breath. I had to pull myself together. *First get the facts, then interpret them*, as Davie had taught me. The fact was: Professor Edwards was dead. That was awful, but it didn't necessarily mean someone had killed him. I could never know what had been going through his mind, so I couldn't rule out the possibility that he had done it deliberately. Again, Davie's voice shot through my head: *Maybe it's what you want to believe. You're looking for an excuse to like him.*

I wished I could deny it, but I knew it was true. I didn't want to believe that the League had anything to do with his death. Not just because the thought itself was sick, or because it would mean they were more dangerous than I had ever imagined, but most of all because it would mean Blake was involved.

He wouldn't do that.

I had to talk to him. First him, then Davie. As I opened my door, I reached for my phone to call Blake.

It fell to the floor the second I entered my room. A clatter on the wooden flooring that I barely heeded, because the moment that swept over me was louder. Paper sailing with a rustle off my desk, scattered by the beating of wings. The twittering that was not quite drowned out by my hammering heart.

Instinctively I closed the door behind me, although what I really wanted was to run. But I couldn't. This was my room. My clothes over the chair, my books on the table, my notebooks on the floor. My little home, the place where I had always felt safe. Until this moment.

Because even as I stood pressed against the door, letting the scene sink in, I knew one thing: I would never feel safe or protected here again. Not when somebody had been in here and left it like this.

It was filled with birds. Real, live, flapping, chirruping birds, fifty of them, at least. Birds with black beaks and grey-brown feathers speckled with fine white dots. I knew this was their winter plumage, and that by summer they would have exchanged it for something much more splendid. Their feathers would turn black, with a sheen of greens and violets gleaming in the sun. The white flecks would fade, and their beaks would take on an intense hue. They would alter their appearance, just as they could alter their song to mimic other species. Just as they continuously altered the shape of their murmurations in the sky.

I knew this, because they weren't just any birds.

They were starlings.

~

Zoe didn't respond until my third knock. Her soft 'yes' was almost swallowed up by the rushing of my pulse. I opened the door and saw her sitting in bed with her laptop and several books on our reading list.

Under normal circumstances I would have been relieved, because only a few days ago I'd discovered she had missed an essay deadline and had been given a few more days' grace. She had refused my offer to help. She was refusing everything I offered her these days. I'd decided to give her some space, but I couldn't afford to be tactful right now. Not when my palms were still chafed and sore from thirty minutes spent scrubbing the floorboards, having taken just as long to shoo several dozen birds out of my window. I supposed I should have been grateful they were still able to fly. My stomach turned at the thought of the blood I'd seen on the last starling's feathers. Still, it was cold comfort. A dead starling couldn't hurt me. A flock of live ones could.

'Did you let anyone borrow my spare key?' I blurted almost before I'd walked through the door.

Zoe wrinkled her brow. 'Huh?'

'Did you give Ashton my spare key?' I didn't have the energy to put it in a nicer or more neutral way. I knew it was them, I just had to know which one. Whoever it was, they'd obviously gained access somehow, and Zoe was the only person besides me and the college porters who had a key. My uninvited guest must have got it from her.

Or they bribed a porter. Or they've got other ways of getting past locks, like you do.

I narrowed my eyes and focused on Zoe, who was staring at me uncomprehendingly. 'Why would he want that? It's over there somewhere, I think, I'm not sure.' She glanced at the desk, which was piled high as always with stacks of paper from seminars. Then she gazed at me. Her face seemed paler again, her eyes lustreless and dry. 'What's up, anyway? Is it ... you've heard, haven't you?'

I stopped, taken aback. 'About Professor Edwards? Yeah, I—' I broke off. This made no sense. Even if word had already got round about the professor's death, it was unlikely to have reached Zoe. She'd been living in her own little bubble recently, and I could tell by looking at her that she hadn't left the room all day. I knew Zoe. She never went anywhere without at least a slick of mascara. 'Wait, how did you hear about it?'

'I didn't,' she replied, sounding just as baffled. 'I've never even heard that name before.'

'Then what are you talking about?'

'Cody rang, he said he's been trying to get hold of you too. He's Davie's emergency contact.' Her expression grew more serious, but even the concern in her eyes seemed washed-out. As if only shadows of emotion were left to her. The thought frightened me so much I could barely focus on what she was saying.

'Emergency?'

Zoe nodded, pushing her laptop aside. It felt like an outworn reflex, as if she knew she ought to be with me for the next words – only, she couldn't quite recall why that was the right thing to do. She stopped at the edge of the bed, just looking at me. 'Davie's in hospital.'

My stomach knotted again, this time so hard I tasted bile. A gag reflex in my throat, a stabbing pain in my knees. I staggered. 'What, why?'

'I don't know.'

'You didn't ask?'

'I don't think so? I'm not really sure, I'm so tired.'

The words were another kick to the gut. I felt like crumpling. I felt like shaking her. But there was something in her eyes that made it impossible to be angry.

Her face was utterly expressionless. She was the most vibrant, colourful and loyal person I knew, but right now I felt like I was looking at a stranger. The Zoe I knew would never just be sitting around like this while a friend was in hospital. She would be doing whatever she could to find out what had happened, she'd be camped out on the ward to make sure she was there if Davie needed her. She would just ... be there. But she wasn't. She was sitting in front of me, but she wasn't there.

Paulina's words popped into my head. *I feel so empty inside. Like I've already ... disappeared.* At that moment, I understood what she'd meant. There was a surge of emotion, pitch-black, blazing: fear and helplessness, hatred and rage. For whoever had done this to Zoe, however they'd done it. For whoever had put those birds in my room to threaten me. Without meaning to, they'd made it obvious that Professor Edwards's death was no accident.

It took all the strength I had to push the thought of Ashton and his friends to the back of my mind. Before I did anything else, I had to find out what had happened to Davie.

'Which hospital, which ward?'

Zoe blinked and reached for her phone to show me a text from Cody. She didn't offer to come with me, and I didn't ask. Right now, the person I wanted with me didn't exist. The thought tasted bitter but true. Perhaps, in the end, the truth was always bitter. Maybe that was why I couldn't bring myself to pick up when Blake called as I was leaving our staircase.

I couldn't ask every question at once. I couldn't cope with every answer at once. Perhaps I couldn't cope with any answers at all, and I'd cracked under the pressure hours ago. Part of me was sure I must already be unconscious, because every action I took now felt somehow drained of conscious purpose.

All my movements felt like sleepwalking. Which made

sense, frankly, because this whole situation ... it was a nightmare. But this time, somehow, I knew there was no waking up. There was only all-consuming darkness, and with every step, every breath, every thought, I waded deeper in.

CHAPTER 22
MABEL

I had this theory that hospitals triggered a different emotion for everybody, one conditioned by memory. The minute I stepped through the door, a memory and a feeling would leap out of some compartment in my mind, try as I might to hold it shut. Me at fifteen, walking down a white corridor that smelt of disinfectant, bandages and peppermint tea, past rows and rows of closed doors. My aunt at my side, her hand on my shoulder. She was trying to show support, but somehow it felt oppressive. Maybe because I was pretty sure I could read what she was thinking in her eyes. A sense of utter helplessness: that was how hospitals made me feel.

I braced myself against it as the lift came to a halt. There were plenty of reasons why somebody would need to go to hospital. Perhaps Davie had food poisoning, perhaps he'd broken his arm or got appendicitis. Perhaps, no, *definitely*, it was something harmless enough that he'd be out again soon. There was no reason to feel helpless: people came to hospitals because they could be *helped*, because they could be saved. Mum had been the tragic exception, not the rule. *Definitely*.

Cody was sitting in the waiting area, next to one of

the unopenable windows, beyond which was the spreading smoke-blue dusk. Arms resting on his knees, face as white as the walls. A weak smile crossed his face when he saw me, and he stood up to give me a hug before sitting back down. 'I tried to call you.'

'Yeah, I was...' I trailed off, because none of that mattered. Only one thing mattered: 'What about Davie, how's he doing?'

Cody's half-hearted smile faltered, slipping to reveal a broken, grief-stricken look. I couldn't remember ever having seen him that way before. Cody had always seemed so enviably carefree. *It'll all work out, Commander*, he used to say whenever Davie was fretting about something at the paper. As if he had a fundamental faith in the universe that everything would turn out right in the end. Now, though, I could find no trace of it. 'They won't tell me anything, we have to wait for his family. But ... I don't think it's looking good.'

All the reassuring thoughts that had kept me going on the way here evaporated at a single stroke. My knees buckled. 'What happened?' I managed to force out, taking a seat beside him.

'Davie was out on his bike today, and he got into an accident.'

A chill trickled down the back of my neck, and I burrowed more tightly into my scarf, despite the radiator gurgling only a few yards away from us. 'What kind of accident?'

'The official version?' He put on an empty smile. 'He was going around a corner and didn't look properly, and he was hit by a car.'

Those words alone tugged at drawers containing other memories in my head, but I shoved them back. 'And the unofficial version?'

'A couple of twats with more money than sense decided to have themselves a little street race. Two cars were seen just minutes before. Unfortunately, I can't prove that they were the ones who hit Davie. So I shouldn't be going round spreading rumours. Or that's what the police said, anyway, when I tried to tell them.'

I swallowed hard. 'Do you know who they were?'

'They were just here. I've seen them before, at uni. I only caught the name of the guy who hit Davie. After the collisions, he crashed into a building. Died on impact. Victor Mason.'

I let out a sound I didn't understand myself, because yet again I didn't understand *anything*. The facts Cody had given me all felt like questions. Even if I hadn't already known Victor's surname, thanks to Davie's research, I would have realised who he was talking about. Nothing that had happened here was a coincidence. Victor had died after running into Davie. Davie, whom the Starlings knew was investigating them. First the professor, then Davie. I thought of the birds in my room, and my mouth was flooded again with the taste of bile. 'What about the other driver? Did the police arrest him?'

'No, like I said, they're assuming it was a straightforward accident, just two people involved. I mean, they say the investigation is ongoing, but if you ask me, it's a cover-up. They've all been paid off. The police officers, plus the only eyewitness to what led up to the accident. I saw him here earlier, you know, chatting away with those arseholes. Guess they just *happened* to bump into each other.' Cody smiled grimly, knocking back the last dregs of coffee in his paper cup.

I could only guess how many he'd had. He looked so shattered – he must have been in the waiting room for hours. I was ashamed I hadn't come sooner. But I was here now, and I'd do whatever I could to be there for him – to help. 'So who's the witness?'

'Jess Holden. On the same course as me. Nice guy, as it happens. But even nice guys can be bought, I guess. You can bet your arse he's just repeating whatever line they told him.' Cody crumpled up the empty cup. Coffee dripped onto his trousers and my skirt. Neither of us paid any attention to it.

Moments like these pared everything back to its essentials. I was so worried about Davie it stifled all my other feelings. Except the helplessness, which grew with every passing second. Every now and then, the automatic doors opened, people in white coats scurried down the equally white corridors, tinny announcements wafted through the space, and the occasional beam of a car's headlamp glanced through the window.

'Go home, Mabel,' Cody said after a while, laying a hand on my shoulder. Even through the fabric of my jumper, it felt cold, like everything inside me.

'Isn't there anything I can do?' I asked, but immediately regretted it. After all, I thought, maybe that was the problem. I had done too much. Everything that had happened today was my fault. Not just the professor's death but the fact that Davie was lying in one of these rooms. If I hadn't pushed him to keep investigating, if I ... if I'd just been better. I should have looked out for him. Like I should have looked out for Zoe. Now here I was, feeling like I'd lost them both, a long time ago. That was at the core of what hospitals did to me: making me realise I was too late to protect the people I loved.

Cody shook his head, giving my shoulder a squeeze. 'I'll stay until Davie's mum gets here. As soon as I know more, I'll give you and Zoe a call.'

'Better just call me,' I answered automatically, getting to my feet. 'Zoe's—Just call me, okay?'

'Will do.' Cody attempted another smile, but it just looked sad. Hopeless. Maybe that was what hospitals did to him: made him realise that things didn't always turn out all right. Sometimes they just got worse and worse, until eventually they stopped entirely.

∼

The rain set in as I made my way home. Threads of grey like a veil across my eyes as I approached the college. I'd got off the bus a few stops early – I needed the walk. As if that could clear my head. As if anything could clear something so clogged up.

I knew I had a lot to do. First, I had to talk to the police and find out if they were going to follow up the lead Cody had given them. I also had to speak to Zoe and make sure she was okay, although I still found her behaviour as hurtful as it was concerning. And I had to be there for Davie, in any way that I could. But how could I focus on any of it when I didn't even know what was wrong with him?

Again I checked my phone, but Cody still hadn't messaged. My eyes paused over the number in my missed calls. Blake had tried to reach me three times. There could be all sorts of reasons – we'd been in touch every day for two weeks, after all. But I sensed it was no coincidence. He knew about Davie's accident. And I realised also what that meant: he knew how it had happened. Because his friends had something to do with it.

Heart thumping, I put my phone away and turned a corner. The park I was walking through suddenly opened up, the trees giving way to a flat space enclosed by a fence. It took me a second glance to realise it was a football field. And a third to see it wasn't empty.

I jerked to a halt. Even if the floodlights around the edge of the pitch hadn't been on, even if the beam hadn't brought out the threads of gold in his curls, I would have recognised him at once. By his laugh, if nothing else, as it drifted over to me, stirring up a burning hatred.

The situation confirmed all my long-held assumptions about Ashton: here he was, larking around with a bunch of other people on a football pitch, and he was ... happy. Even though a few hours earlier, one of his friends had not just seriously injured somebody, but had died himself. What kind of person acted this way? The answer was obvious: they didn't. He wasn't a person, he was a monster. Maybe that was what Professor Edwards had meant when he talked about the supernatural. Maybe it was the reason he was dead now too. Maybe Ashton really was the root of all the evil spreading like wildfire through Cambridge, through my little world.

I knew it wouldn't help, that I could only make things worse, but I couldn't be reasonable. I couldn't be quiet. Not when everything inside me was screaming loud enough to burst my eardrums open and every shred of my soul, too.

Fists clenched, I left the path and strode through the gate towards them. I saw several small groups, but barely glanced at their faces. I had never been as disgusted by anyone than Ashton in this moment, and it was this repulsion that drew me to him.

Ashton didn't notice me until I was almost on him. There was a brief pause, followed by a broad grin. He broke away from the group and came to meet me. 'Mabel. I wasn't expecting the pleasure of your company tonight. Did Blake invite you?'

I hated him. I hated the way he looked at me, as if he saw through everything, even though he knew nothing whatsoever about me and Blake. The way he said his name, as if marking his territory. The way the phony cordiality of his expression transformed into something darker with every second I stared at him. The way that nothing mattered to him. Not me, not Zoe, not Davie – not even his own friends. I hated him and I wanted to watch him burn. The lot of them. And I wanted to set the fire right now.

'I know what you did,' I said, as calmly as I could. 'I know you made June jump off that roof somehow. I know you did something to Paulina too – and then you made her keep quiet about it. I know you killed Professor Edwards because you found out he'd agreed to talk to me. I know you're responsible for what happened to Davie. And I know you let a whole swarm of birds into my room to warn me off. But you want to know something? You can forget it. I will *never* stop.' I broke off, breathing heavily, staring into his blank face, which was bathed in the wan, rain-smeared glow of the moon. There was a faint twitch at the corners of his eyes, nothing more.

'These are rather wild accusations,' he answered with his usual composure. 'They sound a bit – and please don't take this the wrong way – but they sound a bit *crazy*. Zoe did tell me you tend to get obsessive.' He took a step towards me, lowering his voice. 'We talk about it a lot, you know? She's worried you'll go overboard. That things might end badly. For you.' He raised his hand as if to touch me, but before it reached my throat I slapped it away.

'Threaten me all you want, I don't care.'

'I'm not threatening you. I'm reminding you that you have no proof, and that no one's going to believe some poor girl with a vivid imagination.' Ashton smirked. God, how I was itching to wipe the grin off his face.

Instead, I forced a similar expression to my own lips. I wanted to get a reaction out of him, at least – something that showed me he didn't feel untouchable. Because he wasn't. Nobody was. 'You've got no idea how public opinion works, do you? It's not about *proof*. It's about attention. I'll go running to every talk show in the country if I have to, email every single newspaper, contact every conspiracy blog – and I'll tell them the exact same story, over and over again. It doesn't matter how much of it turns out to be true. I just need enough people to believe it to make life really fucking awkward for you. Can't really have a secret society if the whole country's talking about it, can you?'

'Mmm.' Ashton tilted his head side to side, vertebrae cracking. He said nothing else, only clenched and relaxed his fist, repeatedly. Even though he wasn't touching me, it somehow felt that way. I felt a prickle inside me: a tingling that started just between my ribs, burning unpleasantly as it spread.

I lifted my chin fiercely, trying to ignore the twinge. I felt my muscles cramp, I teetered slightly, then my senses began to blur, my vision.

I squeezed my eyes shut. When I opened them again, Norah was standing next to Ashton. Her red hair was in a braid, her watchful eyes on me. 'Ashton,' she said softly, with an odd note of warning. 'She doesn't belong to you.'

He let out a snarl, but took a step back. As he moved away from me, the panic in my chest subsided, leaving in its place the tender feeling of a sore, an uncomfortable but bearable wound, as if something were scabbing over. Not *on* my body, exactly, more ... inside it.

I still felt nauseous. What I really wanted was to sit down, or at least lean against the fence. Instead, I forced out a snort. 'Seriously? I don't belong to anybody, which is why I can do whatever the hell I want. And believe me, I'll do whatever it takes to bring down the League of Starlings once and for all.'

Ashton's nostrils flared, but he managed to compose his face again into its mocking sneer. 'You seem flustered, my love. Perhaps you need to be prescribed a sedative. There's a good hospital nearby, I could give you a lift?'

And then it happened: something in me short-circuited. I wanted to scream, I wanted to start hitting, but instead I rose up onto my tiptoes and spat in Ashton's face.

He didn't flinch, he only blinked and stared at me. Two, three seconds, then the muscles in his jaw began to churn. He wiped the back of his hand roughly over his cheek and loomed in over me. 'That was a mistake, Moth,' he growled.

The same moment that Norah lunged towards Ashton, somebody wrenched me back. Blake's face appeared before mine – just briefly, then he wrapped an arm around my hips and picked me up. This time I did start hitting, and maybe I even screamed, maybe ... I couldn't tell. All that registered was

Ashton's gaze boring into mine, and Blake's grip, which didn't relax until we had left the pitch.

Once we were on the other side of the fence, he set me back on my feet. 'Mabel, calm down!'

The football field was a blur of gold-tinged green in my peripheral vision, but I was still seeing red. 'Calm down? Davie's in hospital and I don't even know how bad it is! If he'll ever be himself again! And all because your friends are a bunch of megalomaniacs who don't give a shit about anybody else!' My eyes were burning. Maybe I was crying, but everything was itching and throbbing and scratching too badly to focus on that. My face was still wet with rain, but I wished there were more of it. I wished a whole flood would come bursting forth between us. I couldn't bear to look at him. I couldn't bear how pin-sharp his outline was, even in the dark, because all my attention was bent on him. I couldn't bear that I *was* looking at him, that I saw and felt him so clearly and yet had the sudden sense I didn't know him at all. None of this made sense. Who he was didn't make sense with who he was *for me*.

'Victor was also killed in that accident,' he reminded me, his voice subdued.

For a moment, I paused. It was true, of course. Blake had lost a friend today. Only ... why couldn't you see it on him? He looked grave and tense, but not distressed. I knew everybody grieved differently, but Blake didn't even seem upset. There was no sign of shock – in fact he seemed maddeningly self-possessed. The composure in his eyes was as intolerable as the smirk I'd just seen on Ashton's face, because both were testament to the same fact: they couldn't care less that Victor had died.

'Right. And you're all so broken up about it, aren't you? That's why your friends are over there *celebrating* like nothing's happened.' I shook my head in disgust. 'You guys really don't give a shit, do you? How can you act like this?'

Blake was silent for a moment, then he took a step towards me, seeking my gaze. 'I thought you said I wasn't like them.'

I thought so, I wanted to say, but couldn't bring myself to. The past tense would mean acknowledging something I still didn't want to accept: I realised now that I'd been wrong about him. Blake *was* mixed up in this whole desperate nightmare. How could I deny it any longer? Even if he hadn't told the others about my conversation with the professor, it was enough that he was here. With them. Whatever he thought of his friends' actions, as long as he stood by them, he was one of them, and if I tried to convince myself otherwise, I was just lying to myself. And I wasn't a good liar, was I? No matter how much I wished I was right now. It was time for the whole truth.

'I spoke to Aspen,' I blurted.

Blake stared at me, baffled. 'What?'

'She showed up at your flat just as I was leaving. And we talked. About you. About what kind of person you are. And were.' My voice broke, the shards embedding themselves in Blake's cheeks. The muscles in them tensed visibly, and he drew back.

'What did she tell you?'

'You already know,' I said. And now so did I. Aspen had been telling the truth. Including the truth she couldn't admit to herself, because she loved her brother too much. In the end, that was what love did, wasn't it? It stripped you of the power to think rationally. Too see the obvious. You gunked up every mirror you held up to a person with a collage of the thoughts and feelings you wanted to associate with them. You only saw what you wanted to see. What you *had* to see in order to love that person unconditionally.

Nobody was perfect. We all made mistakes, we all had flaws. Mistakes could be one-offs or unintentional, but flaws were inherent in our character. They were inside us, in what we might call ... the soul. We all had them, and they made us human. Yet there were some faults that could not be justified, that could not be shrugged off with an, 'I love you because of your flaws' – or even an, 'I love you despite your flaws'. They were too great, too hideous, too all-consuming. What Aspen had implied was exactly that: a flaw that ran deep into the soul.

My body was on fire, my mind a whirl. I wanted to hug Blake and I wanted to push him away from me, I wanted to scream at him and I wanted to cry, I wanted to ask for his help and I wanted to order him never to look at me again. My head was spinning, my heart was in tatters. How much of it was even real, how much illusion? All those glimpses behind the curtain: were they all a sham? Blake had said they were all too real – but what if that was just another lie? What if everything had been a lie? What if the things Aspen had told me earlier were the first truths I'd ever heard about Blake Ames? It couldn't be. Because if that was the case, then none of what had passed between us meant anything. It had never meant anything.

'Is it true? Did you ... did you do it?'

Blake knew what I was talking about. Of course. His expression closed itself off, like a curtain being drawn. Or opened? Was his aloofness perhaps the most honest thing about him? 'Mabel, you have to—'

'I don't have to do anything! Especially since you still haven't given me an answer.' I took a deep breath and forced myself to lift my chin. *Direct question, direct answer.* 'Did you rape that girl from your class in your final year at school?' My voice was cracking again, but when he didn't answer immediately, I compressed the last of it into another word. A word that sounded as desperate and pleading as I felt. 'Blake?'

He closed his eyes. Three seconds. Then he looked at me steadily. 'Yes.' His gaze was as cold and expressionless as his voice. There was no trace of remorse or self-loathing, not the slightest sign that it even bothered him to admit it. 'Her name was Piper. Not that it matters. She wasn't anything special, and she wasn't the only one. Not the first, not the last. It just proved a little more expensive than usual to buy her silence. Irritating, but not the end of the world. My parents took care of it, same way they take care of everything.'

The words were flippant, edgeless, but they hit me hard across the face. There was acid in my head, in my throat, in my heart. Everything burned. Every tender thought I'd ever had about him, every still-more-tender emotion I'd felt in his presence, they all evaporated. Left in their place were the ragged shreds of an illusion I had so desperately wanted to believe in. An illusion that part of me – a part I hated, yet couldn't suppress – wanted to believe in even now.

'No,' I whispered. *No, no, no.* I wanted to cover my ears, but I could tell from Blake's eyes he wouldn't let me. He would compel the words into my head with all his might, each one a crowbar. He wanted to break something. Me, or just my image of him?

'Do you want to know why I did it? I could tell you. I remember every detail – I think about it every night. The way they felt underneath me. The tension in their muscles, the pointless efforts to resist. As if they could ever have more strength than this body. I remember their tears. Their screams. Their moans.' He grinned, broadly and yet ... emptily. *Soullessly*, I thought. 'It's all still there. It's a part of me.'

'Stop it. You're lying.' My voice was thin, barely audible.

Blake gave a harsh laugh, and I winced. 'I know I said I'm a good liar, but I think this might actually be the first time I've told you the truth.'

'It's not possible.' I could hear how despairing it sounded. 'You're not ... like that.'

Blake raised his eyebrows and hid his hands in his coat pockets, although I could still see they were balled into fists. 'Why? Because I didn't want to sleep with you? Look, I'm sorry if you thought you meant something to me. It's just kind of off-putting when somebody's as needy as you are. You've been trailing around after me ever since we met. Did you seriously think I'd be interested in someone like you?' He came towards me, and I shrank from him until my back was against the fence. 'I was only hanging out with you to do my friends a favour, Mabel,' he explained calmly, his voice as dispassionate as his face. Not the faintest tremor, not the least hint that he felt anything. At least, not for me.

'Ashton wanted Zoe around, and you were getting on his nerves. On *everybody's* nerves. So I kept you busy just to shut you up. And I must say, you didn't really ask for much, did you? I guess when you've been ignored most of your life, you're extra eager to jump at the tiniest scraps of attention. You could call it *sad*, really.' He leant in, bringing his mouth only millimetres from mine. Only then did his lips curl into an artificial smile. 'But I think *pathetic* is the right word.'

Everything in me wanted to believe he was lying. That he was just trying to push me away, for whatever reason. But my rational mind was beginning to accept that this was the very truth I'd suspected from the beginning, the truth I'd been suppressing for weeks. My desire to trust Blake had been so strong that I had staked everything on it, against my better judgement. Now here he was, tearing those illusions into little shreds. Until nothing was left. Absolutely nothing, except this pain, this mix of disgust, hatred, shame, sadness, hurt and rage. It was the simplest calculation in the world: if you bet everything, you stand to lose everything.

'How... *Who are you?*' I whispered.

Blake drew back from me, his shoulders slumping. As if relieved to get it off his chest. 'I did tell you to stay away. That I'm not one of the good ones.'

'But you didn't tell me you were a monster.' I knew there were tears welling up in my eyes, and that he saw them. He just didn't care.

He gave a narrow smile. 'I tried. You just never really listened.'

It was true. I hadn't. But I would never let it happen again. From now on, I would listen only to my head, not my heart. I wouldn't let myself be confused, or distracted from what really mattered. For Zoe. For Davie. For myself. For everybody else who was in mortal danger as long as these people walked free, doing whatever the hell they liked.

'You're right,' I said coolly, though inside I was reeling. 'You are one of them. So I'm including you when I say this: I'm going to end you.'

I tried to walk past him, but he moved to block my path. I stumbled away, shocked, until again I felt the chain link at my back. The words caught in my throat as Blake laid his hand on it. How many times had he done that in the past: grazed his fingertips over my artery, smiling, feeling it pulse faster and faster as he looked at me. So warm, so ... happy. As if this banal sign of life was enough to remind him of the good things in the world. His touch had been gentle, light as a breath of wind. Now, even though he wasn't using much force, it felt completely different: threatening. His thumb on my artery was cold, his eyes burning into my face.

'Don't fuck with us, Mabel,' he growled. 'What happened to your friend is just a taste of what we're capable of.'

'Maybe,' I hissed back, 'but you don't know yet what *I'm* capable of.'

I shoved him off me and ran past. He let me go, watching – I felt his eyes as I rushed away into the unlit park.

A passage from *Wuthering Heights* was racing through my head: *I gave him my heart, and he took and pinched it to death, and flung it back to me. People feel with their hearts, Ellen: and since he has destroyed mine, I have not power to feel for him.* I had never fully understood Catherine, but now, suddenly, I knew exactly what she meant. What she had felt. Nothing.

Blake's words, his open threat, left me unmoved. For the simple reason that I could feel nothing anymore, because there was nothing left. Nothing of what I thought I'd seen in Blake. Or, perhaps, in the most naïve way, what I thought I'd had with him. But that also meant there was nothing now to hold me back. I would destroy Blake Ames. I would destroy the League. No matter what it cost.

CHAPTER 23
CLIFF

I'd never much liked London. Something in the air of the city made me wistful. Change, perhaps. Here, time never stood still, because everything and everybody was constantly in motion. New details appeared every time you blinked, while others disappeared. No moment seemed to want to linger very long, so you never really noticed them enough to remember later. I hated that. If you didn't have memories, then ultimately you were left with nothing. Nobody knew that better than me. Than *us*, to be more precise.

I let my eyes drift upwards to the vaulted ceiling, which reminded me of a church. Probably that was the reason why I'd always liked this place. It was at the heart of the Royal Courts of Justice, and because it was open to the public, it was usually milling with people. By this time of night, however, the building had long since closed. Not that it mattered to us anyway. If we didn't want to be disturbed, we weren't disturbed.

I tried not to think about how many security guards were supposed to be here right now, and definitely not about where they were instead. I stared at the windows with the coats of arms, then the oil paintings hung here and there on the stone walls, until my eyes came to rest on the mosaic floor. It was so newly cleaned that I could just make out my own reflection.

I found the sight of it even less bearable than usual. Closing my eyes, I rubbed the back of my hand over my forehead. It felt warm, like the core of my body, which was throbbing more fiercely than usual. Earlier, before we'd left Cambridge, I went downstairs to the café underneath my flat. It was always crowded in there on Saturday mornings, so I could easily brush unnoticed past enough people that they wouldn't suffer for it later. A slight headache, a drowsiness after lunch – nothing a nap wouldn't cure. I would have preferred to pay Matthew another visit, or someone else like him. But I hadn't wanted to risk going anywhere near the colleges for a solid week, except when I absolutely had to. I didn't trust myself enough not to crack and seek out the one person I had to stay away from.

Although I was pretty sure she wouldn't let me near her anyway. Not now I'd told her the truth. Or half of it, at least. The part that mattered: that made me what I was.

I wasn't surprised to hear she'd spoken to Aspen. Or that Aspen had told her about the incident. My sister didn't believe what her own logical mind was telling her. She loved her brother, but she didn't know everything about him. Even during the hard times, she'd never fully lost faith in me, believing that underneath all my shenanigans lay a heart of gold. A good soul. She'd wanted to believe it, just as Mabel had. For two years I'd been trying to reassure Aspen that her faith was warranted, but I'd had to destroy all trace of it in Mabel. Sometimes, all it took was the truth.

I hadn't lied, although I'd wanted to. Everything I'd told her was true. I remembered every detail, I thought about it every night. The way their bodies had felt, the expression in their eyes, the sounds they'd made – so much panic, so much pain, so much helplessness. And the noises that had come from the mouth I'd used to kiss Mabel, only a few years later. The hands that had touched her, the same hands that had hurt those women in the cruellest ways. Those memories were a part of me. The part that made it impossible for me to look in a mirror without self-loathing. That made it impossible for me to sleep with Mabel, although I'd desperately wanted to.

I had told her one part of the truth – the darkest part, the part I was least able to shake off and which clung stubbornly to my heels. Because every truth had a shadow, and the shadow was where we lived. The fact buried deep within it was this: my body wasn't good enough for Mabel. I wasn't good enough.

'If I see one more twat of a cyclist who thinks they can ring their bell at me I'm going to drown them in the Thames with my bare fucking hands!'

I closed my eyes in resignation before turning around to face Ashton. His steps were crisp and resolute, the echo of them drifting up towards the vaulted ceiling. There was no space so large that Ashton couldn't occupy it if he wanted to. His anger put him at the centre of the hall, so that even the conical lights above us seemed to pool their beams around him. I'd hoped a walk would give him a chance to cool off, but apparently it had done the opposite. Normally Ashton liked London. He loved the crowds of people, the frankness of the city and its inhabitants. Of the tourists, above all, who flocked to the city year-round. Fascination and excitement made people more accessible. But today, not even the wildly beating heart of the capital could cheer him up. For a week now he'd been in such a foul mood that I could hardly stand to be around him. Which, of course, was exactly why I didn't want to leave his side. I knew him well enough to be aware that when he was in that state he often made decisions he came to regret. Decisions we all came to regret.

He stopped in front of me, directly beneath the three arched windows, beyond which was the expansive blue of the London night. 'Still no word. Have you heard anything?'

I shook my head. Ashton and I had been in the conference room earlier that evening, briefing the council on the situation at Cambridge. Well, technically Ashton had done the talking, and more soberly than I was used to from him. Henry's gimlet stare was the only thing really capable of keeping him in check – for as long as it was bearing down on him, at least. As soon as we re-emerged, his temper flared again. That was barely two hours ago. If the council didn't decide soon, it wasn't just London's cylists who were in danger, it was the entire contents of the building.

'I'm sure they'll let us know soon,' I said calmly, although I was growing more anxious by the minute.

I had come here to support Ashton, and to keep tabs on how much information he gave them. But I almost wished I hadn't, because he hadn't just told them about Victor, he'd told them about Mabel, as well. In a way that made it clear what his intentions were. He was good at downplaying things, but even better at making them more dramatic. A couple of times I'd nearly interrupted, but I knew the council well enough to be aware of the consequences of that. Disrespect and disobedience were always punished in the same way. I couldn't help Mabel if I was bleeding to death somewhere.

All I could do was hope that the council members would, as usual, make a more level-headed decision than Ashton was capable of right now. He just snorted and ran a hand through his curls. 'Honestly? Right now I don't give a shit what they say. I want her gone.'

'Since when do we make decisions for personal reasons?'

He took a step towards me, so close that I could feel the heat coming off him. Judging by the warmth of his body, he hadn't been on that walk alone. 'Since that bitch spat in my face.'

I looked at the spot beneath his breastbone, which was

giving off an unpleasantly tangible vibration. 'You shouldn't be so hung up on external appearances, remember?'

Ashton snarled and gave me a shove, hand to my chest. 'Fuck you, *Cliff*.'

'All right, calm down.' I followed him as he began to pace back and forth. If he knocked over one of the statues or attracted any other kind of attention, he wouldn't be the only one to carry the can. 'She's just a harmless girl, no danger to us.' Everything about the words tasted hollow. She wasn't just a girl, and certainly not harmless – she was one of the most headstrong people I'd ever met. And even if she wasn't a danger to us, she was most definitely a danger to me. Had been for a while.

'But you know what she said, don't you?'

Of course. Norah had told me everything that happened before I got there. 'She was upset,' I replied soothingly. 'Her friend's in a coma. Because of us.'

Another weight settled over my shoulders at the thought. I'd tried calling Mabel after the accident but couldn't get through. Maybe she was already starting to doubt me. If she hadn't spoken to Aspen and Ashton first, if she'd just talked to me, things might have turned out differently. Maybe I could have been there for her – properly – and not just by trying to protect her from Ashton.

'I mean, maybe if it was intentional. But we both know it was just bad fucking luck that Vic hit that loser.' Ashton grimaced, staring at the chalk-white statue by the wall.

I stepped casually between him and the statue. 'Yeah, but you can't blame her for assuming otherwise. Plus, it happened right after the professor died. Doesn't take a genius to connect the dots. And Mabel is...' I trailed off, because there were too many possible endings to that sentence, and I wasn't allowed to utter any of them. 'She's very intelligent.'

Ashton gave a grim smile. 'If she was very intelligent she wouldn't have thrown it in my *face* like that, telling me exactly what she planned to do with that information. Now she's not just a danger to us, she's a danger to my own personal project.' Again, he jabbed me in the chest. 'I don't care if you've taken a shine to her.' Another jab. 'I don't care if we agreed not to touch each other's moths without permission.' A third jab. '*I. Don't. Care*. Got it?'

On the fourth jab, I caught his wrist. 'Listen, you—'

But I didn't get any further, because Ashton's phone rang. He jerked his hand away and answered the call. The pounding of my heartbeat was so loud I barely caught what he said over the next few minutes. Yet I understood instantly. I could tell from the way the tension ebbed from his shoulders as he listened to Henry, and by the time he turned back to face me, I knew. There could only be one reason for such a broad grin. One that almost brought me to my knees.

'Well, well, well. Today's looking up,' he announced cheerfully. 'Henry says they agree with me. After Victor's little accident we can't afford to draw any more attention to ourselves. Not even if – and I quote *it's just the rantings of an overzealous bursary student*. I've been given the official go-ahead: I can make sure this problem is taken care of.'

I felt a tremor run through me. It took all my strength to stop it reaching my muscles, and especially my face. Yet I couldn't stop it creeping into my next words. 'We can't do that, it would be much too high-profile.'

Ashton rolled his eyes. 'I'll be careful. There are all sorts of solutions, and Victor's preference isn't necessarily mine. I like to go about things with a bit more style. They'll never even find her.'

I tasted bile on my tongue, and took a step towards him. 'Ashton, you can't—'

'I can and I will!' His eyes flashed in warning. 'As soon as the dust settles and this whole accident thing is forgotten, I'll deal with it myself. You'll have to find a new plaything. Or is there some other reason why you're giving me that look?'

Yes, there was. I couldn't put it into words, but the emotion behind it was so powerful I was willing to do anything, risk anything, sacrifice anything to stop Ashton. But that was the problem: there was no anything. There was only nothing. I could do *nothing* to dissuade him. And even if I could have found some way of convincing him to leave her alone, *they* wouldn't. As of this moment, Mabel was officially what our community referred to – with a faintly mocking undertone – as *fair game*. She was as good as dead. And nothing I said now would change that.

'No,' I made myself say. 'Of course not.'

'Then it's agreed. We're disappearing that cunt. I never want to see her again.' He reached into the breast pocket of his shirt, took out a cigarette and tucked it behind his ear before he turned to go. There was a look of such perverse delight on his face that I preferred not to think about what it said about me that he was one of the people I loved most. Pausing in the middle of the hall, he spread his arms wide and threw back his head, bathing his features in the mingled golden-blue light cast by the lamps inside and out. His next words were spoken with a soft, blissful smile: 'And before that, I want her to suffer.'

Ashton left, and I stayed. Mired in the familiar sluggish sense of helplessness. I knew it well: the numbing realisation that it didn't matter what I wanted. Or *didn't* want.

For years I'd been passive, a piece slid around on the board that was my life. I played by the rules, cheating only when I knew it would go unnoticed. I did as I was told, because in some games, there was no way to give up of your own free will. So I had given up on free will instead.

For the first time in many years, I felt something stirring: the urge to fight back. Not on my own behalf – I'd realised long ago that I had lost. But she hadn't. And I wasn't going to let her lose a game she never should have got dragged into in the first place. I wasn't going to let something happen to her just because she'd been unlucky enough to cross paths with us – to cross paths with *me*.

CHAPTER 24
MABEL

My head was aching as I left my final supervision that afternoon. It had been complete chaos in there for days. I was constantly racing down different alleyways of thought, and every single one felt like a dead end. Davie's condition remained unchanged. According to his mother he had multiple broken bones as well as a traumatic brain injury, which was why the doctors had put him in an induced coma. As soon as he was stable enough, they would take him off the meds and let him wake up. Whether it would actually work, they couldn't say. They also weren't sure if he'd be left with permanent damage, assuming he woke up at all. And if he didn't come out of the coma, then... I was overwhelmed by a stabbing mix of panic and desperation, as always when my thoughts began to spiral into what ifs.

I knew it was pointless. I couldn't help Davie like that. The only real help I could give him was trying to figure out who was actually responsible for what happened. The trouble was, I didn't know where to begin. Normally I'd have talked it over with Davie. But Davie wasn't in any condition to talk. And the professor who might have given me more information to go on was dead. Zoe was still miles away, although I hadn't seen her leave our staircase for days. She was constantly skipping class, leaving her seat unoccupied during lectures and seminars. I often found myself staring at the empty chair, at the pattern of light cast through the windows, which reminded me of the deepening shadows on her face. The last time I'd brought myself to ask her what was wrong, her response had been curt. Apparently she'd been to the GP, but he'd found no medical issue and simply advised more sleep and vitamins. Every now and then she asked about Davie, but as far as I knew she hadn't been to the hospital herself. To me that was decisive proof that there was a lot more going on than a slight vitamin deficiency. Still, I hadn't seen Ashton come round since the day of the accident, although I worried he might be dropping round when I wasn't there. It felt as though there was more than just plasterboard and brick between us – there were hundreds more walls Zoe had built up around herself. I couldn't get through to her anymore, and I didn't understand why. What he was doing to her to make her withdraw from her friends and isolate herself.

My temples pulsed. I pressed both hands to them as I hurried down the stairs. I couldn't let myself wallow in the feelings swimming around at the bottom of all those dead ends, especially because I was facing them alone now. If I didn't try to figure out what was going on, nobody would.

Emerging onto the steps outside, I stopped, took a deep breath, and forced myself to run through my to-do list.

1. Shed some light on how Davie's accident happened.
2. Shed some light on what's wrong with Zoe.
3. Shed some light on what else the League of Starlings is up to at Cambridge.

I just wished someone would tell me how you were

supposed to shed light on anything when you were completely alone, trapped in a clinging, pitch-black darkness.

My fingers stroked the bulge in my coat pocket. I hated that I still carried the magpie around with me. I hated that it brought me comfort, although I knew now it was nothing but a way of manipulating me.

I'd heard nothing from Blake since that night at the sports ground, but I still caught myself every night, checking to see if he'd messaged. To say it had all been a lie. That he was on my side. That he was helping me.

But no message came, of course. Of course – I was alone.

As I turned a corner, I saw someone sitting on a low wall in one of the archways.

The young man had both legs pulled up, his back leaning against one stone column and his feet resting against the other. He had rolled up the sleeves of his woollen jumper to examine his forearms. Even from this distance, I could see the skin was dry and blotchy-red. Judging by the look on his face, it was as painful as it looked. He was obviously in no mood for company, but I went up to him anyway, for the simple reason that I recognised him—even though I'd never met him before. I knew him from the Instagram profile Cody had shown me.

I'd been wondering for days how and where I might be able to track down Jess Holden. I knew I needed to speak to him. Cody had been unable to tell me where he lived, and it seemed too blatant to lie in wait for him after a lecture. I couldn't let this opportunity pass me by.

It wasn't until I'd stopped in front of him that he looked up. 'You're Jess, right?' I asked bluntly.

He cocked his head and surveyed me. I couldn't quite read the expression that flashed in his greenish-brown eyes, unnaturally bright in his winter-pale face. 'I'd like to say I'm not, believe me.' He rolled down his sleeve with a sigh. 'How can I help you?'

I pulled back my shoulders, summoning all the authority I had. 'By telling the truth. About the accident you witnessed ten days ago.'

'I already spoke to the police about that.'

I stifled a contemptuous laugh. The officers had told me the same thing when I tried to explain the truth to them. They thought they'd already got to the bottom of it, because there was only one eyewitness and he had described it as an unfortunate accident. In the end, it didn't matter who was at fault, Davie or Victor. Neither was available for comment.

'You lied,' I replied sharply. 'You said what *they* wanted you to say.'

Jess swung down his legs, which dangled. 'And who are *they*?' he asked with interest.

'You know who. You were seen talking to them on the day of the accident.' I took a deep breath, forcing myself to speak calmly. 'Listen. I have no idea what they told you, but if they threatened you, you have to report it. They're not all-powerful – nobody is. If you go to the police, they'll be able to protect you. They can make sure no one else gets hurt.'

The tip of Jess's nose wrinkled, but I wasn't sure if he was annoyed or amused. 'Who says they threatened me?'

I paused, taken aback. What other reason could there be to lie for a group of unscrupulous bastards like them? What would motivate someone to do such a thing, if not fear? The answer was simple, even if I didn't want to believe it. Power.

'They promised you something,' I realised. 'But ... if this is about money, then it's even more straightforward. It doesn't matter how much they offered you, you can't accept it. Nothing in the world is worth selling your soul for.'

Jess gave a shout of laughter that made me jump, but in seconds my confusion had turned to rage. 'It's not funny! My friend was badly injured. He's in a coma, and we don't know if he's ever going to wake up. We can't let them get away with this.'

Jess ran a hand through his ash-blond, faintly greasy hair, then he drew up one leg and rested his chin on his knee. 'The driver's already been prosecuted. He's dead – that's about as punished as it gets, isn't it? Surely that's enough for you, love?'

'Don't call me that,' I snapped, before forcing myself to take another deep breath. 'And no, it's not. For one thing, I know the driver of the second car involved in the race is still around. No idea if it was Ashton Griffin himself or one of his friends.' *Just don't let it be Blake*, a voice whispered in my mind, and again I hated myself for it. 'Not that it matters – they're all in it together,' I reminded us both firmly. 'And I want them held to account.'

Jess regarded me in silence. The corners of his mouth twitched, and part of me was sure he was suppressing another laugh. Finally, he put his leg back down and leant forward. As he did so, the neck of his moss-green jumper slipped down to reveal his collarbone. On it was a tiny, strangely angular freckle. It took a moment to sink in, because I really hadn't seen it coming. Then the sweat broke out on the back of my neck, and I stepped back. There was a roaring in my ears – that freckle changed everything. Because it wasn't a freckle at all. It wasn't a birthmark or a pigment disorder, and it wasn't a mark left by a pen. It was a tattoo.

Dumbfounded, I looked back at Jess's face. 'That's what they promised you? They'd let you join them?'

He tugged at his collar before jumping down from the wall. His eyes held nothing but irritation. I knew now this conversation was futile. He'd already picked his side. Still, I couldn't just give up.

He tried to push past me, but I blocked his path. 'You can't really want that – those people are sick. They only ever bring bad luck, to the people around them and each other. Trust me.'

I grabbed his arm, and instantly recoiled. Even through the fabric, his skin was so hot it felt like touching a stove. He must have a fever. That would also explain the violet circles under his eyes and the strangely murky look in them. Then there was the smell coming off him, which settled unpleasantly in the pit of my stomach. Underneath the sharp scent of his aftershave lay something musty, almost ... rotten.

I made to pull back, but this time he grabbed my arm and bent over me, so close that his forehead nearly grazed mine. 'You trust *me*,' he hissed into my ear. 'Your curiosity is your greatest enemy, Anna Karenina.'

His breath was warm on my skin, but everything inside me froze to ice. I hadn't thought I'd ever hear those two words spoken to me again. Not when the only person who had ever called me that was dead.

I blinked, but there was no sense to be made of it. 'Wh ... what?'

Jess grinned shallowly and let go. I could still feel his fingers burning into my arm, and the hazy heat he radiated. 'You heard me. Better stop wasting your time. Sometimes you've got less of it than you think.'

The tea was lukewarm by now, but I kept stirring the silver spoon. Speculoos tea: Zoe loved the taste, but I found it too sweet and only drank it because I missed her. Suddenly I was missing everything I'd taken for granted only a few months ago. I'd never spent much time in the common room, but I preferred sitting in one of the red armchairs and looking at the gilt-framed pictures than staring at the wall in my room, wondering what Zoe was doing behind it. From my seat by the window, I could see directly into the court. The ivy-covered walls, the dark wooden doors, the grass that looked golden in the summer light and silver in the winter. My little cosmos, my home, where for the first time I felt utterly alone.

As the door opened and I saw who walked into the room, my tea went down the wrong way, and I started coughing. Nothing about this picture made sense, from the Trinity College crest emblazoned on the scarf he wore, at odds with Trinity Hall's coat of arms on the wall behind him, to the smile that broadened on his lips when he caught sight of me. I took my feet off the seat cushion and set them flat on the ground next to my shoes. Ashton's amused gaze lingered over the pumpkins embroidered onto the grey fabric. I lifted my chin defiantly. The socks were a gift from Zoe, and I loved them for that reason alone – I refused to be embarrassed. Especially in front of him.

'Zoe's probably upstairs,' I informed him coolly.

He sat down on the chair across from me. 'Actually, it's you I wanted to see. I spotted you through the window.'

'Should I be alerting the authorities?'

'Don't be silly.' He chuckled, waving a dismissive hand. Our common room was a bit chaotic, the red fabric clashing with the orange-tinted paint on the wall and the blue carpet. It was almost ridiculous how immaculate Ashton still managed to look even in this environment. 'I'd like to speak to you in private. Do you mind if we go to your room?' he continued affably. Too affably – and I didn't buy a word of it.

'No,' I replied in the same tone, layering on a beaming smile. 'I'm definitely not going anywhere with you where no one else can see us.'

Ashton was still smiling, but I saw his eyes narrow. Patience was not his strong suit. It might have been the only thing we had in common. 'Fine, then just listen to me for a minute, will you. I wasn't very pleasant last time we spoke, I realise that. Which is why I've come: to ask if we can put all that behind us and just get along.'

'And why exactly would you want that? You hate me.'

'Hate is a very strong word. We barely know each other, and I think that's because we've never really had the chance. Which is a terrible shame, given how close Zoe and I are these days.'

Everything he said was true, rationally speaking, but coming out of his mouth it sounded like a lie. Ashton was a selfish bastard. For weeks now he hadn't even bothered to hide how much he disliked me, or how little he really cared about Zoe. The mere mention of her name triggered a fresh wave of fury. 'You're not good for her.'

Ashton sighed. 'You see, this is what I mean. You're not even giving me a chance to show you you're wrong.' He rested his elbows on his thighs, palms innocently upturned. I was still expecting him to pull a knife at any moment. 'I know you think she's down in the dumps right now, and that it's because of me, but has it ever occurred to you that I'm just trying to help? To be there for her, especially now that her best friend isn't?'

Was he serious? Was he really trying to manipulate me in such a stupidly obvious way? It wasn't my fault that Zoe wouldn't let me in. It was *his*. 'I'm always there for her. I'd do anything for her.'

'Then prove it, and give me a chance. Almost everything you think you know about me and my friends is bullshit.' He glanced over his shoulder at two students on their laptops, neither of whom paid us any attention. Still, he lowered his voice. 'We're not some weird conspiracy of serial killers. We're just students. So maybe we're a little imprudent every now and then – we make mistakes, like everybody else. We're not perfect, but we're not monsters.'

I flinched, remembering the last time I'd used that word. I went cold, and I wrapped the knitted cardigan more closely around my chest. 'Blake is. I know what he's done.'

Ashton blinked. His hands balled into fists as he leant back. 'He told you about Piper and the others? That's ... interesting.'

'Not the word I'd choose.' Even now, I couldn't follow the

thought to its logical conclusion. It felt unwieldy, painfully sharp. Every time I tried to force it to the surface of my mind, it tore another hole through my memories of Blake, memories that were still more tender than they should have been. It was stupid: you could hate someone, but it still didn't change the feelings you'd once had for them. Some emotions couldn't be put right. The same was true of mistakes. Maybe that meant emotions more generally were a mistake. The ones I'd had for Blake definitely were.

Ashton looked out of the window, beyond which the college had receded into shadow. At long last he shook his head, as if he'd given up trying to understand something, and shifted his focus back to me. 'Whatever. You shouldn't be hanging out with him anyway. You should be hanging out with me.'

I gave a breathless noise, a snort and laugh rolled into one. Of all the weird shit I'd heard Ashton say, this was by far his most absurd idea yet. 'Why the hell would I do that?'

'To make an unbiased judgement – see if maybe I'm a good guy, after all. Come on, just go for dinner with me. You can ask me all the questions you've been stewing over for weeks, and I promise I'll answer them honestly.' He smiled, gazing at me with those beautiful thick-lashed eyes.

It was strange – his almost angelic looks were so at odds with his personality. Not that I knew all the details of it, of course, but I didn't have to. I'd got the rough gist from the beginning, and that was all I needed to know. He'd brought so much grief to other people, including my best friends. Whatever positive qualities he might have, nothing could outweigh that.

Still, I was loath to turn him down. I'd never really hung out with Ashton alone, and although I was sure he wasn't telling me the truth, sometimes just catching someone in a lie was informative enough in itself. Besides, I was out of leads. I couldn't learn much more about the League from external sources, and Ashton was offering me a last chance to discover more. I had no idea what he was hoping to get out of it, but ultimately what mattered was what *I* got out of it. As long as we stayed somewhere public, he couldn't do anything to me. It was worth a shot.

Slowly I got to my feet. 'Let's get one thing straight: there is absolutely no way I am ever going to sleep with you.'

Ashton laughed warmly, revealing dimples in his cheeks. 'I don't know what you usually do for dinner, but that's not what I had in mind. I just thought we could have an innocent little chat. Let's try to bury the hatchet. For Zoe.'

This is not a good idea, warned a voice inside my head. My gut was screaming at me to listen, but I forced myself to nod. 'Okay. Fine.'

Ashton's smile shifted – fleetingly, almost imperceptibly, in a way I couldn't quite define. Yet my stomach knotted, because my first thought was: *triumphantly*. 'Great. How about tomorrow night? Around eight?'

'All right,' I said, although I felt anything but.

Ashton nodded and rose to leave. 'I'll pick you up.' His hand made a move outwards, towards me. Instinctively I reached for my throat, pressing my fingers to it, although I couldn't have explained why. All I knew was that I wasn't going to let Ashton touch me. In any way, shape or form.

His eyes narrowed, but he stopped and shoved his hands into his trouser pockets. 'Until tomorrow, then. I can hardly wait – just you and me, all evening. A frank, open conversation.'

~

Around nine o'clock I went into the shared kitchen to empty my half-full mug and wash it. Just as I was putting it back on the shelf, I noticed a flicker of something pale on the terrace, and realised suddenly that the door wasn't locked, it was just pushed to. A cold gust of wind shuddered through the loose knit of my cardigan as I opened it. There was someone standing outside. A lone silhouette, just below the dimly glowing bulbs of the fairy lights we'd strung above the tables.

A moment passed before I recognised her. Hurriedly, I slid the door all the way open. 'Zoe? What are you doing out here?'

She turned to me with a bewildered look. 'I don't know,' she whispered as I reached her. 'I feel almost ... nothing. I feel almost nothing.' Slowly she stretched out her arms and examined her hands. She wore no jacket, shoes or socks, just velvet trousers and a woolly jumper. Her hair was coming loose from a straggly bun and her face was bare of make-up, palely radiant in the darkness. 'It's cold, isn't it?' she murmured, running her fingers over her bare forearm, which was covered in goosepimples. 'Why doesn't it feel that way?'

There was such a hard lump in my stomach that it nearly made my knees buckle. 'You've been out here way too long. Your toes are all blue, you're shivering. You need to go inside.' I took her hands and held them. Her skin was like ice, and a chill ran through me.

Zoe was staring at our clasped fingers. 'We love each other, right?'

I nodded firmly, although the question brought tears to my eyes. Even just the idea that she could doubt it hurt more than everything else. 'Of course. You're my best friend. The best I've ever had.'

'And you're mine. I know that, but then why'—she was sobbing dryly now—'why can't I feel it? Why don't I feel like I love you or that you love me? Why don't I feel angry when my mother tells me I've put on weight, or happy when my dad sends me photos of my dog? Why don't I feel scared when Professor Martin says I might fail my exams, or nervous when I have to give a presentation? Why don't I feel *anything* anymore?'

Helplessness was the coldest of all emotions. In seconds it had bitten through me with its icy, crystalline teeth. It was an effort to muster up anything encouraging to say, because I knew it wouldn't fix anything. 'You're not well. But you'll get better, any day now.'

Zoe laughed and sniffled at the same time. Her eyes gleamed, as if her body wanted to cry but didn't know how. 'I don't get what's happening. What am I doing here?'

My mouth went dry when I realised what she was trying to say. That she didn't just mean the patio, she meant ... the world. And it scared me so much I couldn't bring myself to answer. I just pulled her into a hug and held her tightly, as if I could drive away the sense we both had that she was disappearing.

'You're here,' I whispered, hugging her close to me, until her cold seeped into me. Because Zoe loved those hugs, and because I desperately wanted to remind her of that. To remind her of the things she loved and hated, of who she was. 'You're here, and you're you. And we'll get through this. Trust me.'

'You promise?' Her voice trickled into my hair, her scent into my clothing. Her scent, which was different than normal. Less intense, less sweet, less ... Zoe. There was just less Zoe there.

'I promise,' I replied. 'Whatever it takes. I'll make sure you get better.'

I stayed in her room that night. Put a hot-water bottle at her feet and read to her until she fell asleep. Then I sat beside her, watching her chest rise and fall with reassuring evenness. The candles on the bedside table cast shadows across walls dotted with polaroids, snapshots of countless memories. The laughing girl in them seemed to have little in common with the one slumped next to me on the pastel-blue sheets. At that moment I didn't care what the League of Starlings was, or what it did. All that mattered was what Ashton had done to Zoe. Whatever it was, I would figure out a way to help her. I had to try. *For Zoe*.

CHAPTER 25
MABEL

Of all the things I'd done over the last few months – some of them of dubious legality, or which at least broke all the rules I'd set for myself – this felt by far the most dangerous.

Stopping outside the main door, I checked the pockets of my coat for the hundredth time. I didn't want to risk pressing record on my phone. If Blake had sussed it immediately, Ashton probably would too. Better to make nice with him for a while before I got down to the important questions. And that meant letting the evening begin the way he wanted. Whatever that was.

With a deep breath, I reached for the handle and opened the door. After Ashton's visit yesterday, part of me had been expecting him not to show up. I'd assumed even he would realise how ridiculous this was. But as I came outside, I saw him: standing in the middle of the grass, dressed in pale clothing, so that he was visible immediately even in the dusk.

His coat was open, his college scarf wound loosely around his neck. He smiled as I walked up and gave him a subdued greeting. 'Fancy a stroll before we go to dinner? There's a stall that sells mulled wine just outside Trinity College. We could grab some and wander around for a bit.'

My first impulse was to walk straight back the way I'd come. The thought of him somehow directing us to an area that was deserted was unnerving. There were always people around the college in the evenings, but still, Ashton would no doubt have figured out somewhere 'suitable'.

'The non-alcoholic kind. And I'll get it.'

I saw Ashton suppress a grin, and he gestured for me to lead on. 'I expected nothing less.'

Snow began to drift down as we left the stall and set off through Trinity Hall. Forgotten Christmas lights still hung between the trees that lined the paths, and the buildings glittered in the hazy moonlight. Every now and then, we passed students bundled up in winter jackets and woolly scarves that hid their faces.

Ashton was much better at small talk than I was. He asked me questions and filled gaps in the conversation with anecdotes about the university and its history, which I would probably have found interesting if I hadn't been so focused on watching his behaviour rather than on his words. But ... there wasn't anything. He seemed genuinely normal: open, friendly, obliging. Which was precisely why I grew uneasier by the minute.

We reached the Bridge of Sighs, the most beautiful bridge in the whole university. St John's College had been founded in 1511, but in the nineteenth century the grounds were expanded to the west side of the river, and a bridge was built to connect the older areas with the new. Today, the covered bridge, built in a Victorian Gothic style, was one of Cambridge's most famous landmarks. Pretty much every punting tour passed beneath it on the Cam, and by day the bridge itself was thronged with students and tourists alike.

Now, in the gloom of a January evening, it, too, felt deserted, although there were at least lights on in the building we passed through to reach it, and the bridge itself was also lit, colouring the stone a warm ochre that was mirrored in the river.

Ashton stopped by the archway at the midpoint, looking out through the gaps in the metal grille. From here you could see the banks of the Cam, and more bridges. Barren meadows, bare, low-hanging branches, wan tracks that petered out into nothingness. The bridge itself opened on both sides onto colonnaded walkways that led to more college buildings and courtyards. I knew what a beautiful place it was, but right now I could only think how lonely it all felt.

'This has always been my favourite spot, out of everywhere in the whole university,' Ashton said after a moment of silence.

'I never thought I'd hear you say anything so clichéd.' I moved closer to him. The bridge was fully enclosed, after all – he couldn't throw me over the edge. 'You know this was Queen Victoria's favourite spot, too.'

He turned to face me, leaning his shoulder against the bars. 'It was named after a bridge in Venice, did you know that?'

I nodded, folding my arms. One look at the deep black water below me and I felt it tugging at my feet. 'They're not very similar, though, architecturally speaking. Except that they're both covered. And I also know that some people say it's only called the Bridge of Sighs because students crossing it think of their upcoming exams and sigh in frustration. And that – twice – students have floated a car underneath it using lashed-together punts and hoisted it up to dangle from the bridge.' At moments like this, I understood why people called me a know-it-all. But the truth was, stating facts kept the gnawing unease at bay. I didn't say things like this to impress other people, I said them to keep myself together, to stop myself from crumbling and losing focus.

Ashton raised his eyebrows appreciatively. '1963 and 1968, to be precise. You really do know a lot about this university.'

I took a step back, away from the balustrade and from him. 'Not everything.'

'No, definitely not everything.' He smirked and took a sip of punch. 'I think what I've always liked so much about this bridge is that it shares its name with something else yet it's totally unique. Makes me believe in individuality, even though this world does its very best to grind down its inhabitants and make them all alike.'

'And I thought you considered yourself a one-off.' I couldn't resist the note of mockery.

Ashton sighed, leaning back against the wall. 'You really don't trust me an inch, do you?'

'Did you think telling me something personal would change that?'

'No, probably not. I'm just trying to get to know you.' Ashton sipped again at his mulled wine. The berries darkened his lips, but his eyes were still bright and friendly. 'I'm sure we must have *something* in common, if we look hard enough.'

'Like what?'

'Let me think.' He grinned softly, the expression at odds with his next words. 'Like a dead mum. Mine died ages ago. How and when did yours die?'

I tilted my head, confused, and the pearls on my hairpin cast a speckled light across our faces. Very briefly I thought of Blake, of the tiny moonspots on the bridge of his nose. I screwed up my eyes until the memory faded. 'Car accident. I was fourteen.' I shook my head. 'But if that's all we have in common, I'm not sure it's a very promising start.'

'Why not? That stuff has a huge impact. The early losses in our lives are the worst. The first time you lose someone in such a final way, it's a sharp lesson in how much pain you're capable of feeling. It's fascinating and also terrifying how powerful the mind is. How badly emotional pain can wound you. More intensely and lastingly than the physical kind ever could.' He sounded more grave than usual, calmer somehow. As if the words came straight from the windless depths of his heart. Although I hadn't meant to, I began to let my guard down. This was the first time I'd seen an emotion in Ashton that felt entirely real. I hadn't expected it to be sadness, of all things. 'Who else have you lost, besides her?'

He was quiet, gazing into his cup. Then he lifted it abruptly and downed its contents. 'Lots of people.' He wiped his mouth and then the fake smile was back. 'At some point I lost count.'

'I'm sorry.' I didn't have to lie, whatever I might think of Ashton. I knew how much that kind of pain could change a person, and at that moment I found myself wondering reluctantly how much of Ashton's manner was shaped by it. Who he would have been if he could have answered 'no one', like you'd hope most people our age could. Like you'd hope anyone could.

'Don't be.' He set the cup down on the ground. 'Once you get over it, you realise you can get through anything life throws at you. Those things aren't important. They don't mean anything.'

'And by "things" you mean emotions like ... love?'

He gave me a pitying look. 'Love is an illusion. Something people want to believe in because they're afraid of being lonely. But in the end, we all are.'

'Is that why you joined the society? To be less lonely?'

'Loneliness isn't the same as being alone. Haven't you ever seen that printed on a postcard?' He winked at me in amusement. 'It doesn't matter how many people you surround yourself with, it doesn't change anything. It's just that there's advantages to not going it completely alone.'

'So all of your relationships have some kind of utility? Even your relationship with Blake?'

Ashton shook his head, his eyes softening. 'It's different with Blake. Nothing about us is temporary – we're bound together, forever. What we share goes beyond any relationship.

Let's call us ... soulmates.' He was grinning wryly, but the word still sounded earnest. He meant it. He did love Blake. Just as Blake loved Ashton – he'd told me so himself. Love was one of those emotions that usually cast everybody in a flattering light, but now it struck an odd note.

'For someone who doesn't believe in love, that's a pretty romantic word to use.'

He raised his hands, laughing, fingers sticky with mulled wine. I thought of bird's blood, and shifted back a little. 'You got me. Don't tell him.'

'I don't plan on ever talking to him again.'

He shook his head slowly. 'Okay, but surely you can see that what he did is a sign that he has feelings for you. A pretty foolish, hopeless sign, sure, but you should definitely take it as a compliment. I can't remember him ever rebelling like that before. And definitely not over a girl.'

I stared at him, perplexed. This conversation was taking a turn I couldn't make sense of. At all. 'That's ridiculous. He lied to me. He used me. How is that having feelings for me?'

'He was trying to protect you by keeping you away from us.' Ashton took a step towards me. 'By keeping you away from me, to be more specific.'

My heart skipped two beats, then instantly began to race. I felt a tingling at the nape of my neck, but forced myself not to back down. The bridge was narrow. I sensed the metal bars behind me, only centimetres away. 'What are you trying to say?'

Ashton hesitated. His eyes searched the empty archways at either end of the bridge, then snapped back to my tense face. He studied me briefly, then sighed. 'I had other plans for this, but maybe I don't need to bother.' In a flash his gaze turned dark and smooth. 'What I'm saying is that you get on my nerves, Mabel. You really fucking get on my nerves – and I'm reaching the end of my patience.'

I wasn't surprised, but I didn't understand why he'd gone

through this whole performance when we both knew what was at the bottom of it. 'Then why did you drag me out here? If you're so sure I can't do anything to hurt you, you could have just left me alone. You'd never have to see me again.'

I heard footsteps somehere beyond the bridge, echoing hollowly down the covered walkway. Ashton's eyes darted towards the sound, but besides a shadow flitting past, we remained alone. 'Let's just say that my relationship with finality is different from other people's,' he said, when the shadow had gone. 'There are enough commas in my life already, so I prefer to put full stops wherever possible.'

'Then don't talk to me in question marks,' I hissed. 'What does that actually mean?'

'What do you think it means?'

The answer was so trite that my brain refused to think it: the most effective way to put a full stop was to end a life. The cleanest cut, the ultimate conclusion.

I found myself recoiling, and promptly bumped into the bridge. Although I'd spent weeks thinking the worst of the Starlings, turning the possibilities over in my mind, they had never coalesced into a feeling. But they did now. And it was cold and clammy and spreading at unpleasant speed throughout my body.

'So it's true,' I blurted hoarsely. 'You killed June. And the professor. And you tried to kill Paulina and Davie as well.'

Ashton put his hands into his coat pockets and moved slowly towards me. 'Yes, yes, yes and no. Believe it or not, what happened to your friend was a regrettable and ironically coincidental accident.'

'And the others?'

'Well ... Victor overestimated June's ability to resist, so in a way that was unintentional too. Jack wanted to get rid of Paulina, and Victor egged him on to choose the most effective route. That was ... ill-considered. Impulsive. And the professor, well, that's on you, I'm afraid. He'd been on our radar for years, but he wasn't a threat. We knew he'd keep his mouth shut. Until you came along. There's something about you that makes people disregard their own safety. Maybe that's why bad things tend to happen to the people around you, have you ever considered that?'

My mind reeled as I tried to process the barrage of information. But how could they have done it so quickly? How could they have done it at all? It was crazy. It was ... sick. But as I looked at Ashton now, I realised I didn't doubt for a second that he was capable of it. 'It was you. You killed him.'

Ashton ran both hands through his curls, pushing them back from his face. In the dim light I saw an unfamiliar edge to his soft features, and the look in his eyes was both amused and exasperated. 'It doesn't matter which of us made him jump off that balustrade. With us there is no I or you, there's only we.'

'But ... how did you do it? How did you make them want to take their own lives?' Blake had sworn to me Victor hadn't done anything to June, and although I had no reason to believe him, I did – about that, at least. And even if he had lied to me, what could they possibly have done to Professor Edwards to make him kill himself when he'd only been back in Cambridge a day?

Ashton sighed, audibly impatient.

'It's tricky to explain, and anyway, it's beyond the scope of this conversation. Let's just say that ... a soul is made up of energy. It's like we've all got this sort of vessel inside us, just brimming over with waves. When you siphon some of that off, every bit of it takes away a nuance of the individual's personality. Their beliefs, their traumas and fears, their character – everything fades. Their very will begins to fray. It varies from person to person, but generally speaking, the more energy you take from someone the easier they are to manipulate. Once you lose enough of it, you don't really know anymore who you are or what you want. It's a relief when someone tells you what to do. So if you order someone like that to jump over a railing or off a roof, they don't hesitate.'

The words rolled off his tongue, like he'd learnt them all by rote or used them many times before. It was by far the most insane thing I'd ever heard. What did you have to do to someone to take a part of their *soul*?

'I don't understand. What did you actually do to them?'

He tutted, closing more of the distance between us. 'I just answered that question. You just don't want to understand, because you've spent your whole life thinking in the patterns that have been laid out for you, and now you can't stop.'

He paused, still a step's length away from me: an eloquent look, a jeering smile. I almost laughed when I realised he wasn't speaking in metaphors. The image he had used was, for him, a mirror of the truth.

I let out a breathless sound. 'You're serious? You think you can get into other people's souls and ... drain their energy? And you're saying that's what you're doing with Zoe?'

Ashton's lips twisted into a look of mock contrition. 'I admit, I've bent the rules with her a little. We're not really supposed to feed on any one moth for too long. Gets a bit dicey – you might burn them so badly they just drop dead. But Zoe is exceptionally strong. Anybody else would have died ages ago, the amount of energy I've been draining from her over this span of time.'

Impulsively, I moved towards him, until our bodies were almost touching. 'She is dying. She's almost gone.'

'Hmm. I suppose I have been overdoing it a bit lately. Your fault again.' He raised a hand and stroked my hair, so fleetingly that I couldn't tell if he had actually touched me. 'I can get a bit tetchy when someone's trying my patience. Zoe was just a way of making up for it. If it's any consolation, I'l keep my hands off her from now on. After tonight, I can't afford any more involvement with your social circle. It would raise too many questions.'

I didn't fail to notice the threat in his words, but all I could think about was Zoe. For months, Ashton had been the centre of her emotional life. She had readily made excuses for him every time he let her down, saw depth in every word he said, no matter how shallow, spun rose-tinted magic out of every meaningless moment. She had been sure he liked her just as much as she liked him. She was *in love* with him, and he had deliberately exploited that, while feeling nothing remotely comparable in return. While feeling nothing for her *at all*.

'You couldn't care less about her, could you?'

Ashton laughed softly, and for a fleeting moment I hoped he would deny it. Despite everything I knew about him, despite all I'd just learnt, I would have preferred to know that even a psychopath like him had feelings for her than to have it confirmed he didn't give a shit.

'Of course not. We couldn't care less about any of you, Mabel.'

And just like that, the last trace of hope I'd had in him was gone. Right from the start, Ashton had struck me as unnatural, like an over-elaborate, perfect image of a human being. An artifically created construct designed to put forward an illusion that adapted to other people's desires. A fake smile instead of a filter, charm instead of Photoshop. Blake may have been a liar, but Ashton was an actor. Someone who could slip on personalities like masks. But this, this was his true face.

Ashton sighed. 'Don't look at me like that. I'm not crazy, I'm just honest. That's what you wanted.'

'And why are you being honest? Why are you confessing to multiple murders?'

The corners of his mouth lifted. 'Oh, come on. Don't disappoint me.'

I'd read enough thrillers to know what he was implying. Even so, it was an effort of will to say it out loud. It was just so absurd. I was twenty years old, an ordinary student at an elite British university. I was standing in front of an educated, affluent young man my own age – with a friendly smile and nails that were better manicured than mine. And yet the truth lurking in his eyes was this: 'You're saying I won't get the chance to tell anybody. You don't want to have dinner with me. You want to kill me.'

'Blake was right. You really are very intelligent.' Ashton cocked his head, and the light from the lamp behind him dazzled me.

I lifted my chin. Whoever he thought he was, I was still me, and I was in control over how this played out. 'Then let me make one thing clear: you will never get me to jump off a bridge or a roof or even a table. I will never do what you tell me.'

'I will admit you're tough to get at. Some people lock their souls away in little cages, you know. Not brittle little walls of glass, but metal and concrete. Tough to break open. We all sensed immediately what a challenge you would be.' He tapped at the hollow of my throat, which was bared between my scarf and the collar of my jumper. 'Shall I tell you something interesting? You made those walls thinner for one of us. Being around Blake made you open up. That's why he had such an easy time with you. Easier than I'll have, and tonight hasn't done anything to change that.' He let out a noise of resignation. 'But, oh well. I'm strong. Stronger than you, that's for sure.'

I struggled to take what Ashton was saying seriously, but at the same time, nothing about him suggested he was joking. I went hot, then cold, when I realised what that meant.

I was on a bridge in an empty corner of the university, alone with a man who had just announced he was going to kill me. Beyond the flickering lamplight, the world around us was bathed in the colours of night, a painting in shades of blackish-blue and shadow. The sky was starless, the water beneath us clouded and murky, and the cold came creeping towards me through the metal bars on either side. It pinched at my calves through my tights, as if trying to make me run. Yet I couldn't even bring myself to move aside.

'You're completely out of your mind,' I blurted. 'You can't seriously think that's true. That you can make me do whatever you want.'

'Of course I can. And I'm not just going to make you jump. That would be far too quick.' Again, he leant in, this time so far that the tip of his nose almost brushed mine. Despite the cold, it wasn't red. Traces of mulled wine lingered at the corners of his mouth. 'I want you to suffer while you lose everything, so I'm going to really take my time. Only then will I take the final piece of your soul, so that nothing will be left of you once you finally fade.' His voice grew quieter with every word, until it died away completely. Its waves lapped against my face. They were ice water. I shivered.

'You're sick,' I whispered.

A smile played around his mouth. 'I'm powerful. Sometimes it's easy to get those things confused.'

My heart hammered in my chest, but I didn't move. Part of me sensed that Ashton was waiting for the fear to take over. That was why he'd sown the seeds of it inside me instead of just doing what he was going to do. He was enjoying this. He wanted to see me afraid. And although I knew I should be, my mind refused to fully yield. Every ounce of pride and self-control I had was tearing it up at the roots. Not all of it, but some. And that was all it took. Too much fear was paralysing. But a little of it awoke the urge to act. To fight back.

My hand closed more tightly around the cup, as liquid spilt over the rim. 'So this is where the nice part of the evening ends, is it?'

'This is where everything ends, Mabel,' Ashton replied, his voice still friendly.

I nodded. 'Okay.' Then I flicked my wrist.

Ashton didn't cry out. Even now, I couldn't get anything deep or genuine out of him. But the cooling mulled wine hit him square in the face, and within seconds it was in his eyes, in the curls that hung down over his forehead, in the fabric of his jumper. His whole upper body was drenched in berry blood, but he only gasped under his breath and took two steps back. Still, it was enough.

I dropped the cup, turned, and then ... and then I ran. The moment pooled, thick and obscure, as if someone had poured tar into it. The cold wall beneath my fingers as I sprinted off the bridge towards the walkway. Warm brown around me, inside a stinging red. My pulse was unsteady and my vision went in and out as my heart boomed in my ears and in my head. I saw the expanse of Third Court before me: paved paths, squares of scant, wintry grass. Only a few yards, then I was in Second Court. My eyes swept across the brick walls of the enclosing buildings, the mullioned windows, the towers with their pattern of white stones. Lights were on in some of the windows, but there was no one to be seen anywhere. All I could hear was the echo of my footsteps and my own panting breaths. My lungs were burning, there was a stitch in my side and between my ribs, but I forced myself to run faster.

I could see the passage leading to the next court, a dark tunnel, and beyond that a glimpse of the court itself. From there it wasn't far to the main gate and the city centre: well-lit streets full of restaurants and other people. Rescue, safety, protection. I could already see it all before me, a bright glimmer in the distance, when it happened.

Midway through the passage I felt such a pressure in my chest that I nearly tripped over my own feet. It felt like somebody was using a crowbar inside me, prising me violently apart. I fought it, but I was too weak. Something in me gave way and exploded. Next came a thousand pinpricks boring in between my ribs, and then a terrible burning. I gasped, staggering into the wall next to me and clutching my chest. Seconds later, it was on fire. I felt tongues of flame licking at me from the inside, spreading to all my senses. I was sick and dizzy at the same time, and every time I tried to run, I stumbled again.

What was that?

I was so busy trying to locate the source of the burning sensation that I didn't hear the voice until it was already next to me. 'Not very nice of you, Mabel.'

The taunt reached me only faintly. The pain had now acquired a sound, a buzzing in my ears. I pressed my hands to them, then to my chest again, where everything was on fire. I let out a whimper, my body sliding down the wall as the feeling chewed through all my muscles. Through *me*. All my thoughts, all my instincts, all my reflexes, all my emotions. I was coming apart, and I could do nothing to stop it. No. *No, no, no.* I forced myself to push back with all my might, heaping my strength on the flames, bracing my mind against the pressure threatening to tear me apart. *I. Will. Not. Give. Up.*

A panting breath reached my ears, but I wasn't sure if it was mine until I heard his voice again. Barely more than an exasperated growl. 'You could have made this less taxing for both of us if you'd just opened up to me a little. But no, you've got to be so fucking suspicious. I'm genuinely curious: what was it about Blake that made you more tractable with him?'

Ashton was standing next to me. I sensed his presence like a cold, damp cloth, but I wasn't able to look up at him. Even with my eyes closed, everything was spinning. The darkness was giving way to memories, which began to spill out. The pain was dragging out of me everything I'd kept pent up over the last few months: the worry, the unease, the nervous curiosity, the clammy fear. All the dark, but also all the light. All the ... beauty. Memories of Zoe before she slipped away from me, of Davie before I almost lost him, of Heathcliff before I'd realised he was only ever Blake. Of him, especially, and for the first time, I fully embraced the feeling that came with them. With him. I had always known that falling in love could be disastrous, but now I realised how dangerous it truly was. Because it had brought me here. To the brink of the darkest abyss I'd ever glimpsed: the one yawning inside myself.

I gasped, whimpered, cried soundlessly, did everything I could to keep my mind away from the edge. To cling to my own will, because I could sense it slipping further through my fingers with every passing second.

Ashton had squatted down in front of me, but I didn't notice until I felt his breath on my face. 'You stupid, stubborn girl.' He took my head in his hands, wiping my damp cheeks. I barely felt it – my skin seemed wrapped in cotton wool, like Ashton's voice as it slunk into my ears. 'Just let go.'

I wanted to say *no*. I wanted to scream it, lash out at him, fight, defend myself and ... my mind reeled, my muscles went limp.

I felt my face resting in his hands, because I no longer had the strength to hold up my head. Because I had no strength at all. Because everything was pointless, exhausting, futile. Because I didn't stand a chance anyway. Because I couldn't do it anymore. I didn't want to keep fighting. I didn't want anything anymore. Just for it to stop. Maybe ... forever.

'There, finally.' Ashton's voice grew softer, almost tender, like his touch on my cheek. I felt the tips of his fingers glowing on my skin, and realised it wasn't his heat. It was mine. I felt it: warmth seeping out of me, drawing the energy in its wake. My will, my strength, my ... soul?

My head slumped back against the wall. Ashton's hand slid under the scarf to my neck, where the artery thrummed wearily. He sighed. The sound was gentle, satisfied, yet he was pushing me relentlessly towards the abyss. I stumbled, my muscles twitching, my hand fumbling at his. He was burning; I was cold. My fingers dropped. And I tumbled ... into myself. Sometimes falling felt like floating, sometimes like endless impact. This kind was almost unbearably soft, like plunging through cloud, and for some strange reason I could not name, I knew the landing would be all the more brutal. But I didn't care, because I didn't care about anything. Because I was disappearing, in the quietest, most gossamer way. Second by second, breath by breath, I was dissolving. My body grew heavy and numb, until I felt nothing anymore: not the cold stone beneath and behind me, not the icy January wind that engulfed me, not the hands holding my head and stroking my throat, not my artery, which still throbbed lethargically.

There was nothing left, nothing, only ... a voice. 'Get back – now!'

I was almost sure I was dreaming it. Except that this dream felt more like waking up. The cotton wool inside me dissipated, so that the pressure returned. Fingertips gouging between my ribs – not from outside, but as though a hand were rooting around inside me. I let out a gasp of air, realising that if I could still do that, then I must be breathing. Which should have been a good thing, except that all I felt was how much it hurt. Every breath was agony, as if my lungs were on fire. Or the air. Or my chest. Or ... everything.

'Not her, Ashton.'

I knew that voice. I liked that voice. Maybe I even loved that voice. Maybe I didn't want to, and yet I was thankful for it, because it reminded me that I was capable of it: love. *And hate*, I thought, as the other voice responded. Close by, just as deep, warning and ... angry. 'That's not for you to decide.'

'Yes, it is. This time, it is. I've called the porters – they'll be here any minute now.'

'Are you serious?'

'Dead serious. You know I love you, but if you don't let go of her right now and get out of here, I'm going to hurt you. In every way you can think of. You know I can. So don't push me.'

Silence, the pressure inside me building until I felt like screaming. I let out a murmur, that was all, and then ... it was over. The pressure eased, the hand withdrew.

A gust of wind on my face, my lolling head. My eyes tried to open, but the lids were weighted with stones. My darkness circulated, not black now but a deep and lightless brown that somehow still seemed light. Warm. Protective.

There were more words, but they were drowned in the sea of pain inside me, the waves reluctant to calm. I was vaguely aware of more hands cradling my face. Cooler hands, gentler hands. And then that voice again, so close that I could feel it on my skin. 'Pica.'

I smiled inside, but the corners of my mouth didn't lift, because my mind was slipping away once more. Again, the sense of falling, but this time I felt no fear. Because my last thought was that there was someone there to catch me.

CHAPTER 26
MABEL

From one darkness to the next. The thought flashed through my mind as I blinked. Close to my face was dark green, a slant of light dancing across it, moving swiftly towards me. It was dazzling, and I squinted. Just a few seconds, then the light had moved on. With it went the sound of an engine, reaching me from far away.

I rolled my head towards the window with an effort. The curtains weren't fully closed, and the colours of the street were cast into the room. Car headlights, lampposts, traffic-light red. The different shades swirled unpleasantly in my brain. I pressed my hands to my throbbing eyes, trying to remember. Where was I?

My thoughts felt soft, deformed somehow, as if still marked by someone else's fingers. Maybe because I could still feel that alien hand so clearly in my chest.

I sat up with a jolt, but immediately regretted it as a sharp pain burst through my temples and between my ribs. Panting, I pressed both hands to my frantically beating heart, trying to make sure I was still in one piece. Each breath was a burning ache, but otherwise I felt unharmed, and like myself.

I was still here, even though ... *Ashton Griffin had just tried to kill me.* The thought felt more like a nightmare than a memory, but I knew instinctively it wasn't. If I had woken from a dream, I would have been in my own bed, and not one I'd never seen before.

Taking a deep breath, I threw back the duvet and set both feet on the floor, one after the other. My head began to swim, my vision went fuzzy. I blinked until it cleared, then looked down, seeing with relief that I was still fully dressed. Only my coat and shoes had been removed, replaced with thick socks.

The only object in the room, except the bed, was an oak wardrobe with gold knobs. I opened it and looked inside. Muted colours, shades of olive and brown, lots of black. My fingers skimmed the expensive fabrics, increasingly reassured. I knew who these things belonged to. Not because of the garments themselves, but the scent that lingered on them. Warm, woody oud, spicy cinnamon, a note of bergamot and a hint of lavender. I had smelt it many times before, but it was most intense here: in the home of the person it belonged to.

Relieved, I closed the wardrobe and went over to the door, beyond which I could hear muffled noises. Blake was at the stove. He had his back to me, but I knew he sensed me the moment I entered the room. I had been here often, but never in his bedroom. Almost as if he was trying to lock away the thoughts that loomed behind it.

As soon as I reached the kitchen island, he turned to me. Studying me, stirring a saucepan on the hob. The air was rich with the warm scent of milk, and my muscles relaxed a little.

'How did I get here?' My voice was hoarse, and I cleared my throat.

'I brought you here, after...' He trailed off, shoulders hunching. The memory bore down on them with all its weight. I could almost see it, although I'd glimpsed what happened only at the edges of my perception.

'After you stopped your best friend trying to kill me,' I finished matter-of-factly. Oddly, I was long past the point when those words felt difficult to accept.

One corner of his mouth lifted, a sorry attempt at a smile. 'You really are quite strong. You shouldn't even be able to remember that.'

'You're not even going to deny it?' Until now, Blake had always tried to defend Ashton.

'I thought we'd leave all that behind us, at last. Doesn't matter now anyway.'

'What do you mean?'

He opened a cupboard and took out a mug. 'Like I told you, I was just trying to protect you by keeping you away from me. But after what happened tonight ... that's no longer an option.'

When he turned to me again, I smiled grimly. 'Good.'

'Good?' he replied sceptically.

'Yes. Like I told *you*, that isn't what I want.'

For a moment we looked at each other in silence, then he gestured to a stool in front of me. 'You should sit down. It'll take your circulation a while longer to recover.' He went up to the island from the other side and slid a notepad and a book aside as I climbed onto the stool. A flare of dizziness, and I grabbed the edge to support myself.

Blake reached reflexively for my hand, holding it tight. His skin was so warm that I flinched. But it was probably just because mine was so cold. There was a shiver caught inside me, which kept sending waves of gooseflesh over my skin. Blake let me go at once and stepped back. 'You don't have to be afraid of me,' he said tonelessly, reaching again for the spoon.

'I'm not,' I replied, surprised to realise I meant it. 'You wouldn't have saved me from Ashton if you were planning to kill me yourself.'

'I didn't just mean that. It's also ... what I told you about Piper and the others. I would never ... touch you.' His voice was shot through with hesitation, as if there were truths hidden in those silences he didn't want to share.

But what he'd said already was enough to send another shiver down my spine, because I realised it hadn't even crossed my mind when I first woke up in his bed. I'd felt no trace of fear that he might have done something to me, although I knew he was capable of it. I tried to tell myself I was just confused, but I knew better. My feelings for Blake weren't confused. Despite the chaos all around us, what I felt when I looked at him was simple. Even if it was wrong, it was real.

I narrowed my lips and said nothing. I couldn't leave now, anyway. Not just because Ashton might be waiting for me outside the house, but because I believed Blake when he said he was tired of secrets. And so was I. After everything that had happened tonight, I needed answers more urgently than ever.

Blake took two pot holders off the hook and poured the milk into the mug, then added several tablespoons of honey and stirred. 'Here, drink this,' he said, setting it in front of me. I could see how careful he was not to look at me or touch me. 'It helps.' He gave me an encouraging nod, and I tried the milk. It was too sweet, but after the first taste I could already feel the soft honey soothing the roughness inside me.

'I don't understand how Ashton did it,' I whispered after a few sips, which cleared my mind a little. 'I didn't let my drink out of my sight, how could he possibly have slipped something into it?'

Blake leant against the kitchen counter, arms folded across his chest. He still wouldn't look me in the eye. 'He didn't give you anything, he took something from you.'

'Come on, don't tell me he siphoned energy out of my soul to make me easier to manipulate.' I laughed aloud, a brittle noise. When I saw that Blake didn't respond, it turned to ash in my mouth. I swallowed heavily. 'Again, you're not denying it.'

'I don't like lying, remember?'

I stared at him in horror. Even if I could accept that someone had tried to kill me, that didn't mean I could accept ... *that*. It wasn't possible.

'Do you want to leave?' Blake asked, as if he knew very well I was questioning his sanity.

'Would you let me?'

At last he looked up. His eyes were dark, the expression in them at once exhausted and alert. 'As soon as you leave this flat ... as soon as you leave *me*, I can't protect you anymore. So please don't force me to choose what to hate myself for.'

'Well, anyway. I don't want to leave. Not until I know what's going on.' Now it was my turn to nod promptingly as I took another sip of milk. Each one made the shiver in me easier, more bearable.

'If I tell you everything, you won't want to believe me. It goes against everything your rational mind tells you about the world. And I know how much that matters to you.'

'The truth matters to me more. So. Try me.'

Blake nodded hesitantly. 'What Ashton told you about souls is true. It's also true that he ... that we have the ability to access the energy inside them and take some of it for ourselves.'

I felt several impulses at once: walking off without a word and bursting into laughter were the two strongest. Suppressing both, I counted to ten in my head before I trusted myself to answer. 'Why would someone want to do that?'

Blake was watching me closely. 'Feeding on other people's souls energises you. It clears your mind, gives you a sense of vitality, euphoria, strength. It's like ... a kind of high. A special drug that only a handful of people are able to consume.'

'So how come you guys figured it out, then?' I tried my best to sound diplomatic, but it wasn't easy. I didn't doubt Blake believed what he was saying, but surely he must realise how it came across.

'My ancestors were very spiritual. These days we might

call them witches, but that's misleading. What they practised wasn't magic. They just understood how nature really works – how the universe works. They realised that human beings are made up of two elements that don't necessarily have to be connected.' He paused, as if I should be able to figure out the rest. But I hadn't followed a word of what he was saying. 'The body isn't axiomatically bound to the soul,' he continued slowly. 'In theory, the two can exist independently of one another. And while the body is limited to a certain lifespan, the soul itself is eternal. So they began to wonder how they could free the soul from the mortality of its shell.'

The look on my face was starting to give me away. Was he really talking about ... *immortality*? 'How is that possible?'

'Several of them imbued their combined life force into an object, letting all the energy in their souls flow into it.'

'You mean they sacrificed themselves?' I asked, appalled.

Blake nodded. He still hadn't moved a muscle, as if it was taking all his focus to keep talking. 'It created a sort of tool, which enabled the other participants in the ceremony to liberate their own souls from their bodies.'

My mouth opened and closed several times without producing any sound. My mind raced with a hundred questions and objections, but I forced myself to put them aside. If I wanted to understand what was going on here, I had to be open to what Blake was saying. No matter how far-fetched it all sounded, I had to at least try to keep an open mind. I could decide at the end what to think about it.

'Okay,' I said, deliberately matter-of-fact. 'But a soul without a body, can it survive?' I'd read that some cultures and religions believed the human soul detached itself from the body after death. But as far as I knew, it then either passed into the afterlife or was reabsorbed into the natural cycle, ready to inhabit the world again into some other form.

'No, it has to ... anchor itself in another body, otherwise it breaks apart. Permanently.' Blake's voice broke on the last word, as if it were an oath. Or a curse.

'So it has to enter the body of another person? Like a ... corpse?' My mouth twisted, and I quickly took another sip of honey milk to mask it.

Blake pushed away from the lip of the countertop and came towards the island. I tensed, but he just pulled one of the stools aside to sit down. 'No, it doesn't work that way. A body has to be alive to be habitable.'

'But if we're assuming every human has a soul,' I began tentatively, 'then surely that means there's one inside it already?'

'Yes.' Blake was running his thumb absently over a nick in the wood. 'The moment a second soul enters the body, it's sort of superimposed over the weaker one. The first soul is still there, like a flimsy veil, but essentially it's no longer ... animate. It's a shadow of its former self. The soul that lays claim to the body takes the reins, as it were. It takes over the person's life.'

I frowned, baffled. My head was beginning to ache, and I felt dizzy again. 'But if you're effectively erasing someone's soul, then that's pretty much just ... murder, isn't it?'

Blake nodded. His face had gone pale, making the scar on his temple dark and prominent.

'Why would someone do that? Just to have a different body? A lot of effort to go to for some plastic surgery.' I forced out a smile, but Blake still wasn't looking at me.

'It's not about any one body. It's about being able to keep switching to a different shell before it dies.'

His words thickened between us until they were the only thing in the room. Everything else faded. The light above the island flickered, the fridge's hum fell to a whisper, my heart thudded dully in my ears. I gripped the mug more tightly, but not even the warmth reached me. It took all my focus to assemble a thought from the pieces I'd just been given.

Blake was telling me that these people had figured out how to put their own souls into strangers' bodies, making them … immortal, because only the body died, not the soul. The soul could move on, and begin a new life. One after another, while the original people … wasted away in their own husk. Rationally, I could entertain the thought, but I couldn't grasp it. How could I? It went against everything I knew about life, death, nature. But that was exactly the point – Blake was talking about something *supernatural*. Just like Professor Edwards had said.

I felt sick, pressing the back of my hand to my mouth. 'That's insane,' I whispered.

Blake smiled faintly. 'I told you, you wouldn't want to believe it.'

It had nothing to do with wanting to. The question was, was I even capable of believing? How could I accept something so far-fetched as the truth? Something for which there was no evidence, besides the word of a person who had told me many times what a good liar he was?

'If all this is really true'—I hesitated—'then what has it got to do with you and your friends?'

He closed his eyes. 'You already know.'

I clenched my teeth, hissing out a single word: 'No.'

Blake looked down at me. I wished he hadn't. I didn't want to see the raw, open look on his face, I didn't want to see that he was fighting back tears, I didn't want to see that his whole expression was more intent and honest than ever before. 'Yes, Mabel,' he said roughly.

I pulled my hands into my lap, fingernails biting into my skin. I had to feel something to distract me from the pain of this absurd revelation. 'So, you're telling me you're some kind of wandering soul that infests other people's bodies so you can live forever?' My voice quivered with the effort of stifling a frantic laugh.

'We call ourselves soul-jumpers. But yes, that's essentially the gist of what I am.'

I stared at him. There was no twitch at the corners of his mouth, no trace of amusement or derision. He wasn't making fun of me, he wasn't lying. He was telling me something he considered to be true. I didn't want to believe him, but suddenly I wasn't sure how not to. What did he stand to gain from telling me this story? It was bonkers, sure, but at the same time it explained so much. Everything I'd been trying to make sense of for weeks. I'd been missing the glue that held together all the things I'd heard and witnessed. Ashton and his friends' behaviour, June's death, Paulina jumping after her conversation with Jack, Professor Edwards's death, my research with Davie, Blake's hints and attempts to push me away, Zoe's condition, which was getting worse the more time she spent with Ashton.

If I accepted the idea that the League of Starlings could mess with other people's energy, it all made sense. But if I accepted that, I had to take the rest of Blake's story seriously. I had to ... believe him. Even if it meant forgetting everything else I thought I knew.

'How long...' I couldn't bring myself to finish the sentence.

He understood me anyway. 'There's only one generation of us. The original ceremony released us from our bodies, and we've been using the artefact to jump ever since, but it no longer allows us to make new soul-jumpers. The League of Starlings has consisted of the same members from the very beginning: today there are one hundred and seventy-five.'

My heart was droning in my throat, and I pressed my hand to it. 'How long?' I repeated tonelessly.

Blake's eyes gleamed. 'The ceremony took place in 1867. I was twenty-three.'

'So you're telling me'—I took a deep breath—'you're nearly one hundred and eighty years old?'

Blake's lips twisted. I was still wishing he would burst into a laugh instead. 'Depends how you look at it. The bodies were never older than twenty-five when I left them again. But if you're counting by the age of my soul, then yes.' Again he smiled, a bit more genuinely this time. 'I don't think you can measure it in years, though. There are too many other factors involved.'

'Like what?'

'Experiences, memories, emotions you've gone through. The way you've come to know the world, how many layers of life's meaning you've already witnessed. And what you're like more generally.' He shrugged. 'Each individual has a different personality, a different depth to their soul. A totally unique way of thinking, feeling, living. I've met eighty-year-olds with the cheery, superficial souls of teenagers. And children who have a way of looking at the world as if they've been here for hundreds of years.' His voice trailed off, as if he were thinking in that moment of the hundreds of people he had met. Over the last *one hundred and eighty* years.

God, it was so... I pressed the heel of my hand to my temple. *First get the facts, then interpret them.* I pointed at him. 'So ... that's not your body?'

'Well, that also depends how you look at it,' he replied, studying his hands. Or ... *not* his, actually? 'But no, it originally belonged to someone else.'

'Blake Ames,' I choked out. The words had never caught in my throat like that before. 'Then, that's not really your name?'

'You knew that already, too.'

Yes, I did. I knew because he'd told me the night we met. Our first glimpse behind the curtain had perhaps been the truest of all – at least, until now. 'Cliff,' I whispered. 'Your real name is Cliff.'

His expression relaxed, as it always did when I called him by that name. 'We're not supposed to use those names anymore. We're essentially ... actors. When we take on another body, we immerse ourselves into that person's life. Which means we have to give up our own lives, the ones we had before, time and time again. I've played many roles over the decades, but Cliff...' He shook his head. 'I haven't been Cliff for a very long time.'

'And yet it's the name you gave me when we first met. Why?'

'I've been asking myself the same question. There was no reason, it didn't even make sense. I was just talking to you, and for the first time in ages, I felt like ... myself. A self I had to leave behind an eternity ago. A self I've had to disown every day for over a hundred years in order to survive.' He smiled, and his eyes were almost cautious. 'There was no reason, Mabel. There was only you.'

At that moment, I realised how right he was. This thing between us had never been logical, it was always about emotion. We had seen each other, really seen each other, from the very first glance. There had been no masks, no front, no attempt to seem better or even merely different from what we truly were. What we had shown each other that first night was the core of our real selves. And despite the walls of lies we'd built up later, we both knew it was true. We both knew *each other.* Which must have been why – without reason, with only my heart and every feeling in my body – I decided to believe him. Even though it was far-fetched, even though it went against all the convictions of my rational mind: I believed him.

I drank down the last of the honey milk, trying to wash away the shouts of *crazy, crazy, crazy* echoing in my head. 'Did you choose this? Did you know what was in store for you?'

'No.' Blake was eyeing me warily. Probably he was unsure if I believed him or was just trying to stall. Or he was still expecting me to make a run for it. Which was fair enough, really: after all, he'd just confessed that he was essentially a supernatural being, and also a murderer. One or both of those things should have terrified me, yet somehow I felt safe. I wasn't afraid of the truth. And I certainly wasn't afraid of ... Cliff.

'My parents were the ones who initiated the ceremony. They sacrificed themselves to create the artefact.' He rubbed his eyes, as if trying to erase the pictures behind them.

I wondered if memories were altered when you took them from one body to another. When you left the body that had seen a moment – heard it, smelt it, tasted it, felt it – did you also leave behind gauze-thin layers of its perception? Or was it true what they said, that memories were stored ... inside you? In what we called the heart, which was really something else entirely: the soul, perhaps? I would have liked to ask, but I didn't want to interrupt. I could see it cost him something to keep going.

'I just did as I was told. At the time I had no idea what the point of it all was. To be honest, I knew next to nothing about my parents.' A bitter grimace played across his lips. 'But it would be too easy to say I'm innocent. I went along with it, even enjoyed it, for a while. There's a special magic to realising you're no longer bound to the mortality of the body. That you can live forever. It felt like a blessing. Until I realised what it really is: a curse.'

'How so?' I asked carefully. Immortality was a popular motif, and not just in myths and fairy tales. In the real world, too, we were obsessed with growing as old as possible and being able to live a long, fulfilling life. I was sure many people would do anything to achieve a thing like immortality.

He fell silent for a moment, then got up and took my mug. Reaching the sink, he put it in, along with the saucepan, before turning on the tap. His voice was nearly lost in the running water. 'I can live forever, but not properly. None of the lives I live are ... real. I slip into them, run them day-to-day, take on the person's family and friends, but none of it is my decision. I'm a puppet. I do what I'm told.' He switched off the tap, but kept his back to me still. 'Our council chooses the bodies we inhabit: it's always about power, money and contacts. About making life as comfortable as possible for ourselves.'

That explained why the members of the League were in such high-level positions, even though at first glance they were not connected. How could anybody on the outside ever guess what linked them together?

'And none of it lasts,' Cliff went on, his voice low. 'Just as I'm getting used to a life, I have to leave it again. Every time I ... meet someone, I know that soon I'll have to ... stop seeing them.'

I went rigid as it dawned on me what he was saying. That he was talking in part about us. How whatever this thing was between us, it had never stood a chance. 'That sounds like a lonely life.'

Slowly, he turned to me. 'I told you Ashton and the others are my family. And in my case, I really can't choose them. We only have each other.'

'But you can decide to stop jumping,' I said. 'Live a life to its end, and ... go.' Whoever this council were, they couldn't force him to live out an eternity he didn't want. Could they?

Cliff shook his head, wiping his hands on a tea towel. 'No, that's not possible.'

I frowned. 'Why not?'

He opened his mouth, then closed it again. Tossed the rag onto the countertop and returned to the island. 'They'd never let me. I tried to run away once before. To dodge the ceremony. It took Ashton less than two weeks to find me, even though I'd left the continent. We know each other in a way so deep I can't really describe it. We're ... bound together.' He didn't sound reverent or ecstatic. More resigned, as if he'd come to terms with it as fact.

'Soulmates. That's what he called it.'

'Whatever it is ... I can't stand him sometimes, but I'll always love him.'

I felt like listing everything that was deeply unlovable about

Ashton, in my opinion – everything from abusing my best friend to trying to kill me – but stopped myself. I knew that wasn't how feelings worked, and anyway, I knew only a fraction of Cliff's and Ashton's past. Whatever they'd been through together, it ran deeper than it seemed today. *To truly love means to forgive.* I thought of Mum's words. Probably they were more important the more time you spent with someone.

'Are you afraid yet?'

I studied his face. The defined jawline and sharp cheekbones, the straight nose, the thick eyelashes, as dark as his brows and hair. I found it hard to get my head round the idea that none of it was really him – but then again, perhaps that wasn't true. A face was like a photograph: no matter how beautiful it was, it was lifeless without the personality that shone through the features. I had never been interested in the face itself, only the person whose brow furrowed in that pensive way, who wore a muted grin at the corners of his mouth, who looked at me as if he took for granted I would always be the centre of attention, even in a crowded room. I had never been less afraid of him than in that moment.

I couldn't help smiling. 'No. I'm not even as overwhelmed as I probably should be. Somehow, it all makes sense.' I shrugged and sat up straighter, only to promptly lose my balance.

In a flash, Cliff's hands were on my shoulders. 'Come on, let's find you somewhere with a backrest.'

Instead of taking me to the bedroom, Cliff led me to the sofa. He moved as if to sit in the armchair, but I grabbed his hand and pulled him down next to me. A little reluctantly, he sat, leaving a foot or so between us.

'There's one more thing I need you to explain,' I began, pulling the woollen blanket draped over the backrest onto my lap. 'What Aspen told me. About Piper and the others. That was him, wasn't it? Blake?' My heart began to beat faster: I couldn't help it. Logically, it had to be true. Aspen had said her brother changed completely after he met Ashton, which must mean all those terrible things happened when he was still ... him. Still, I needed to hear it from his own mouth.

Cliff gripped the backrest, his knuckles whitening. 'Yes. A few decades ago, I started speaking up about what body I wanted. There are so many people with such ... dark personalities, especially in the so-called upper classes. People who have done ugly things. Blake spent his whole life taking what he wanted, because he knew no one would stop him.

'*You* stopped him.' Even I could hear that my voice had softened – with relief, with affection.

'That doesn't make it any better what I did to him, Mabel. Nothing justifies murder. I was just trying to make the guilt easier to bear. I suppose it was selfish, really.'

I grabbed his hand and held it firmly as he made to take it off the backrest. I ran my fingers gingerly over his knuckles, over the tiny freckles on the back of his hand, the delicate grooves of his skin. I understood now why he'd said I wouldn't want to be touched by them if I knew what they had done, but ... he was wrong. These hands were not the acts that had been committed with them. This body bore no guilt. It wasn't dangerous. *Cliff* wasn't dangerous. And he wasn't a monster just because he'd done a few bad things. Not that I could ignore what he'd done, of course. If all this was true, he was responsible for taking lives. That wasn't right, but it didn't mean everything about him was wrong. Or that he could never do anything right ever again. Someone who reflected on his guilt and despised himself for what he'd done wasn't a fundamentally evil person. Maybe it was naïve to think that way, but even if it was, it didn't matter. It was what I believed. And I knew how stubborn I was when it came to my beliefs.

'I don't think so,' I whispered. 'Doing bad things doesn't necessarily make you a bad person.'

'That's just what you want to think.'

'I want to think it because it's how I feel. Because I've seen the way you talk about Aspen. I've seen how deeply you care for me – so much so that you'd rather let me hate you than put me in harm's way. I've seen the way you act when you think no one's looking, and I knew from the moment I laid eyes on you that you're a good person. You can't change your past, but your future ... that's up to you.' I clasped his fingers in mine. 'No matter what other people try to tell you. And your present, you took control of that today, didn't you? You stopped Ashton and saved my life.'

Cliff's lips were tightly compressed, silent. For a while he studied our hands, self-loathing oozing out of him every single second. The expression beneath it was no less dark: worry. 'I don't know how to protect you from him,' he confessed softly. 'How to protect you from *all* of them. The council approved Ashton's motion, and they decided to eliminate you.'

I wondered what was wrong with me, because I wasn't even all that concerned. Something about Cliff's nearness made it impossible to be afraid. 'But you've decided not to go along with it.'

He gazed at me in despair. 'But I don't know how I'm ever going to do it alone.'

'You're not alone.' I did my best to smile serenely, although I sensed fatigue creeping back over me. My mind was overwhelmed, and the rest of me was exhausted. Whatever Ashton had done to me, it had left a mark. 'I'm here. And we're going to figure this out, together. In case you haven't noticed, I'm pretty clever.'

Cliff smiled and raised his free hand, brushing my fringe back from my face. He ran his fingers over the string of freckles across my temple, the way he often did to his scar, which was in the same place.

'Your scar,' I said, going on instinct. 'Aspen said you came home one day and you were different. Did you do it to yourself?'

He nodded. 'My own body had one. Since then, I've taken it with me whenever I—'

'Whenever you move?' I completed the sentence with a half-grin that slid into a yawn.

Cliff was watching me, equal parts amused and exasperated. 'Your clever brain won't help us much if you're not on top form.'

I wanted to argue, but instead of a sentence, out came another yawn. Cliff drew back his hand as if to let me go, but I allowed myself to be led by the movement and leant in towards him. He stiffened briefly, before at last he sighed and opened his arms so that I could nestle close to him.

'Your survival instincts are looking pretty rusty,' he said, smoothing my hair carefully over my shoulders so it didn't get caught.

I couldn't help laughing, burying my face into the fabric of his jumper. His scent dispelled the last remaining trace of unease. It was impossible for someone bad to smell so good. Absolutely impossible. 'Hopefully, Ashton disagrees.' It felt like an eternity since then, although it had only been a couple of hours. Gingerly, I prodded around again in my insides. At all the places that had hurt while Ashton tried to break me open. 'The parts of ... my soul that he took, are they gone forever?'

'Energy is pretty fluid. Ashton didn't take as much as he could have, and you're tough. You just need to get your strength back.' He kissed the crown of my head, then rested his chin on it.

'And what about Zoe?' The thought suddenly occurred to me. 'Do you think he's taking it out on her?'

'Don't worry. It's more likely that he's at the pub, feeding on several different people at once. He's impulsive, but he's not completely reckless.'

Relieved, I pressed my ear against his body, at the exact spot where I felt his heart beating. Whatever he said about his body, that was definitely *his* heart. It had to be, because it beat faster as I let my fingertips wander over his jumper. For a few minutes, we just lay there, then I forced myself to lift my head again and look at him directly. 'If I fall asleep, is there anything I need to be afraid of?'

Instantly he tensed. 'I would never—'

'I didn't mean that,' I interrupted quickly. 'Just ... you might decide you regret this decision.'

I knew he understood what I meant. Not just saving me, but how close he was letting me get to him right now. The way he held me in his arms, stroking my shoulder with his thumb, his eyes fixed on mine. On what was hidden in them. Not on my face, only on me.

'It doesn't matter if I regret it, or wish I'd done it differently,' he said softly, caressing my cheekbone. 'I made my choice the moment I first saw you. And there are so many reasons why this can't work, but ... here we are. And here we'll stay. As long as we can.'

I smiled, murmured, 'Here we'll stay.'

Cliff slid further down onto the sofa and pulled me in tighter. His heart against mine, his *soul* so close to mine that I was sure they must have interwoven. 'Go to sleep now, Pica.'

I snorted, my eyelids drooping of their own accord. 'Only because I want to. Not because you're telling me to.'

'Of course.'

His smile was the last thing I saw before I drifted off. In the arms of an immortal soul-jumper, in the arms of a multiple murderer. I had never felt safer than in this embrace. It had been a crazy night, but that was the craziest thing of all.

CHAPTER 27
MABEL

I woke to a bluish light seeping through my eyelids. I blinked languidly, just in time to see Cliff lock his phone and place it on the sofa beside him. Beside us. My head was still resting on his chest, my whole body on his. My eyes wandered over his jumper, which smelt so unmistakeably of him, to the clock on the wall next to the front door. It was just past four – I'd been asleep for several hours.

I leant back to look at him. His eyes were only half open, but the expression in them was sharp and alert. 'Did you sleep?'

'Not really.' His hand slid to the nape of my neck, gently stroking the vertebrae towards the neck of my jumper.

'Hmm.' I knitted my brows. 'So what have you been doing, then? Not nibbling away at my soul?'

Cliff frowned, visibly torn between scepticism, mirth and concern. 'You know, there's really something wrong with you. You're taking this a bit too well.'

I laughed. 'Sorry. It's just … I love to think logically, right? And as absurd as the truth is, it's the only explanation that makes sense. Which means believing it is the most obvious course of action.' I shrugged, but instantly regretted it when a sharp pain sliced through my neck. 'Maybe we should go and lie down in the bedroom, I've already got a crick.'

'I don't know if that's such a good idea.'

It took me a moment to put two and two together: his answer with the uncertain expression on his face. And I wasn't sure if I was more embarrassed or weirdly ... flattered. I sat up a little, still on top of him, and grinned crookedly. 'Don't tell me you'd feel tempted in a bed like that?'

'I'd be tempted anywhere if you're there too, Pica.' His fingers were exploring under my collar. The hairs beneath it stood on end, and I shivered and felt a swell of heat at the same time.

Without stopping to think, I bent down towards him. My hair grazed his cheeks, my lips brushed his face. I kissed the scar on his temple, his cheek, the corners of his mouth, then the mouth itself. Cliff wavered briefly, then pulled me in closer. The kiss tasted of honey, and felt like it, too – warm, soft, golden and ... healing. All lingering trace of unease, fear and stress dissolved, purely because he was kissing me. Because his teeth were tugging gently at my bottom lip, because his hands were wandering all over my body, pressing me to him firmly, because I could sense every part of him, absolutely *every* part, and because, strangely, it let me sense every part of myself as well. Everything Ashton had jumbled up, his touch slid back into place. Everything that last night's revelations had stirred up inside me was smoothed out under a pleasantly heavy blanket of warmth and ... desire.

I sighed against his lips as he slid his hands underneath the hem of my sweater dress. Instantly he stopped and jerked his head aside. Worried, I pulled back. 'What's the matter? Did I do something wrong?'

'No. It's just—' He broke off and ran a hand through his hair, then pressed his fingers to his eyes.

'Cliff?' Gently I took his wrist and guided his hand away

from his face, trying to catch his gaze. I couldn't, because it was fixed on his own hand. Only, it didn't feel that way to him. My chest tightened when I realised that was exactly the problem. 'It's about what he did, isn't it? Blake?'

He strained at his hands until I let him go, but when I began to slide off his lap he held on to me. 'What I told you on that football pitch, it wasn't a lie,' he said hoarsely. 'Those memories are real. And they're in me, because they were in him. Because they were his deepest, core memories. The ones he ... liked the best. The ones he savoured, over and over again.'

'So you remember all his experiences too?' Perhaps it was true, then, that our memories were bound to our bodies. Perhaps they embedded themselves in our cells as well as in our minds. It seemed only logical, after all, that they would leave their traces everywhere. The way that certain scents or tastes could evoke an intense emotion associated with them, even though we might not be consciously aware of where it came from. Memories were more than just images of the past: they shaped the way we moved through life. What we saw, felt, thought, existed differently because of the things we had experienced. And Cliff ... Cliff had experienced more than other people. It must be confusing, carrying so many memories around with him, many of which weren't even his.

'No, it doesn't work quite like that. As the soul's energy fades, so does the body's capacity for memory. Let's put it like that. Only shreds remain. A scent triggers a familiar feeling. You see a place and you remember abruptly what it looked like the last time the body was there. And ... you remember the things that shaped the original soul most deeply. Often, the good things and the not-so-good things balance each other out, but with people like Blake ... even his best memories are cruel and dark. They *all* are.' He leant his head back against the armrest, swallowing. 'It's as if my soul is in this container, and the images are ingrained into its walls. So it feels as though they're burnt into my retinas, overlaying the way I see the world.'

I wanted to touch him, but didn't dare. 'That must be awful.'

He twisted his lips into an unconvincing smile. 'It's fine.'

'Cliff.' I hesitated briefly, then raised my hands and cradled his face. 'I know you think you deserve this, but that's not true.'

'It's fine,' he repeated, closing his eyes as I stroked his cheek. 'Just … this, this isn't.' He took my fingers away from his face, interlacing them with his own, as if the trace warmth of my skin made him feel guilty.

'Why? It doesn't have anything to do with you. They aren't *your* memories. They aren't things *you* did.'

'But they're the same hands.' He smiled bitterly, holding them up as if expecting me to see the guilt on them as clearly as he did. 'It's the same mouth. The same body, Mabel. How can I touch you with it without thinking about everything it's done in the past?'

I studied the despairing look on his face. The face he thought was someone else's, although all I could see was him. His way of smiling, so enigmatic, as if secrets were hidden in those dimples. His way of looking at things as if he saw more than others did, because his gaze bored beneath the surface. The way his brow furrowed or his jaw tensed, or the tip of his nose crinkled subconsciously. His habit of brushing back a lock of hair from his forehead or stroking his fingertips along his scar. All of that was Cliff, none of it was Blake, that was for sure. And when we were together, he was never rough or selfish. In every kiss, in every touch, I could tell he was paying attention to what I liked. He would never have done anything I didn't want. In fact, he'd done *less* than I wanted. So why did he seem to despise himself for things he hadn't done?

'It's not just that, is it?' I realised. 'It's not just about what he did. It's also about what you … might do.'

Reluctantly, he met my eye. 'Genetics is a complicated thing. Not even we really know what effect it has on our souls when we occupy a body. Nobody knows how much of our personality or our actions are influenced by our physical form. Like taste preferences, for instance? That changes every time. There are some things we can't control.'

'Like an aversion to raisins, for instance?' I remembered the forlorn look in his eyes when he told me he wished he liked them. It was only dawning on me now that it would have been a sign he was still himself.

The corners of his mouth lifted in a sad smile. 'Exactly. So ... what if I've changed in other ways, too, and I don't realise until it's too late? What if that violence, that darkness ... that urge, what if it's rooted in this body? What if it originates deep in these cells? What if I suddenly lose control?'

'Does that mean you haven't had sex since you've ... been like this?' I had understood by now that his friends only organised parties to feed unnoticed on the souls of unsuspecting guests, not because they were after anything else, but that didn't mean they all refrained. Their souls might have been old, but their bodies, at least here at the university, were in their twenties. I was pretty sure that at least some of them had ... natural urges to grapple with.

Cliff's smile deepened. 'It's only been two years, the blink of an eye for me. And before that ... I've inhabited the bodies of some pretty amoral people in my time, but the memories were never like this. It's never been this intense, this bad.'

'Even so.' I was watching him, intrigued. 'There must be ... hormones circulating in this body, right? Don't you ever want it?'

He laughed and pulled me suddenly close, burying his face in the hollow of my neck. 'After everything I've just told you, you're still thinking about that?' His breath tickled my skin, as heat began to spread downwards from my belly. *Deep, deep down*. Especially when he looked up and stared into my eyes. 'And yeah, I want it, Mabel. I want it every time I look at you. When you rub your lips together to blend your lipstick. When you're thinking and you get this look on your face, so rapt and focused. When you give me your opinion, because you've got so many fucking opinions. I find that pretty ... attractive.' There was still the trace of a laugh in his voice, but it sounded oddly harsh in a way that made me uneasy. Which is ... *frustrating*.

I swallowed. 'Is that so?'

'Mhm.' He stroked his thumb over the curve of my lips. 'And obviously I want to when we kiss. When I touch ... *you*.'

I felt a clench between my legs. I wanted to touch him too. Needed to touch him. After everything he'd told me there was so much to think about, but right now I wanted something else. I wanted to feel. I wanted to feel *him*. 'So ... just theoretically speaking, of course ... do you want to right now?' I had to know if it was just me. 'I know a lot has happened and it's all really confusing and chaotic and crazy, but do you want to, even just a little bit?'

His fingers skimmed my cheek to reach my throat, my neck. 'Yes,' he whispered. 'I really do.'

I put my hand on his. 'But you're afraid.'

'Yes.' He smiled faintly. 'I really am.'

'You're not going to hurt me.'

'You can't know that.'

'Yes, I can. Because I saw you for who you are before we even knew each other. So listen to me.' I pushed him firmly away from me so I could sit up straighter. 'You are *not* him. This body is *not* what you are. And it certainly doesn't control your actions.' I took his face in my hands, looking him dead in the eyes. I didn't care what happened or didn't happen in that moment – only that he understood me, here and now. 'You are you. Just you. And you won't hurt me, Cliff. I trust you. So please, trust yourself.'

For a moment there was silence, then he took a deep breath. 'Mabel—'

Instantly I jerked my hands back, cupping my elbows. 'I mean, we don't have to, obviously. Not now, not ever. But ... you want to, and I want to, and I think we can try it. We can always stop if you don't feel comfortable. Really, whenever.' I could see how tense he was, and I hurried to shake my head. 'Forget it. Obviously I don't want to talk you into doing something you don't want to do. I—'

He silenced me with a kiss. I was pretty sure it was the only interruption I would respond to with a sigh rather than indignation.

Cliff pushed my hair back over my shoulders, drew his lips away from mine and brushed them along the sweep of my neck. Although I knew my beating pulse had some other significance for him, I felt not a trace of fear that he would do anything but feel me.

Slowly he pulled my dress over my head, then he straightened up and looked at me. A stain of my red lipstick on his mouth, his own red flush in his cheeks. He was glowing in the most attractive way, and it made me burn too. Still, I grabbed his hand as he slid two fingers under the strap of my bra. 'Are you sure?'

'Yes.' He smiled, a genuine, happy, almost astonished smile. The most beautiful smile I'd ever seen on his face. 'I want this so much. I want *you* so much.' He bent towards me again, kissing the corners of my mouth, then full on my lips, long and intense. He slipped down the waistband of my tights and helped me shimmy them off, until they dropped onto the floor beside the sofa. Meanwhile I was tugging at the hem of his jumper, much more inelegantly and feverishly, until he pulled back and took it off himself.

'Let's go in there,' he murmured into my lips. 'I think I might be a bit too out of practice for this.'

'Who'd have thought? That I'm the more experienced one here, even though you're *so* much older than me.' I laughed, the sound slipping into a moan as he gently bit the crook of my shoulder.

'Careful, Pica,' he murmured, then grasped my thighs and held me firmly as he stood up.

I wrapped my legs around his hips and my arms around his neck, not breaking the kiss. I'd never clung to anyone so tightly, and although I knew we might both go tumbling over the edge, I wasn't scared. Not with him.

My back knocked against the bedroom doorframe, and Cliff swore. I smiled and kissed him again. Kissed him as he laid me down on the bed and bent over me. Kissed him as his hand slid under my back and undid my bra. Kissed him as he ran his hand over my breasts, with just the right pressure, gentle yet urgent, so that my pelvis bucked to meet him.

My thoughts swam in the sensations of the body, what it felt and wanted, but when I blinked and looked up at Cliff's face, something held me back from sinking into it fully: the crease between his brows, the way he avoided my eye. He was obviously trying to give himself over to the moment, which existed purely between us. But he was still torn between what he was and what he thought Blake might make of him. I wished I could make him understand that his body didn't matter. That nothing mattered except what we truly were.

Swiftly making up my mind, I pushed him off me. 'Wait, let me try something.'

Cliff watched me, frowning, as I climbed out of bed and went to the wardrobe. 'What are you up to?'

I ignored him, sliding the hangers one by one until I found what I was looking for. Carefully, I removed two ties and went back to him. 'Trust me. Close your eyes,' I said sternly, when I saw the confused look on his face. He hesitated, but nodded. I tied one tenderly over his eyes before doing the same to myself. 'I don't have to see you to see you, right?'

The way he pulled me close and kissed me: on the cheek, on the chin, at last on the mouth, said: *right*. Or maybe I just thought so because it felt that way. Felt right, felt like us.

His hands rested a gentle pressure on my shoulders, so that I fell back onto the pillow. I felt the warmth of him as he leant over me, then his weight on mine. He was pressing me into the mattress, but somehow I felt like I could breathe more easily than ever before. With agonising slowness he slid one knee between my legs and stroked upward from my bare waist, moving along my arms until he found my hands.

His fingers dwelt on my wrists, his thumb on my pulse, his breath on my mouth. 'If I do anything you don't want me to—'

'I'll let you know.' I smiled and reached for him, kissing his neck. 'And you let me know. Okay?'

He took a deep breath, his chest brushing mine. 'Okay.'

And then we were silent. There was only the rustle of the sheets and the last of our clothing falling to the floor, the sounds of skin against skin, of our lips as we kissed, caressed, felt everything our eyes could no longer see. No arms, only tensed muscles, no breasts, only gooseflesh, no legs, only shudders, no mouths, only stifled moans, no looking, only seeing. No bodies, just us.

Eventually Cliff rolled off me and on to his side. There was rattling as he tried to open the drawer in the bedside table. The rasp of wood, then the crackle of plastic. Again he was on top of me, the tip of his nose against mine. 'Sure?'

'Yes.' I put my arms around his neck. 'You?'

I knew he'd nodded without having to look. I could feel it, as I felt everything we were thinking and wanting in that moment. I was *so* sure about this. About us. We kissed again, then he grabbed my thigh and pulled me closer underneath him.

Forehead to forehead, mouth to mouth, one shared breath. And then, finally, he was inside me.

I had only slept with a couple of men in my life, but I was used to it feeling a bit uncomfortable for the first few seconds: not that it hurt, necessarily, but it was always a strange, alien feeling. As if there was something inside me that didn't belong. That didn't belong to me. This time, with Cliff, it was different. Of course it was, because everything with him and about him was different. It didn't feel strange that he was inside me because in other ways – more intimate ways – he was a part of me already. Even when we were still trying to keep a distance between us, we had been close. If I could believe in such a thing as souls, then I could believe they sometimes recognised each other deep down, before the conscious mind had even realised.

I couldn't see Cliff's face, I would never be able to see his own face, but at that moment, as he thrust into me, careful yet assertive, I was more sure than ever: I saw him. I saw him with all my senses, with everything I was. I sensed his muscles under my fingertips, his breath on my face, his lips on mine, his heat and skin on mine, his whole self in each movement, in each gasp and moan and sigh that mingled with my own. Until we were truly together, in every way.

After a while he slid a hand between us, running it up my thigh to the point where the throbbing was building more with every second. I helped him find the best place, showed him the right pressure, wordlessly, because we didn't need words. I let out a gasp as he rubbed, faster and faster.

The tingling between us heightened, unfurling itself between our bodies like barbed-wire velvet, growing ever more intense and heated with the friction of our skin until it was so unbearable I whimpered softly. Cliff stopped moving, but increased the pressure of his thumb. My hips bucked, but he pushed me back against the sheets, kissed me more deeply, more breathlessly.

I moaned, feeling the sound itself make the hairs rise on his body – and I knew, I just knew, that in this moment he felt that it was truly *his*. That what we were doing belonged to us alone. The wash of realisation was too much. I moaned again, or maybe I was screaming, maybe I was sighing, maybe ... I didn't know. For a heartbeat my mind was suspended, everything ran into everything else. The burning flooded my body, searing into every cell, every thought, every feeling. I was standing in the flames, and I loved it, I loved it so much because I knew I wasn't in them alone.

Cliff waited until the quiver in my toes had relaxed. Then he began to move inside me again, slower now, but a little deeper and harder. I shuddered with every thrust, especially when, minutes later, I felt him tense above and inside me. His teeth grazed mine as he kissed me again, just at the moment he came. And I ... I wondered if he, too, realised in that instant why people called it *coming*. Because, with the right person, it felt like you had reached somewhere, in so many ways that mattered.

My heart was beating softly, palpably, like a rubber ball bouncing around in my chest. A warm languour trickled through my body, into all the places that had been tingling seconds before. I traced invisible patterns on the muscles of Cliff's back, waiting for his breathing to slow.

He kissed me lingeringly on the forehead, then he pulled away and flopped down onto the mattress next to me, still not letting me go. His hand reached around to the back of my head and undid the knot in the tie.

'Hey.' His face hovered close to mine. No crease between his brows, no strained focus in his eyes. Just a light film of sweat on his forehead, a mark on his cheeks from the tie, and a look of relief and happiness.

I smiled, because I felt the same. Carefully I brushed the hair back from his forehead, tracing the delicate scar that originated at his browbone. 'Everything all right?'

He just nodded, and kissed me briefly on the mouth. I was so hot that my cheeks must have been on fire, but even that wasn't unpleasant. I was naked and myself and ... happy. I was *so* happy, in spite of everything. For a while we lay side by side, fingers roaming over each other's warm bodies, kissing sometimes, exhausted in the most wonderful of all ways.

'What's the deal with the tattoos?' I asked, resting my thumb on the mark below his collarbone.

'We've all got one,' he explained quietly.

A flash of Jess came into my head, along with guilt – Zoe was still ... lost, and Davie was still in hospital. His condition unaltered, although I hoped for better news every time I visited him.

Cliff continued. 'If you put them together, it forms our coat of arms, the starling. Every time we enter a new body, we get it tattooed. A constant reminder that we're only complete when we're together.'

'You don't need them to be complete,' I objected, kissing the scar on his temple. The part that belonged to him, to him alone, and not them.

'Yes,' he murmured. 'I'm starting to feel that, for the first time in ages.'

I propped my head up on my hand, amused. 'Just look what a bit of sex can do. Guess it's like riding a bike, even at your age.'

Cliff groaned and laughed at the same time, putting his arm over his face. A wash of colour clung to his cheeks. He had never been more handsome than in that moment. 'Doesn't that bother you?'

'What, that you're a hundred and sixty years older than me?'

'Yeah?'

'No, oddly enough it doesn't. The stuff about your "family"

wanting me dead, however, that does give me pause.' I tried to keep my tone light, but Cliff was instantly on edge.

'I won't let them hurt you,' he said, so earnestly that it felt at odds with the situation.

I knew he meant it, but at the same time, it wasn't a promise he could make. I still wasn't sure I really understood the League of Starlings, but what I did know was enough to realise that these people, if you could call them that, were willing to go to terrible lengths to protect their secrets. Or even just for their own enjoyment. They didn't care about the lives of others.

'You know this isn't just about me, right? They're a threat to everybody. After what Davie and I found out, I'm pretty sure what happened to June and Paulina isn't a one-off. Even just what happened to Zoe ... they can't, I mean, *you* can't use people like that, Cliff. It's not right.' Whatever my feelings for him, I couldn't separate him entirely from his family.

'I know.' He nodded slowly. 'But I don't know how to stop them. What I told you is true: leaving isn't an option. We all have to stick to the rules the council has set for us. If we defy them, then—' He broke off and shook his head, before rolling onto his back and staring up at the ceiling. 'There's only one way to truly destroy the League.'

I sat up, instantly alert. 'And what's that?'

Cliff was silent. Strips of light broke again through the window, creeping across the bedding and his face, painting bright shadows on his pensive features. For a moment, I thought I saw a pang in his eyes: as if he were reaching a decision that caused him physical pain. A second later, he took a deep breath. 'The artefact. We have to destroy it. Without it, we can't switch bodies anymore. We'd be tied to the ones we're in. Until ... the end.'

My heart began to race. It sounded like a near-perfect solution. If we bound the soul-jumpers to their current bodies, they could all finish living out those lives. That meant making decisions, taking responsibility, discovering what they wanted for themselves and acting accordingly. They'd be stuck with the same struggles as the rest of us, forced to give this one lifetime their best shot. It wouldn't undo the suffering they'd caused in the past, but it would stop them from ever doing it in the future. Then again, it would upend Cliff's whole life, bring down everything his ancestors had built. Everything his parents had ... died for. I eyed him uncertainly. 'Is that a price you're willing to pay?'

He stroked my cheek. 'I'd pay any price,' he said, with an almost reverent smile. 'It's the greatest gift you could give me. To have something finally worth risking everything for. Without that ... it's no life at all.'

Tenderness curled its warm fingers into my chest, and I kissed him. I paused, my lips still close to his. 'I know you have your issues with this body, but I would help you learn to love it. I promise. Then you can live a normal life in it. Make your own decisions, your own mistakes, choose your own family. You can grow old.'

He clasped my fingers in his and pressed his mouth to the back of my hand. 'Is it weird that that's my greatest wish?'

'No. It suits you, somehow. I can see you as an old man on a patio somewhere, doing a crossword puzzle.' I let myself drop back onto the mattress. 'How come you never go past twenty-five?' Lots of people said your twenties were the best years of your life, but I'd never really believed it. The older you got, the more you found yourself. Personally, I was just happy I'd found myself enough that I no longer felt at sea in the world – no matter how chaotic it got sometimes.

'The council decides what role we play. Some of the older members inhabit the bodies of very prominent people, which is how we expand our sphere of influence. Ashton, Norah and I were among the youngest of our original group, so we have to wait until we're allowed to move up to a more senior level. Until then, we play the spoilt children of wealthy, powerful families, siphoning off money and influencing our parents... It's all a bit trivial, really. Basically house arrest for soul-jumpers.'

'So why haven't they let you guys move up the chain yet?'

Cliff sighed quietly. 'Henry – that's the head of the council, and one of the founders of the League, the only one chosen to survive the ceremony—'

'Wait,' I interrupted, snatching at a memory as it flitted through my mind. 'I saw a Henry. At the Christmas party. He looked late thirties, at the most.' My lips pursed as I remembered our encounter. He'd more or less told me with a single glance that he thought I was worthless.

'His current body, yes. Benjamin Colton, he's an MP. Henry's actual body was in its mid-forties at the time of the ceremony. He's my uncle, and Ashton's father.'

'You're related?' I asked, taken aback.

Cliff nodded. 'Our fathers were brothers. And Ashton's relationship with Henry is complicated. He's always felt this need to prove himself. The rest of us could have applied to be moved up a rung, but we didn't want to leave Ashton. He needs people around him who love him, and who are kinder about showing it than his dad.'

'There are limits to my sympathy for Ashton.' Which was putting it mildly.

Cliff gave a half-hearted smile. 'He's complicated. Like everybody else. But he isn't all bad. This life just has a different way of shaping you. A crueller way. We were all just trying not to die. And Ashton's had a tough time.'

'In what way?' I asked reluctantly.

Cliff sat up, leaning back against the headboard. 'At the time of the ceremony, in 1867, he was seeing this girl. She was a soul-jumper, too. They were more or less inseparable for a century.'

I felt a queasy flip in the pit of my stomach. I sat up too, pulling the duvet around my chest. 'What happened?'

His eyes were far away, different. Something told me he was delving deep into memories that had nothing to do with his body – and everything to do with his soul. 'She was the wildest, freest person I ever met. Open-hearted, brave, confident, but rebellious almost to the point of danger, and ... reckless. She just did what she wanted. Acted without thinking. I never met anyone who lived like she did.' He rubbed his eyes with the back of his hand. When he looked back at me, his expression was troubled. 'Problem is, there are certain rules we *have* to follow. Like for instance, there are limits to how much energy we're allowed to absorb. If we feed on others unchecked, the vessel that contains our soul can't handle it – it's like it cracks open. It leaks out, and corrodes the body we're living in.'

I tried to follow what he was saying, confused. 'But then, can't you just switch to a new body?'

'Not if the soul is already trickling out. Then you're stuck in that body, trapped as it slowly but surely falls apart.'

'And that happened to her? Ashton's girlfriend?'

Cliff nodded. 'She overdid it. Ignored the warning signs and kept on going, because for her, it was always about the next thing, she never stopped and took a breath – let alone a step back. Until it was too late, and her body was on the verge of collapse.'

'So she died?' I couldn't stop a note of sympathy from softening my voice. Despite how I felt about Ashton, I hadn't forgotten the look on his face when he was describing what he'd lost. The pain etched on his features in that moment had been real. And probably the most human aspect of him I would ever see.

'She killed herself,' he corrected. 'Here, in Cambridge. We were at university here then, too. We celebrated this existence so hard, you know? We felt invincible. We relished every second of these stolen lives, because we didn't care we'd taken them from someone else. We didn't care about anything.' He laughed, a hoarse, discomfortingly sad sound. 'Until one of us decided out of nowhere to start a fire and die in it.'

My mouth fell open when I realised what he was talking about. 'Hang on ... do you mean Amelia Wallingford? The student who died here? 1982?'

Cliff smiled lopsidedly. 'Too crazy?'

'Maybe a bit,' I murmured in agreement. 'Wait.' I fumbled for my bag, which was lying next to the bed. It took me a moment to find the picture on my phone. It was blurry, but the only one I'd been able to snap of the article before it was burnt along with the rest of Davie's files. Zooming in on the faces of the five students, I held the screen out to Cliff. 'So these are all people in the League of Starlings?'

He nodded and took the phone, holding it so we could both see it. 'Nox,' he began, from the left, 'Norah, Ashton, Heaven and ... me.' He tapped the man in the middle before handing me back the smartphone.

I gazed dumbfounded at the figure I'd mentally labelled as Cedric Landon Wells, although somehow he'd felt oddly familiar to me this whole time. It was nuts: suddenly, in this oh-so-bizarre way, everything made sense. 'I knew there was something about him nagging at me.'

'The scar. You can just about see it,' Cliff said, pointing at the pixellated face.

And sure enough, I could make out a faint line on his temple, but I knew that wasn't what had struck me. 'No, that wasn't it. It was something about the look on his face. It's the look I've seen so often on *your* face. So brooding.' I shot him a teasing grin, before examining the other faces with fresh eyes. When I reached Arthur, I paused. He had his arm around the shoulder of the woman next to him, and his eyes were fixed on her profile, the expression in them soft and full of open tenderness. If I hadn't known it was Ashton, I never would have guessed. I had never seen such devotion on his face. I hadn't even thought he was capable of it. 'He loved her, didn't he?'

'More than anything,' Cliff said quietly. 'We all did, but Ash took it hardest of all. When she disappeared, a part of him went with her.'

'Disappeared?'

'I like to think that souls don't die, they just go somewhere else. Many cultures believe they reappear eventually – in a person, in another living creature, as some energy of the universe. Some souls are older than others.' He nodded at me with a grin. 'Like yours, for instance. It feels ancient.'

'Charming.' I pursed my lips and locked the screen. I didn't like how sorry I felt for Ashton. It was easier to see him as an emotionless, unscrupulous monster. 'Did Ashton have that bench put up for Heaven?'

'No, that was me and Norah. We tried to be open about how much it affected us, losing Heaven. After all, the five of us had been practically joined at the hip since we first started jumping. What happened to her changed things, for all of us. But Nox threw himself into the security of the council's rules and regulations, and began pursuing a career in the League. And Ashton just pretended like nothing happened. Ever since then, all he wants to do is live for the moment, and he never really lets anybody get close to him. He's been struggling with it for nearly forty years, but he won't let anybody try and help him.'

'But that doesn't give him the right to take it out on other people.' No matter how much Ashton had suffered, was still suffering, perhaps, it didn't justify inflicting pain on others. Nothing did. 'I need to protect Zoe from him. We need to protect *everybody* from him. From him and from … the rest of you.'

'You're right. I've known for a while now that this can't go on.' Again, I thought I saw a shadow flit through his eyes, but before I could reach for it, he blinked it away. 'But the artefact is under twenty-four-hour guard. It's impossible to get to it. Unless...' His face twisted, as if a bitter thought had occurred to him.

I was instantly on edge. 'What?'

'Very soon, they're going to hold an emergency ceremony.'

'Emergency?'

He hesitated. 'You're not going to like this.'

I gave him an incredulous stare. 'You think I like any of this?'

He sighed again. 'During the accident, when Victor hit Davie. At the moment Victor's body was injured, he tore his soul out of it and jumped into the only undamaged person he could find nearby.'

This time I was quicker to put two and two together. I didn't like what I got, but I wasn't surprised. 'Jess Holden, the witness. I spoke to him – he called me Anna Karenina. So that was ... Victor?' Part of me had suspected after our conversation that there was something deeper going on. But how could I have persuaded my rational mind to accept it? I could never have made it fit with what I thought I knew of the world, but it did fit perfectly with what I knew of Victor. With his disregard for others. Not only had he come within a hair's breadth of killing Davie, but he'd murdered the real Jess to save himself. I felt sick, and hugged the duvet around me more tightly.

'Yes,' Cliff replied cautiously, as if he knew exactly what was going through my head. 'Emergency jumps like that are risky. They're not always successful, and even when they are, they're short-lived. If you jump into a body without preparing the ground first – by weakening the soul inside it – then the energy is still too present. And it's too overwhelming for the body. You have a few weeks at the most before it dies.' He snapped his fingers, and I winced.

'So they're going to let Victor change his shell? And they're bringing the artefact here to do that?'

'The ceremony won't work without it. The trouble is, they

won't let me take part. My body ... I still have a couple of years left in it, and the protocol is absolute. The artefact must be protected at all costs, even from us. After all, we might be tempted to take it for ourselves, run off and jump as much as we like. Only one member of the council, the jumpers, and the people whose bodies they want to occupy can be present.' His fingers were drumming on the duvet, and I had to restrain myself from grabbing them. Something told me he was only moving them so he wouldn't have to stop and face the thought that was spreading like a dark cloud across his eyes.

'What is it?' I asked bluntly. 'Something else I'm not going to like?'

He stopped, caught. 'It's *me* that doesn't like it. But if we're going to save you and destroy the artefact, it's the only option that might conceivably work.'

I didn't fail to notice the hedging, but I ignored it and lifted my chin. 'All right. Then let's do it.'

His eyes wandered over me, darkening, second by second. It took me a moment to realise there wasn't affection or concern behind them, but something more overcast. Something I had never seen in him this strongly before. Maybe because he'd been hiding it from me, or maybe because he hadn't felt it this powerfully in the time I'd known him.

'I'm afraid,' he whispered. 'It's been a long time since I've known fear, but then you came along, and suddenly my list of things that make it all worthwhile boils down to you, and pretty much nothing else.'

My heart turned heavy and soft at the same time when I realised what he was referring to. I remembered the way he'd looked at me on our walk, when I told him the things on my own list. Admiring and almost envious, as if he longed to find something to put on his.

'I know how ridiculous it sounds, but it's true,' he went on, when I said nothing. 'And that's exactly why I'm scared. You really terrify me. I don't want to lose you. I *can't* lose you.'

I was able to move again, at last. 'You won't.' I let go of the duvet and climbed onto his lap. I didn't care that he was seeing me naked again – I'd always felt bare, exposed, before him anyway, ever since the night we met. 'We'll get through this together, and afterwards we'll just do really boring stuff. Revise together, eat one a.m. pancakes, start a Brontë book club. And do this.' I pressed my lips to his. 'A lot.'

'Sounds tempting. And in between *this*'—he put a hand on my lower back, pressing me in closer, and I sighed, and he smiled and gave me a fleeting kiss—'we can go travelling. I'd like to show you a few places that in my opinion you definitely can't miss.'

I grinned. 'Sound great. We'll have to wait until I've saved up for it, though. I don't care how filthy rich or ancient you are, I'm not letting you pay for everything. But we've got time.' I nuzzled the tip of my nose against his. 'Not eternity, but ... a lifetime. That's enough, right?'

He closed his eyes and slid his face past mine, nestling his forehead into the hollow of my neck. 'Mabel.' His voice tickled against my skin, and beneath it.

I'd never thought my name would feel so meaningful to me. As if it truly did belong to me alone, and said so much more than I had ever realised. Those two syllables contained everything he saw in me, which in turn was everything I was. It sounded like the most beautiful compliment I'd ever heard, yet at the same time the most despairing cry.

'What?' I asked, with a lump in my throat and a knot in my chest. Both relaxed a little when he drew away and looked directly into my face. There was a last trace of sadness in his eyes, but the smile in them was stronger. Even in the dim room, it brought a light to them, and for a brief moment nothing about our situation seemed crazy, weird or hopeless. For a brief moment, everything was fine. Just because he was looking at me like that, like he was telling me how sure he was that this – that *we* – were worth overcoming anything.

'Mabel,' he repeated gently. This time, it sounded like a promise I still could not fully understand. 'I think, with you, everything is enough.'

CHAPTER 28

CLIFF

Happiness and misery weren't mutually exclusive. For a long time I'd assumed you could only feel one or the other, but now I knew that wasn't true.

Since telling Mabel the truth, I'd felt better than I ever had. The moment she realised what – and *who* – I was, but had still decided to stand by me, something that had long been rattling loose inside me had fallen into place. I felt like myself again. Like the self I had believed for many years was dying, as time wore away more and more of its layers.

Maybe it was as simple as that: we had lost Heaven, I had lost myself. I had found Mabel, I had found myself. What I felt with her was more than happiness. It was like coming back to life after an eternity in which I'd felt half dead. Yet I knew what it would cost me to hold on to this feeling. Who it would cost me.

This would be the hardest thing I'd ever done. Probably the worst, too, although I'd done so many unforgiveable things in my life – in my many lives. I knew I shouldn't feel this way, but hurting strangers was different from hurting the people you loved the most. Nothing was crueller than betrayal.

Still. It was the only right thing to do. I just had to forget everything I had internalised over the past one hundred and sixty years. I had to throw out every rule, every code of behaviour, every pattern of thought that had been indoctrinated into me. For the first time in forever, I had to listen to my own instincts. To what *I* wanted, even if it destroyed everything my community had built. If it destroyed *us*. The fact was: I was about to change the course of one hundred and seventy-five lives, permanently – including the lives of the two people who were the closest thing I had to a family.

The guilt had been heavy on my shoulders ever since last night, when Mabel and I came up with our plan, and with every step I took towards the building, it weighed me down further still. Even so, I never doubted I'd go through with it. I had to do this. I had rediscovered, finally, how it felt to believe that doing the right thing was worth enduring anything. Or no, I hadn't *rediscovered* it: Mabel had brought it back to me. Just the thought of her made me breathe easier. *This is worth it,* I thought, opening the door. *She's worth it. I'm worth it – the me I want to be.*

Norah had texted to say where they were. I'd asked her to keep an eye on Ashton last night, after Mabel had dozed off on my sofa. She hadn't asked why, but I assumed Ashton had told her. When it came to words, he wasn't good at self-restraint – especially not when he was angry.

Reaching the door of the room where we sometimes held our parties, I paused. One last deep breath, and then I opened it and stepped inside. My eyes dwelt briefly on Norah, sitting at the piano by the window, before they found Ashton on the sofa.

'You shouldn't be smoking in here,' I said, gesturing at the cigarette between his fingers as I shut the door behind me.

He growled, but otherwise did not respond. Instead, he took a pointedly long drag.

'Come on, people. We know each other too well for all this passive-aggressive bullshit. Talk it out.' Norah's gaze lingered on me. Evidently, she'd heard enough to know I'd have to apologise before Ashton would even talk to me. In all these years, I'd never dared to oppose him like that. Mabel was a first for me, in more ways than one. And in one specific way, a last.

I forced myself to nod, coming further into the room. 'Norah's right. I'm sorry, Ash. I lost control and took it too far.'

'That's one way of putting it.' Ashton stubbed out his cigarette on the armrest of the sofa. It took all my self-control not to step back as he got up and came towards me. 'What the hell is going on?' he asked sharply. 'Do you have feelings for her or what?'

It was obvious from his tone how ludicrous he found the very idea of it. Of course: in all the years of the League's existence, nothing like this had ever happened. Relationships between members and outsiders were either inherited from the original owner of the body or served a clearly defined purpose: the spouses of the bodies we inhabited, relationships that benefitted us or helped us network. I had never heard of a soul-jumper falling in love with someone outside of that. Perhaps no one had let it get that far, because we knew nothing could ever come of it.

And yet here I was, unable to deny it. 'She was the first ... moth I'd had in decades,' I replied evasively. 'I'm not used to how intense the bond can get when you keep one for that long. I got mixed up.'

Ashton's brows knitted warily. 'But you're not anymore?'

'No.' That, at least, I didn't have to lie about. My mind had never felt clearer than it did in this moment. 'You're right. Mabel won't stop until she's dragged the truth into the light. She can't stay.'

Ashton crossed his arms and took another step towards me. A pulse was beating from the core of his chest: too weak to be fresh, but strong enough that I knew how much he must have absorbed recently. As it dawned on me that this was Mabel's energy, I clenched my fists. When I'd found him with her last night, I was so worried about her it overshadowed everything else. Now a different emotion flooded through me, all the more powerful: rage.

'And this revelation just came to you, did it?' he asked, before I could do anything stupid that might give me away. 'After you rode in to rescue her like a knight in some stupid fucking TV drama?' His breath was on my face. Smoke and gin, as well as a hint of Mabel's own unique scent, which had never felt so unfamiliar to me.

I felt sick to my stomach, but I didn't blink. 'I wanted to keep her, but I see now it'll never work.'

He inclined his head and dropped back onto the sofa. 'So where is she, then? Why didn't you bring her?'

'Because I thought we might make it work a different way.' I sat down in the armchair next to him. I had to wet my lips before I could bring myself to say the next words. The ones that would make or break everything. 'I want her face. Not for myself, though. I mean ... near me.'

Norah let out a gasp of astonishment, but I didn't dare look in her direction. My whole focus was on Ashton. He stared at me incredulously for about fifteen seconds before he burst out laughing. 'She's a bursary kid. Her family's dead, and they were a bunch of nobodies to begin with. She's nothing.'

Everything, I thought. *She is everything*. I gave a deliberately casual shrug. 'I know, but we've always made exceptions. When it's important. And this is important. To me.' I rested my elbows on my knees and leant in towards Ashton. 'She reminded me why I love this life. Why I ... love my life with all of you. Give me a little time with the part of her I can have.' I put a hand on his shoulder, hating myself for it. 'Please, Ash. Talk to Henry.'

He pulled a face, but I saw the way his eyes softened. Even if

Ashton liked to pretend he didn't care about anything, nobody knew better than me that it wasn't true. He had come to bring me back after I'd made the decision to leave. He had given me as much leeway as he could, covering for me with the council and his father so that I could take my time finding my way back to them. He had waited for me because he loved me. That's why I knew the plan would work. And why it was the worst thing I had ever done – or would ever do.

'Even if I could get Henry to agree,' he replied sceptically, after a pause. 'Who'd take on that body willingly?'

That was the one problem I didn't have a good solution for. Before I could come up with something, Norah cleared her throat.

'I'll do it.'

Everything inside me froze. It was an effort of will to lift my hand from Ashton's shoulder so that we could both turn to look at her. She was standing, arms crossed. Her mint-green dress fluttered in the draught from the window, but her eyes were firm and resolute.

'What?' Ashton asked slowly.

She shrugged. 'I'll take her face. It's pretty, and I don't mind wearing plainer clothes for a while. Besides, I don't mind Cliff staring at me.' She smiled gently. 'The three of us are best friends, aren't we? This is the kind of thing we do for each other.'

'Norah...' My voice broke, and so did a part of me. I'd known this would be painful, but this ... this was more than I could bear. More than I could inflict on them.

'What, *Blake*? I'll do it.' Seeing the fierceness in her eyes, I swallowed all my arguments.

Ashton was looking from one of us to the other, bemused. 'Are you sure? She's not a redhead. Definitely not your type.'

She snorted and pushed the hair back from her forehead. 'If

you want to talk tradition, you broke your own a long time ago, *Arthur.*'

She was right, although I knew he wouldn't like to be reminded of it. We had all found ways of making the bodies our own. I gave each of them the same scar, the one I'd got falling out of a tree in my first lifetime. Norah sought out women with the same fox-red hair as her own. And Ashton had always chosen someone with the same or a very similar name to the one he was born with. At least, until the day Heaven left. Something in his eyes told me he was thinking of her too. That he couldn't lose another of us.

He threw back his head with a groan. 'Okay, fine,' he said resignedly, getting to his feet. 'I'll talk to Henry. If that's what it takes to get you back, then I'll do what I can.'

I pushed out a smile, although guilt tugged heavily at the corners of my mouth. 'Thanks.'

Ashton waved a hand and stalked out before either of us could say a word. These days he never lingered in a situation once it started to feel too intimate, but I had never been more grateful for it than in that moment. One more question and I would have cracked and told him everything. It was true: being good at lying didn't mean I liked it. And with them – the people I was supposed to be completely open with – it was even harder. I felt wretched and relieved at the same time.

The minute the door swung shut behind him, I exhaled. 'Norah,' I began again, but I couldn't find the words. Although perhaps I didn't need to, because no one knew me better than she did. Norah knew my ugliest secrets and my loftiest thoughts, and she always understood me – maybe even the things I couldn't explain.

'It's okay.' She came towards me, resting a hand on my cheek. 'We love you, Cliff. And you love us.'

I grasped her fingers tightly. 'You're not going to ask, are you?'

'Like I said: we know each other too well for that.'

Instead of answering, I stood up and pulled her into a hug. I shut my eyes and rested my head against hers. Funny: she'd been using the same perfume for decades, but it smelt different on every body.

'I'm tired too. It's all right,' she whispered, pressing a kiss to my collarbone. The tattoo pulsed, but at that moment I felt more powerfully than ever before that this fleck of ink wasn't what connected me to Norah. It was so much more. It ran so much deeper.

Maybe Norah sensed what I was planning, or she was taking a chance because she trusted me. Either way, it didn't change the fact that I was going to betray her.

We had lived our lives together from the beginning. Here in Cambridge, nearly forty years ago, Heaven's death had changed things in a way that could never be undone. It had taught us that even eternity was not untouchable. And here it would come to an end, once and for all: our lives, our friendship, our us.

I couldn't help thinking of the words Heaven always used to say: *eternity is poised upon this moment.* And I knew: *this is the one that's going to bring it down.*

CHAPTER 29
MABEL

The next two weeks felt like a sort of trance. I spent most of my free time with Cliff. He went out of his way every morning to walk me to the faculty building, kept me company between seminars, picked me up from the library in the evenings. He said he wanted to spend time with me, but we both knew it was more than that: he wanted to make sure Ashton didn't run out of patience and take matters into his own hands. For the same reason, I spent most of my nights at his place. I slept beside him, with him. For the first time, I felt like I truly understood why they called it sleeping with each other. It wasn't just about the sex, it was about the before and after. The sense that you were sharing something beyond the physical. When I fell asleep in his arms, I felt like our minds were interweaving. As if, although it was unconscious, although it went unremembered, we even shared our dreams. Whatever this thing was between us, it was bigger and more powerful and more beautiful than anything I'd felt with a man before. In the presence of his soul, I felt my own soul coming to rest, and somehow ... coming home.

Nobody noticed I was spending the majority of my free time

away from college. Davie was still in a coma, and Zoe had gone back to her parents' house the day after my confrontation with Ashton. She still wasn't feeling any better and the college had insisted she take a leave of absence. I'd told her I thought it was a good idea – Cliff had promised me she'd recover quickly once Ashton was no longer feeding on her soul. That thought was the only thing that let me relax even slightly as the date of the emergency ceremony loomed.

It felt like we were on a chessboard. Cliff and I on one side, the rest of the Starlings on the other. Although we were the only ones aware we were playing, I still felt like we were at a disadvantage, because on a fundamental level, we didn't know the rules. We had a plan, but it relied largely on improvisation. The only real move we had was to get me into the same room as the artefact. Everything that happened after that depended on me.

As much as I liked taking matters into my own hands, I couldn't stop them shaking when I thought about that. Like right now. I clasped them uneasily over my stomach to keep them still.

Cliff noticed anyway. With a glance up and down the empty street, he interlocked his fingers with mine. 'The car will be here any minute.'

'I know, that's why I'm nervous,' I muttered, looking around. It was early twilight, and Cambridge lay before us in shades of grey and blue, only the evening sky shot through with soft violet.

Cliff had told me the council moved the location of the ceremony every time, making it harder for anyone who might be planning to disrupt it. This one would take place somewhere near Cambridge, because Victor's body – *Jess's body* – was already too damaged to withstand a long journey, but the exact location had not been shared with Victor or Norah. All we knew was that I'd be picked up in about ten minutes.

'There's something else.' Cliff stepped in front of me, shielding me from the street. 'They'll notice if your soul is untouched. I have to take some energy from you or they'll get suspicious.'

I swallowed, my carotid pulsing dully. 'Okay.'

'Just a bit, I promise.' Softly he cradled my face, letting two fingers slip down to the artery in my throat. I'd realised by now that made it easier for them to reach the soul.

My pulse slowed beneath his touch, and I smiled. 'I trust you, remember?'

I closed my eyes as I sensed a gentle pressure inside my chest. It felt completely different than it had with Victor and Ashton. Cliff didn't hurl himself against my soul, he knocked cautiously. I didn't try to push him back, I opened it for him. After all, he was already in there, although in a different way.

It lasted just a few velvet-flowing seconds, the heat streaming from me and into him. I was flooded with a pleasant kind of langour, sinking against him, breathing him in, absorbing his closeness – the same thing he was doing, just differently.

Carefully he disconnected, although he held my body more tightly than ever. His breathing deepened, maybe because of my energy, maybe because we both sensed this was a goodbye. He wasn't taking part in the ceremony: if he tried to follow us, it would raise questions. It was safer for us and for the plan if he waited here. Still, it felt awful.

'I don't know if I can let you go,' he murmured. 'If something goes wrong—'

'It's our best option, isn't it?' I broke in calmly. 'I mean, you can't keep me out of this now, I'm in too deep. You said it yourself – the council wants to get rid of me. And I'm not going to hide from them. We both want a real life, don't we? And we can't do that if we're on the run. We have to strike first. We have to stop them. This is the right way. Logically, it's the only thing that makes sense.'

He pushed me gently away from him, looking at me. 'This has nothing to do with logic, Pica.'

'Yeah, I know. Emotions are such a drag.' I rolled my eyes, knowing he would see in my face that I didn't mean it. Not anymore. Not when it came to him – to us.

'Promise me you'll be careful. That you'll do everything you can to protect yourself. If you have to choose between destroying the artefact and saving yourself, you choose yourself, okay?'

I forced myself to smile. 'Sure.'

Cliff pressed his forehead against mine. 'You've always been a terrible liar.'

'All right, then listen to this: I'm coming back to you,' I replied, with all the certainty I had. 'Was that the truth or a lie?'

Instead of an answer, he gave me a kiss. Maybe he really could hear what I was thinking: that it wasn't either of those things. I wanted to mean it, but I couldn't promise. I had absolutely no idea what was going to happen once I got into that car.

Just as Cliff let me go and took a step back, it appeared at the end of the road: a black vehicle with tinted windows, which pulled up beside us. Cliff's expression shut down, and I knew the curtain had fallen back across the window. Once again, he had made a mirror of himself, reflecting whatever it was that others wanted to see. Reaching for the rear door, he opened it for me.

I knew I couldn't afford to turn a hair, couldn't make the slightest protest: my soul was supposed to be drained, and I had to act accordingly. Meekly. I lowered myself slowly into the car, staring rigidly ahead at the rolled-down partition while Cliff flicked the door shut beside me. Leaving me like it was nothing. Even though I knew he'd drawn the curtains of distance and indifference on purpose, I felt sick. I hoped desperately this wasn't my last true glimpse of him.

∽

I couldn't tell how long we'd been driving. The landscape slipped by outside the tinted glass like a featureless grey ribbon, and I didn't let myself glance at my watch. Not until the car began to slow did I risk a proper look out of the window. In the blue dusk I saw the outline of a manor house. Low lamps illuminated the gravel driveway that led up to it, bathing it in a warm coppery glow.

We pulled up just outside the steps leading up to the enormous double wooden doors. A moment later, the door opened next to me and a man peered inside. His eyes swept over me, then he took my arm and pulled me out. Everything inside me was screaming to tear myself free, but instead I walked on up the steps beside him without a murmur.

The interior of the house was as chilly and imposing as the exterior had suggested. The man led me silently down red-carpeted corridors, past walls covered in paintings, galleries of pale statues, and nooks crammed with brocade armchairs, as I struggled to take note of my surroundings without seeming too alert. After we had descended a flight of stairs, he stopped and turned me around, yanking my arm so roughly that I hit my back against one of the sculptures. For the first time, I allowed myself to look at my escort, and I noticed the bird-shaped pin on the lapel of his jacket. It was exactly like the one Heaven had worn in the picture of her, Cliff and the others.

'Wait here until someone comes to fetch you.'

I didn't have to decide whether to risk a reply, because he had already turned on his heel and was climbing back up the stairs.

Just as I was about to take my phone out of my jacket pocket to text Cliff, I heard more footsteps down the hall. Taking a cautious step away from the statue, I peered out into the corridor. Two men were standing a few yards away from me by a half-open door. I could only see one of their faces, which glowed pale in the dim light of the gilded sconces between us. His eyes swept glassily along the corridor and over me, as if he didn't notice me at all.

A second later, the other man grabbed him by the shoulder and pushed him down onto a bench, saying something. I froze when I realised who it was. Just as he straightened up and saw me.

How could I have spent even half a second talking to Jess and not realise? That smirk on his face: derision camouflaged as pleasure, so insincere that the skin around his eyes never even creased. The way he tucked strands of hair behind his ear, even though they were too short and immediately fell out again. The way he appraised me, as if he both hated me and wanted me for himself. None of that was Jess. It was Victor. Or ... the soul I thought of by that name.

He stopped just in front of me. 'Well, well, well. Who'd have thought we'd end up here, eh?' He wound his fingers around a lock of hair and tugged hard.

My fingers twitched. I dug them into my palms and bit the inside of my cheek, trying not to make a sound. He was so close to me now that I could see what Cliff had meant when he said the body was falling apart. His skin was sloughing off in reddish-purple scales, his cheeks were sunken, his eyes deeper-set than normal. The corners of his mouth had cracked, as had his nails and the skin around the cuticles. The unpleasantly sweet odour was even more pungent than before – it made me think of overripe fruit. *Rot*, I thought instinctively. *That's what rot smells like*. I breathed through my mouth, lowering my gaze, because I wasn't sure what to do. What I would be like if I ... wasn't myself anymore.

'I'd have bet money Cliff would give in to temptation and accidentally kill you,' he murmured, running two fingers along my cheek towards my throat. 'The way he looked at you ... I haven't seen him show that much emotion for years. He wanted your soul so badly – I'm astonished he wanted your face more. As if this were worth anything.' He flicked my cheek before he let me go. 'He's stupider than I thought.'

Rage flared up inside me, forcing my lips apart. 'Shut your mouth.'

Victor frowned. 'Excuse me?'

I knew I should leave it, but I just couldn't bring myself to. My gaze bored into the washed-out greenish-brown of Jess's eyes. 'Don't you dare talk about him like you actually know him. You don't know anything about him. Or me.'

A look of bewilderment crossed his haggard features. At that moment, I realised he wasn't even really listening: it wasn't what I'd said, it was *how* I'd said it that was the fatal mistake. 'You still seem a little too clear-headed to me.'

'I don't know what you mean,' I replied, and regretted it immediately. Even I could hear it now: there was too much edge to my voice, it was too cold. Not half as vague as it probably should have been, given that my soul had supposedly been blotted out to make room for Norah's in my body.

Victor frowned, and I felt sick. Moving with deliberate slowness, I tried to take a step past him, but he blocked my path. 'What are you doing?' This time my voice was unpleasantly thin and reedy.

'Something I've been wanting to do for a really long fucking time,' he replied with a grim smile, before he reached out and clutched my throat.

I tried to push him off me, but he shoved me back against the wall with a thud. And then ... he hurled himself against me, without coming even a centimetre closer. He clutched at something inside me with unimaginable violence, far more brutal than Ashton had been a few days earlier: I felt the full force of him slamming against me, so hard that I felt my soul transforming into a pulsing bruise.

I had to... But my thoughts crumbled, becoming a thick layer that coated my whole mind. My eyelids grew heavy, my knees weak. I collapsed, and I would certainly have fallen if Victor hadn't held me up.

'Stop that immediately!' The bright voice shot swift as an arrow through the pain vibrating through me. My brain tried to connect it to a face, but all it managed was the thought of red hair like a fairy's.

Victor sighed, but his grip relaxed inside me, even as his hand tightened around my neck, still holding me up. 'I was just preparing the body for you. Cliff was a bit sloppy.'

'He wasn't sloppy,' the other voice snarled. *Norah* – of course. 'He was just leaving some for me. Unlike you, he respects the fact that I like to do it myself. I'm the one spending the next few years in this shell, after all – it's my right to prepare it the way I want!'

'Fine, fine. There's still some of her left.' He grabbed my shoulder and shoved me over to Norah.

My knees were still too weak, and I sank helplessly against her. Norah grabbed my arms and held me upright. Vaguely I felt her fingers skim my throat. I thought I heard her say something else, but I was too far away to reach for the words. Everything around me interwove into a blanket of cotton wool. There was a buzzing in my ears, and inside me, too. Perhaps it was the echo of my heartbeat, which was the last thing I really registered.

At the fringes of it all, I sensed us moving. A breath of wind on my cold face, Norah's warmth, which never left my side. Behind my closed eyelids was a spreading darkness, shot through with a few dabs of gold. More voices drifted loosely past me, but I made no effort to catch them. I didn't want to hear anything, I didn't want to feel anything, I didn't want to ... be anything. I didn't want anything anymore.

I wasn't sure how much time had passed before I felt another touch on my neck. With an effort, I made my eyes blink open, and blearily I recognised Norah's face in front of mine – creased brow, narrowed eyes. She leant towards me until her mouth hovered close to my ear. Her fingers were resting on my carotid artery, where my pulse thudded with all its might against her touch.

Something strange was happening: the longer I felt her touch, the more I grew warm. It didn't feel like she was taking energy from me, more like ... giving it back. I gasped as a wave of strength surged through my exhausted body. Reflexively, I struggled to break free of her embrace, but she held me tightly, pressing her lips closer to my ear. I sensed her breath, her fluttering heartbeat, and my own, growing stronger with each and every thud.

I blinked, turning my head to look around. We were in a round room lined with floor-to-ceiling columns. The black stone at our feet was inlaid with gold decoration, and all around us were pillar candles, the only source of light. I took this in only vaguely, because my attention was drawn to the middle of the room.

On a waist-high marble plinth was a vessel made out of slate-grey glass. The size of an ostrich egg and quite unremarkable, yet I couldn't take my eyes off it. As I moved, the candlelight fell on the material, bringing out faint grooves. I had to squint hard before I realised it was words – in a language I didn't understand.

Victor's eyes met mine from the other side of the plinth. He grinned, before my eyeline was blocked by the back of a man I didn't know. The guy who had been with Victor earlier was now lying motionless on the floor beside him. Slowly it dawned on me the situation we were in: we were standing in the room where it was going to happen. Where ... Victor was going to take over his body, and Norah mine. Panic convulsed in my muscles, but so weakly that all I did was begin to tremble.

Norah increased the pressure on my throat, snapping my focus back to her. At that moment it hit me with a certainty that made me gasp: I didn't stand a chance – I never had. How could Cliff and I ever have hoped otherwise? I was only human, and neither my body nor my soul were at their strongest. My muscles felt limp, my insides skinned and sore, my mind spinning. I was *so* tired. It felt like part of me was missing: the part that had housed my resolve, the part that had promised I'd do everything I could to get out of this situation.

I had wanted to fight, but now I just wanted it to stop. Everything. Deep down, beneath the exhaustion, something whispered to me that it made sense: what Cliff had taken from my soul had been a tiny sliver, but what Victor had ripped out had left a hole. An aching, pulsing breach that leaked its agonising nothingness across the surface of my mind. Whatever Norah had just done, it wasn't enough. I didn't have the strength to pull this off alone. There was no way I could hold my own against all these people in this state, no way I could destroy that thing.

'Listen: you have to concentrate. When I say *now*, you have to do it. You have exactly one chance, so don't hesitate.' Norah's voice flowed softly into my ear, a salve to my raw thoughts.

Her gaze focused my eyes – focused my soul. It felt like she was reaching out a hand and trying to bind the loose ends back together.

'Got it?' she hissed.

I wasn't sure I had. It made no sense. As far as Norah knew, my only plan here was to die. She couldn't know what we intended. And even if she did – surely, she wouldn't be on our side.

I parted my lips, but at that moment I sensed the person at my back.

'Ready?'

Norah's eyes were still locked on mine as she nodded. One by one, she took her hands off me. I staggered a little, but stayed on my feet. Norah took the box from the man, wincing faintly as she did so. Even though she was standing at a distance from me, I felt the heat radiating from the wood. My eyes slid past her. Victor wasn't standing on the other side of the artefact anymore. A second glance, and I realised he was lying motionless on the floor beside the other man. Instinctively, I knew that one was unconscious and the other was dead. Victor had left Jess's body and was now ... in the glass vessel on the plinth? I narrowed my eyes, catching a glimpse of the silvery gleam that seemed to float inside it. So that must be ... his soul? I felt like laughing, somehow like crying, too, but it was taking all my concentration just to breathe.

'Horatio?' asked Norah tonelessly, interrupting my thoughts.

He had already taken a step towards me, but now he stopped. 'Yes?'

Just as he turned in her direction, Norah looked at me and said, 'Now.'

In the same fraction of a second, she lunged out of nowhere, raising the box to bring it slamming down on his head. The edge of it struck his temple, and he let out a groan. Wide eyes staring at her in shock, he sank helplessly to his knees.

Norah's lips clamped as she struck a second time. 'Do it,' she hissed, just as Horatio's body finally hit the ground.

I still wasn't quite sure what was happening, but a switch flicked and I sprinted into the middle of the room. The heat of the artefact was gathered like a cloud around the plinth, trying to thrust me back, but I plunged headlong into it anyway. It had a taste: ashes and iron; a sound: a low hum; a colour:

shimmering silver. It wound itself so tightly around me that I lurched over the final few steps.

Seeing nothing, not hesitating, I reached out to grasp the vessel with both hands. It was heavy and hot, and within seconds, a barbed pain was tearing through my skin. Struggling, I squinted against its light. My nostrils filled with the smell of charring as somewhere, dimly, I registered my singed hair. Everything inside me screamed at me to put it back or let it drop, but I gazed spellbound into its depths. Into the gleam that was a whole existence. A soul. A life. A person.

This is murder. The thought darted through my head. *You're killing Victor.* Part of me didn't want to, despite everything he had done. But what I'd said to Cliff before was true: logically, this was the only right thing to do. I had a choice, and every available option made me someone I didn't want to be. I had to choose the version I could live with.

I narrowed my eyes until the silvery glow was barely more than a thread. I thought of the scar on Cliff's temple as I tightened my grip on the artefact, raised my arms above my head and flung it to the ground.

The humming cut out the moment the vessel hit the tiles, escalating seamlessly into a shrill noise like a shriek. I didn't know what had caused it, I just knew that the sound pierced straight into my head, every thought now bristling with thorns. My brain furrowed under every attempt to think, and I gave a muffled groan.

Something was shattering into infinite pieces, and at the edges of my perception I realised it wasn't just the vessel itself. It was what it had contained. Victor's soul, perhaps every soul it had ever held, perhaps especially those sacrificed to create it. Perhaps, in that moment, they all felt it: perhaps the wave of light that burst through the room forced that pain into every Starling in existence.

It knocked me back a little, too, more from shock than pain.

Briefly all my senses were engulfed in the cloud, which whipped up in seconds into a towering storm before – quietly, abruptly – it dissipated. The silence was almost more painful than the din that went before it. It crept into my brain like a roar, forcing me to my knees. Bracing myself with all my strength against the dizziness, I turned.

Norah was kneeling next to an unconscious Horatio, whose chest rose and fell shallowly. She was doubled over, clutching her body with both arms as if trying to subdue some pain within. Or ... to hold herself together?

'Norah?' My voice sounded as broken as the vessel, the shards of which were scattered around the room like a carpet of glass. My shoes crunched as I walked towards her and crouched down.

'It's really over,' she whispered, sinking forward until her forehead was resting against my shoulder. Even through the layers of fabric, I felt the cold streaming out of her. My throat tightened, and carefully I held her in my arms.

Only for a few seconds, then she pulled away. Staggering to her feet, she glanced around her. For a moment, her eyes lingered on the corpse – the one she saw in the body, and the one reflected for her in the shards of the artefact. A look of grief flashed across her face, before she hid it again behind the smooth familiar mask of determination and aloofness, which I had never fully understood. At that moment, I thought I did understand. It was self-protection. Norah locked away her true self from the outside world because it helped her cope, both with what was happening inside her and around her. She was playing a part, even now. Only, this time it was one she'd chosen for herself.

'What about him?' I asked hoarsely, pointing at Horatio. 'Won't he know you hit him?'

'I took some of his energy. With any luck, his memory will be foggy. It'll buy us some time.' Still expressionless, she held out her hand to me. 'Still, we'd better get out of here before the guards show up. Give ourselves a head start before they start asking questions. We're going to need some pretty watertight answers.'

Reflexively, I took her hand and let her draw me upright, following her out of the room and along the looping corridors of the building. I didn't dare ask what answers she had in mind. Cliff and I had talked for ages about what would happen if the League found out the artefact had been destroyed – especially after a ceremony in which I was supposed to die had apparently failed – but we could never come up with a satisfactory answer. *One step at a time*, I'd said eventually, with more confidence than I felt. I knew that even with Norah's help, there would be holes in our story.

We could do our best to make it watertight, but they'd try to drown us anyway.

CHAPTER 30
MABEL

Once we'd reached the main road, Norah called us a taxi for the way back. While we were waiting, I texted Cliff to tell him it was done, but I felt none of the expected sense of relief.

It was impossible to relax. What had just happened settled like a cold damp hand on the nape of my neck. The plan had worked, but I knew it was far from over. Norah had managed to get us out unnoticed, but what we'd left in the room would raise questions. The thought of the dead body made me strangely nauseous. One corpse, two dead people. I was thinking mostly of Jess, and I knew Norah was thinking of Victor. The glassy look in her eyes as she stared out of the taxi window reflected memories left unsaid. To me, Victor had been a monster; for her, and for Cliff, he was a friend. Yet they had still allowed me to destroy the artefact. I thought I understood why Cliff had made that decision, but … not Norah.

'Why did you help me?' I asked, keeping my voice hushed so the driver couldn't hear us.

Slowly, she turned her gaze on me. Her red hair shimmered

like copper, and the shadows under her eyes were deep. I had never seen her so ... tired. At that moment, it was easy to imagine how old her soul must be. 'Cliff loves you. I know that because we're so familiar with each other we can see these things. It was obvious he would never sacrifice you like this. He'd have tried to run off with you rather than give up your soul without a fight.'

I blinked, taken aback. 'Then ... you knew what we were planning? So why did you go along with it – why did you help? You don't even know me.'

'I don't have to. No offence or anything, but this isn't about you. It's about Cliff. And about ... myself.' She smiled dully, running a hand over the smooth skin of her cheeks, as if she could feel the mask slipping with every word. 'When you've lived as long as we have, eventually you come to realise what really matters to you. For a long time, I thought I wanted all the things the League was created to provide. But after what happened with Heaven, I realised that wealth, power, eternity – they mean nothing. Not if you can't spend that time with the people you love.' She gazed again into the reflection of her own eyes. I wondered how many faces she saw when she looked at herself. If maybe, even after all these years, she sought her own true face in each reflection. 'When we lost her, I chose friendship,' she whispered, as midnight-blue billboards swept past outside. Lie after lie, all trying to sell you something, and Norah's pale features overlaid across them. Her face had never looked more honest. 'That's why I did it.'

I had never seen anyone more loyal. Cliff hadn't told her what he had in mind, yet she'd not hesitated to support him, even though she knew it would change her own life forever. More than that: if she helped him, there would be no forever. I wasn't sure if I liked Norah, but from that moment on, I felt more respect for her than for almost anybody else.

'Thank you, Norah.' I hesitated. 'I mean, is that your ... real name?'

'Who's to say. It wasn't my first, but it looks like it'll be my last.' Her smile faltered, and she swallowed heavily. 'Be good to Cliff, okay? He's the best soul of us all. He always was. He deserves things to end happily.'

I returned her piercing look, not understanding. 'What do you mean, end? I know it's your last life, but it's only just beginning. You have so much time left.'

She looked at me with strange perplexity. Before I could ask again, the car stopped and the driver turned to us expectantly.

Cliff was waiting for us outside his building, and hugged first me then Norah. His expression was a mosaic of relief, guilt and weariness as he stepped away from her, his hands on her shoulders.

She smiled crookedly and adjusted the collar of the dark shirt poking out from underneath his jumper. 'I'll try to put Henry off the scent, but you know what he's like. I'm afraid that sooner or later they'll want to talk to you. And to her.' She lowered her voice, and I took a step away from them. Not just to give them some privacy, but so I could pretend I didn't know they were talking about me. I didn't want to think about what happened next.

'I know. I'm ready for whatever's coming.' Cliff hesitated, then he hugged her again. His voice was mostly lost in her thick hair, and the rest was plucked apart by the gust of winter wind between us, so that it reached me only in fragments. 'Thank you. And ... forgive me.'

'There's nothing to forgive,' she replied just as quietly, before she pulled away. 'But you know he won't see it like that.'

He nodded slowly. 'Like I said: I'm ready.'

We watched Norah until she had vanished into the densely woven network of passageways. For a few minutes more we lingered there, standing close yet in our own separate worlds, then Cliff took my hand. 'Milk and honey?'

I smiled and squeezed his fingers. 'Sounds good.'

~

I sat down on the sofa while Cliff heated up the milk. When he brought it in I was just finishing a brief conversation with Zoe. I accepted one of the two porcelain mugs gratefully, drawing up my feet so he could sit next to me.

'Zoe's feeling better,' I told him after the first sip. 'She's staying at her parents' place for another week. At least Ashton won't be able to take his temper out on her when he finds out what we've done.' I hesitated, setting the drink down on the table.

'You want to tell her the truth,' he said, before I could go on. He didn't sound troubled or surprised, more like he'd seen it coming.

'I don't think I have a choice. Zoe needs to know why she has to stay away from Ashton. Even if you can't leave your bodies anymore, he could still try to drain her energy. Or he could use her to get revenge on me in some other way. I have to protect her.'

He stirred his milk pensively with the silver spoon. 'Do you think she'll believe you?'

'She believes in *astrology*,' I replied, giving him a look. 'If I can believe it, she definitely can.'

Cliff smiled and put his mug down, too. 'All right, then go for it.'

I sat up straighter, astonished. I'd been expecting a lot more resistance. We'd struck a fatal blow to the League, but even so, I assumed the Starlings would be none too pleased about me spilling their secrets. 'You don't mind?'

'It doesn't matter anymore who knows what. I mean, we

probably shouldn't go to the newspapers with it, but—' He broke off when he saw my face change, twisting with pain the way it always did when I thought of Davie.

'I'm sorry.' He stroked my hand, which was clenched rigidly around my knee. 'He could still recover. Anything's possible.'

I noticed the deliberate subjunctive. He knew as well as I did that he could make no promises. My only hope was that Davie would be as tenacious now as when he was chasing down a story.

I forced myself to smile. 'I know. And when he does, I'll ask him to be discreet. Davie's pretty good with secrets, as long as he's in on them.'

'All right, let's do that. I don't want you lying to your friends for my sake.' He grinned half-heartedly. 'Plus you're still pretty crap at it. You're not going to fool anybody even if you try.'

'Hey,' I began, mock-outraged, then broke off instantly when the doorbell rang.

I hadn't realised it was possible to ring a doorbell angrily – until now. Whoever it was, they were holding down the button while hammering against the wood with their other hand. Cliff and I exchanged a look. I swallowed; he ran a hand through his hair. *Whoever it was?* Bullshit. We both knew exactly who it was.

'Maybe you shouldn't answer,' I whispered. 'Wait until he's calmed down.'

Cliff shook his head and stood up. 'You don't know Ashton.' He stopped just before he reached the door and turned to me. 'Look, stay back, all right? And ... I'm sorry.'

Confused, I opened my mouth, but he was already turning away again and reaching for the handle. It happened so quickly that I didn't catch on. I sat immobilised on the sofa, watching as Ashton pushed Cliff back into the flat and followed him inside. As the door was still falling shut, he swung. There was an unpleasantly dull crunch as his fist hit Cliff's nose. Cliff grunted, and I pressed both hands to my mouth to suppress my scream. Still, Ashton's voice rose above everything else.

'*After. Everything. I've. Done. For. You?*' Each word was a snarl, the sentence punctuated by blows. Two more to the face – one in the eye, another just below the cheekbone. Cliff's head snapped to the side, then Ashton's fist struck him in the ribs and stomach. Cliff sagged a little, but he didn't fight back. No raised hands, no attempts to get away. He staggered against the wall, letting Ashton pin him there, his forearm across Cliff's throat. 'Was it worth it?' he spat into his face. 'Was her shitty life worth betraying all of us?'

'Ash—' Cliff broke off when a fist slammed into the wall beside his head. One of the frames wobbled threateningly – like my knees, when I finally managed to stand up.

'Let him go!'

Ashton shot me a glare over his shoulder. His usually light eyes were incredibly dark, as if the pupils had blown out and begun to leak. Hatred had contorted his angelic features into an expression that looked more like a devil's. 'I'll get to you later, Moth,' he snapped, before turning his attention back to Cliff.

Cliff put a hand on the forearm crushing his larynx. 'She had nothing to do with this.'

Ashton laughed jarringly, not pulling back an inch. 'Are you for real? Do you seriously think I don't know what happened? Henry just called and told me how the guards found the ceremony chamber: Horatio and the host body were lying unconscious among the broken shards of the artefact, Victor's dead, and Norah and your fucking moth were nowhere to be found. Don't tell me this was an accident, *Cliff*. We both know it was absolutely deliberate. This was the plan all along. You lied to me! You took advantage of our friendship and tricked me into giving your friend the chance to destroy it!'

Again he punched the wall, so hard that his skin split and

blood spattered across the wallpaper. Feeling sick to my stomach, I took a step towards them.

'You're right,' Cliff said, his voice rough. 'But it was *my* plan. *My* decision. If you want to find them a scapegoat, take me. She had no idea what she was doing.'

'That's not true!' My heart was racing in my throat, but I forced myself to take another step towards them. I'd have been lying if I said I wasn't scared of Ashton, but I was still going to intervene. Cliff and I had made this decision together, so we'd face the consequences together. 'I knew exactly what I was doing,' I went on, as Cliff gave me a warning look over Ashton's shoulder. '*I'm* the one who broke that thing. I know you're angry that you don't get to keep switching bodies, that you've got to stick with this one for the rest of your life, but if you're going to take it out on somebody, take it out on me.'

Ashton's body went visibly stiff, then he let go of Cliff and turned to me. His gaze seemed to bore through me, and my stomach fluttered uneasily as I remembered what he did the last time he'd scowled at me with that kind of rage. Yet he made no move to grab me, inside or out. He only looked at me, brow furrowed, and ... laughed again. The sound was clear as crystal, and so cold that it sent a shiver down my spine. 'She doesn't know, does she?'

'What don't I know?' I looked uncertainly from Ashton to Cliff, who had taken a step towards me, so that he was now standing between us. I could only see the back of him, but I could tell that the muscles in his neck were tense.

Ashton shook his head. The echo of a sneer lingered at the corners of his mouth, and his eyes still gleamed darkly. 'What it is you've really done.'

'Ashton, don't.' Cliff reached out a hand towards him, but Ashton shoved it roughly aside and pushed past him, coming straight to me.

'Doesn't she deserve to know what she's actually

responsible for doing? You won't be able to hide the consequences from her, mate.' He slid his hands into his pockets, stopping just in front of me. 'When you destroyed that artefact, you didn't just kill the person who was mid-jump. You ruined any chance of any of us ever changing host again.'

'I know. You'll have to live ordinary lives in your ordinary bodies. What a terrible tragedy. Welcome to the normal world, Ashton.' I tried to take a step past him, but he seized my arm. His knuckles were bright red, and the metallic scent of blood filled my nostrils, forcing me to breathe through my mouth.

'Normal?' He loomed over me. 'Let me tell you something about *our* normal. Because there's still residual energy left over from the original souls that inhabited these bodies – *our* bodies – they age differently than they otherwise would. It's like they're burning up from the inside out. The energy in them is too much. We can bolster them by absorbing energy from other people, but after a certain point, we're powerless against nature.'

His words were a river in my mind: a terrible roar that drowned all the meaning in those letters, until I could make no sense of them. 'I ... d don't understand,' I stammered, although I was beginning to sense that wasn't true. I did understand, deep down. I just didn't want to admit it, so I was holding the knowledge beneath the surface with all my might.

Ashton's grip tightened, his mouth twisting into a furious smile. 'Oh, come on. I thought you were supposed to be clever. Surely you can work out how stupid you've really been.'

I swallowed hard. What he'd told me reminded me of something Cliff had said about Victor and unplanned soul-jumping. He'd said that if the original soul hadn't been weakened beforehand, the body would decay more quickly than usual. But Ashton, Cliff and the others had done it properly. I'd assumed they only changed bodies so frequently because the council insisted: because that way they could take over whatever lives were most useful to them at the time. But if what Ashton had said was true, that wasn't the only reason. If the original soul's energy weakened the body more quickly than normal, that meant it would age more rapidly. Which in turn meant—

'Your bodies are going to die sooner?' I whispered hoarsely. My eyes darted past Ashton to Cliff, who had turned his face away from us. As if he couldn't bear to look at me. 'But … when?'

'Generally speaking you've got about three to five years after a jump before the body becomes uninhabitable. Until the soul has to move on, if it doesn't want to die too.' Ashton let me go. He must have known those words would hurt me more than any physical pain he could inflict. It felt like I was poised on the edge of a cliff, every syllable pushing me closer to the brink. I staggered, barely managing to keep myself upright. Until he leant in towards me again. 'And you've made that impossible for us now, haven't you?'

That was the last nudge: my mind toppled over the edge, and I fell and fell and fell – until I hit the realisation of what that meant. What I'd done. I let out a sob, and pressed a hand to my mouth. Tasting bile and blood on my tongue. Maybe because I'd bitten my cheek, maybe because I had so much blood on me now. Not just on my hands, everywhere. I breathed guilt, and it tasted of iron and ash and pain.

Ashton stepped back, gazing down at me. 'We've been in these bodies for two years already, Mabel. So enjoy the next few months with your boyfriend, because soon you'll be watching him die a miserable death in front of your very eyes. And you'll know it was your fault.'

My cheeks burned, my vision blurred. I was dimly aware of Ashton turning on his heel and walking out without another word. He slammed the door behind him, and the picture frames trembled again. So did I.

I stared at my hands, winter-pale, library-pale, but I could still see the blood. These were the hands that had destroyed the artefact. These were the hands that had made sure no soul-jumper would ever leave their body again. I'd thought that meant they had one last life to live. With a bit of luck, and universe willing, they'd have another forty to sixty years, just like the rest of us. A normal life, a normal death. I thought I'd done the right thing. Logically I knew that was still true: these souls didn't have the right to eternal life at other people's expense. I had protected countless people from them. I had protected Zoe. I had done what I set out to do. But I hadn't known what price I'd pay for victory. What I was sacrificing for it. *Who* I was sacrificing. If I had ... I wouldn't have thought of it as a victory at all. You couldn't call it that, not when you were losing this much.

'Mabel.'

I didn't even see Cliff until he was standing right in front of me. He reached out to me, but I flinched away. How could he have talked about his own struggles with guilt, only to let me bring the same guilt upon myself?

My vision was still distorted. I could barely focus on him, but I registered the marks on his face: the swelling under his eye, the split lip, the red cheek. Despite it all, I was sure I was more badly hurt. I had so many feelings: rage, despair, sorrow, pain and ... betrayal. 'You knew.' I had to force out the words, still backing away. 'You knew my biggest fear is to lose someone I love! And you still ... you did this to me? You let me *kill* you?'

I didn't care what I was confessing to him, I didn't care about anything. I felt like I was choking. My head was pounding, my heart raced, its beat a constant pressure that fractured every positive emotion I'd ever felt. There would never be anything bright, pure or good in me again.

'You haven't killed me, Mabel. If you think about it, I should have been long dead by now anyway.' He came towards me, but I recoiled until my back hit the wall. A picture frame jabbed into my shoulder, and I wished the pain had been more intense. I would have felt anything to distract me from the burning inside me.

'But you're not dead. Just, now ... now you're dying. Because of me.' As my voice cracked, so did something inside me: the last piece of armour protecting me from the full impact of this feeling. It was like someone had sliced through me with a knife. Not just through my chest, but my belly, my lungs, every single cell in my body. It made sense: I felt Cliff everywhere, so of course I'd feel it everywhere when I lost him. And I had lost him, in the most final possible way, and by my own hand. I'd seen Victor before the ceremony – I knew what would happen to Cliff once his body gave up. In a couple of years, maybe even months, he would die a horrible death. And it was my fault. My fault. My fault. My—

'Not because of you.' Cliff took my face in his hands as if trying to halt the spiralling thoughts behind it – or to save me from falling.

But I already had. I had already hit the ground and shattered, and I knew I'd never be fully whole again. A part of me had broken forever.

'Because it's right,' he said. 'We don't deserve to live this life at other people's expense. What we're doing is murder. I've been murdering people for one hundred and sixty years. It's time to put a stop to it, you said so yourself.'

'But not at any cost, not this!' I tried to push his hands away but he wouldn't let go, so instead I punched his chest, kicked his shins, fighting tooth and nail to break free of his grip. Cliff didn't retaliate or defend himself, any more than he had with Ashton. He just stood there calmly while I hit and scratched and kicked him, until at last I began to cry. Soundlessly, wet-cheeked, shoulders quivering and lips clamped shut. My hands slackened against his body, and in that moment he drew me close. Wrapped his arms around my back and pulled me into a tight hug.

'I can't lose you. I can't.' My voice was lost in the fabric of his jumper, but he heard me.

His mouth grazed my temple. 'Listen. This is the way life is supposed to be: none of us know how long we've got left. We can't control how long we live, only *how* we live. Who we live life with. And I know that two or three real, honest years with you are worth so much more than anything else could be.' Gently he let go and stepped back to look at me. He stroked the hair back from my damp face and touched his forehead against mine. 'I don't need eternity, Pica. I just need a bit more time with you. Will you give me that?'

I felt like shoving him away – I felt like throwing my arms around him. Like scratching out his eyes and closing his mouth with mine. I wanted to kiss him until my body was nothing but that gentle burn and pleasant throb, not this sharp pain. I wanted to scream that I would never forgive him, I wanted to whisper my confession that I was in love with him – because I hadn't said it yet, not directly and honestly, and suddenly I realised I didn't have as much time as I'd hoped.

I had always known it was dangerous, opening yourself up to other people. Once they get comfortable in there, sooner or later they get tangled up with you. They start popping into your head as you move through the world. I would never see a magpie again without thinking of the one I always carried in my pocket. Fitting neatly in my hand, in my heart. I would never eat a pain aux raisins without thinking of how much he wanted to like them, and wishing I could share my enjoyment of it with him. I would never hear organ music or smell honey without feeling a tug of longing in my stomach. I would see Cliff in every silver-shimmering scar, because his flaws were what made him most beautiful to me. I supposed that was what it meant to love someone.

What Cliff's *soul* was, all those tiny details, had woven itself through my perception of the world. If he was torn away, it would leave a ragged hole inside me, trailing loose threads. Losing him would rip me apart, even as I was just beginning to feel like I'd been put back together – like I'd found myself again. I didn't want to lose that, him and me. Us.

Fresh tears welled up, and I did nothing to stop them. 'It's not fair.'

'I know.' Cliff nodded and closed his eyes, but I saw a few tears run down his cheeks too. He didn't try to hide them. This was the end of all lies. This was the final truth, and it was true what people said: most of the time, that truth was ugly.

'I wouldn't have done it if I'd known...'

'I know. That's why I couldn't tell you.' He kissed my forehead, the bridge of my nose, briefly and firmly on the mouth. He tasted of blood. We both did.

My lips quivered. So did my voice. 'Just a short time won't be enough.'

'I know.' He smiled weakly. 'But that's true for everybody, always. To have something you can lose is the most precious thing there is. I know you don't get that right now, but I do, because it's been so long since I had something like that: underneath, the pain is how you know you've lived a full life. That you've got something you love so much you can't bear the thought of losing it. You've given that back to me, Mabel. And ... I know it's going to hurt like hell when I have to leave you, but ... it's worth it. So, if a short time is all we've got, then it'll have to do.' The colour of his irises blurred into an eddying darkness, but something about the look in them was bright enough to light up the gloom of my thoughts.

I was still in despair, still shocked and angry – at him, at myself, at the absurd situation we found ourselves in, where doing the right thing had led to something so horribly wrong, painful, cruel. But ... I was still glad he was with me. It hurt, but

Cliff was there. If I pushed him away while I still had the chance to be with him, I would never forgive myself. Maybe it was naïve to cling on to something I knew would soon be ripped away from me, but Cliff was right: what we had was worth it. It wasn't perfect, it wasn't easy, but it was real. And that was what life was about, wasn't it? Finding something real.

I closed my eyes and forced myself to nod. 'Okay,' I whispered.

'Anyway, time is relative.' Cliff smiled into my forehead. 'If I've learnt anything, it's that. And I know everybody's always wishing it would stand still, but for years now I've been wishing the opposite. That it would start up again. That ... that I would start up again.'

I thought of Cliff's watch, and how he'd told me it had stopped working the night that Heaven died. Suddenly I understood why he had never got it fixed. His world had been shaken to the core that night, and in a way, his life had stood still, too. He had realised what this existence truly meant, and it had stopped him dead. After all those decades of playacting his way through other people's lives, he wanted to lead one of his own, at least for the short while that remained to him. A few years in which every sentence would be his, not the lines of a role he'd been forced to play – years when every step was chosen by him, every decision made by him. He just wanted to be himself once more. And that self wanted to be with me. I was the first decision he had made for himself in a very long time. And he ... he was mine. No logic, no rationalisation, just the feeling that it had to be this way. We had to be, we wanted to be, and we could be. For a while, at least. Maybe that was all you could ever expect from life. In the end, there were never any guarantees, promises or certainties. Each life was a leap into the unknown. At some point you were going to hit the ground, and there was nothing you could do about it. All you could do was choose whose hand you were holding as you fell. And if you chose right, for a while, it might not feel like falling. It might feel like flying.

I took his face in my hands, one thumb on the silver scar at his temple and the other touching his moonspots. It wasn't his first face, but it would be his last. And his truest, because it was the one he'd worn when he decided to take his life back.

Here he was. Here I was. And here we remained, even as we drifted on – even as we fell.

I took a deep breath, closed my eyes, and ... leapt. 'Then let's make the most of our own little corner of eternity.'

MABEL

Two months later

The starlings came back. Cliff and I had seen them for the first time a few weeks ago, while we were revising on the banks of the Cam. For a moment I'd thought the spring sky was clouding over, but when I looked up, I realised the shadows speckling my notes were something else. Countless birds, flying in extravagant formations across the blue. In that moment I had understood why the League of Starlings had chosen that name. Not because they were the most talented mimics. Individually, the black dots in the sky were nothing special, but together they formed an impressive and powerful work of art.

Cliff had watched them, too, until they disappeared from sight beyond the college walls. He'd said nothing, but from the way his lips narrowed, I could tell he, too, thought it might be a bad omen.

It had been almost two months since I'd destroyed the artefact, and every day of them we'd been expecting delegates from the council to show up and ask questions. So far, nothing had happened. Norah had said she'd try to buy us time, but we knew it couldn't last. Just like the real starlings, returning a hundred-fold with the advent of spring, the members of the League would eventually return to find out what had happened. And the trail would lead them to us. No matter what Norah had told them, no matter whether Ashton covered for us or denounced us. Sooner or later, they would come.

I wanted to say I wasn't afraid, but unlike the birds in my room, which I now knew Victor had put there, these Starlings could be dangerous. For me, and for Cliff. It probably didn't say much for my survival instincts that I was more worried about him than about myself. And I was pretty sure Cliff felt the exact inverse. The day we first saw the birds, he asked me if I wanted to go travelling with him during the Easter break. *There are some places I'd like to show you*, he had told me as we lay in bed together. It was one of those warm, languid moments when our eyes were shut and we were naked, inside and out, while the world beyond – the sounds of rain and the dull yellow beam of headlights – passed us by outside, crossing through our own dark quiet.

I still wasn't keen on him buying me things I couldn't afford, but I couldn't bring myself to say no. Perhaps because I knew he, too, was trying to outrun his fear of the future, at least for a little while. Or because I knew now that our future together was going to be a lot shorter than I'd wanted.

So I agreed, and now here I was a few weeks later, standing in my room with my bags packed, gazing out of the window. No starlings in the sky, only a magpie perched on a tree in the court, polishing its feathers. If bad omens existed, there had to be good ones too, surely?

I smiled as I saw a figure slip behind the reflection of my own face, and I turned around. Zoe had just walked into my room. Her hair was intricately braided, and her lids gleamed as golden as her enormous hoop earrings and her eyes. No more poorly concealed dark circles, no bitter twist to her lips, no distracted sheen in her cornflower-blue eyes. Having Zoe back, really *back*, reminded me every day why it had all been worth it.

'Shouldn't you be on your way by now, my little globetrotter?' The teasing note in her voice was gentle: Zoe was almost more delighted than I was that I was finally spending a holiday away from college.

'Almost. How about you? Are you going home?'

'No. Home isn't ... it isn't the greatest for a holiday.'

I gave her a worried look. 'Why, what's wrong?'

Zoe shook her head, coming towards me. 'Nothing bad, and nothing important.'

'You sure?' I did my best to wipe away the plastered-on smile, trying to see the truth beneath. Although Zoe had been more open lately about her family issues, she still didn't really like to talk about it much. 'It's not too late to come with us. I bet the rooms we booked have a sofa bed.'

Zoe snorted. 'Oh God, please no. I love you, but there's no way in hell I'm coming on holiday with you and BC. It'll make me feel even more single than I already do.'

My mouth twisted. 'Stop calling him that.'

'It's the safer option. If I start calling him Cliff with you, I'm one-hundred-per-cent going to forget I'm not supposed to call him that in public. And if I keep on calling him Blake, I have to see him flinch every time like I've just insulted him.' She sighed theatrically. 'Your boyfriend is super complicated.'

I couldn't help laughing. 'I mean, you're not wrong.' Hesitantly, I took her hand. 'Speaking of complicated, have you seen Ashton recently?' I didn't like saying his name in front of her, but it was the only way to find out if he'd tried to get in touch. We hadn't spoken to him since the night he showed up at the flat, hitting Cliff with his fist and me with the truth. Cliff said Ashton was ignoring his attempts to get in contact. I knew it bothered him, but I still found it hard to see Ashton as anything more than a ruthless bastard. At least Zoe and I finally agreed on that.

She smiled grimly, but I saw the muscles in her jaw tense, as if the thought of him was painful. 'No, don't worry. And if he ever dares come round here again, I'll beat the shit out of his stolen arse.'

I didn't know whether to laugh or shake my head. Zoe had taken the whole crazy truth much better than I'd expected. Obviously, she'd been pretty sceptical when I said the word *supernatural*, but after Cliff and I spent a few hours explaining it all to her in detail, she decided to believe us.

You're my best friend, she had said with a shrug. *If I'm not going to trust you, who can I trust?*

I got the feeling it also helped that the truth finally gave her an explanation for Ashton's confusing behaviour, and especially for why she'd felt so strange around him. In any case, it had been enough to make it clear to her that she had to stay away from him. I was relieved, but worry still niggled at the back of my mind. Zoe made out like she'd put it all behind her, but I knew her well enough to see that she was hurt. Ashton had used her for months, treating her even worse than the previous guys she'd had bad experiences with.

As if she could hear what was going through my head, she rolled her eyes and gave me a poke in the ribs. 'Don't look at me like that. From now on I'm going to take good care of my soul. And my heart.'

I smiled. 'Glad to hear it. And I'm going to help you.'

'I know you are. But first you're going to have a lovely Easter holiday with your mystical bird boyfriend. I guess after one hundred and eighty years he must be a fount of information as a travelling companion. He's almost as old as the stone circles you're going to see.' She wiggled her eyebrows humorously, and again I wasn't sure how to react.

'It's so weird, isn't it?' I said sceptically.

'Completely,' Zoe agreed, taking my shoulders to pull me into a deep hug. 'This whole relationship is the craziest fucking thing you've ever done, probably ever will do. Which is why I'm just so happy you're doing it.' She kissed me on the cheek, then took my hand and led me towards the door. 'Now get going, all right. Don't waste any time.'

I didn't argue. I just picked up my stuff, made her promise once again to keep me updated on Davie, and left. If there was one thing I'd learnt by now, it was that each and every second was precious. And I wanted to spend as many of them as possible with Cliff. For as long as I could.

Outside, I took out Mum's mirror and gazed into it. My lips were a rosy pink. *Soft Love*. It had been my favourite shade ever since Cliff had been just Cliff. I smiled, knowing that if the forces of the universe were real, if Mum really was looking back at me through the mirror, then she was smiling, too.

I snapped it shut, blinking in the spring sunshine. It flooded the grass with an orange tint reflected in countless windows and the pendant on my necklace. I held the flat gold bar, stroking my thumb acros the delicate engraving.

Cliff had given it to me. A few weeks ago, without any particular reason or explanation. I had found it in my jacket pocket one evening after he picked me up from the library and walked me home. He loved small gestures like that. Holding the door open for me, ushering me wordlessly to the side of the pavement furthest from the street, smuggling coffees into the library for me, which I drank surreptitiously in the hazy light between the dusty windows and stacks.

My everyday routine carried on as usual, of course, and Cliff made no attempt to stop it. He fell in with my habits, keeping me company while I worked or waiting for me in the evenings when the libraries closed. And I was careful to give myself more breaks, because I realised now that there were things that mattered to me outside of books. Things I wanted to appreciate and enjoy. Those brief moments were the best part of my day: even if it was just ten minutes to talk to him and see him and kiss him, and remind myself that I was allowed to do all of that now. We weren't a secret anymore, yet what we shared still felt immeasurably precious, special. Worth protecting. Like the necklace he had slipped into my pocket that evening. The pendant was about the size of my thumb, with engraving so fine that you could only read it if you turned the metal to the light: *whatever our souls are made of...*

I knew *Wuthering Heights* well enough by now to finish the quotation in my head: *his and mine are the same.*

I had smiled when I read it, and then cried. The line captured so perfectly how I felt when I thought about Cliff: unmistakeably, inexplicably, unshakeably certain that we saw and understood each other. It was the most wonderful feeling I could imagine, and at the same time the most painful, because the idea of losing him so soon was unbearable. The thought loomed over us like a grim cloud, although I did my best to push it to the back of my mind. I simply refused to accept that the storm brewing inside it would eventually burst and engulf us. Nothing had happened yet. Anything was possible. Our story had to have a better ending than Catherine's and Heathcliff's. It just had to.

Cliff was waiting on the road outside the college, leaning against his car. When he saw me, he pushed off it and came to meet me. The closer we got, the more his smile faded. Whatever he saw in my face, it brought a frown to his. 'Everything all right?'

I smiled hurriedly, letting him take my bag. 'Fine, yeah. I was just wondering how many more of these trips we could take before...'

My voice broke. Cliff hesitated a moment, then he put down my bag and drew me towards him, fingers curled into the sides of my open coat. 'A few years is a long time.' He kissed the freckles on my brow. It was strange, but every time he did that, it felt like he was taking away some of their darkness and the thoughts swirling beneath. 'Who knows what might happen.'

'Right.' I smiled. 'Plenty of time to hunt down a few more mythical artefacts, for example.'

'Pica.' He cupped my face in his hands and pressed his forehead fleetingly to mine. He did that a lot: mostly when we disagreed about something. Which we still did, often. Especially when it came to this particular topic. 'How many more times are we going to argue about this?'

'I'm not arguing, I'm just saying.' I pushed him firmly away, palm to his chest, but then immediately took his hand and led him towards the car. It was parked underneath a blossoming-pink chestnut tree. 'You should have figured out by now that I don't give up. As long as we've got time left, I'm not going to stop searching for a loophole. This isn't over yet.'

Cliff sighed, reaching past me to open the passenger-side door. 'Of course not. What we have between us is only just beginning.' He pointed inside the car. 'Now, get in. I want to go on holiday with my girlfriend. Like a completely ordinary person.'

I could have told him he wasn't an ordinary person. That because of that, I would never make peace with the idea of letting nature take its course. His whole existence, after all, was *super*-natural. But instead I kissed him lightly on the chin and got into the car. I wasn't going to back down, but I also didn't want to spend every moment arguing about it. There was still time to make him understand that I wasn't going to just resign myself to fate. It really wasn't over. Our ending had yet to be written, and I had no intention of letting it be dictated to me. We would create it for ourselves, no matter how time-consuming or exhausting it would be to find the right words.

As Cliff walked around to the other side of the car, I held the pendant in my palm again. I knew one thing for sure: whatever our souls were made of, I would give everything I had, until the very final second, to save his.

ONE MORE CHAPTER

YOUR NUMBER ONE STOP
FOR PAGETURNING BOOKS

The author and One More Chapter would like to thank everyone who contributed to the publication of this story...

Analytics
Imogen Wolstencroft

Audio
Fionnuala Barrett
Ciara Briggs

Contracts
Laura Amos
Inigo Vyvyan

Design
Lucy Bennett
Fiona Greenway
Liane Payne
Dean Russell

Digital Sales
Laura Daley
Lydia Orulnge
Hannah Lismore

eCommerce
Laura Carpenter
Madeline ODonovan
Charlotte Stevens
Christina Storey
Jo Surman
Rachel Ward

Editorial
Janet Marie Adkins
Rosie Best
Kara Daniel
Emily Thomas
Charlotte Ledger
Jennie Rothwell
Sofia Salazar Studer
Helen Williams

Harper360
Emily Gerbner
Ariana Juarez
Jean Marie Kelly
emma sullivan
Sophia Wilhelm

International Sales
Peter Borcsok
Ruth Burrow
Bethan Moore
Colleen Simpson

Inventory
Sarah Callaghan
Kirsty Norman

Marketing & Publicity
Chloe Cummings
Grace Edwards
Katie Sadler

Operations
Melissa Okusanya
Hannah Stamp

Production
Denis Manson
Simon Moore
Francesca Tuzzeo

Rights
Ashton Mucha
Alisah Saghir
Zoe Shine
Aisling Smyth
Lucy Vanderbilt

Trade Marketing
Ben Hurd
Eleanor Slater

**The HarperCollins
Distribution Team**

**The HarperCollins
Finance & Royalties
Team**

**The HarperCollins
Legal Team**

**The HarperCollins
Technology Team**

UK Sales
Isabel Coburn
Jay Cochrane
Sabina Lewis
Holly Martin
Harriet Williams
Leah Woods

**And every other
essential link in the
chain from delivery
drivers to booksellers
to librarians and
beyond!**

ONE MORE CHAPTER

One More Chapter is an
award-winning global
division of HarperCollins.

Subscribe to our newsletter to get our
latest eBook deals and stay up to date
with all our new releases!

signup.harpercollins.co.uk/
join/signup-omc

Meet the team at

www.onemorechapter.com

Follow us!

@onemorechapterhc

Do you write unputdownable fiction?
We love to hear from new voices.
Find out how to submit your novel at
www.onemorechapter.com/submissions